BAD ASS MOMS

THIS BOOK IS A REAL MOTHER

EDITED BY MARY FAN

CRAZY 8 PRESS

For all the moms out there. You're bad ass.

TABLE OF CONTENTS

RUTH

MICHAEL JAN FRIEDMAN

HALFWAY UP THE ROAD FROM the ocean walk, Ruth stopped, put down her worn leather briefcase, and took off her glasses.

I could see her eyes in the bright, brittle sunlight. Like pieces of a broken Coke bottle, sharp and ready to cut. It was the way they always looked to me.

Even that time they brought Reese down from the Mountain. Mourning him turned me inside out, but not Ruth. She seemed to feed on her grief, to draw strength from it.

As we stood there in the salt air, she took out a tiny cloth and cleaned her lenses. When you walked the ocean walk on a breezy day, you got sprayed by the surf pounding against the bulwark. If you wore glasses the way Ruth did, you found yourself looking at the world through droplets of dried ocean water.

Of course, there were other ways to get to the courthouse in Vista Azul. Upland ways. But the ocean walk was the fastest for those of us who lived in the *vecindario*, and the flattest, and outside of the spray the least demanding.

"You all right, Lyndita?" Ruth asked, allowing her gaze to drift in my direction.

"As right as I'll ever be," I said.

Ruth nodded. Then she replaced her glasses on the bridge of her nose, picked up her briefcase, and started up the hill again.

"Miss Ginder?" someone called.

I turned in the direction of the voice, thinking someone might be addressing *me*, until I saw Paulie Sorenson, all long, skinny arms and legs. He'd left a couple of other kids behind to come shambling in our direction. Paulie was Ruth's biggest fan. Everybody knew that.

"Good morning, Paulie," Ruth said when he'd gotten close enough.

"Can I carry your bag?" Paulie asked her, his chin slick with spittle.

She waved away the suggestion. "I can manage, Paulie. Thanks all the same."

"You sure?" the boy asked. "Dad says at your age you need all the help you can get."

Ruth chuckled. "Your dad's a good man, Paulie. But he's wrong about my needing help. I can handle my own things. Always have, always will."

Paulie shrugged his bony shoulders. "Okey doke," he said, grinned at Ruth, and ran off to rejoin the other kids.

Ruth watched him go for a moment. Then she said, almost beneath her breath, "At *my* age."

Ruth was old when she gave birth to Reese. Almost forty, I'd heard folks reckon. And we'd celebrated Reese's thirty-eighth birthday a couple of months earlier, so his mom had to be pushing eighty. She never said, of course, but she had to be.

At that age, I'd have let Paulie Sorenson carry my briefcase. Then again, I wasn't a Ginder. Not by blood, I mean.

"Come on," Ruth said, and started up the road again.

———— ·•· ————

The courthouse had more than its share of cracks in its white, stucco walls. People said it was just a matter of time before some hidden sinkhole sucked the place down into the ground. And it was true that the ocean was constantly undermining buildings along the ocean walk, slowly folding them in on themselves.

I didn't know if the courthouse would crumble someday. I was just glad it had lasted this long. Because without it, we'd never have had a chance of seeing justice done for my Reese.

As we entered the courthouse's slate-floored lobby, two uniformed guards nodded at us. They were on loan to us from Sacramento. Dave, the tall one, had lived in our town till high school, so he knew his way around. Simon, the stocky one, was from way down the coast, where things were *really* bad.

"Ladies," said Dave.

We greeted him in turn. But not in a cheerful way. We weren't there for a cheerful reason, after all.

Beyond the lobby was a set of double wooden doors, and beyond them the courtroom.

As we walked inside, Judge Jurn was turned away from us, bent over an old book.

Ruth cleared her throat.

"I hear you," the judge said, and put the book away.

Bradon Jurn was a blond, square-jawed man with a twitch in his left eye from Bell's Palsy. He hadn't changed much since the day he presided at my wedding, which he'd been glad to do for free because of how much he admired Ruth.

I remembered the judge wishing, as he stood there in front of me and Reese and our families, that the union he was making official would bear fruit. Apparently, he did that at every wedding he presided over—wished the bridge and groom healthy issue, and plenty of it.

Pitifully, few of them got what he wished for.

As we watched, Jurn stood up, took his black robe off a wooden coat stand behind him, and slipped it on, covering his work clothes. He'd been harvesting crops that morning, like everyone else in the uplands. Sweating, getting his hands dirty, taking care to preserve every last runty strawberry. But now that we'd entered his courtroom, he was all business.

He eyed Ruth. "You look like you could use some water."

She shook her head. "Don't need it. Have some yourself, if you want."

Jurn chuckled. "If an old bird like you can go without, so can I. Go ahead, have a seat. Both of you."

We sat down behind a table in the front of the courtroom, Ruth and I. Then she said, "You're going to tell me there's a problem."

"You don't need *me* to tell you," said the judge. "You've been doing this long enough to know it for yourself."

"There's not enough evidence," Ruth conceded.

"There's no evidence at *all*," said Jurn. "Look, I'd like to put this sonuvabitch away too. You know that. But we're lacking here. We've got half a dozen witnesses among those who followed Reese up the Mountain, but none who saw the actual murder."

"They saw Darron shoot," Ruth insisted. "They saw my son fall."

"But not so they could say unequivocally it was Darron who killed Reese. He wasn't the only one shooting, after all. There was only one man close enough to know for certain, and—"

"And he's up on the Mountain," Ruth said.

Jurn sighed. You could hear the sound come up from his heart. "That's what they said. I'm sorry, Ruth. I really am."

She pointed a spindly finger at the judge. "You're not going to let Darron go." It wasn't a question.

"I'm not going to have a *choice*. The world may be going to hell but this is still a courtroom. I can't send a man upstate without evidence."

"You're *not* going to let him go," Ruth repeated.

Jurn sat there for a while, meeting her gaze, his eye twitching every so often. Then he said, "I'll keep him as long as I can. But it won't be much—a couple of days at the outside. You know that."

Just then, the court clerk—a bony, blonde woman named Abigail—came in. She nodded to Ruth and me. Then she handed the judge a folded piece of paper.

Jurn read it. Without looking up, he said, "He's asking to speak with you." He cleared his throat. "With *both* of you."

"Darron...?" I blurted.

"Yes," said the judge. He looked up at me. "Mind you, you don't have to if you don't want to. But—"

Ruth held a hand up. "*I'll* speak with him. That's all. There's no way. My daughter-in-law—"

"It's all right," I said.

Ruth shot me a sidelong look. "You certain, Lyndita?"

I hated the idea of seeing Darron. But if I saw him, he might say something that would incriminate him. I didn't know—I wasn't a lawyer like Ruth. But maybe.

"Yes," I said. "I'm certain."

As we walked into a little side room, I saw Darron. He was sitting in a wooden chair with his hands manacled and placed on the table in front of him.

His lawyer, a man with a large, grey moustache and a paunch, was there too. Dave stood in the corner, his hand on his gun, making sure Darron didn't try to hurt us or anything.

Like he could have hurt us more than he already had.

Darron was the same as I remembered him—ruddy, mostly bald, with broad features and big, pale blue eyes. The kind of eyes one would expect to see in the face of a child.

But he was no child.

It hadn't been easy for the cops to get their hands on him. Apparently, he'd had a girlfriend outside town that no one knew about. He'd made her mad somehow—mad enough to tell the authorities when he was paying her another visit.

It was a stroke of crazy good luck, one shot in a million. And even then, Darron had almost gotten away. He was strong, slippery, smart—which was how he'd gotten to be who he was, I figured.

"Whatever you have to say," Ruth told him, "say it quickly."

"You don't have to do this," Darron said—to both of us. He spoke softly, evenly. There was no threat in his voice, no emotion at all.

"Don't I?" Ruth asked.

"You're thinking about what happened on the Mountain," he said. "I don't blame you. He was your son. But there are other things to consider."

"Not for me," Ruth snapped.

"You know what kind of world this is," Darron continued. "How important it is to keep healthy bloodlines going. And your family's *known* for the health of its bloodlines."

A muscle quivered near Ruth's eye. "My... family."

"That's right."

I understood where Darron was going with this. So did Ruth, it seemed. "And if I see you pay for your crime," she said, "my family's future will suffer."

He shrugged. "It's a certainty."

7

She planted her blue-veined hands on the table and glared at Darron. "You honestly think what you're saying is going to change my mind?"

"It should," he said, still unruffled. "Unless you're not as smart as I thought you were."

A bitter smile spread across Ruth's face. "I'm smart enough to *convict* you. Think about *that*."

Seeing he wasn't going to get anywhere with Ruth, Darron turned to *me*. "I'm sorry about your husband," he said in the same soft, unoffending voice. "It was just something I had to do."

I believed he thought so. It didn't change anything. "You didn't know him well enough to be sorry," I said. Darron looked like he was going to object, but I didn't give him a chance. "So let me tell you about him. He was kind and loving and generous, and he had a laugh loud enough to frighten dogs, and he wanted more than anything to have a family and watch them grow." Tears rolled down my cheeks. I couldn't help it. I wasn't Ruth. "And you took that away from him. And from *me*."

Darron was silent for a moment. Then he said, with just a hint of an edge in his voice, "What I told her about her family's future... make sure she thinks about it. Make sure she thinks *hard*."

As if I was on his side. As if I was one of the low-life scum who worked for him.

I could feel my anger and grief and despair climbing the inside of my throat, threatening to drown me. I tried to say something in return, but I couldn't. I couldn't get a single word out.

The next thing I knew we were out of the room, and Ruth was grabbing my sleeve. "Are you all right?" she was asking.

I drew a ragged breath. "I'm fine."

She didn't argue with me.

"What are we going to do?" I asked, a whimper in my voice.

Ruth frowned. "I have an idea. But first I need to see Ralph."

* * *

Once, Vista Azul had been a tourist town, where people came to sit on the beach and swim in the ocean and forget the weight of their city jobs. But that was a hundred years earlier, when the ocean was farther away and a lot kinder to us.

Since those days the Pacific had eaten up the beach and the lower half of town. Not all at once, of course. Year by hard, dismal year. It had salted our ponds and our streams. It had even invaded the water table so we couldn't get drinking water from our wells.

People were healthier before the waters rose. At least, that's what you hear. They gave birth more often, and to healthy babies, who grew up to become healthy adults and make more babies.

Not everyone. Just most people.

The world had changed in that regard. And not just our part of it, though I couldn't say I'd seen it with my own eyes. But it made sense. If the water rose in one place, it was bound to rise in others.

So maybe it was all over the world that families with healthy babies had become an uncommon thing, and getting more uncommon all the time. People went to a lot of trouble to marry into those families. They were the ones that were likely to go on, after all. They were the future, if there was one.

Families like the Ginders. Darron had been right about that. The Ginders were rare in the way they knocked out one healthy baby after another. But even they couldn't have survived without the River.

It might have had a name at one time. Now folks just called it by what it was: the River.

Folks who were dead now used to say they had seen the start of it, way up in the hills, and how it flowed clean and clear until it mixed with the brackish stuff in town. When everything else was ruined by the rise of the ocean, it became our only reliable source of drinking water. That made it precious to us.

So precious that greedy men saw an opportunity in it.

Darron wasn't the first of them. There were water lords before I was born, men who'd gotten the idea to control the River after drinkable water became scarce. But Darron was the best there'd ever been at squeezing the opportunity for all it was worth.

He moved boulders and sealed up the cracks between them, and finally dammed up the River so not a drop reached Vista Azul on its own. He knew full well what a cruel thing he was doing, but he knew too that there was no law against it. Then he raised the price of the water.

Nobody had to buy it. Unless, of course, we wanted to live, and to see our families do the same.

The only other water available to us was bottled stuff that came in a truck from up north. But it was more expensive than what Darron charged us, and it wasn't always as clean as it might have been, and lots of people wanted it up and down the coast so you never knew when it would be available.

And one day someone attacked the truck and killed the men on it, and spilled all its water on the ground. Someone who was never identified, of course. So even the truck was no longer an option. At that point, Darron controlled *all* the water.

And in doing so, he controlled life itself.

————— ··· —————

Ruth didn't linger long at Ralph Tarr's place. Twenty minutes maybe.

When she came out, big old, white-bearded Ralph had a meaty arm around her. He usually walked with a crutch, but not when he was around Ruth, I'd noticed.

"You know," he said in that playful way he had, "you're still a fine-looking woman, Ruth Ginder."

He said it loud enough for me to hear, and winked at me for good measure. Ralph loved an audience, after all.

Ruth shot him a discouraging glance. "And you're still a damned awful liar, Ralph Tarr."

He laughed. "I'd defend myself, but it'd be in vain. No one in his right mind goes up against Ruth Ginder."

And yet Darron was about to walk free.

On the other hand, Ruth had said she had an idea. I wondered what it was.

"Has she told you what she's up to?" Ralph asked me, as if he'd read my mind.

I looked at Ruth. "Not yet."

Ralph sighed at Ruth and shook his head. "She doesn't want you trying to talk her out of it, I guess."

Ruth scowled at him. "Mind your business, Ralph."

"You *are* my business," Ralph said.

Back when he and Ruth were young, they were friends. *Close* friends. There was a time when it seemed they'd get even closer. Then Ralph went off to join the army. And by the time he came back, six years later, Ruth had met her husband and given birth to a son.

But in their old age, the two of them had grown close again. Ruth had even gone with Ralph to Los Angeles to have his leg worked on—for the fourth time, she'd said.

When Ralph was in the army, he'd gotten stationed in Spain. Joined the bomb squad, whose job it was to defuse explosives the enemy had laid in the army's path. One day, one of the bombs took part of his leg off. Since then, he'd had problems with it. Doctors kept taking a little more of it each time.

Still scowling, Ruth patted Ralph on the arm. "See you later," she said.

He smiled in his beard, but it wasn't a happy smile. It was something else. Uncertain, I thought. "Yeah," Ralph said. "Later."

As Ruth and I negotiated the dirt path that led from his house to the road, Ralph didn't go inside. He stood there on his artificial leg, watching us go. Sadly, I thought, like that "later" would never come.

"What's going on?" I asked Ruth.

She stopped by the side of the road and stuck her thumb out to get us a ride, just like she'd done to get us to Ralph's place. "You'll see," she said.

We got out of our ride a little before we got back to town, at a bend in the road. It was just forest there, and had been for a long time. Maybe forever—we only knew so much about the times before the water started rising.

"*Now* you going to tell me?" I asked.

Ruth eyed the gentle, wooded slope above us. "I said I would, didn't I?" And she told me.

I looked at her, then looked up the slope, then looked back at her again. "You're out of your mind."

"All the more reason for you to stay in town," she told me, and started making her way up the slope.

It wasn't easy for her to climb, old and stiff as she was. But it was clear she wasn't going to let her frailty get in her way.

"No," I said, even louder than I'd intended.

Ruth stopped and turned to me. "My mind's made up."

"I know," I said. "But I'm not going to let you do this alone."

She held up a bony hand. "I don't need your help, Lyndita."

Yes, I thought, *you do.* But what I said was, "I loved him too."

Ruth eyed me for a while. A long while, it seemed to me. Then she said, "What the hell," and beckoned for me to come with her.

I thought Ruth would slow down, despite the determination with which she'd started out. She didn't.

She didn't go fast, but she didn't stop. And she didn't make a single sound of complaint, not even after an hour or more of trudging up the hill. Unless, of course, you counted the huffing and the grunting. She couldn't seem to do anything about that.

It didn't seem like it would be much farther before we reached the highest point we could see. But after that there would likely be another stretch of slope, and then another. We didn't know how many.

All we knew was that it was far. Almost a thousand feet of elevation, people said, before you reached Darron's dam. But Reese had made it to that point, or close to it, so I would too.

Of course, he'd had others with him—some of them out-of-uniform police officers, some just farmers, all of them bent on breaking Darron's hold on the River. Liberators, men and women alike, moving up the Mountain under a starless sky.

But Darron's men had spotted them. They'd fought. And Darron had won.

Now Ruth and I were making our way up the hill to meet Darron's army. But we weren't going to fight them. How could we? Two women, unarmed... one elderly...

And we weren't scaling their hillside by night, as Reese had. We were doing so in broad daylight, making no attempt to conceal our approach.

The morning drew on, the sun climbing in the sky. Every so often, I'd ask Ruth how she was holding up. I took the occasion to ask again: "How are you doing?"

Before she could tell me, a man's voice crackled in the autumn air: "Stay right where you are."

Ruth stopped in her tracks and put her hands up. My heart banging in my chest, I did the same.

A man stood up from cover maybe fifty paces up the slope and to our right. He was small and thin, wearing a camouflage jacket that was clearly too big for him, but he had an automatic rifle trained on us.

Don't let them think you've got a gun and we'll be all right, Ruth had told me a while back. I raised my hands even higher.

If Ruth had come up with an armed escort instead of me, they could have cut the man down. But what good would that have done? There were a dozen more like him concealed on the hillside above us, ready to shoot at the first sign of trouble. I couldn't see them but I knew they were there.

"Don't move," the man said.

Ruth remained still but not silent. "I want to speak with Legler."

The man didn't lower his gun. "What for?"

"I'm here to speak with Legler," Ruth repeated. "No one else."

I heard a laugh from off to our left. Another man rose out of the bushes, this one bigger and broader, with bright red hair down to his shoulders. "Ornery for a little bitty woman," he said, "ain'tcha?"

"They want to talk to Legler," said the smaller man.

"Yeah," said the bigger man, "and I want me a dancing girl with long, blonde hair. They'll talk with who we say they'll talk with, or they'll go home empty-handed."

"We're not here to buy water," Ruth said.

That took the redhead by surprise. "Then what are you doing here?"

"I'm here," said Ruth, "to see Legler."

The red-haired man laughed again, even heartier than before. "That's not happenin', lady. Turn around and go back where you came from."

"Our name's Ginder," I said.

I hadn't intended to speak. It just came out.

Ruth looked at me, a little half-smile on her face. As if to tell me I hadn't done anything she wouldn't have done.

"Is this a joke?" the redhead asked, a note of uncertainty in his voice now.

"It's no joke," Ruth told him.

The two men exchanged glances. The smaller one shrugged. Then the bigger one turned back to us and said, "Come with me."

We did as we were told.

We climbed the slope for another half hour or so, me helping Ruth over the rough spots, of which there were more and more the higher we went. In that half hour, we saw another thirty men with rifles, and there had to have been others we didn't see. I had no idea how many.

At the top of the hill, there were more men waiting for us. A knot of a dozen or so, half of them with their rifles trained on us.

Reese had had eighteen guns besides him. *Eighteen*. Had Reese known how well defended Darron's dam was? Had he known how outnumbered he would be?

As we approached that close-packed group at the top, they all had the same look on their faces—narrowed eyes, hard-set mouth. A look of suspicion. Then again, one probably didn't thrive in their line of work unless one had a healthy capacity for distrust.

I could see the dam behind them. Mostly grey stones mortared together, but chunks of cement too. It looked strong. But then, it had to be to hold back the River.

I saw a wooden shack too. It sat to one side of the dam.

One of the men above us, a tall one, came down to where we were. Unlike the others, he carried a sidearm in a holster. "I'm Legler," he said in a rasp of a voice. "You wanted to see me?"

He was older than I'd expected. Old enough to have a receding hairline and some grey at the temples, and crow's feet at the corners of his chocolate-dark eyes.

"You know who I am," Ruth said.

Legler nodded. "What I don't know is what you're doing here."

"I need to speak with you in private."

"Why?" Legler asked.

"You'll know that when we start talking."

Legler's features hardened. "I don't like your tone."

I bet Ruth didn't like his either. But she needed him, so she refrained from telling him what she didn't like.

14

A couple of Legler's underlings laughed at her silence. "Guess you shut her up," said one.

"How about we hang her from a tree?" said another, a fellow with a big hoop of an earring. "You know, the way she's hung some of our friends?"

Ruth shot him a look. "I don't see people hanged. I see them put away."

The man with the earring turned red. "That's what you *say*. All I know is no one ever catches a glimpse of them again."

"You'll get a glimpse," she said, "when you're arrested the same way they were. Everybody in jail sees everybody else. Hard not to."

The man's eyes looked like they were going to pop out of his head. "I oughtta—"

Legler chopped at the air, gesturing for the man to stand down. "No one here's going to jail. And no one's getting hanged either. That's not what Darron would want us to do."

I didn't know Darron well enough to say if Legler was right. But the men on the hill went silent at the mention of Darron's name, so there was that.

Ruth looked up at Legler. "So?"

He eyed her for a moment. Eyed me too. Then he jerked his head in the direction of the shack. "Up there."

"Watch she don't pull a knife on you, Brom."

Laughter. But muted. Legler had already made it clear what he thought of their banter.

I moved forward alongside Ruth—until Legler held his hand up. "You wait down here," he told me.

"I'm not leaving her," Ruth said.

For a moment, Legler looked like he was going to hit her. But in the end, he didn't. "Fuck it. The more the merrier."

And he led the way up the hill.

———————— ••• ————————

Once the three of us were inside the shack, Legler closed its door. Then he leveled a long, thick finger at Ruth. "You show me up again in front of my men, and I'll shoot you like a dog," he grated. "I don't care *who* you are."

Ruth nodded. "I hear you."

"Now," said Legler, "what's so important that you've got to talk to me in private?"

"I'll be honest with you," said Ruth. "We've got a problem. You know we've got Darron on trial, right?"

"Yup."

"We've got witnesses that can place him on the mountainside during the shootout. But nobody who can say it was Darron who shot Reese Ginder."

Legler grunted. "Sounds like a problem, all right. What's it got to do with me?"

"I want you," said Ruth, "to testify against Darron."

He broke into a grin. "Seriously?"

"Seriously."

"Just walk into your courthouse and do that. Like I'm that stupid."

"I'm not asking you to walk into the courthouse," Ruth said. "All you have to do is record your testimony. That will be good enough."

"That simple, eh?"

"That simple."

"Do I look like someone who's tired of living?" Legler asked. "All Darron has to do is hear I cooperated with you and I'm a dead man."

"Unless I put him in prison for the rest of his life. Then you've earned yourself a promotion. *You* can be the King of the Mountain—not just till your boss comes back, but permanently."

I saw a flicker of greed in Legler's expression. But it was extinguished by his instinct for self-preservation.

"And what if something goes wrong," he asked, "and Darron walks? Then I'm the King *Under* the Mountain."

Ruth shrugged her narrow shoulders. "Maybe you don't have a choice."

Legler's brows beetled together. "What do you mean?"

"Maybe I tell Darron you worked with me—gave me whatever I wanted as long as it meant you could take his place here."

"Except I *didn't.*"

"How is he going to know that?" Ruth asked.

Legler's eyes narrowed. "Then maybe I don't let you go back to see Darron."

"Now you're sounding like your men. *Stupid.*"

It was the last straw. Next thing I knew Legler had jammed the business end of his gun under Ruth's jaw. I started to move, to try to stop him from hurting her, but Ruth waved me off.

"I oughtta kill you where you stand," Legler growled.

"Go ahead," Ruth said, her words constricted by the gun barrel pressing against her throat. "Then there'll be no one with the starch to bring a case against Darron, and he'll walk. And he won't be happy when he hears about the blood you spilled."

"Maybe he'll make an exception in this case."

"Is that what you think?"

Legler swore under his breath. Then he put his gun back in its holster. "Goddamn you," he said, his mouth twisting like a slug on a bed of salt. "You're a nasty old bitch, aren't you?"

Ruth smoothed the front of her jacket. "That's what they say."

Legler looked at her, weighing this possibility and that one, and probably liking none of them. Finally, he said, "What do I have to do?"

Ruth reached into her pocket and took out the recorder she'd been carrying. It was small, light. It had to be. She could barely drag *herself* up the mountain.

Then she said, "Tell me what you saw the night Reese Ginder was killed."

———————— •••• ————————

It was late in the afternoon by the time we got down from the Mountain.

Judge Jurn was surprised to see us back in his court room, despite the warning Ruth had given him to expect us. "You all right?" he asked her.

"Why wouldn't I be?" she returned.

"Well, to be honest," said the judge, "you look like hell." He glanced at me. "Both of you."

Ruth ignored his comment. "I'm ready to start the trial."

Jurn nodded. "All right, then. I'll get us going."

Darron's lawyer had said he'd be in the coffee house up the block, but he wasn't. Finally, Simon got ahold of him in a bingo parlor, which was where he went after he got bored sitting in the coffee house.

That done, Jurn gave Darron and his lawyer a few minutes to talk. Then he called the two of them into his courtroom.

"Have a seat," he told them.

Darron's lawyer sat down, but Darron himself stayed on his feet. "If it's all the same to you," he said, "I'll stand."

Jurn shrugged. "Suit yourself."

Despite the manacles on his wrists, Darron didn't look the least bit flustered. He just stood there, probably thinking he held all the cards. Last he'd heard, there was no evidence to convict him.

He's about to find out otherwise, I thought.

There was a time, Ruth told me once, when the court system was different. A jury decided if people were guilty or innocent. And the rules of evidence were pretty strict, so it was harder for a prosecutor to convict someone.

In our time, it was different. There was no jury. People were too busy trying to survive. And judges accepted all kinds of evidence—whatever made sense.

Jurn turned to Ruth, who was seated next to me at our wooden table in the front of the room. "I understand you have something you'd like to introduce into evidence."

Ruth nodded. "That's so, your honor." She put the recorder on the table. "The testimony of an eyewitness to the murder."

"Who's the witness?" the judge asked.

"Brom Legler," said Ruth.

Darron's features froze. Obviously, he hadn't expected Legler to turn on him. At least not this way.

Darron's lawyer objected. "How do we know that's Brom Legler? It could be anybody."

"I've known Brom Legler," said Jurn, "from the time he was a boy until he went up the Mountain. If it's him, I'll know it. And if it's not, I'll know that too."

Darron's lawyer bubbled, but he had nothing else to object to.

"With the court's permission?" Ruth said.

"Go ahead," Jurn told her.

Legler's voice filled the courtroom. You could hear in it that he wasn't happy about talking, but he talked.

He said how he had seen Reese and his men come up the mountain, and how Darron had led *his* men down to meet them. And how there was lots of shooting, and some folks falling on both sides.

But Reese hadn't stopped coming. I believed that when I heard Legler say so up on the Mountain. Once Reese started something, he wasn't the kind to stop before it was finished.

Legler said he himself had taken a couple of shots at Reese, but he'd missed. And so had some of the others shot at Reese, with the same result.

But Darron was like Reese in that he wasn't going to back down. So he kept going too. Suddenly, before either he or Reese knew it, they were just a few yards apart, and nothing except a few branches standing between them.

"For a moment," said Legler's voice on the tape, "they just stood there looking at each other. Then Darron fired. He was too close to miss."

"Could it have been someone else's bullet that hit Reese first?" Ruth asked on the recording, her voice amazingly businesslike under the circumstances.

"No way," said Legler. "Darron was the one. I heard only one shot. Then the cop—Reese—fell backwards. He wouldn't have fallen that way if someone had shot him from a different angle."

Ruth tapped the *stop* button and regarded the judge. "An eyewitness account."

Jurn nodded. "It's Brom Legler, all right. And this is pretty compelling evidence."

Darron laughed. "Are you kidding me? Legler's got everything to gain by lying. It's your *duty* to see he doesn't get away with it."

Ruth glared at him. "Nobody's getting away with anything today."

The judge banged his gavel. "That's enough." He regarded Darron. "I don't need anybody telling me what my duty is in this court. Understand?"

Darron didn't say anything. But his head fell to one side, as if he was telling the judge, *Go ahead, I dare you.*

Jurn saw Darron's look and had to know what it meant—that if Darron got the chance, he'd make the judge pay. And with all the power he'd have, even in jail, he might get that chance. But Jurn didn't back down.

"We don't have much left to us here in Vista Azul," he said, his voice echoing in the courtroom. "Most was taken from us by the greedy and the ignorant long before you thought to take the rest. But we've got one thing, and that's justice. That's not a thing you can dam up or divert. That flows from the highest places to the lowest, and eventually it finds everybody." The judge's hands had become fists. "You understand? *Everybody.*"

We were all quiet for a moment. Even Darron.

"This court," said Jurn, "finds you guilty of the murder of Reese Ginder. The penalty is life imprisonment without possibility of parole, to be served at the state penitentiary in Bakersfield."

Darron shook his head. "You've made a mistake." He said it slowly, so the judge knew what he was talking about.

"Then," said Jurn, "that makes two of us." He pointed to the door. "Take this man away."

Dave took Darron by the arm and led him into the aisle between the defendant's table and the prosecutor's. Darron didn't resist. Not at first, at least.

But as he went past Ruth, he stopped.

Unlike Legler, he didn't threaten her. He just stood there, staring at her. At some level, deep inside where he hadn't yet become a thief and a killer, where he remembered love of family, he had to feel betrayed—and by the last person a man should be betrayed by.

Mother. He almost said it. But in the end, he didn't.

Dave finally told him to get moving again. And he did.

Ruth watched him go, all the way through the doors of the court. Then she nodded. After all, the man had killed her son.

But she'd had another son, one she had lost long ago. And in that moment, she had to be mourning that son too.

Especially since he was the only one capable of extending the Ginder bloodline.

———————— •••• ————————

It was getting to be twilight. I was hungry, and I needed a bath. But Ruth insisted that we stay in town.

"For a little while," she said.

I was too tired to argue with her. And who ever won an argument with that woman anyway? So we sat down on a wooden bench at the base of the Mountain, by the concrete channel where the River used to run through town, and watched the light thin in the sky.

"You know," I said, "this isn't over. Legler will become the new boss of the Mountain. And you have something over him, something that can hurt his standing with his men. He can't allow that. He'll come after you."

Ruth shrugged, as if it were a thing of no importance. "He can try."

"You're not worried?" I asked.

"What was the alternative?" she asked. "To let Darron go free? And forget what he did to Reese?"

Reese is dead, I thought. *And you're alive.*

I was about to say as much when I heard a boom. Like thunder, I thought. But there wasn't a cloud to be seen in the sky.

"What was that?" I asked.

Unlike me, Ruth didn't seem surprised. She just sat there and stared at the sky.

Then I heard another boom. And another, right after it.

"Not thunder," I said, thinking out loud.

"No," said Ruth, "it's not thunder." She put her hand on my arm. "Can you hear it, Lyndita?"

"What?" I said. I was sure she didn't mean more booming.

"Listen," said Ruth, a hint of a smile crossing her lips.

And I heard it: A hissing sound. Like a powerful wind rushing through the trees, bending branches, rustling leaves. But the branches on the trees were still. So it couldn't be that.

Then I saw what it *could* be.

A rush of silver and gold, painted by the last light of day. A rush of silver and gold finding its old bed, which had lain dry and empty for the longest time but was still there under the brush and the leaves, willing to forgive and forget.

It cascaded over rocky ledges. It slithered and rolled past the debris that had taken its place. And finally, it ran into the concrete channel in front of us, sweet-smelling and free—ran tripping all over itself, frothy as any milkshake, all the way down to the ocean.

I wanted to jump into the channel and feel the River wash over me. I wanted to scoop it up in my arms and save it, because water was so precious. Once it mixed with the salt water, it would be useless to us.

Then I looked up the slope of the Mountain again, and I realized it was okay. The water wasn't stopping. It was still coming. There was more of it. *Plenty more.*

People came out of their shops and second-floor apartments to see.

They were amazed, struck by how their lives had changed, and without warning. But no more amazed than I was.

I turned to Ruth and began to ask how this could be. And it came to me in a rush, just like the River.

Ruth hadn't climbed the Mountain just to talk to Legler. She'd had a bigger purpose in mind. She hadn't made the bombs. She wasn't capable of such a thing. But Ralph...

Back in Spain, he'd gotten to know explosives inside and out. So he would've had more than enough know-how to make the kind Ruth needed. Little ones, small enough for an old woman to carry under her coat without anybody noticing, yet powerful enough to do some serious damage.

No one had suspected. Not even me.

Legler would rebuild, or try to. But it had taken Darron a good couple of years to dam up the river, driving his men hard day after day, and he had been twice the leader Legler was.

Would Legler's followers have the patience to do all that work? Or would they abandon him to find easier ways to fill their bellies? I'd have bet all my money on the latter option.

Even if Legler's men stayed, we knew what was at stake now. We were forewarned. We wouldn't let them build their dam a second time.

I put my hand on Ruth's, felt the bones under her cool, paper-thin skin. Her eyes were dry. She wouldn't shed a tear, not even then. Not even after all she'd done that day.

It was all right. I was willing to cry for both of us.

A couple of weeks after the trial, Ruth fell in front of the theater. She was there with Ralph to see a Michael Niosi festival, because Michael Niosi was his favorite from back in the day.

She didn't trip. No one knocked her down. She just fell there on the sidewalk.

My fear was that she'd broken a hip, which would have been bad enough. But it was more than that. She'd lost consciousness.

They took her to the hospital. The doctors there examined her. Closely, as they hadn't for years.

At that point, she could no longer keep it to herself. She was sick. The kind of sick you don't come back from.

They made me wait a couple of days to see her. I didn't yell too much because I was feeling kind of poorly myself, and I didn't want Ruth to catch anything. But on the third day, I went to see her.

She looked small in her bed, even smaller than when I watched her climb the Mountain. She had suffered for a long time without telling anyone. When her sickness finally caught up with her, it did so quickly.

"Ruth," I said, "I have something to tell you."

She couldn't speak. It was all she could do to keep from groaning. But her eyes slid in my direction so I could tell she was listening.

"Ruth," I said, "I saw the doctor yesterday. I'm *pregnant*."

She looked at me for a while, doing her best to absorb what I had said. *Pregnant?* She mouthed the word.

"Yes."

A tear trickled down her cheek and got lost in the folds of her neck. I could see her doing the math in her head.

It'd been a couple of months since Reese's death. He and I had made love the night before he went up the Mountain. I don't know if that was the time that his seed took or some other time, but that was the time I wanted it to be. The time I remembered.

And from what the doctor told me, it *could* have been that time.

There would be a Ginder in the world after Ruth and I and Darron were gone. A Ginder who, with some luck, would never know the tyranny of the Mountain, who would grow up big and strong if the family's bloodlines held true.

A Ginder who would know what his grandmother was like, if I had anything to say about it. And I would.

Ruth was happy about what I'd told her. And sad, no doubt, that Reese would never know his child, but more happy than anything.

I could see it in her Coke-bottle eyes.

RAISING THE DEAD

HILDY SILVERMAN

IT WASN'T EASY RAISING A dead girl, even in a town that claimed to welcome all beings. A pecking order still existed, and my Resurrected daughter Jenni was at the bottom. Which was why I found myself yet again meeting with Principal Steif and members of the P.C.T.A. (Parent-Creator-Teacher Association) at Piscataway Integrated High.

"Mrs. Domingues." Ms. Steif leveled a stare through black-framed glasses that likely petrified students but, given what I'd survived, didn't faze me. "I thought we'd resolved Jenniflore's situation last meeting. Which was only"—she flipped dramatically through her desk calendar then pointed at a page—"last month."

"Except nothing's improved," I said. "Jenni is still being harassed daily. She can't even walk to class—"

Behind me, someone scoffed, "She means shamble, right?"

I clenched my fists in my lap. "—without being assaulted."

"Ah, c'mon." I shifted to face Jack Hoffman, a werewolf who in his day form was burly, and hairy save the top of his head. "Back in my day, kids tussled on the reg'lar. Now it's *assault*?" He looked away, muttering, "Buncha snowflakes."

I'd intended to remain calm so no one could accuse me of being "hypersensitive" this time, but fur-for-brains worked my nerves. "Yes, Mr.

Hoffman. It's assault when students jab objects into my daughter's back because she can't feel them or when they pelt her with rubber brains."

Distinguished Lord Frederic Drayven, blood father to the vampire students, shot Jack a scornful look. "*I* am terribly sorry to hear of Jenniflore's woes. However, the principal is quite correct. This is the third time we have met on the subject, and the school year is not even halfway complete."

"It isn't like anyone can actually hurt that thi… your daughter." Sandy Loew was mother to one of the minority human students. Her wide brown eyes remained in constant motion, gaze darting from one P.C.T.A. member to another. "I mean, what's so bad about tossed brains? That's what she eats… right? I always forget who eats what." She caught the principal's pained expression. "Am I being insensitive again?"

Principal Steif ignored her. "Of course this teasing is unacceptable. P.I.H. prides itself on being egalitarian and accepting of all students regardless of race, beliefs, or dietary preferences. However"—she furrowed her brow—"maybe we are expecting too much regarding Jenni."

By *we*, she clearly meant *me*. "So now it's *Jenni's* fault your bunch of bullies hound her?"

"*Hound*? What're you implying?" Jack growled.

"I am certain you do not mean *my* offspring," Lord Drayven intoned. "My blood children have impeccable manners."

"My Robby doesn't have a mean bone in his entire body!" Sandy waved her hands and half-rose from her chair. "Besides, how exactly does anyone bully a freaking *zombie*?"

The group fell as silent as Hannah Goodwin, the one parent who had yet to say a word in this or any prior meeting. The *bokor*, as her kind were called in LeRoi's native tongue. My heart ached, wishing my ex was by my side fighting for our daughter like he once did so heroically.

Principal Steif cleared her throat. "All I'm saying is that as the only *Resurrected* student"—she glared until Sandy shrank back into her seat—"maybe it's too much to expect Jenni to fit in here."

"What do you suggest?" I tapped her desk. "Jenni needs an education to find jobs and support herself for… who knows how long." An ache filled my chest. *Someday I'll be gone. What happens if Jenni doesn't have friends capable of living—existing—as long as she will?* I feared what endless isolation could turn her into.

"Viable alternatives to public school exist." Ms. Steif shrugged. "Have you considered private options?"

I half-laughed, half-choked. "And where do you suppose I can find a private school that accepts the Resurrected? Never mind how I'm supposed to afford it."

"Don'tcha get support from your ex?" Jack sneered. "Most divorced guys wind up on that hook."

I shot him a dirty look. "Not when they're confined to mental health facilities." Jack had enough decency to look embarrassed while I fought back tears.

LeRoi just hadn't been able to handle what his pumpkin became after an ill-fated family reunion in Petit Goave, Haiti. Jenni and two cousins, who were never found, took a wrong turn walking back to their grandparents' house after a party one night. Our family, armed with machetes, searched until we found the *bokor* camp. We chased them off and freed Jenni before they finished the ritual to wipe out her memories and self-awareness, but we were too late to prevent the physical transformation.

Guilt, coupled with our subsequently futile quest to reverse Jenni's curse, broke LeRoi. He became convinced the only solution was a machete. I couldn't allow that, so I committed him.

I thrust my dark memories down. "We were encouraged to move here because Piscataway promotes itself as a model of human-nonhuman integration. Now, my daughter is a citizen with full rights and protections under the law, which includes a public education." I rested my elbows on the principal's desk and leaned in. "I will *not* look into dead ends like private school. What I *will* do is investigate every legal option to ensure my daughter's safety while she pursues equal educational opportunities right here at your *egalitarian* school."

The principal slumped in her chair. "Fine. I will hold *another* assembly tomorrow and remind students they must treat everyone with respect."

"That's lovely." I nodded. "And what will be the consequences for continued mistreatment of my daughter? Encouraging sensitivity is nice but useless without enforcement."

She pinched the bridge of her nose. "Any student harassing another will be subject to an immediate two-week suspension. Repeat violation extends it to a month."

I raised my left eyebrow.

"The third time," she added quickly, "they will face expulsion."

"Hold up!" Jack sputtered. "J.J.'s the school's best running back. Even a one-week suspension could get him kicked off the team!"

"Then make it crystal clear that if he's harassing Jenni, he'd better cut it out!" Ms. Steif snapped.

Sandy had wrapped her arms so tightly around herself I doubted she could breathe. "Well, I'm certain this won't affect *my* boy. He knows better than to mess with anythi… one here, especially a zom… Resurr-whatever."

"Wonderful, Mrs. Loew." The principal looked to Lord Drayven.

He shrugged one shoulder. "This ruling is acceptable."

All attention shifted to the silent witch. "What say you, Mother Goodwin?"

Looking at her stirred such anger it took all my willpower to remain seated. Hannah Goodwin had straight blond hair, pale skin, and violet eyes. She barely resembled the European colonizer *bokors* who'd tried to enslave Jenni, but all I saw was their spiritual sister.

She clearly didn't need magic to sense my loathing. She licked her lips, and when she spoke, it was barely above a whisper. "What happened to your daughter was an abomination. We call those… traffickers who harmed her, and so many others, warlocks and consider them enemies of witchkind. Me and mine would *never* commit such a perversion of nature or taunt its victim."

What does she expect, applause? "I don't care what you all call each other so long as you leave my daughter alone."

She pressed her lips into a straight line and nodded.

Principal Steif clapped. "Fabulous. We're adjourned." She picked up a random file and began studying it as though we'd all ceased to exist.

Whatever. I'd accomplished what I came for and couldn't wait to go home and tell Jenni.

"Mo-o-om." Jenni dragged out the vowel as only teenagers can. "Why'd you do that?"

We were sitting on the well-worn couch in our small apartment's living room. Evening light shone through the window, casting shadows across her gray face framed by short, stark-white braids. I longingly remembered her warm brown skin and black hair. "Baby, don't you see? Now they'll leave you alone."

Unblinking eyes with dilated pupils set in pale red irises stared into mine. "That's not how it works. You don't tell kids they'll get expelled if they're mean to the school freak."

"Don't call yourself that! Besides, compared to the majority, what makes *you* the freaky one?"

She rolled her eyes. "Not the point. Now they'll know I tattled to my mommy!"

"Of course you told." I raised my hands, palms up. "What were you supposed to do?"

"Ugh, you just..." She inhaled deeply; a dramatic affect since she didn't breathe. "Let me put it clear as I can. Narcing on kids? Makes them hate the narc *more*."

I dropped my hands into my lap with twin *thwaps*. "What did you want me to do? Nothing?"

She clapped and nodded vigorously. "Yes! Exactly."

"Baby, that's... no. Hell, no!" I stood and paced, shaking my head and making *mm-mm* sounds until I found actual words. "No one ever solved anything by doing nothing. Otherwise, wrongdoers don't learn, and nothing changes.

I cupped her chin in my hand. *I'll never get used to how cold she feels.* "I simply can't stand by and watch you suffer."

"Neither could Dad."

I flinched and released her. "Your father—"

She cut me off. "You're gonna tell me not to blame him for what mental illness drove him to the attempt." She studied her hands like she didn't recognize them. "But I actually *do* believe that while you totally don't."

I almost denied it, but I didn't like lying to my daughter. "This has nothing to do with your father."

"Doesn't it?" She hung her head. "Daddy thought I'd be better off not being... this."

My gut clenched. "Your father wasn't in his right mind when... he never would have *suggested* let alone tried—"

"Mom?" Jenni stood and gazed up at me. She'd never reach her full height, which her pediatrician once estimated as half-a-head taller than me. "Maybe he was right."

"Don't you say that, *ever*!" My voice cracked. "Baby, I know this isn't the way you want to be, and I'd give anything, *everything*, to undo it. But at least you're still—"

"Alive?" She shook her head. "I'm such a monster I creep out other monsters! How do you think my pseudo-life is gonna go?"

"Not how we expected." I couldn't keep my tears from falling but swiped each one away as it betrayed me. "But you can still finish school and graduate—"

"And what?" She shrugged. "Have a career? Have my own family?"

All that and more, if you'd been allowed to live the life you were meant to. It struck me then—the root of my constant sorrow and impotent rage.

My daughter was dead.

The girl who'd loved strawberry cupcakes on her birthday and made the crayon drawings stuck with magnets on our fridge. Who'd wanted to be a teacher or maybe a famous singer when she grew up. That girl, my *original* Jenni, had died more than a year ago.

"There it is." She nodded. "You're realizing what I see every day when I look in the mirror. When I don't sleep or feel pain, cold, heat—anything." Her voice cracked, and if still capable, she probably would have wept too. "Undead? Is still mostly dead. That's it, that's what I am and will always be unless someone chops me up or… I don't know, maybe the world ends in a nuclear explosion. 'Til then, I'm just a dead girl walking."

I squeezed my eyes shut. *Different ain't dead! Dead means gone, and she's still here.* I'd said that to LeRoi more than once. Now *I* needed to believe it. We both did.

"Jenniflore Angela Domingues." She met my gaze reluctantly. "You are my daughter, my whole heart, now as much as ever. It's understandable if sometimes you think you'd be better off gone, but *never* think for a second that's true."

I hugged her tightly, wishing I could transfer my warmth and life into her. "I love you and want you here enough for the both of us."

"I love you too. At least I can still feel in that sense." She gently pulled away. "I get that you did what you thought was best today. Still wish you hadn't… but I understand."

I brushed her braids back. "It's early in the school year. If the bullies back off, then you can still make friends. A lot of those kids know what it's like to be—"

"Terrifying?"

"*Different*. In time, they'll see the real you." I tapped her chest. "The person still inside. My sweet baby girl."

"M-o-o-m." This time, she smiled while drawling it. "You're so much."

"I'm so right. As usual." I glanced at my smartwatch. "Now go get your homework done. I'll have your dinner ready at six."

"Let me guess. Raw meat?"

I tried to put a positive spin on it. "Picked it up today, so it's really fresh."

"Yum." She headed into her room and closed the door.

———————— •••• ————————

Weeks later, Jenni started mentioning a girl, Mercy, who'd chosen her as a lab partner. Friendship appeared to be blossoming, and for the first time, Jenni seemed eager to go to school.

So, when she announced that she and Mercy would be staying late to work on a chemistry project, I thought nothing of it—until Hannah Goodwin called.

"I am sorry to disturb you. It's... my daughter told me she was working on an experiment with Jenni tonight, but when I went to school to pick them up—"

The back of my neck prickled. "Hold up. Mercy's *your* daughter?" I checked the time and realized it was later than Jenni had said she'd be home. "Where is Jenni? If your daughter's done *anything*—"

"Mrs. Domingues, please! I swear, Mercy only wishes to be Jenni's friend. She felt terrible for ignoring her before. She only did so because I told her... I said she should stay away given the sensitivity around how Jenni became... as she is."

I struggled not to hyperventilate. "If that's true, why are you worried?"

"The girls weren't waiting in front of the school as planned. I tried going in, but not only are the doors all locked"—she hesitated—"it's warded."

"Meaning—"

"Sealed against magical entry." Anticipating my response, she added,

"*Not* by Mercy. The caster's signature is unfamiliar. I also failed to reach her through telepathic bond or text."

My stomach roiled. "Did you call the police?"

"I doubt they're capable of dealing with whatever this might be."

"Then what the hell do you suggest?"

"Since this is centered around P.I.H., we should summon our fellow Association members."

I was already shrugging on my coat while pinching my cellphone between chin and shoulder. "Call them. I'm on my way."

She didn't waste time trying to dissuade me from coming. "Meet me at the track behind the school."

"In ten." I dropped the phone into my palm, pocketed it, and almost headed out before realizing what I needed to bring. A quick rummage through my bedroom closet yielded LeRoi's machete.

Now I was ready.

—————————————

Hannah, Lord Drayven, Jack in his huge, silvery-black furred werewolf form, and Sandy Loew joined us in the field behind P.I.H. Their kids had given them the same story about working late on projects. None had responded since.

Lord Drayven levitated to the school's roof for recon through various skylights. He soon returned, hissing, "*Witches* have our offspring trapped in the gymnasium!"

"No," Hannah said. "They must be warlocks. Curse it, how could we not know they were in town?"

"Warlocks showing up where a half-turned Resurrected child resides." I stepped up to her. "Some coincidence."

Hannah flexed her fingers. Sparks arced between them. "Meaning?"

I clutched my machete tighter. *Bitch might have magic, but I've got a mother's righteous fury.* She'd never get to spit out a spell's first syllable.

Shockingly, the next person to make a move was Sandy. "Cut the crap!" She glared at me. "I get your hating Hannah because people like her messed up your daughter. But *she* didn't!" Sandy turned to Hannah. "And—normally—all the power Mrs. Domingues has is the ability to hurt your feelings. That's *nothing* compared to what you could do to her. So, *you* quit wasting time sniping at the wrong person, and *you* get over feeling insulted and focus on saving our kids!"

Well... damn. Worry over Robby clearly outweighed Sandy's usual skittishness. I lowered my machete, face warm with embarrassment.

Hannah met my gaze ruefully. "She's right. We must work together." She addressed Lord Drayven. "How many warlocks are there?"

"Seven." He scowled. "Also ten Resurrected. Unlike Jenniflore, they appear fully turned."

"Oy, yoy, yoy." Sandy dropped her face into her hands.

Jack growled, low and deep.

"And our children?" I asked.

"My *filis sanguis*... blood son appears magically suspended." His fangs shone in the moonlight. "Jack's pup is keeping the Resurrected at bay." Jack bobbed his muzzle, conveying *that's my boy* pride. "Mercy is just behind J.J., and Mrs. Domingues—"

"Raquel," I said.

He nodded curtly. "Jenniflore is lying within an upside-down pentagram surrounded by black candles and other... paraphernalia."

That sounded horrifyingly familiar. "They're trying to complete the zombification ritual." My knees buckled.

Hannah caught me. She spoke softly but emphatically. "I will *not* permit it, Raquel. Whatever it takes, this I swear."

Despite everything, I believed her.

"And my Robby?" Sandy demanded.

"Wisely hiding behind the bleachers," Lord Drayven answered.

"My smart boy."

"Indeed," Lord Drayven said without a hint of sarcasm.

"So, how do we get inside?" I looked from witch to vampire to... *wait. Where's our werewolf?*

An explosion answered me. I whipped around just in time to see a bushy tail disappear through the huge hole where the school's back door used to be.

Lord Drayven groaned. "So much for strategizing." He disappeared after Jack in a blur.

"Go," Sandy said. "I'll call for backup."

"You should probably stay with her," Hannah said. "This fight isn't for humans."

"I'm sure you're right," I said.

She smiled briefly. "You won't, though."

"Hell, no."

"Then remember, unlike Jenni, these Resurrected are mindless killers. They cannot be saved and will tear you apart on command." She nodded at my machete. "Don't hesitate."

"Got it."

She extended a hand. "Brute force is well and good for creatures like Drayven and Jack. I prefer stealth. And since Jack destroyed the ward—"

I took her hand. "Let's go."

A disorienting moment later, we were behind the gym bleachers. I choked back vomit as a red-haired boy sitting cross-legged on the floor squealed. "Oh, good." His shoulders sagged. "You're just moms."

"Hello, Robby." Hannah reached for his hand. "I will take you to safety. I'll be right—"

"I can't go." He pointed to an old book across his lap. "I got to finish this."

"What?" Hannah peered at a page, and her eyes widened.

"Yep." Robby grinned proudly. "Handed down through my pop's family for generations."

I had no idea why, but Hannah seemed impressed. "Your mother never mentioned this."

"Eh, she'd rather forget Pop's family legacy. But I've been studying his ancestor's book on the sly for a while." He briefly met my gaze. "I figured it could help. We came tonight to cure Jenni, but these witches advising us turned out to be dicklocks. So now"—he nodded at the book—"I'm gonna use this to stop their zombies instead."

Terrified for my daughter, I gave up trying to decipher what Robby meant. Instead, I peered around the bleachers and saw the scenario Lord Drayven had described, only with additional chaos.

Werewolf Jack wrestled against a Resurrected. Lord Drayven hurled a male warlock into a wall with such force, his crunching bones echoed across the gym. Meanwhile, Mercy stood chanting and waving her hands, which was somehow keeping three other warlocks from reaching Jenni.

I heard her sobs above the fray. Seeing my poor girl lying with limbs outstretched in the pentagram, unable to move, my reason fled. With a shout, I charged toward her.

One of the warlocks spotted me and chanted. A Resurrected—*no, a zombie, that's all they are*—sprinted at me despite his... its stiff legs. It ran with arms outstretched and mouth snapping like a shark swimming through chum.

I swung the machete, sheering off the fingers of its right hand. Instead of slowing down, it grabbed for me with its left.

I hacked and slashed until chunks of flesh littered the floor, to no avail. It would pull me apart like taffy if I didn't take off its head, but that proved easier said than done.

It caught me, pulled me close. Teeth clashed inches from my cheek—

A huge, furry form slammed into the zombie, knocking it away. Jack's powerful jaws clamped shut, and the zombie's head toppled to the polished hardwood floor. The body dropped a moment later.

"Th... thanks," I wheezed.

A swish of his tail, and he turned to face two more zombies speeding our way.

A slightly smaller wolf—Jack Jr., I assumed—bit one of the warlocks who'd been circling behind Mercy's invisible shield. He screamed.

A zombie tackled J.J., forcing him off its master into a rolling ball of flailing limbs and fur.

A yelp spun me around. The zombies had Jack pinned. Apparently, they were just as strong as a werewolf with the added advantages of being unable to feel pain or weaken from injuries.

My heart told me, *Go after the warlocks and protect Jenni!* But my head reminded me, *You owe Jack.* Plus he was closer—and in more immediate danger.

I swung the machete down on the zombie atop Jack with all my weight behind it. Its head split like an overripe honeydew.

Partially freed, Jack twisted around and over the remaining zombie. His jaws opened abnormally wide and snapped shut around its entire head. He spat it out with a triumphant howl.

"Help your son!" With that, I ran over to my daughter.

A female warlock spotted me and flicked her fingers. The machete flew out of my hand to embed itself in the nearby wall. Unruffled, she turned to Mercy. "Stop playing games, little witch. Give us our property."

"She's *nobody's* property, bitch!" Nearly blind with fury, I launched myself at her back.

Without sparing a glance this time, she chanted something. I went tumbling up and over to slam into the wall.

Several moments passed until my vision cleared. I was stuck to the wall near the rafters—but not alone. "Humiliating, isn't it?" The lanky teen boy—or at least teenage-appearing; you can never be sure with vampires—looked miserable. "I am Charles. You must be Jenni's mother."

"Yeah." I struggled not to panic at being magically suspended so high up and surveyed the situation below.

Five chanting warlocks closed in as Mercy trembled visibly. Another warlock lay crumpled with dark fluid spreading from his neck. Lord Drayven was barely visible beneath three zombies pummeling him. Across the gym, Jack huddled motionless, while his son howled and charged the zombie trying to finish him off.

"Hannah!" I understood her desire to protect Robby, but still—the warlocks nearly had our girls, and our strongest fighters were overwhelmed.

A voice out of nowhere: *"Almost ready."*

I looked around wildly before realizing she wasn't actually there. "Whatever you're doing, hurry!"

Electricity crackled and the atmosphere… shifted. The still-functioning zombies snapped upright as squiggly symbols emblazoned themselves across their foreheads.

Lord Drayven took immediate advantage and ripped the head off one of his assailants. Before he got to the second, Hannah appeared beside him. "Stop! We need them." She looked up at me and traced a pattern in the air.

I glided down to the floor with Charles, who muttered, "Oh, thank the Dark Lord."

The warlocks moved to confront Hannah, except for one tall man. He sketched a pattern with his hands, and Mercy abruptly lurched forward. The warlock grabbed her, and his wide mouth curved into a malicious grin.

"Charles, a hand?" I nodded at my machete lodged in the wall. He vanished momentarily then returned, presenting it like a knight offering his sword to a queen. "Thank you kindly."

He asked, "May I?" I barely had time to nod before he wrapped his arms around my waist. We took off at vamp speed.

I was already cocking my machete when we arrived right behind the tall warlock. He spun around, holding Mercy in front of him. She only came up to his chest.

I grinned. "You didn't think this through, asshole."

My blade sliced deeply into his neck. He gurgled and staggered back, blood spurting from the gash. Charles took it from there.

I held Mercy by the shoulders. "You all right?"

"I… yeah. Th… thank you." She regarded me with the same violet eyes as her mother's, only shimmering with tears. "This is my fault. I was trying… Jenni wanted to be human again, and I thought, if we found experts in her condition, there might be a way."

"Despite my explaining there wasn't." Hannah joined us. "Your intentions may have been altruistic, but your actions were reckless." She looked so furious, I immediately released Mercy and backed away.

The remaining zombies herded the surviving warlocks into a circle, from which they shouted spells and waved their hands impotently. Jack hobbled to us with J.J. and Lord Drayven. The latter's bespoke suit was torn in several places, but he seemed unharmed. Charles strolled over, licking blood from his fingertips, and bowed to his father. Robby also join us, pumping his book overhead. "*Ya-a-as*! It totally worked!"

"What—" I shook my head. "Never mind. Hannah, can you free Jenni?"

She waved her hand, and the black candle flames snuffed out. "Jenniflore, you are unbound."

Jenni flexed her fingers, sighed with relief, and stood. I hugged her fiercely. "Baby, tell me you're okay!"

"Well, still undead, but other than that…" She hugged me back so hard my ribs protested, but I didn't care. She was still herself.

"What in the *hell* were you thinking?" I held her at arm's length. "Sneaking out, breaking into school—"

"We didn't! We just stayed late and, um, hid in the bathrooms until everyone left."

"*Not* better!"

Hannah wagged a forefinger at Mercy. "Consorting with warlocks, are you *mad*? You could have cost Jenni her soul, not to mention gotten the rest of you slaughtered! How did you even find them?"

"Through an online hangout for witches worldwide," said Mercy. "It's supposed to be for cultural exchanges of arcane knowledge." She glared at the trapped warlocks. "They catfished me."

"And how did you and J.J. get sucked into this?" Lord Drayven demanded.

Charles shrugged. "As the offspring of an esteemed member of the school's leadership committee, I endeavored to improve relations with my fellow student as ordered." He nodded to Jenni then shot J.J. a knowing smile. "*He* had other... motives."

Jack growled and cuffed J.J. upside the head. He yelped then scooted closer to Jenni and bumped his oversized head against her shoulder. She smiled shyly and scratched behind his ear.

That's going to be a discussion, I thought. "So, everyone's heart was in the right place. Just your brains fell out."

"My coven will take these warlocks into custody." Hannah's expression turned feral. "Take heart, Raquel. They will face a reckoning you could not conceive of in your darkest nightmares." She turned to Robby. "How do we release the zombies?"

"Just a little erasing." He pointed to one of the heads on the floor. "The Hebrew symbols you inscribed on their foreheads—if you erase the first letter, the meaning changes and they die. Permanently."

He noticed the rest of us looking bewildered. "Oh, right—none of you are Jewish." He shrugged. "I'm a descendant of Rav Loew, kind of a master of mysticism, who lived in Prague long ago. He figured out how to raise and control... not a zombie exactly, but a not-alive, not-dead creature."

"Are you saying you're a witch?" I couldn't imagine Sandy taking that well.

"Nah. There's all kinds of magic users. Some good, and others"—he raised a middle finger to the warlocks—"not so much."

Despite the near-dire outcome, I couldn't help but rejoice. *My daughter finally has friends!* And, judging by J.J.'s lolling tongue and wagging tail, maybe more.

I told the parents, "You saved my daughter. Saying thanks isn't enough." A knot formed in my throat.

"In this town, we protect our own." Lord Drayven bowed his head.

Hannah said, "I'm sorry it took so long for Jenni, and you, to feel accepted. I shouldn't have been so indignant at being, I felt, unfairly blamed for the actions of others."

"It's hard not to blame everyone with power for what those who abuse it do." I smiled. "But you aren't a collective. You're Hannah, and she's Mercy."

"And I'm Jenni. I'm never going to be what I was, but after seeing how things could be"—Jenni nodded toward the zombies and shuddered—"*way* worse, I can accept that now."

Sandy Loew charged into the gym waving a baseball bat and leading a posse of our neighbors.

"Ma!" Robby called. "Chill, it's all over!"

She skidded to a halt. The rest of the townsfolk gathered in the back of the gym except for several witches led by a woman I recognized as Jill, the short, brunette mother of another kid in Jenni's class. I'd known Jill was a tour guide for the local historical society but the fact she was also a witch took me completely by surprise. She nodded to Hannah and guided the coven toward the trapped warlocks. Hannah quickly excused herself and joined them.

"Robby!" Sandy dropped the bat and embraced him. "You're all right?"

"I helped stop zombies with multiple-great grandpa's book!" he said cheerfully.

Sandy stumbled back, clutching her chest. "You did *what?*"

Leaving the cleanup in our neighbors' capable hands, I led Jenni outside. "You know there's going to be consequences for lying to your mother, right?"

"I know."

"And you'd best believe we're going to discuss this... thing with the werewolf boy."

She rolled her eyes. "Mo-o-o-o-m!"

WHAT WE BRING WITH US

DEREK TYLER ATTICO

THE LITTLE GIRL SQUEEZED HER mother's hand tightly as the last slivers of daylight faded through the trees, and the sounds of the night awoke around them in the forest.

Naima Ajaje' stopped and smiled. "It is only the song of the night beginning, little one—there is nothing to fear."

The child looked up with soft brown eyes that mirrored her mother's. Spreading her small arms wide, she reached out for the only love she'd ever known.

Naima shook her head, even now she could see so much of herself in her daughter. The child insisted on having short hair like her, and could be relentless. "No Imari. You are five years old. You're not a baba anymore, I cannot carry you, your brother is heavy enough." The baby boy in the red and brown kanga wrap on Naima's back slept unconcerned through the negotiation.

The little girl kept her arms out as she looked up at her mother.

Naima reached down and picked up her daughter, balancing herself between the sleeping bundle of love on her back and the joy she now held in her arms. The child yawned as she nestled her head into her mother's neck and began to fall asleep.

"Imari, don't go to sleep—the village is not that far," Naima said. The young mother took a step forward and then stopped.

The forest was silent.

No. Not silent. The nocturnal sounds of the woods had been replaced by something… unnatural. Three, perhaps four predators were approaching. Quickly spotting a rotted-out husk of a tree, the young woman moved toward it. As she bent down beside the husk, her daughter stirred, yawning loudly.

Naima covered her daughter's mouth to silence her as she tried to do the same with the panic that was growing inside of her. "Shhhh baba, mamma needs you to be quiet."

Naima knelt as she gently untied the kanga wrap while cradling her son. Quickly re-wrapping the baby, she handed him to her daughter. "Take your brother, Imari."

The little girl struggled with the sleeping bundle that was her baby brother. "He's heavy," the five-year-old protested.

Ignoring her tightening chest, Naima smiled a mother's smile as she helped her children into the small space. "We are going to play a game. I need you and your brother to be very quiet, no matter what you hear. If you do as I say, you can both have sweets when we get back home."

Imari's eyes brightened as innocence wiped away her uncertainty. "Yes, mamma," the child responded dutifully.

Naima Ajaje' returned the smile that mirrored her own as she pulled up a nearby bush and placed it in front of the husk's opening and then placed rocks in front of it.

Sealing them in.

Putting her back to the husk, Naima did her best to push away the thoughts of her children alone in the small, dark space. As she stepped back into the clearing, dusk had slipped into a cloud-filled, moonless night.

Naima found herself enveloped in darkness.

She felt it before she could see or hear it. It came from behind and above her like some winged beast swooping down to take her away from her life, her children, her home.

A net.

Muscles reacted without thought. The ever-expanding web reached out for her, scraping up against her, but landed behind her, unable to claim its prey.

She expected them to rush out of the cover of night and attack her, and when they didn't, she could see why. The moon was appearing from behind a cover of clouds, and her attackers could now see whom they were trying to catch.

Naima spoke into the dark forest just beyond the clearing. "Yes, I am a Dahomey warrior. Leave now, and it will be with your lives."

Their response glinted off of the emerging moonlight an instant before it reached her. Unlike the net, the spear found its mark, just below her ribs. Its force nearly took her off of her feet.

She could see them now, three slavers surrounding her. The man in front of her was well over six feet, with a width born out of his profession. His face was a mass of hair that his eyes and teeth peered through. The second slaver was off to the side, moving slowly. This bald man looked soft and out of place, like he was more comfortable giving orders to those that stole people than doing it himself. The slaver behind her wasn't approaching, from his laughter she could tell his attention was on something else.

The husk.

Time appeared to slip away as the young mother glanced behind her to see the slaver's shirtless, scarred back to her. He was tossing the rocks aside as whimpers from inside the hiding place grew louder.

In one swift motion, the Dahomey warrior backed away from her aggressors as she eased the spear out of her side. Then, she swung its blunt end across the face of the slaver in front of her, blood and teeth spraying from him in a shower of red and white.

Ignoring the blood on her hands and the warmth she felt running down her side, Naima stepped to her right as she swung the spear around and behind her, pushing the blade through the neck of the man that was now holding her daughter.

With the blade still in the slaver, Ajaje' twisted the blade as she arced the spear toward her next opponent, beheading the man instantly. The severed head landed at the feet of the final slaver—both men sharing the same shocked expression on their faces.

The last slaver held his hands up defensively in front of the spear, his eyes wide with fear. "Wait, please! Wait! We didn't know we were this close to the Dahomey village. I'm sorry!"

Naima Ajaje' held the tip of the spear in front of the bald man's hands. Her side felt as if she'd been mauled by a lion, every breath a chore; but in truth she could only think about one thing. "Do you hear that?" the young woman said, and without taking her eyes off of the slaver, motioned her head toward the direction of her two children. Her daughter was making low whimpering sounds not unlike a cornered animal in pain, and her infant son, feeling the fear of the moment but unable to articulate it, was simply crying.

Without looking at the children, the slaver began to cry.

"That," Naima said quietly, "is what you and your kind have caused. That can never be undone." Naima pushed the spear tip through the slaver's hand and into his face. The body staggered backward and slumped to the ground. "And no, I don't believe you are sorry."

Naima turned toward her children, and when she did, the Dahomey warrior disappeared. As she approached her son and daughter, the little girl grew silent, and her eyes widened as she now saw her mother in a different light. Ignoring the reaction, Naima put herself between her children and the decapitated body. Kneeling beside her daughter, she smiled as she wiped away her tears. "I am so proud of you, Imari. You were very brave."

The little girl looked up at her mother. "Can I still have sweets?"

Naima laughed. "Yes, baba, you can." Taking her son out of the kanga wrap, the mother was surprised how quickly the baby began to settle down in her presence. After using the wrap as a binding for her wound, the warrior-mother stood up, cradling her son against her with one arm while holding the hand of her daughter.

As the song of the forest began anew, Naima Ajaje' felt a semblance of peace and security return to her now that she was once again holding her children.

But for how long would it last?

TODAY

The world around Major Amari M'Basa swirled in a collage of images.

Her wingman spread across the sky in a cloud of flame and debris. A convoy of dead troops on the ground below. The Gariep Dam, crucial to South Africa's economy, vulnerable and exposed.

As she regained control of her JAS 39 Gripen jet fighter, she could see three of them on either side, about ten feet in length and half as wide, closing in.

Drones.

But unlike any she'd ever seen before, black with their delta design, they looked more like miniature versions of the old triangular B-2 stealth bomber. Even in the midst of the chaos around her, their simplicity made sense to her. Terrorists didn't need million-dollar aircraft, just something relatively small and very fast with radar-absorbing paint, rigged to explode on impact. Line-of-sight was the only way to spot them, and her wingman had never seen his death sneaking up on him.

Now the vultures were closing in on her.

M'Basa placed her hand on her stomach and took a deep breath. "Okay, okay, we got this. Let's see if you bastards can go supersonic."

The young pilot eased the accelerator on her left forward while pulling back on the flight stick between her legs. The single-engine, single-seat aircraft responded immediately, pulling into a vertical climb. A half-second later, her flight suit began to inflate as four times her weight forced her back into her seat and the bird broke the sound barrier, hitting Mach 1.

Pulling away from the Gariep Dam, M'Basa could see all six of the drones were still on her tail. Her plan was working; whoever was piloting the drones thought killing her was more important than crippling the South African economy.

For the moment.

Unexpectedly, the two drones closest to the Gripen dipped under the aircraft and out of sight.

"Fuck!" The pilot spat into her oxygen mask as she instinctively yanked back on the stick, taking 7Gs as her craft accelerated, leaving the explosion meant for her behind.

Major M'Basa strained to look over her shoulder. What would have been an effortless turn of the head a few seconds ago was now excruciating with seven times her weight bearing down on her neck and shoulders.

Four drones were still on her tail, and closing.

The inflated flight suit and oxygen mask were working hard to keep her conscious. The South African blinked hard; the sustained 7G climb was catching up with her, and a peripheral of darkness had begun to seep into her already graying vision. If she slowed down now, the drones would catch up, but if she pushed forward, she might kill herself in a sustained G-climb. Somewhere probably close by, her adversary, the pilot of the drones, was trying to turn her cockpit into a coffin.

The sounds of M'Basa's rapid, stressed breathing filled the small cockpit. What she did next would seal her fate and quite possibly that of all of South Africa. "Okay, we can do this, we can do this!"

The Major hammered the accelerator forward.

Nearly instantaneously, the Gripen hit 9Gs and Mach 2, climbing again. Amari ignored her own groans of pain and the crushing weight on top of her as she placed both hands on the stick while eyeing the altimeter as it approached 50,000 ft. The Gripen didn't have special combat and stealth technology like the American F16 or F35 jet fighters, but with its speed and maneuverability it wasn't necessary; it could hold its own against any aircraft in a dogfight. But this wasn't air warfare of old—the Gripen pilot was fighting the future.

And gravity.

At twice the speed of sound with over nine times the force of gravity bearing down on pilot and aircraft, both were approaching their limits. M'Basa was close to G-lock—Gravity-induced loss of consciousness was closing in, and she only had a second or two before—

"So?"

The man sitting across from Major Amari M'Basa stopped reading and looked up to answer the pilot's question. "I think you already know the answer." Closing the Major's file, he removed his glasses, folding them calmly, and placed them next to her folder on his desk. "How many did you say you took?"

Amari stared at the picture of the young woman stapled to the folder. Lieutenant Amari M'Basa looked like a child. Her round face and wide eyes, eager to take in every challenge life had to offer. She hadn't cut her hair yet, and even pulled back tightly into a bun her dreadlocks announced her audacity; but that was before she realized flying was more important than breathing. The pilot shifted uneasily. She didn't like the chair she was sitting in; it was roomy and plush, yet full of expectations and stigmas. The only seat she felt comfortable in was in the cockpit of her Gripen. That seat was control, that seat was freedom. "Three. I took three tests. How far along?"

Doctor Cohen ignored the emotion in his patient's voice. "Four weeks. Of course, the choice is yours with how we proceed, but if you decide to go forward, there will be stipulations if I clear you to fly."

The doctor was talking to her like they were scheduling the best time for dental surgery. In the real world, Amari knew she was the only woman in a "Males Only" club and a woman of color. She'd worked twice as hard as them to get her foot in the door and didn't want to have it shut back in her face. But she wasn't going to let fear of that control her either.

"Okay, talk to me about flying."

"Well." Reading the anxiety on the young woman's face, the doctor sighed. "There would be stipulations. I wouldn't want you pulling anything over 3Gs, and certainly not for sustained periods. If you decide to do this, I can get you transferred to something with a low threat assessment, like flying dam patrol for the next few weeks and then aerial refueling as things progress."

"As things progress" was one of the many wonderful perks of living on an Air Force Base that was ninety percent male. This was a decision that could change her life and her dreams while creating a new life with its own hopes and dreams, and her assigned doctor could barely look her in the face. "Anything else I should know?"

The doctor put his glasses back on, picked up Amari's folder, and began reading again. As an afterthought, he stopped and answered the question. "Well, you might want to wake up."

She could feel herself twisting, turning. Like the autumn leaf, destined to fall, destined to die.

Major Amari M'Basa awoke in freefall.

A hurried glance at her instruments told her only a few seconds had elapsed since she'd lost consciousness, the altimeter said the rest. She had maxed out at around 52,000 ft., the Gripen's engine had stalled out, and now, with no engine, she was dropping, back toward the drones.

The mechanical assassins couldn't match her top speed; she'd left them behind, but now, was falling back toward them. Instinctively, the Major placed her finger over the engine ignition switch but paused. She needed the engine, its power and expensive gyroscopes, to get back into the fight.

Or not.

Without the engine, the only things that worked would be the oxygen to her flight suit and her guns; everything else would be stick and rudder, no different than 1903 and the Wright Brothers. More importantly, to her adversary piloting the drones, she'd look dead.

And maybe, have a chance.

M'Basa grabbed the flight stick with both hands and struggled to regain control. The beast she sat atop bucked wildly beneath her as she began to go into a tailspin. She could feel G forces once again pressing into her as gravity accelerated the aircraft's decent. "Come on girl, don't do this to me."

Instead of trying to pull out of the tailspin, M'Basa thumbed off the gun safety and embraced the chaos, coaxing the flight stick to roll with the spin, not against it. "Come on girl, give it to me goddamnit."

Almost imperceptibly, she could feel it, the machine relenting under her. She was still falling, spinning, but she was in control.

M'Basa lined up with her targets. The drones that had been specks in the distance were now visible targets seconds away. A pair rushed up toward her on an intercept course while the last two were headed back, toward the dam.

Time was running out.

The Major squeezed the trigger of the Mauser BK-27 revolver canon and watched as its rounds erupted from the Gripen, first shredding and then detonating both drones. As she shot past the falling debris, M'Basa reignited the engine and watched the Gripen roar to life as if awakened from a deep slumber.

That was when she saw it.

Her onboard communications picked up a powerful radio signal about ten miles from the dam. More powerful than a cell tower, the signal was exactly what you'd need to pilot six drones.

Doing a visual check, she could see the last two drones were headed west toward the Gariep Dam. With their head start, she wasn't sure she could catch them both in time—but the signal was due east, only a few clicks from where she was.

"Please be right," Amari whispered as she pulled the stick to the right; turning, the Gripen east. Dropping to under a thousand feet, she scanned the South African countryside for anything unusual, and she almost missed it. A camouflage tarp, covering a school bus.

With an antenna dish on the roof.

M'Basa locked onto the target and fired two sidewinder missiles; she could feel vibrations course throughout her ship as they detached from under her wing and their rockets ignited. The missiles sped away from the craft as if the Goddess Oya herself had unleashed their fury.

Confirming missile signal lock, the Major jouked her craft west in a hard 5G turn. A cone of pressurized air formed around the craft as it went supersonic. M'Basa gritted through her teeth as she accelerated. "Come on!"

The drones were in sight, and just beyond them their target.

The Gariep Dam.

Amari knew missiles would take out the drones, but she dared not use them for fear of missing and doing the terrorists' job for them. Switching to guns, the young pilot was about to pull the trigger, then stopped. She realized she was now traveling faster than the top speed of her munitions if she fired. Physics told her the only thing she might shoot down was herself. At that same moment, her weapons board registered that the sidewinder missiles destroyed the school bus.

But the drones were still flying.

"Fuck!" M'Basa screamed into her oxygen mask. It was over, she'd lost. All she could do now was watch the drones impact the dam and throw South Africa into an economic freefall.

But that didn't happen.

Like a maneuver gone wrong at an air show, the drones crossed each other's flight paths, clipping each other in the process. One drone exploded right there, most likely from its payload being hit. The other spun wildly end-over-end and descended toward the dam, and as constructed, exploded on impact.

Just outside the dam walls.

It was only now with the threat averted that Major Amari M'Basa, callsign: Longshot, allowed the last few minutes to hit her. She could feel her face was wet and welcomed the emotions she'd been holding back. Reducing the throttle, the mother to be made a leisurely turn back to base. "I think we're gonna be okay."

TOMORROW

Oddly, having a gun pulled on me wasn't what surprised me. What surprised me was where it happened.

There aren't supposed to be any guns here on Mars, or on my ship. The *Persistence* was NASA's multi-billion-dollar solution to getting humans to Mars safely, and as mission commander my job was keeping us all alive during our stay, including myself.

A minute ago, I thought I was working an unexpected comm problem with my two Fulcrum crewmates, but the gun changed all that.

Captain Connor Shepherd held the weapon the same way he ran his team, with authority. West Point graduate, turned war hero, turned private astronaut for Fulcrum. Control was something he was used to, and I was getting the impression he didn't like sharing. At six feet and two hundred pounds, Connor towered over my thin five-foot-seven frame; it always seemed to bother him that this didn't bother me.

It was clear the gun had been printed; from the looks of it, it was a Sparrow PPC, the first printed weapon to be used in a presidential assassination attempt. And now it was on Mars.

Pointed in my face.

"Give me your command codes, Monroe." Shepherd demanded.

NASA's blue-and-gold uniforms didn't have any logo or rank; it was the same for the blue-and-red Fulcrum suits. Just a simple raised seal of Earth and under it the Latin inscription: Pro Ominbus Hominibus—For All Mankind.

I was starting to think Shepherd didn't agree.

His charm and southern hospitality had disappeared; I was pretty sure this was our first true introduction. As the commander of *Persistence*, there was only one possible reason he could want my codes. Ignoring the request, I looked past the weapon to the man holding it. "How'd you print the gun, Connor? It's not in our database."

He gave me that smirk set in a square jaw under intense blue eyes. It was the same smirk he'd given when we were introduced, the one that said I should be thankful I was breathing the same air he was.

Shepherd smiled. "Not in yours, Asha. The Fulcrum Industries database is independent of NASA."

Fulcrum Industries, commonly known as Fuck You Industries. What started as a fly-by-night 3D toy-printing business was now a trillion-dollar company printing everything from apartment complexes to rocket ships. The mega corporation was everywhere back home, and like its namesake, the company used its money and power to pivot into key governments and organizations around the world, regardless of who they stepped on.

The backup Shepherd had brought with him to the command deck for his coup was unexpected. Engineer Tony Dalmatian (yes, like the dog), fresh into his thirties, sweet as hell, and loyal as his namesake. Tony was so happy just to be on Mars, he might have pulled the trigger himself if Shepherd had asked. With my team outside repairing solar panels, Shepherd had picked the perfect time to do this.

I tried to ignore the gun in my face and the smirk on Connor's. "Look I get it, we've been here a year, ten people, two teams working every day, another eighteen months before we get relieved. It's stressful, but both teams need each other on this expedition." I exhaled and actually managed a smile. "Let's go somewhere and talk this out, in private."

Connor thumbed off the safety on the Sparrow; a small light on its side went from red to green. "We're not going anywhere, Commander, but you and your team are. You're going back to Earth. Today."

And there it was. Even hearing it out loud, it was hard to believe. "What are you talking about?" I said.

My disbelief must've shown because Connor actually seemed pleased. "Fulcrum Industries wants to thank NASA for assisting with getting our infrastructure in place, but we can take it from here. We've already grabbed two of your crew, John Smith and Michael James. They're at the *Audacity*, prepping for launch. Give me the codes, and this can be an easy transition for everyone."

It was a lot to take in. NASA had refused Fulcrum's bid for a joint first mission to Mars for years, and then the private company did the unexpected. Fulcrum built the *Audacity*, an expedition ship exactly to NASA specs, and then publicly launched it unmanned to Mars. The *Audacity* was a display of Fulcrum's commitment to work with NASA and a (free of charge) ready-to-go fail-safe should anything unexpected happen on Mars; how could NASA refuse? On top of that, Shepherd already had two of my crew and was trying to send all five members of the NASA team back to Earth.

Now it all made sense. "Fulcrum is making a play for Mars. I'm not going to let that happen," I said.

The look on Shepherd's face told me he had moved on from our conversation. "I'm going to make this really simple for you, Monroe. The system will only accept my command authority to launch if I have those codes, or if you're dead. I'm fine with either to achieve my objective." Shepherd put the gun to my temple. "So, what's it going to be?"

I stared at Shepherd. "Are you really going to commit the first murder on Mars?"

The West Point graduate shrugged. "You leave me no choice. Someone's got to do something, and you're standing in the way of progress."

Progress.

It took a long, long time for the world to accept that I could be the mother of two boys, have a wife, and be mission commander of the first human expedition to Mars.

But *that's* progress.

For him, the word meant a manifest destiny, replete with discovering places other people lived, strip mining landscapes, and miseducation.

I took a step into Shepherd's personal space, ignoring the pistol. "Yeah, I'm sure someone told Native Americans the same thing. Look Shepherd, you may be upset that the best man for this job is a woman, but you're not getting those codes," I said dryly.

Connor stiffened, his face reddened, and for the first time he was visibly angry. Then, like wiping away facts off a whiteboard, the emotion was gone, replaced with the rehearsed smile. "Goodbye, Monroe."

"Wait!" Dalmatian yelled.

Dalmatian wasn't looking at me or Shepherd. At first I thought he couldn't bring himself to watch what was about to happen, but then I realized he couldn't take his eyes off the central view screen. "Is that what it looks like?" I said.

Dalmatian was rapidly working the keyboard under the main screen. "No, it's much, much worse."

Shepherd kept his weapon trained on me as he stepped backward toward Dalmatian, and then he lowered it as he stared at what we were looking at. "Fuck," he whispered.

Every second of every day, Mars is trying to kill us. If it's not the toxic atmosphere or the lack of resources, then it's the weather. Today, that worked in my favor. I shot a glance over to Shepherd as I kept my eyes on the Martian landscape and the rover's steering controls. "Tell me again," I said.

Shepherd's voice was different now, less confident. This wasn't the way the captain had planned today. "I had my team kill the comms and loop the sensors at the launch site so no one would realize what was happening until it was too late."

I looked over at the Fulcrum captain. He kept his eyes straight ahead on the Mars terrain. "Right, except you didn't plan for a dust storm the size of Asia to blow in while our people are unaware at the launch site when they should all be at basecamp. How much time?"

I could hear it now. It wasn't just a lack of confidence—he was scared. "We'll be there in four minutes; this is going to be tight."

Needing verification, I tapped in a few commands and confirmed on the rover's HUD display. We were four minutes out from the launch site and fifteen minutes ahead of the largest storm we'd ever seen since being on Mars. If everything went as planned, we'd pick up everyone from the *Audacity* and be in the dust storm no more than four or five minutes before making it back to basecamp, we hoped.

Connor swiveled in his seat and faced me, and after a moment of just staring at me in silence, he spoke. "I need to know why you brought me with you and not Dalmatian. Better yet, why you didn't just use the pistol on me yourself."

He was right. Except for the two members of my crew he abducted, the rest of my team was outside basecamp working on solar panels. It only took a few minutes to get everyone together and bring them up to speed. Before that, seeing the storm had Shepherd so dumbfounded, I could've grabbed the Sparrow pistol, used it, and claimed self-defense on behalf of myself and the Red Planet. I'm even pretty sure Dalmatian would've backed me.

"My ancestor was a Dahomey warrior, from a tribe of African female warriors that *protected* their village and others," I said.

Connor's face contorted. "Okay, I don't understand what that has to do with this. If anything, it shows you should've used the gun."

I ignored Shepherd and continued. "My grandmother was a fighter pilot, and when I was a little girl she always used to tell me to be careful what I bring with me. It wasn't until I was an adult that I understood what she was trying to tell me."

The captain had a blank stare on his face. "Well, I have no idea what you're trying to explain to me, Commander."

I could see that Shepherd was sincere, which somehow made it worse. "I've always known the biggest threat to this expedition wouldn't be what challenges we found here on Mars, but what we brought with us. It took us seven months to get here, and we're sixty million kilometers away from the place of our origin, where everything we've ever known has happened. I brought the legacy of my family with me, and you brought a gun."

THE SONGBIRD AND HER CAGE

JOANNA SCHNURMAN

"Encore! Encore!" The cries that beckon me to reappear on the cavernous stage are accompanied by thunderous applause, filling the ornate theater with a raucous mélange of sound. I breathe deeply before taking a sip of fresh water from the crystal glass my attendant placed in my gloved hands as I exited the stage moments before. The newly installed electric theater lights gleam, illuminating the carved mahogany theater walls and the rich crimson velvet curtain separating me from the crowd of well-dressed aristocrats.

"Bella!" The audience rhythmically begins chanting my name. One more aria.

I draw in a deep breath and plaster a broad smile on my face before stepping back onto the hardwood stage, the satin of my elaborate emerald-green bustled gown swooshing with every step. The stagehands heave the rope on either side of the stage, and the heavy fabric of the curtain parts with a dramatic flourish. I place my gloved hand on my chest, grazing the lace décolletage of my bodice. Dipping into a practiced curtsey, I thank the quieting crowd. I nod to the maestro, one of the golden curls that frame my face briefly bobbing out of place. It's a rare imperfection in my routine. A reverent hush falls over the crowd, and I sense thousands of eyes on me. Goosebumps rise on my skin at this sensation that has taken half a decade of performing to become accustomed to. Yet, my heart still quickens at their rapt attention. The orchestra swells as they begin the lush musical introduction. Letting my voice soar through the theater, I navigate the rich melismas of the love song I've chosen for the finale.

I have methodically practiced this piece for years now, my expressions and movements carefully honed over countless hours of rehearsals. I clasp my hands to my chest as the orchestra crescendos before throwing my arms wide. A triple forte high note bursts from my lips, my own ears vibrating from the sound. As usual, the audience erupts with cheers as the note fades into silence. Dragging my gaze upward, I acknowledge the box seat belonging to the theater's impresario, my husband, Bruno Capaldi.

I pull off one of my gloves and press my scarlet-painted lips to the moon-white skin of my palm before blowing a kiss to his imposing form shadowed at the edge of the box. His portly frame dominates the space as he stands and steps into the light, removing his top hat. He nods shallowly so as to not expose his thinning black hair, combed over to hide his bald pate. He gestures behind him, ushering in a small girl who bounces into the box with exuberance. Her golden curls are trussed up with bows that bounce with every movement, shining under the lights. Nanetta, my daughter, grins widely and waves down at me. I blow one more kiss to the box. And for a moment, I see what the audience sees, what Bruno wants them to see: a perfect, loving family.

I smile tightly before exiting the stage one final time, already pulling the other stifling glove from my sweating palm so that I may begin to unlace the bodice constricting my rib cage.

I step briskly to the stagehand near my dressing room, eager to remove the layers of cosmetics and fabric confining me so completely so that I may see my daughter before dinner. "Thomas, please fetch Bess. I would like to change into my dressing gown immediately."

"I am sorry, Madame Capaldi. Master Capaldi has summoned you to his suite." Thomas stops me with his words. My husband usually spends his evening drinking and gambling away any profit we made from the performance. What's different about tonight? I sigh in resignation before giving a curt nod. Steeling myself, I turn to the stairs that lead to my husband's private rooms.

"Bravo, darling." Bruno grips my arms and kisses my cheeks wetly. "Bellissima. But please, I told you to begin the final aria with a pianissimo crescendoing to fortissimo."

"Yes, my love." I choke the words out. "It's the corset; it was laced too tightly. Next time, I will be better."

Bruno tightens his grip on my arms, and I wince. Holding me closer, he whispers in his deep, lightly accented voice, "No excuses. You want to look and sound the part of songbird, not elephant."

He releases his grip and gestures for me to sit at the foot of his long linen-covered dinner table, laden with sumptuous-looking bread, no doubt shipped here to London from his native Naples. I notice there are three cloches instead of two. I look up at my husband hopefully, his depthless brown eyes meeting my sapphire ones.

"Si, mi amore. Nanetta will be joining us this evening." He snaps his fingers at the stoic attendant by the door, and my daughter is ushered inside.

"Mamma!" she cries, only to be silenced by a severe stare from Bruno. "Sorry, Papa."

Bruno grips her hand like a vice and nearly shoves her into the third bulky chair at his dinner table. "Children are to be seen and not heard. I will not mention this again."

I ball my hands into fists but lower myself into my chair as Bruno's eyes meet mine again, full of silent command. Bruno's chair creaks as he does the same, a bead of sweat dripping from his top lip. The cloche on each of our plates is removed with a flourish by the attendant, and I frown at my meal. A small portion of roasted vegetables from our hot house. Again.

"Bella, my dear." Bruno's sharp voice punctuates the silence, garbled by a bite of rich gravy-laden roast beef. "It's a shame to see such an ugly expression on such a beautiful face. You must smile."

"But, darling—"

"Good seamstresses don't come cheap, and I'll not pay to have them let out your dresses and costumes because you have no self-control." A dribble of gravy slides from his elaborate mustache as he spits his reply.

"Of course not. How could I have been so silly." I spear a green bean onto my silver fork, hoping this is enough to avoid a conflict.

"Indeed. You'll give our Nanetta all sorts of ideas. No wonder she speaks so brazenly without permission," he grumbles before returning to his meal.

Our Nanetta. *Our* Nanetta. I grit my teeth, choking back the words that threaten to escape from my lips. I reach over to Nanetta, my beautiful girl, and run my fingers along her golden curls. She grins at me, exposing a few gaps where her teeth have fallen out. She's growing so fast, and I'm running out of time.

"My dear, speaking of Nanetta, I worry that her gowns are falling out of fashion." I speak softly and peer through my lashes at Bruno. "Why, I saw Lady Martin's daughter tonight wearing chantilly lace! I'm afraid Nanetta's dresses look drab in comparison. With the Queen's gala coming so soon…"

Bruno's face reddens until his doughy face is almost purple. He cannot stand the thought of being looked down upon as an outsider in the aristocracy, and the Queen's lavish birthday gala will be an important event for the theater. Our image is always perfectly maintained. I, the ingénue discovered among the young ladies in a rural British conservatory by Signor Capaldi, the master musician and impresario of the little-known Capaldi Theatre. After he found me, I performed lead roles for his theater, drawing increasing numbers of high-class aristocrats with each recital and opera performance. He sculpted me into a prima donna, and we fell in love immediately. Our darling Nanetta was born not even a year later. From student to prima donna, wife, mother, and the toast of the town. A fairytale story with as much truth as a fairytale indeed. I know Bruno won't dare risk a crack in that gleaming facade.

"Well then, take her for a fitting at once!" He scrambles clumsily from his chair, drawing up the sole key to his safe from a long silver necklace he wears underneath his frilly white shirt.

My eyes narrow as he fumbles for his safe behind a false panel in the wall, retrieving a few coins.

"That won't do at all, my love. Chantilly lace is worth far more—"

"This had better be worth it, Bella." He grabs a fistful of coins and crosses to me, shoving them haphazardly onto the table.

Nanetta squeals from her chair, her small bowl of porridge empty, "A new dress! Thank you, Papa!"

"No speaking until you are spoken to, Nanetta. You are just like your mother. You never learn proper respect. Get out and go straight to bed."

Bruno clenches his jaw, no doubt upset about having to dole out more of his dwindling reserves of money. He really must stop gambling.

I move to take Nanetta's hand to lead her from the room. There's still time enough for me to read her a bedtime story. There's nothing I love more than those moments I can hold my daughter close and tell her stories of adventures in far-off lands.

"I did not dismiss you, Bella," Bruno says coldly as he returns to the table. "Sit."

Hesitating briefly, I perch on the edge of my seat. Bruno is in one of his moods, and the only way to escape is by weathering the storm. "Thank you for dinner, my lo—"

"If you do not get your daughter under control, I will be forced to send her away to school." He places his large hands on the arms of the chair to either side of me, penning me in.

"I will speak with her." I lay my hand on his, placatingly. Peering up at him with wide eyes, I silently beg him to let her stay. He can't send her away. I won't allow it.

"She was playing with her dolls on the catwalk above the stage this afternoon. And the stagehands have reported her running down hallways like an absolute heathen in between acts. It won't do, Bella." Bruno grits his teeth before standing and crossing to the other side of the table.

"It won't happen again, I promise. Please, Bruno..." Trailing off, I meet his dark stare. I know what is coming next.

"Without me, you both would be living on the street. When I first found you, you were pregnant and alone, wandering the streets selling little songs and picking pockets with those filthy hands of yours. I took you in and made you a prima donna. But one word from me and you will be back in the gutter with that mutt of yours." Bruno's fist slams into the table and the dishes tinkle, a crystal wine glass slipping off the edge and shattering on the floor.

It's always the same threat. I close my eyes, my mind wandering to life before Capaldi swept in. I was young and alone, waiting for my lover to return to port as my belly swelled more each day with our child. My wonderful, kind Phillip would never get to meet our child. Unshed tears sting my eyes as I recall the day his ship sank to the bottom of the frigid water. Without Bruno, I'd be raising Nanetta on the streets with naught but the coins I made from singing on street corners and filching unsuspecting aristocrats' wallets. Sometimes, especially on nights like this, I wonder if we'd have been better off that way.

Using the theater training Bruno instilled me with, I cross the room with graceful movements. I reach Bruno and let my nimble fingers trace through his sparse strands of raven hair like they used to trace the pockets of aristocrats' coats. I press myself against his portly frame and brush my lips against his cheek lightly, whispering, "I promise, my love. It won't happen again."

His eyes widen and his cheeks flush. My distraction is successful; perhaps he will forget about sending Nanetta away.

"You will stay in my chambers tonight." His tone has softened, and I know I've diffused his anger. He strides from the dining room without a second glance.

I nod anyway and pocket the coins he so carelessly dropped on the table for Nanetta's new dress. Half will go toward the dress, and half will join the pile I have stocked behind a loose brick in my dressing room. I smirk and saunter from the room behind him.

———————◆•◆———————

"The Queen and her retinue will arrive in one hour, Madame Capaldi." The short seamstress hooks the last button through the eyelet at the back of my gown and spins me to face her assessing gaze. After a moment of appraisal, she brushes a strand of frizzy gray hair from her face and continues, "You look spectacular."

I pat the woman on the shoulder fondly. "Thank you, Bess."

"You're so sparkly, Mamma!" Nanetta's crystal blue eyes are round and wide as she runs her fingers over the beaded ivory skirts of my gown. It was commissioned by Bruno especially for my performance in this evening's gala for the Queen's birthday. Of course, instead of the designer he asked for, I hired a promising apprentice and hid the extra coins.

"Thank you, sweetheart." I smile down at my daughter, who is beaming in her new pink dress. My eyes dart to the loose brick to the side of my mirror, and I stare, picturing the small pouch of coins hidden behind it. The sack is filling enough that Nanetta and I will be able to escape this jeweled prison within months. Nanetta follows my gaze, and I quickly look away from the hiding spot.

"I will tell Master Capaldi you are ready for your audience with the Queen." Bess nods at me, then Nanetta before taking her leave.

"Mamma, what's this?" Nanetta's bell-like voice sounds from behind me, and I turn to face her so quickly that one of my curls comes unpinned from an elaborate updo. She's moving the brick back and forth, and my heart drops. I waste no time in running to her, my feet nearly catching on the yards of beaded fabric adorning me.

"Stop that!" I pull her from the wall before she can remove the brick completely.

Her brows knit as I set her down, and she peers up at me confusedly. "Mamma, did I do something wrong? You're always looking at that spot, and I saw you playing with the brick yesterday. Is it a game?"

"No—Yes." Biting my lip to keep from trembling, I kneel before Nanetta. How can I keep her from revealing my damning secret? I whisper conspiratorially, "Yes, my darling, it's a game like hide-and-seek, but even more secret. The only way to lose the game is to talk about it."

Nanetta's eyes go wide, and her mouth opens, "And how do we win the game?"

I put my finger over her mouth. "We win the game by seeing who can keep the brick a secret for the longest. Do you think you can beat me?"

Nodding vigorously, she bobs up and down in excitement. "What do I get if I win?"

"Darling, you will have all the candy in the world. Now, will you go fetch Bess and ask her to bring a pitcher of water to my dressing room?"

"Yes, Mamma." Nanetta smiles and skips to the door. I turn to the wall and begin to push the brick back into place, my hands still shaking.

"Papa!" Nanetta's voice peels through the air, and my heart plummets again. I drop my hands and look to the dressing room door.

Bruno is standing in his finery, a hand around Nanetta's arm. What did he see? I can only hope I was fast enough, and that he hasn't noticed what I concealed. His dark eyes are locked onto me, and without breaking his stare, he says with frightening quietness, "I told you no running in the theater, Nanetta."

"I'm sorry, Papa." She frowns up at the only father she's ever known.

My heart squeezes as I think about the despair she will feel when I take her from her "Papa". I know it's for her own good, but still, I never want my daughter to feel the loss that I've hidden from her since my Phillip, her true Papa, perished at sea. The loss of a father.

Bruno's jaw clenches, and Nanetta grimaces as Bruno grips her arm tighter. I hold up my hands in a placating gesture, but he barrels toward me, dragging Nanetta behind him. He stops before me, his gaze settling on the ivory silk of my glove. I realize too late that dust from the brick clings to the fabric. I move to brush my hand on my dress, but Bruno is shockingly fast for someone of his size. He catches my fingers in a crushing, vice-like grip, some of the dust falling from the silk.

"What could Mamma have been doing, Nanetta?" Bruno tugs her forward to stand between us. Nanetta's eyes gleam conspiratorially, and she grins up at me, her finger covering her mouth just as I'd shown her moments before.

"Whatever are you talking about, darling?" My voice doesn't tremble like I think it will, my years of vocal training at work.

"Do not play me for a fool. What do you take me for?" He releases my hand with a thrust and pushes us closer to the wall. "Nanetta, what was Mamma doing?"

"I don't think I can say. I want candy for winning the game!" Nanetta looks from Bruno to me, confusion in her eyes.

Bruno's eyes narrow as he focuses his attention on me once again. He brushes his fingers across my cheek and whispers, "Keeping secrets, my love?"

"I—" My sentence is cut off as Bruno's meaty hand moves from my cheek to my shoulders with a violent shove. The silk of my dress grates against the brick wall, and some of the beads clink as they hit the floor, ripped from my gown. I try inhale, but the wind has been knocked from me.

"I will not ask you again." Bruno's fingers clasp my jaw and tilt my face up, forcing me to look at him.

"Papa, please! It's just a game!" Nanetta tugs on his waistcoat. "I give up. You can have the candy if you want. Mamma was playing with her special brick."

My stomach knots as Bruno's eyes follow where Nanetta points, right at the loose brick. Abruptly, he lets me go and I sink to the floor, gasping for breath. Tears sting my eyes, but I refuse to let them fall. My mind races to find a solution or a distraction. But my thoughts are slow as I catch my breath, and I watch in horror as Bruno feels the wall, finding the telltale looseness of the brick.

With one motion, he yanks it free and it drops with a thud as he squints into the dark cavity. I hold onto the irrational hope that he will somehow miss the pouch, but alas, a second later he has snatched it free and pours a few coins into his hand. He looks from me to the coins incredulously before turning beet red with anger, his jaw set in an expression that promises violence. He takes in my appearance, and the beads surrounding me on the floor, and something in his expression cools from red-hot rage to icy fury.

He places each coin back into the pouch and deliberately tucks it into the pocket of his waistcoat before kneeling in front of me, his face just an inch from my own. He declares, too low for Nanetta to hear, "I always knew you were the same guttersnipe I met years ago. Nothing but traitorous filth. How dare you betray me after all I've done for you and the girl."

I'm quivering uncontrollably now. I don't care what happens to me, but what will he do to my daughter?

"Get yourself together. You're a mess. Look what you've made me do." He gestures to the beads on the floor. "You're meeting the Queen in one hour, and then you will give the performance of your life. I will deal with you later."

My breath hitches again as he stands and saunters to the door, my pouch of coins, my only hope jangling in his pocket.

"Papa, I'm sorry that Mamma made you angry. She shouldn't have done that. I'm sure she's sorry too." Nanetta pleads to Bruno's back and, to my horror, he stops, seeming to remember her presence.

"Nanetta, have Bess pack your bags. You leave for boarding school in the morning." Slamming the door behind him, his flat, cold voice seems to linger in the air around us.

Nanetta dives into my arms, and I hug her tight as she sobs.

"Do I really have to go away, Mamma?" She asks me in a timid voice, but I don't answer. My mind is reeling. How could things have gone so wrong in the blink of an eye? Despite Nanetta being sent away, all I hear in my head is one phrase over and over. *I'm sorry that Mamma made you angry. She shouldn't have done that. I'm sure she's sorry too.*

The words that left my innocent daughter's lips wrap around my heart and settle there, squeezing like an iron vice so tightly I want to scream. How could I have been so blind? How could I have missed that witnessing Bruno's behavior was slowly but surely poisoning my daughter? My eyes rove over the luxurious furnishings in my dressing room. All this time I thought I was protecting her, providing a father and a better life for her by enduring mistreatment. I was wrong.

I take a long breath, finally regaining the air in my lungs, and I think of a plan. I know what I must do.

———— •·• ————

The atmosphere is austere as Bruno leads me to the luxurious room where the Queen will receive me. I'm told she would love nothing more for her birthday than to meet the greatest prima donna in the country and hear her sing.

Gossamer floats behind me, hiding the swaths of missing beading from Bruno's attack. Bess had shaken her head as she pinned the extra material to the back of my gown. The remaining beads hiss against the floor as we arrive.

The Queen's personal guards open the double doors to the ornate room, lined with panels of gold and illuminated by crystal chandeliers. I step forward, my eyes cast downward from the Queen's small frame, which is laden with jewels, from her diamond cuffs to her ruby necklace and of course, her signature tiara. She emanates a sense of power that fills the room of tittering courtiers. As I step forward from Bruno, she offers her delicate hand to me, and I curtsy low to the ground and lightly press my lips to the finest satin of her glove for a moment longer than I should.

"It is lovely to meet you, Madame Capaldi. I was quite delighted by your performance of Ariette last Spring." The Queen's voice is rich and warm. She eventually seems to remember my husband's presence and waves him up from the deep bow he's been straining to maintain. "Ah yes, and you, Maestro Capaldi. How lucky you are to have such a songbird."

Bruno's eyes dart to me with a momentary gleam of antipathy before he clears his throat. "Yes, Your Majesty. Quite lucky indeed."

"I wonder, Madame, if you would indulge me in a pre-performance chanson? Your French art songs are impeccable." The Queen asks with authority. I contain my grin at the perfect turn of events.

"Of course, Your Majesty. It would be my sincerest honor." I bow my head quickly before moving to the center of the room. I make a show of preparing to sing, then wobble a bit on my feet. One of the Queen's personal guards moves to steady me, an action she seems to note as coming from her own retinue rather than my husband.

"Are you quite well, Madame?" the guard asks me gently.

"Yes…" Breathily, I make sure the room takes in my valiant effort to continue. I draw another breath and close my eyes, promptly falling. I'm caught just before I hit the ground by the guard's firm hands.

"Someone fetch a physician!" one of the courtiers intones, and I snap my eyes open. That won't do.

"No… no… I'm simply lightheaded. I had somewhat of an eventful afternoon." I glare quickly and imperceptibly at Bruno as I stand. I pat his chest lightly. "Perhaps my husband might keep you company while I rest before my performance? If that pleases you, Your Majesty."

"I trust your word, Madame Capaldi. Please, do take your time getting ready for the performance. I shall… enjoy your husband's company." She looks my husband up and down with a doubtful expression. He is splotchy and red now, beads of sweat pouring from his forehead. I know he is incensed that I've caused a scene, despite the fact that had I actually fainted, it would have been his fault.

"Thank you, Your Majesty." Bowing, I try not to take my leave too hurriedly. I step at a steady pace from the room, careful not to let my hand graze my prize, having slipped it into my pocket as I fell moments ago. Biting my lip as I leave the room, I hope that the Queen won't notice quite yet that her diamond cuff no longer resides on her wrist, but in my skirts. I move in the opposite direction of my dressing room, having one more stop to make before I can be rid of Bruno and this theater forever.

* * *

"Mamma, please slow down," Nanetta pleads as she pants to catch her breath. We run at breakneck speed down the corridor that leads to the back exit of the theater. Our faces are both hidden under the hoods of our dark winter cloaks.

"Sweetheart, you must run faster. It's another game. Whoever leaves the theater first gets a brand-new doll." I tug her onward, seeing the doorway at the end of the long hallway.

"I didn't like the last game." Her tone is tremulous, and I squeeze her hand in comfort.

"I know you didn't. But this game is different... it's much better." Shoving the door open, I nearly push Nanetta outside the confines of our gilded prison. "Let's go!"

Our footsteps echo off the cobblestones, which are luminous with rain. The light from the streetlamps reflect in them like watercolors. I inhale deeply at the fresh air. Freedom.

With a jolt, I'm hurled forward, catching myself before I hit the pavement as someone brutally yanks at my voluminous skirts.

"Brava, carina." Bruno claps slowly. "What a lovely performance. But did you think I was a fool? As soon as the Queen sent her guards to find her missing bracelet, did you think I'd not realize just what kind of dirty filcher stole from her?"

My hands tremble as he approaches, stopping just a hair's breadth away from my face. He kisses me deeply before whispering into my ear, "You're mine. You both will always be mine."

He pulls away and sadistically slaps my cheek. Nanetta's scream pierces the night air.

"It'll be all right, Nanetta. Just stay behind me." I put a hand against my throbbing cheek, and I feel the tender flesh swell.

"Quiet, woman. I should have you jailed for life. Where is it?" Bruno searches the pockets of my skirts but finds nothing. Just like I knew he would.

"Where is what, darling?" I say, my words dripping with disdain.

"Don't play-act with me. Where's the bracelet?" He shakes my shoulders.

"Bracelet... bracelet..." I tap my chin in a faux ponderous motion. "Oh... do you mean, this?"

Bruno's eyes widen as I grasp the chain around my neck, pulling the key to his safe from where it lay hidden under my dress. He grits his teeth, "Why you little—"

I casually swing the key in a circle and the chain wraps around my finger. A guard's whistle blows from behind us in the direction of the theater. "You really should be more careful with this key, darling. Anyone could take it from you and plant anything they wanted to in your safe. Like, for instance, a diamond bracelet."

Bruno steps backward, and his expression slackens as realization dawns on him. "That moment you patted my chest in front of the Queen…"

I smirk and step forward, continuing with mock innocence, "You see, when I found out my husband invited the Queen to his theater just to steal from her, I was shocked."

"What—" Bruno begins, but I saunter closer.

"I always knew my husband gambled, but I didn't know he would plan to steal from Her Majesty. When I found out, I alerted the guards promptly." I'm close enough now to share breath with Bruno, and I manage to look down my nose at him despite his height. I brush a tendril of his sparse, string-like black hair behind his ear and whisper into it, "We were never yours."

"You'll never get away with this!" Bruno's face is purple with rage.

"I already have." I simper before knitting my brows together and using my performance skills to cause tears to well. I touch my cheek as the guards finally catch up to us and restrain Bruno.

"He's here, just like you said Madame Capaldi. I'm sure we will find the bracelet in his safe where you warned it would be." A guard nods at me then tilts his head, noticing the bit of swollen, red cheek I allow to show between my fingers. "Did he hurt you, Madame?"

"Y-yes. He threatened to harm my daughter and me when he found out I told you about his horrible crime." I sputter and sob with a dramatic flourish while still being believable. I should thank my husband again for the theater training. I pull Nanetta close to me and hug her tightly.

"You little guttersnipe! It's not true! She's behind this. She even has the key to my safe!" Bruno points at me accusingly. But where the key was just swinging around my finger lies empty space.

I shake my head in mock resignation, trying to hold in the grin of satisfaction threatening to curl my upper lip. "Darling, do you mean that key around your neck?"

Sure enough, he looks down and finally notices the chain I slipped around his neck as I'd distracted him by whispering into his ear. I pat my skirts, and a faint jingling noise escapes from the coin pouch I'd picked from his pocket at the same time. His mouth falls open in disbelief, and he sputters his innocence as the guards drag him away.

"I'm sorry you've had to endure this, Madame." A guard nods at my sore cheek. "Her Majesty appreciates your loyalty in turning in your own husband, and she would love to reward you personally."

"Please tell Her Majesty, it is naught but my civic duty to honor my Queen." I look down humbly, and the guard nods once again at me, then Nanetta, before returning to the theater.

"Mamma, what will happen now? Where is Papa going?" Nanetta peers up at me wide-eyed, and I bend down to scoop her into my arms, hugging her tightly to my chest. I know that however painful, this is for her own good.

"Papa is going away. It's going to be just you and me now. We are going on an adventure." I lean my head into her curls and smile.

"An adventure?" She pulls back and looks me in the eye, hopefully.

"Yes, a grand adventure." I put her down and take her hand. We walk down the alley, and into our new lives, together.

HELLBEANS

JENIFER PURCELL ROSENBERG

SATURDAY BEGAN LIKE ANY OTHER. The kids had woken up early, noisily whispering at each other to be quiet as they raided the cabinets for sugary cereal and tracked crumbs to the living room to watch YouTube videos of people playing video games on the TV. The cats had sprawled across the bed, taking up so much space that Miranda and her wife were both teetering on opposite sides. The dog was on the couch with the kids, sneaking as much spilled cereal as possible, and causing peals of laughter every time he farted. Miranda had eventually gotten up and poured herself some micro cold brew before reminding her offspring to sweep up the fallen crumbs.

Once everyone was up and dressed, time was taken to make certain every one of the children had completed their homework. A little more focus was needed for their first-grader's handwriting practice. The second-grader had completed everything as assigned and was reading ahead in her advanced reading chapter book. The fourth-grader was less than thrilled about learning the difference between acid and alkaline, and just wanted to watch more YouTube. Everything was sorted by lunchtime, and the kids happily devoured some riced cauliflower stir-fried with veggies and tofu.

By two in the afternoon, Miranda was sitting on the porch halfheartedly reading over an expense report for work while the kids raced around the yard with their friends, pretending to have a space battle. Miranda's wife,

Cat, was pruning the rosebushes by the driveway, her thick curls pulled back into a puff at the nape of her neck. They had purchased purple roses, with thick vibrant plum-colored hues, only to discover that the luxurious roses they had paid for were grafted onto a cheaper, smaller red rose varietal. Miranda grinned quietly and patted the dog gently while Cat could be heard cursing the garden center from across the yard. She was sure she had noticed the neighborhood busybody Mr. Jenkins peeking out from behind sheer green nylon curtains disapprovingly, but then, what else was new?

Miranda and Cat's three children, Ruth, Simone, and Robin, were happily rolling around in the yard, grass stains and smears of dirt covering their overalls and striped t-shirts (the perfect outfit for any child!). They were joined by the twins from the house on the left, Shelly and Adrien, and three kids from different houses across the alley behind their two-story craftsman in a small Midwestern college town. Miranda had never expected to be able to have this life, and as she sipped her third cold glass of coffee, she mused over how lucky she was to be here and now, and not living in a time where she would have been punished for marrying the love of her life.

As Cat walked up the path to the porch, shaking a branch with an anemic red rose and singing a song about painting roses from an old animated movie, Miranda laughed heartily. If only she could capture all of these little moments on film! As she began to sing along to the jaunty tune, she realized the sky had darkened a bit despite no visible clouds. When she breathed in deeply to determine if the scent of impending rain was in the air, there was an unusual, almost tinny scent instead. A hush fell across the neighborhood as everyone paused to assess the weather and wonder how far off the local forecast had been this time.

The silence was pierced by the sounding of tornado sirens, blaring a robust, ear-splitting warning loud enough to carry from the small town and out to the neighboring farmland. People throughout the neighborhood peered toward the sky again, shrugging and shaking their heads when they saw there were no dangerous clouds, and it wasn't as if everything were that pre-tornado shade of green. The sirens continued to wail, and Miranda motioned for the kids to come inside. It was probably a computer error, if the switches had ever been upgraded. Miranda remembered the time a spider had gotten into the old analog switchbox when she was a kid back in the 80's, and how the sirens kept going off randomly until someone figured it out. Nevertheless, on the off-chance there really was a tornado, it would be best to have the kids inside. It would be quieter, too.

Miranda counted off the children. Her three, the twins from next door, plus Brynn, Adara, and Jake. That was all eight of the usual crew. "Who wants popcorn?" she called, and they shouted in unison, "MEEEE!" As children began racing around the living room, she pulled the air popper down from its place in the cabinet and began measuring out popping corn. The sirens continued to blare outside, and Muggle, the lovable mutt they'd adopted from the local rescue, was howling along. Never a dull moment!

She ran her hands through her short green hair, took a deep breath, and bounced on the balls of her feet a few times. She'd learned to channel her anxiety through action back in high school, which was probably why she had been so active in sports. She realized the amount of coffee she regularly consumed wasn't helping the anxiety, but she didn't get as anxious as she used to. Having Cat in her life had really made a difference. She smiled as the first kernels of corn began to frantically bounce against the clear yellow top of the popper, and ping into the bowl she had waiting.

While the corn was popping, Miranda noticed movement outside of the kitchen window. It looked like one of those shiny plastic balls for sale from a big wire cage in the supermarket, only an extreme shade of black—the kind of shade famous artists might get into a feud over. The ball was not moving normally, however. It was moving slowly through the air. Was it a balloon, perhaps? She shifted to look more closely and realized that there were several of these dark orbs lazily floating through the neighborhood. She heard the front door slam, and it must have slammed hard to be heard over the sirens, the kids, and the popping kernels. Cat ran into the room, short of breath, her amber eyes wide. "Let's get the kids in the basement," she gasped. "One of those floating things just... swallowed Mr. Jeffries!"

Mr. Jeffries was the busybody neighbor who was always snooping around. He was always overly concerned about what everyone else in the neighborhood was doing, and he made a point of making passive-aggressive comments about having a same-sex couple on his street. If he had his way, women would marry men, stay home to mind the children, and never be caught with short green hair—so Miranda was one of his least favorite neighbors. Most people in the neighborhood enjoyed making jokes about how Mr. Jeffries could "sod off" when he complained about the lawns of those who lived around him. Despite the older man's cantankerous nature, Miranda had always made a point of being kind to him, assuming he must be a lonely soul to spend all of his time foisting his ideas on others. As Cat grabbed the bowl of popcorn and some board games to help shepherd the kids into the basement, Miranda went outside to see for herself what was happening.

Mr. Jeffries was standing in the front yard of Miranda's house, staring directly at her. He was soaked with a glistening slime, his small side-tufts of dull grey hair plastered to his ears, his skin shiny like a freshly waxed car. He was shuffling toward the house slowly, limbs shaking with obvious tremors. Miranda watched in horror as her senior neighbor opened his mouth as if to speak, and a viscous black ooze spilled out. With sirens still blaring, and orbs still floating through the air, Miranda wanted to run inside and lock the door, but she felt rooted in place. As Mr. Jeffries shambled forward, it became obvious that his eyes, instead of being their usual pale rheumy blue, were now smaller, bulging versions of the deep black orbs.

A sudden movement startled Miranda into action. Chris, the father of the twins currently hiding in her basement, had run outside frantically calling for his daughters. "It's OK, Chris!" she called, "Shelly and Adrien are safe here!" Relief washed over her stocky red-haired neighbor, and he waved his thanks. As he stood there, however, one of the orbs floating near him glommed on to his outreached hand. As he struggled to pull free, the orb began to melt and ooze, enveloping his arm. Chris's wife Lisa ran out of their house with a shotgun in hand. "Let go of my husband, you freak!" she screamed, and fired the gun. The shot passed right through, coming out the other side slowly, covered in the dark goo and floating away.

Without thinking, Miranda reached inside and grabbed her keys and the softball bat that Cat kept by the door in case of intruders. She locked the door, pocketed the keys, and ran across the yard to her neighbor's. Swinging the bat hard, she battered the orb that was trying to cover Chris. It felt like trying to hit a volleyball with a stick, and the bat bounced back. She struck the orb again, harder this time. The side of the orb dented slightly, but otherwise the blow had no effect. Chris was looking paler than usual, and sweating as he struggled against the alien orb. Miranda worried that he was going to throw up the alien slime like Mr. Jenkins had just done.

Glancing back to make sure Mr. Jenkins was not still approaching her house, Miranda noticed a twenty-something woman whom she knew lived in the duplex down the street was approaching the older man with concern. Mr. Jenkins reached out toward her, grabbing her arm. When this happened, the young woman spilled the overpriced boutique coffee she'd been holding, and it splashed over them both. Mr. Jenkins began emitting a horrible screech, and the alien matter began to drip from his eyes and nose, sloughing off of his body like a chunky, gelatinous snakeskin. Miranda glanced at Lisa, and they seemed to have the same idea. Time to get some coffee!

Lisa ran over to where the young neighbor was still gawking at Mr. Jenkins, pulling her away from the affected man. "Is there any coffee left in the cup?" she demanded. Miranda rushed back to her house, unlocked the door, and ran inside. "Cat!" she called. "I need your help!" Cat scrambled up the stairs, worried for her wife. "These things don't like coffee!" Miranda said. Cat glanced outside and saw Lisa dumping the dregs from the coffee cup on Chris's arm, and the orb shrinking back and releasing him. It then began to float off, but was dripping slime as it went.

"Do we know if it's the acid, the heat, or specifically the coffee?" Cat asked. Miranda, who was dumping instant coffee she'd gotten for a garnish on a chocolate recipe into an empty cleaning spray bottle with water she had just boiled in the microwave, shrugged. Cat saw the spray bottle and had an idea. They had several, which they often filled with vinegar and hot water for cleaning the windows and counters. More eco-friendly and cost-effective than buying harsh cleaners. She filled it with straight vinegar. Calling down to the kids to stay put, they went outside to test their options.

As they were leaving, Lisa was running toward the house. "Chris is making coffee," she said. "I want to stay with the kids." They let Lisa in the house and locked the door. She had a genetic condition called POTS that caused her to faint sometimes, and was safer and more helpful with the kids anyway. Miranda ran into the yard with her bottle of coffee and the softball bat, and Cat grabbed a cultivating rake that was on the porch with some of her other garden tools before heading out to test the vinegar. They moved carefully past Mr. Jenkins, who was now sitting on the ground as a thick trail of black slime inched away from him like a slug.

The tornado sirens stopped abruptly, and screams, cries, and emergency vehicles could be heard echoing through the streets. Hundreds of orbs were floating through the air, and people were hiding in houses and cars to avoid them. Miranda pulled the lever on the spray bottle and squirted at one of the orbs a few feet in front of her. The horrible screeching sound that had occurred when the coffee hit Mrs. Jenkins was repeated. The orb stopped moving and paused, dripping like the one that had released Chris. While it was still, she hitched the lever for the bottle on her belt and smacked the orb as hard as she could with the bat. Instead of denting it like a ball, the bat went completely through the orb, causing it to explode into a spray of gelatinous goop. Perfect!

Cat was going in the opposite direction. She'd noticed Chrissy and William, two preschoolers who lived at the end of the block, were running from their babysitter. She raced toward the little ones and stood between them and the shaking, slimy college student that was in pursuit. Aiming the bottle of vinegar, she pulled the trigger. Nothing happened. She glanced down and realized that the nozzle was turned to "off." She twisted it and tried again, this time creating a mist. The babysitter pulled back for a second, but then lunged again. "Crap!" shouted Cat, and she quickly moved the indicator to "stream" instead. She began to frantically spray at the sitter, hoping that the vinegar would be as effective as the coffee had been. The answer was no. It was far more effective.

The stream of vinegar hit the sitter on the forehead and ran into his glistening black eyes. As it ran down, thick streams of jet black liquid began to pour off of his skin, and a horrid, guttural keening sound reverberated from within him. Within seconds, he was unconscious on the ground. The liquid that had poured off of him half evaporating, and half congealing on the ground. Cat dropped her rake, held her spray bottle precariously in her teeth, and grabbed each child under one arm, running back to her house. Lisa had been watching out the window and opened the door to bring them in to safety. "Call everyone," Cat said. "Tell them that it's acid. The stronger, the better!" Cat ran in to get the two-gallon jugs of cider vinegar that were under the sink, and decided to go ahead and grab the brown squeeze bottle of malt vinegar they kept for fries as well. Lisa locked the door behind her.

It was easier to do damage to these things if they had been hit with something acidic, that was certain. But would the acid be enough? Could these things be killed? How many were there, and how many people had they gotten to in the past, what? Half-hour? Hour? Everything seemed to be dragging and rushing simultaneously. Would these things make inhabited humans break into houses? Would anyone be able to get the rest they needed to keep fighting? She was terrified of the notion that the world was ending today, but she wasn't about to stop trying to save it. "Get vinegar!" she screamed. "Acid makes them weaker!" She noticed a few faces peering out windows and disappearing. Hopefully, more people would spring into action.

A sudden tingling sensation on the back of her neck gave her pause, and she turned around slowly to realize that one of the orbs was right behind her. She stared in horror at the glistening, deep black sphere, feeling rooted to the spot, her limbs ensconced in the pins-and-needles sensation you get when leaning on your arm too long while reading, or sitting cross-legged on the floor to do a puzzle with small children. Her chest was tight, and she became aware of the fact that she was wheezing while breathing. Vinegar. She needed to use the vinegar. Hadn't she just been holding two gallons? Had she dropped them somehow? She fumbled her tingling hands around, aware only dully of sensations, but mostly of the stinging agony of touching anything. Was this thing controlling her mind? She began to think as hard as she could, struggling to focus. Forcing herself to think the word "NO!" with all of the power of full concentration.

As she was focusing, she felt the numbed sensation of something brushing against her hand. The malt vinegar was in her sweater pocket! She fumbled to grab it, feeling as if she were an intoxicated person trying to operate keys. Finally, she felt she had a grip on the bottle, and pushed up to open the flip-top cap. The sharp scent of malt vinegar hit her nose, and immediately a palpable sense of having a little more control of her mind helped her renew her attention to the task. She lifted the bottle and squeezed as hard as she could, even though her hands felt like they were full of electrified ground glass. She watched the tawny liquid gush against the mirror-shine of the glistening ball, and saw that the areas touched by the acid lost their shine. As the vinegar coursed against the surface of the orb, the prickling feeling in her body pushed away. She had a mental image of putting a drop of soap in oily water, and how it caused sudden separation, all of the grease fighting to get away from the chemical agent. This was the effect acid had on these things.

As she was standing there, her sensations returning to normal, she became aware of the fact that her hearing had ceased while she was in the thrall of the floating entity. She jumped in surprise at the sudden cacophony of sound, people screaming, car alarms, emergency vehicles, helicopters, and her wife! Miranda was screaming profanity and running straight toward her with an iron fire poker raised above her head. "LEAVE MY WIFE ALONE, YOU FREAKING EVIL KICKBALL!" She swung downward sharply, hook end of the poker first, and managed to slice right through the thing. It fell to the ground with a dull thud, its insides thick and viscous and an eye-straining shade of bright pink. It pulsed for a few seconds, quivering like neon pudding, and then shuddered to a stop, losing its glow. It made a crinkling sound, and transformed, like a time-lapse film of something decaying, into fine-grain pebbles in a dull shade of brown – not unlike the dirt on an ant hill.

The women stared at each other for a second, bewildered by what they had just witnessed. Miranda kicked at the pebbled debris, scattering it. They began running, door to door, to make sure that everyone knew what to do. It was imperative to get the upper edge before dark, and before too many people were overtaken by these things. When Cat knocked on Susan Weber's door, she screamed when she was greeted by a glistening woman with skin covered in shining inky slime, wearing a rubber swimming cap on her head and what appeared to be a diving suit. "Don't worry, Catty Cat!" the older woman shouted. "It's one of them charcoal face masks to remove sebaceous deposits! I figured those creepy things in the sky might ignore me if I prepared! My grandkids live on the other side of Ninth Street, and I fully intend to go make sure they're safe because my daughter isn't answering her mo-bile phone!"

Cat figured the fact that Susan's eyes seemed fine, and she was smiling and talking, meant she was probably telling the truth. She cautiously reached out and touched Ms. Weber on the nose. Completely dry, just a shiny mask. She stepped back as the woman lugged a large plastic bin full of a light greenish powder out of the front room.

Helping her neighbor lift the bin, which was surprisingly light, she asked, "What's in the bin, Susan?"

"I heard y'all yelling about acids, so I've spent the past half hour emptying all of my single-serve powdered lemon and lime packets into here. I buy them in bulk!"

Cat nodded. "Good luck! Might need to get it wet so you can splash the things."

"You betcha!" Susan said.

Cat went to the next house. Within a matter of minutes, half of the adults and several of the teens on the block were outside, armed with acids and weapons. Little grains of aerated dirt were piling up as everyone followed the acid-douse-and-thwack method Cat and Miranda had discovered. Super-charge water squirters were being loaded with vinegar, lemon-shaped bottles of juice were being squeezed, and interesting items like pickle relish and mustard were being slung about. Miranda helped a couple of sisters who supplemented their household income by making bath bombs to empty bags of citric acid into buckets half-filled with water to make some more liquid. They'd tried just throwing the powdered acid at the creatures, and it wasn't as effective as a wet application.

"Whatever happened to acid rain?" asked Chris.

Miranda nodded, and wondered just how acidic rain was these days. After all, recent relaxations in environmental standards were making air and water less clean—it was possible that a good raincloud could help wipe out the creepy space ball population.

The neighborhood resembled a massive battle scene from some sort of surreal video game. People with all manner of weapons and condiments were rushing about attacking the orbs. Ms. Weber had been tossing shovelfuls of her citrus mixture at them and shouting, "DIE, HELLBEANS!" as she obliterated them with the edge of the same shovel. Chris and some of his gaming friends were hitting the things with a Sriracha and Tabasco mixture, and then grinning while they called, "I ATTACK THE DARKNESS!" A hairdresser from the salon at the end of the cross street was using hairspray as a makeshift flamethrower, and showing that flame was also helpful, turning the orbs into charcoal-like powder. Miranda and Cat were operating as a tag team, with Cat spraying and Miranda hitting. Others were dragging people who, like Mr. Jeffries, had been attacked, to the safety of front porches and parked cars.

Whatever the floating spheres really were, they must have had at least a modicum of intelligence, or a hive-mind perhaps, because they began floating away from the neighborhood. Miranda watched them float up and over the houses, all heading in the direction of the university. Had they originated there? She hadn't noticed them until they were already in the neighborhood, so she didn't know which direction they'd originally come from. She also noticed that there were several children, including her own, faces pressed against windows, watching the drama unfold in their own front yards. Why hadn't Lisa kept them in the basement? Well, to be honest, how had Lisa managed to keep them confined for so long to begin with? Mrs. McMullan had taught her daughter well, but we were talking about eight children! At least they were still safe in the house. She inhaled deeply, smiling at the sharp scent of condiments and citrus strewn across the neighborhood. Everyone's lawns were going to die, but maybe it would be a good opportunity to convince people to replace lawns with natural native plants and hearty perennials that were better for the bees. Many of the car alarms that had been sounding had settled down, and the emergency vehicles had either shut off their sirens or just left the area. The hospital and police station were on the other side of the university.

Suddenly, the ground began to shake. At least, that was how it seemed. The two women looked at their feet and saw that the Earth was solid beneath them. There was a loud, rhythmic thud heading toward the neighborhood. As it approached, they could hear people from further up the hill shouting in fear. They looked up in horror to see the entire men's college basketball team was marching down the middle of the street approaching them, their colorful uniforms dulled by the grimy sheen of the orbs. It was one thing to smack a strange floating ball. These, however were real people. These were the local heroes of the top-ranked basketball team, and they were all in peak physical condition. Nobody was going to want to fight possessed humans, especially not the local sports legends! A murmur went up around the assembled neighbors.

"This is some shit right here," said Chris.

Seemingly out of nowhere, there was a high-pitched keening sound. Lisa came rushing up, wearing what appeared to be Miranda's catcher's gear for softball and wielding one of the massive neon-colored water canons called a BFG Splooshify. She pumped the canon rapidly, aimed it at the approaching team, and screamed, "I lost fifty bucks when you punked out on the game last week!" A thick stream of what appeared to be red wine vinegar cascaded over the first few players. The assembled neighborhood watched in awe as slime seemed to ooze from their pores, creating a thick, congealed look like a blob fish before falling to the ground in quivering chunks. When the ooze had dropped, the college athletes appeared dazed and staggered back, only to be shoved out of the way by the still-possessed members behind them. This wasn't just the top team you saw on local television; this was an entire university basketball program. People rushed to usher the dazed players away.

There was another voice following the marching mob of possessed ballers. Miranda stepped aside to try and hear what was happening, and see where the shouting was coming from. She realized that it was the head coach of the basketball team, Alan J. Brava. He was a local legend. At 6'7", he had led the college basketball team to a national victory back when he was a student in the seventies. Now he was America's favorite basketball coach, and he was frantically chasing his team of slimed athletes. "Stop! Wait! Don't hurt them!" he was shouting. Miranda turned back to helping the vinegar efforts.

Cat noticed that the limbs that came in contact with the vinegared players took on a sheen as if they were beginning to lose some of the viscous alien matter. It gave her an idea. Grabbing up one of the jugs of vinegar someone had carted out, she held her breath and poured it over her head, then rubbed some mustard on the softball bat that was usually by the front door. She was ready for battle. As she was about to rush forward, she saw several quickly moving and brightly colored orbs, very small in comparison to the ones they had been fighting. They flew through the air in an arc, landed on or near the team members, and exploded! Turning to glance back, Cat felt her fear melt away when she realized several of the high school kids from the area had started filling water balloons with vinegar using the water cannons and were lobbing them at the approaching horde of ballers. She smiled. Smart kids! She held the bat out horizontally in front of her and approached the guys who had not yet been hit. One, Number 43, reached for the bat and got slippery handfuls of yellow mustard. As intended.

The gleam in Number 43's alien-possessed eyes dulled for a second, and he looked at Cat in alarm right before a bright blue water balloon collapsed on his head and caused the extraterrestrial goop to vacate his body. Cat knew what she had to do. She flung the bat out of the way and marched headlong into the remaining pack. Why were there so many people on the team when only a handful ever played in the games? They all reached for her, trying to either injure or infect her, but then backed away when they touched her vinegar-soaked body. She started to grab them one at a time and hold them still for either vinegar balloons or canons. Once one target had been hit, she would grab the next. Miranda, wielding a basket full of vinegar-soaked sponges that she was distributing, smiled and called, "Doing great, love!"

As she smiled back, Cat slipped on some of the underfoot goo and fell hard on her butt. When she did, the impact of her fall turned the matter into the strange aerated dirt again. "HIT THE SLIME!" she shouted, as several of the remaining players began to shed the goop. Many neighbors, after pouring vinegar on their shoes, began stomping on the quivering bits until they turned to dust. Ms. Weber used her trusty shovel and began smacking the alien substance until it was mere soil. More shovels, bats, and even brooms were employed in the task as the community came together to finally defeat the invasion for good.

Once every last player, as well as the assistant coaches, had been treated with acids and were sitting on the ground recovering, the assembled neighbors began to relax. Perhaps this surreal nightmare was over. When crop dusters began flying over town spraying vinegar over everything, people started dancing in the streets. Their gardens would be fried and their lawns smelled like pickles, but they were alive and well.

Susan Weber was pumping her fists in the air triumphantly and smiling up toward the raining acids. "OPE! I got it in my eyes! Real smart there!" she said.

Miranda and Cat, hand in hand, smiled at each other, feeling that they were now safe and could return to life as usual, though a lot of gardening would be in order.

The official news reports of course tried to play the events of the day off as some sort of horrible prank involving chemicals being used to make bubbles. Everyone knew this was a cover-up, as the science building had a huge hole in the side and a gigantic sinkhole in the middle. Videos online of the orbs pouring from the building were quickly taken down, and a giant privacy fence and scaffolding went up around the building, which was now under guard as several military and unmarked vehicles traveled up to campus every day. An environmental agency came and removed the soil from the yards of neighborhoods that had been invaded by the orbs, and new truckloads of clean soil were brought in. Miranda and Cat convinced several neighbors to plant native grasses and wildflowers instead of regular lawns, and several people planted new trees as well.

For their part, Miranda and Cat weren't publicly recognized for discovering the solution, but when a member of the city council had seen their family seated nearby at a restaurant a week later, she arranged with the manager to pay their bill. Sales of vinegar nationwide increased as the story of the orbs spread through social media. But mostly, life went back to being almost the same as it had been before the orbs came. The people in the neighborhood had a better sense of unity now, and everyone knew each other's names. Mr. Jenkins had stopped being fussed over everyone else's business and was very grateful when his neighbors helped to design a beautiful bee- and butterfly-friendly garden in his front yard. Children were once again playing outside, but instead of space battle, they pretended to battle the Hellbeans.

KRYSTA, WARRIOR PRESIDENT

PETER DAVID

STONN

S TONN WAS ACCUSTOMED TO EATING alone. It was pretty much standard operating procedure for him.

The fifth grader sat at the table in the cafeteria, eating the lunch that had been prepared for him by the White House chefs. It seemed such a waste of their time, as far as Stonn was concerned. He was surrounded by kids who were eating lunches out of paper bags that had been crafted for them by their parents. Peanut butter sandwiches, or tuna. Cold cuts in some cases. Some of them came with notes of affection from whomever made the lunches in the first place.

The White House chef never left him notes.

"You okay?"

The question came from David Webb, one of his Secret Service guards. With his salt-and-pepper beard and glasses, David stood serenely behind him, keeping a wary watch on the surrounding lunchroom.

"I'm fine," said Stonn.

"You don't seem to be eating."

He wasn't. He was just poking at the sandwich without much genuine interest. It made sense. He wasn't really hungry.

Then he looked up in surprise.

There was a girl standing a short distance away. She was quite an attractive young thing, with short, brown hair and a round face that seemed capable of boundless empathy to the world around her. Of course, that might have just been his imagination, but it was possible. She was holding her lunch bag with both hands and studying him openly.

The girl wasn't approaching. She was just standing there, staring, with her head slightly cocked. He realized she was waiting for him to acknowledge her in some manner. He nodded slightly and waggled his finger in a "come here" manner and instantly regretted it. It was as if he was summoning her, and that might be viewed as condescending.

But if she was offended, she didn't indicate it. Instead she headed straight over to him. He heard David take in a sharp breath, and it was all he could do not to smile. "I'm reasonably sure she's unarmed, David. Please take a couple of steps back so you're not breathing in my ear."

David seemed about to protest, but instead he nodded and stepped back a few feet.

The girl plopped down in a seat opposite him. She wasn't carrying a tray of food; instead, she had a brown bag that was curled shut at the top. "Hi," she said. "You're him, aren't you. The First Son."

He stretched out a hand and shook hers. "My name is Stonn," he said.

"Do you have a last name?"

He shrugged. "Not sure why I'd need one. Everybody knows who I am. Plus, how many people do you know named Stonn?"

"That's true, I guess. My name's Dany, by the way."

"Dany."

She undid the top of her lunch bag and withdrew a sandwich. "Why do you always sit by yourself?" she asked.

"I don't do it deliberately. People just choose not to sit near me."

"Why? I mean, you're the First Son. Isn't that enough to get people interested in you? I think your mother's amazing."

"Thanks," he said, shrugging slightly. "I'm not sure everyone around here agrees. A number of kids here, they have one or more parents who work in the government or are politicians, and they come into conflict with her about stuff."

"What kind of stuff?"

"All kinds. I mean, she's the President, so it's kind of her job to be involved with everything. Like a queen. Except she's governed by laws instead of being the law."

"Oh yeah, I know that. Although didn't she used to be a queen? Or a princess? Something like that?"

"She never liked to use that title. Princess. She preferred the title that the queen gave her: Warlady."

"Warlady?"

"It's like 'warlord' but..." He shrugged again. "Y'know, for ladies."

"You never really answered my question. Why are you eating here all alone?"

"I'm not really that big on making friends. Everybody seems to want something."

"Is it wrong of me to still be so interested in your mother? I mean, I don't want you to think I'm like those other kids. You know, that I want something."

"Do you?"

"Well, good grades. And world peace. But I'm figuring the grades are more likely."

"Based on the history of humanity, I'd say so." Stonn shook his head. "I've studied a lot of history, believe me. Kind of my hobby. What I've found hasn't been especially encouraging."

"Speaking of history... your mom..."

"*That's* a smooth segue."

"Well, I was just wondering. I mean, there's so many books about her, so many stories, and some of them conflict with each other. And I figured you'd know all about her."

"Why? Because I'm her son?"

Dany blinked in surprise. "Well... yeah. Obviously."

"Doesn't necessarily mean much. Mom isn't always the biggest talker. Especially about the past. She worries mostly about the future. Which we have arguments about because I always say that knowing about the past is the only thing that helps us avoid making mistakes in the future. But, y'know... go argue with your mom."

"So you don't know anything about her past? About how she wound up becoming President?"

"No, that I know about. God knows I've talked to enough people who were there who were happy to answer my questions." He cocked an eyebrow. "You wanna hear it?"

"Yes, please," she said eagerly.

He sat back, interlacing his fingers. "Well... it started when she saved Eloise Colson."

ELOISE COLSON
THIRTEEN YEARS EARLIER

Eloise Colson could feel the energy sweeping into her from the crowd. She felt as if it was actually giving her additional physical dimension. She had always been something of a slight woman, but she had come to regard that as a strength rather than a weakness. As unthreatening as she was physically, her personality and sense of will always stood her in good stead when she faced off against the various powerful Goliaths in the government.

The governor of Colorado was on the stage introducing her. It was merely a formality; she was Colorado's senator, after all, and had been for eight years. So naturally, everybody out there knew her.

One of her handlers, Michelle Crichton, was trying to push through the array of individuals who were in the way. She shoved them roughly, her long auburn hair swaying into her face, not giving the slightest of damns who they were or what their purpose was. Colson's bodyguard interposed himself in her way at first, but then recognized her and wisely stepped out of her way. He was paid to intercept brutes with knives and guns, but the petite assistant? He cleared out of her way immediately.

Michelle was waving her iPad with clear excitement.

"What?" said Eloise. "What is it?"

"New poll numbers. We're at fifty-five percent!"

"My God," said Eloise, taking the iPad from her hands and staring at the specifics depicted on the screen. "This is... it's incredible."

"Five points in two days. And we're still five months out from Election Day." Eloise was grinning ear-to-ear. "This is fantastic."

The governor was wrapping up his introduction, espousing her tireless support for the people of Colorado and her efforts on their behalf all these years. It was all stuff that she knew he was going to say, but she still loved hearing it.

"We're going to do it," said Michelle. "We're really going to make it all the way."

Eloise felt a need to try and rein her in. She placed her hands on Michelle's shoulders. "That's an eternity," she said calmly. "A lot can happen. A lot can go wrong. Things can turn on a dime, so we can be happy, we can be appreciative, but we can't assume it's all going to go the way we want. Understand?"

Michelle bobbed her head, but she was still grinning so stupidly that Eloise was sure nothing she was saying was getting through. "Understood, Senator," she said, clearly not really listening.

Eloise shifted her attention away from Michelle and back to the situation at hand. Other advisors of hers were approaching, each of them showering her with advice that doubtless meant a lot to them but nothing to her. She wasn't focused on any of them. Instead her head was, as she liked to say, in the game. Their babbling about last-minute meetings, about polls, about various people who wanted five minutes of her time in order to pester her about their individual concerns... it all dissolved into one mass of white noise that she was able to thrust aside so she could focus her attention elsewhere.

These were the people, *her* people. Her followers, her base. Furthermore, she knew that CNN, Fox, and all the major cable news networks were carrying this as well. This was her first rally since actually winning her party's nomination for the presidency. The attention level to be showered on her had been ratcheted up to an eleven.

And she was ready for it.

She still remembered being a child and telling her parents she wanted to be President. You'd think her mother would have supported her while her father dismissed the idea, but actually it was the other way around. Her mother had laughed skeptically, but her father had nodded and said, "I believe in you," and had never wavered in his support. Yes, Mom had eventually come around as well, but it had been her dad who had supported her without question. And then the bastard had died the previous summer. That was what upset her the most; he would have loved to see this. This entire campaign was for her dad. When she was standing there, taking the oath of office, she would imagine that he was sitting there with a broad smile, nodding in that way he had whenever she did something he approved of.

That was when she felt the beginnings of the earthquake.

It wasn't as if earthquakes were unusual in Colorado, nor were they as common as they seemed to be in Los Angeles. She had endured more than a few during her sixty-plus years of existence, but nevertheless something felt slightly wrong this time. She didn't know what that was, exactly. But the first tremors didn't feel... normal.

And she had no idea why.

The people surrounding her seemed to sense it as well. Her security guard placed a cautionary hand on her shoulder as if worried she was going to topple over. She brushed it aside; she was confident she could remain on her feet.

Then the vibration ceased, but oddly enough, the rumbling continued. She heard confused murmurs from the crowd, people asking each other needlessly if they had "felt that," wondering aloud what was causing the rumbles. No one seemed to be panicking, but there was a definite lack of comfort.

Eloise saw that the governor was likewise looking nervous, and realized that she had to do something immediately to settle down the crowd. He had not completed his introduction yet, but to hell with that. Eloise needed to take charge. Then again, she was running for President, so who else better to do so?

She moved Michelle aside and strode out onto the stage, smiling and waving to the crowd. Her presence had the effect that she had hoped it would. The crowd immediately started to cheer, shouting "El-Oh-Weeze!" repeatedly, which was their typical way of greeting her. She was fine with that; anything was better than shouting "Lock her up!"

The governor smiled when he saw her and was furthermore relieved because the distant rumbling ceased. It was as if her appearance alone was sufficient to quell the anger of the Earth gods. "Welcome Senator Colson!" he said cheerily, which wasn't really necessary since they were already in the process of doing so. For a moment Eloise felt almost godly; the ground itself had attended to her appearance and ceased its quaking. How wonderfully cool was that?

"Glad to be here, governor," and she came forward and shook his hand.

"Thanks for that wonderful introduction. And thank you, Colorado!" she turned and waved to the crowd. They waved back in response. The governor nodded and backed away, crossing offstage and dropping into a chair that had been set up for him.

She interlaced her fingers. "So… let's talk about the President. Or rather, the idiot who has taken up residence in the White House and sworn fealty to a document that he has neither read nor would understand even if he did read it. It's—"

Suddenly, the ground began to tremble as violently as it had earlier, and possibly even more so. The audience was immediately stricken with uncertainty, unsure if they should stay where they were or flee. The problem was that even if they did run, they hadn't the slightest idea where they could go that they would be safe.

That was when the ground in front of Eloise Colson erupted. Dirt and debris sprayed all over, knocking people off their feet, and something gargantuan exploded from beneath.

Eloise's green eyes widened in shock.

It was a huge, white, furry creature. It seemed at first glance to be some manner of gargantuan rodent, but the damned thing had to be fifty feet long. Its body was adorned with thin white fur on its loosely hanging skin. It had twin massive teeth projecting from its jaws that were covered in dirt; obviously that was how it managed to dig its way through the ground. Its eyes were slitted and small, and it clearly did not like the bright sun that was beaming down on it.

People were screaming and running, and then Colson realized she was being dragged offstage. Her bodyguards had emerged and come running out to pull her to safety, even though she had no idea where safety might be provided.

The beast fully emerged from the hole, and it had a long pink tail that whipped around. It shattered the half of the stage that Eloise and her protectors had been running toward, and they ground to a halt as they saw that their progress had been blocked.

That was when she saw that the creature had a rider.

He was perched atop its neck, just beyond its head. He was dressed in some manner of purple robes, and a thick gray-and-black beard adorned his face. He was grinning dementedly, looking around, trying to assess what he was seeing. He likewise squinted in the bright sunshine, and he was wielding a staff that had the carved head of some sort of animal on the end of it. He brought the staff up, waved it toward the sky, and immediately thick clouds drifted in front of the sun, blocking the rays and bringing some shade to the day.

Oh my God, thought Eloise, *he controls the weather.* Which she knew was patently ridiculous. Weather controllers and the like were things that were cast up from fantasy novels and movies. They didn't exist in real life. None of this existed in real life. This gigantic mole creature that had materialized, it made no sense, it...

Mole creature.

It's a blesmol, she realized in shock. *It's a gigantic mole rat.* She remembered seeing one in a zoo a year ago, but it had been normal sized. Six to eight inches; not the size of a freaking bus.

There were Secret Service agents on either side of her, and they both had their guns out. They could get off the stage on the other end, but it would require them getting closer to the beast and its insane rider.

The rider took notice of Eloise when he saw that she had guards. The beast he was riding was hissing and snarling, but he managed to quiet it. People were screaming as they ran, and he bellowed *"Shut up!"* so loudly that it actually managed to carry over the hysterical voices that surrounded him. He shifted his briefly diverted attention back to Eloise. "Are you someone important? You appear to have guards." His voice was thickly accented, and Eloise couldn't place its origin. It sounded like a combination of Russian and German.

The Secret Service agents weren't having any of it. They both had their guns out and leveled at the intruder. *"Get that thing out of here!"* the slightly taller one shouted in warning.

The robed man cocked an eyebrow. "And if I don't?" he inquired.

That was clearly more than enough for the agents. Deciding not to take any further chances with this insane situation, the agents opened fire.

The man did not seem the slightest bit concerned. He simply stared at them and then, to Colson's shock, both agents staggered. Their guns slipped from their hands, and there were gouts of blood on their chests, from bullet holes that had appeared from absolutely nowhere. One of them pitched backwards; the other fell to his knees and tumbled to the side.

Slowly the gigantic mole rat began to slink toward Eloise. Its huge legs propelled it forward in what resembled to Eloise the movement of a snake. She started to back up but then remembered that the stage behind her had been shattered. There was nowhere for her to retreat to.

"You," he said, his voice a silky purr, "could make a most attractive hostage."

Eloise Colson drew herself straight up, unsure if any eyes were upon her, uncertain if anyone could hear her, and as her protectors writhed on the floor at her feet, she stared straight into the eyes of this monster of a man that hell itself had apparently spat out.

"Go fuck yourself," she said.

That was the moment that a high-pitched howl of fury erupted from nearby, and the face of Eloise's attacker switched from self-satisfied to fearful. His head snapped around, and that was the same moment that Eloise saw what it was he was staring at.

It was a blonde-haired woman, or at least she seemed to be blonde; her hair was stained with dirt as if she had just clawed her way to the surface. She was wearing an outfit of black leathers, and she was wielding the strangest sword that Eloise had ever seen. It was two serrated blades, side-by-side, projecting from the hilt. Each blade seemed to be a little over two feet long, but if it had any weight, no one would have known from the way that the woman was wielding them. She also had a short blade strapped to her right thigh. She was wearing a golden tiara around her head with a single, glittering red gem smack in the middle of it. "*Cyprian!*" she shouted, her voice rising above the roaring of the creature and the terrified shouts of the crowd. "*This ends today!*"

He scowled upon seeing her, clearly not thrilled over her arrival. "You don't know when to give up, do you, Krysta?"

"I do. I give up when you're dead!"

She charged at him.

The blesmol had spun to face her, baring its teeth accompanied by a deep-throated roar. Its tail whipped around, and the woman identified as "Krysta" leaped over it without slowing. The tail snapped back, and she rolled forward under it this time, and then she flipped over onto her back and snapped the blade around. It cut through the tail, severing it in half. The blesmol let out a high-pitched screech of agony as drops of blood the size of small boulders went flying from the stump that was lashing back and forth.

It bellowed defiance at her, and its head jutted forward. It snapped its jaws repeatedly, and Krysta kept dodging, staying out of its way, looking for an opening. In the meantime, the man she had called Cyprian was gesturing with his staff, muttering a string of words in a language that Eloise could not begin to discern. Dark clouds were rolling in from all directions, and suddenly a series of lightning bolts came crashing to Earth.

Krysta displayed an ability to dodge damage that seemed to border on the psychic. Every time a lightning bolt slammed down, Krysta had vacated the area where it had hit. The mole rat began to get more cautious, trying to fake her out, snapping its head this way and that, hoping to get her to commit with one defensive maneuver and then attack from another direction. Eloise watched with silent astonishment, no longer thinking about trying to find a way off the stage. She watched as if she was observing an adventure unfolding on a movie screen.

The mole rat faked left, came in right, and Krysta dropped onto her back even as she swung her sword. She cleaved right through the monster's lower jaw, and it thudded to the ground.

"*You bitch!*" howled Cyprian, but his excoriation of her was drowned out by the mole rat's ear-splitting shriek of agony. Blood spouted from the lower half of the beast's face, and Krysta did not hesitate. She sprinted forward and leaped, landing squarely on the creature's tongue as it flapped down to the ground with its lower jaw no longer there to contain it. Keeping the head momentarily immobilized, she drove her sword upward, presumably straight into the monster's brain.

Its narrow eyes widened in shock, and its entire body began to tremble violently. Cyprian leaped clear of his position atop the beast's head, and then with one great, final roar the monster pitched forward.

The full weight of the creature's skull landed atop Krysta. She was unable to clear out in time, and she was pinned beneath it.

Cyprian climbed down from atop his now-dead mount. A twisted snarl of triumph was upon his lips as he slowly approached the trapped Krysta. He chortled in delight as she tried in frustration to shove the beast's corpse off herself and failed. "What did you think would happen here, Krysta? Did you think you could destroy me? The greatest sorcerer in the history of your world? Of all the foolish—"

That was as far as he got before the crack of a gunshot lanced through the air, and blood welled up on his right shoulder. He stumbled, fell to his knees, and whipped his head around.

Eloise Colson was standing on stage, holding the gun from one of the agents firmly in both hands. She was aiming it straight at Cyprian, and she cocked the trigger. "Couldn't make a bullet bounce away if you weren't watching, huh," she snarled.

"I'm watching now," he said, and began to stretch his staff forward.

Eloise shifted her target and aimed it at the head of the staff. A bullet spat out, and the staff's head shattered as the bullet struck it. Cyprian let out a startled howl of fury.

"*Try firing one of your lightning bolts now, dumbass!*" Eloise bellowed.

That was when, accompanied by a grunt of effort, Krysta straightened her coiled legs and scampered out from under the beast's lifeless head. She scrambled to her feet, bringing her sword around, ready to swing it at Cyprian. "You killed Markos," she said tightly, hatred dripping from every syllable. "I'll kill you for that."

"Maybe, child," retorted Cyprian. "But not today."

Once more the ground began to rumble savagely all around them, and then a hole collapsed directly underneath Cyprian's feet. He did not seem the slightest bit perturbed by it; instead, he laughed loudly. Krysta shielded the lower half of her face as a great gust of dust and dirt blew up, briefly obstructing her view. She brushed it aside, coughing violently, and stumbled forward.

The ground had converged in front of her. She clawed at it, trying to shove it aside, but there was no use. Cyprian had vanished into the Earth, and Krysta had no means of pursuing him.

She let out a frustrated howl and continued to try and dig her way through, but it was useless. She could have utilized a jackhammer and she wouldn't have been able to penetrate the mass of rubble that was obstructing her.

"Damn it! *Damn it!*" she shouted, and sagged to the ground. She sat there, shaking her head.

Then she glanced up.

Camera crews were moving in around her from all directions. She stared at them uncomprehendingly, clearly trying to determine whether they represented a threat or not. She quickly bounded to her feet and whipped the sword around. "Stay back!" she warned, and that was all that was required for the cameramen to stop precisely where they were.

But now reporters were surging forward, thrusting their microphones at her, shouting a series of natural questions: Who was she? What had they just witnessed? Where did she come from? Who was she rooting for in the Presidential election?

She scowled at them and was clearly considering hacking them to bits with her sword, and then Eloise shoved her way through. "One side, one side!" she shouted.

Krysta stared at her. "You were the one who stopped Cyprian," she said, "with that... that odd weapon."

"It's called a gun. Come with me," said Eloise. Some of the personal guards from the governor had stepped in to replace the wounded agents that were being held for medical attention. "Let's get you away from here."

"To where?"

"Anywhere but here."

Krysta seemed about to protest, but then she nodded in understanding and accompanied Eloise.

Minutes later, they had retreated to Eloise's private dressing room. Michelle was there as well, guarding the door from the virtual army of people who were standing on the other side, demanding to know what the hell was going on. Krysta sat in a chair, breathing hard, staring in confusion at the wet wipe cloths that Eloise had handed her to clean the dirt from her face. She studied the dirt, then held the cloth up so that she could see it more clearly. "Hmmf," she said.

"Who are you?" said Eloise.

"I am Krysta. I am a princess from the land of Saguenay."

Eloise blinked. "That's in Quebec, isn't it? Off the Saguenay River."

Krysta stared at her. "What is Quebec?"

"It's in Canada."

"What is Canada?"

"It's another country," Michelle said helpfully. "Up north."

"No," and Krysta shook her head. "It's there," and she pointed straight down.

"Spell it," said Michelle as she readied her iPad.

Krysta clearly had no idea what the device was, but she did as she was requested. Eloise was relieved that somehow this woman knew English; it saved them a hell of a lot of time. Within minutes Michelle had pulled up a Wikipedia article. "'According to the Iroquoians, there was a kingdom to the north, of blond men rich with gold and furs, in a place they called Saguenay,'" she read.

"'Jacques Cartier first described finding the Saguenay River on his second voyage in 1536; he had with him Chief Donnacona's sons who told him it was the way to the Kingdom of Saguenay. While imprisoned in France in the 1530s, Donnacona himself also told stories about it, claiming it had great mines of silver and gold. French explorers in Canada looked for this kingdom in vain. Today, it is typically understood to be entirely mythical, a European misunderstanding (or made up), or an Iroquoian attempt to trick or confuse the French.'"

"Well, it obviously wasn't mythic," said Eloise. "I mean, she's from there, and she's sitting right here." She turned her attention back to Krysta. "So who was that... that magic user you were fighting? What did he want up here?"

Krysta shook her head. She was staring at the cup of coffee that Michelle had placed for her at the table next to her. She lifted it slowly, sniffing it in an experimental manner. Then, very meticulously, she sipped it. Her eyes widened, and she licked her lips. "What is this?" she said in wonderment.

"It's called 'coffee,'" said Eloise.

"It's amazing. I've never tasted the like." She sipped it once more, then put it down and shifted her attention to Eloise's question. "I have no idea what Cyprian wanted here. To the best of my knowledge, he was trying to escape me and my vengeance."

"Vengeance." Then Eloise remembered something that Krysta had said. "Markos."

Krysta's gaze fell to the floor. The coffee was clearly now forgotten. "Markos was my lover," she said softly. "He was a brave and valiant warrior. Cyprian killed him. Threw him into a volcano. I didn't see him die, but I heard his voice screaming my name. He was... he was glorious. And I chased Cyprian to avenge Markos's death. But I failed, and he got away, and now I can never go after him."

"Why not?"

"He buried the entrance!" Krysta said with an air of impatience. "You saw. There's no way I can penetrate the ground and go after him. I'm shut off from him, from my land. From everything I've ever known." With a roar of anger, she swept the coffee cup off the table. Eloise barely dodged it as the hot liquid sprayed everywhere. "*I have nothing!*"

Slowly Eloise approached her and rested a hand on her shoulder. "You have me," she said firmly.

"And who are you?" asked Krysta.

"My name is Eloise Colson, and I am running for… leadership of this country."

"Running for? Is it fleeing?"

Eloise chuckled at that. "It means we are having an election and I am trying to convince a majority of Americans to vote for me."

"You vote for your leaders?" Krysta appeared incredulous. "You mean leadership is not an inherited title?"

"In some countries, yes, but not in this one."

"Hunh." Krysta gave it a moment's thought. "How has that worked out for you?"

"It's had its moments," Eloise admitted. "Some leaders are better than others. Everyone's tried to do their best, and that's all you can really ask of anybody."

"No." Krysta shook her head. "Ask for better than they can give. If they are a true leader, they will rise to the demand."

Eloise chuckled at that. "Perhaps you should run for leader."

"Perhaps I will," said Krysta.

AFTERMATH

"And she did, obviously," said Dany.

"Well, not immediately," Stonn corrected her. He slurped the last remains of his apple juice from its bottle and then set it aside. "She became an advisor to Eloise. It was a way to keep herself occupied. But she became a media sensation. Every article about Eloise wound up talking a lot about my mom. And when they found out she was pregnant with me, then that kicked her to a whole new level."

"And your father was...?"

"Markos. Her lover. The one Cyprian killed."

"Oh. Sorry," she said softly.

He shrugged. "It's not like I mourned him. I never knew him. He was never part of my life. I mean, I appreciate the sentiment but I never really give him any thought, y'know."

"I guess."

"Anyway, Eloise won the presidency, but many people claimed that it was mostly because of all the attention Mom got. Mom reflected well on her. She wound up becoming Eloise's 'special advisor,' whatever that was supposed to be, and she was always in the public eye. People were more interested in what she had to say about pretty much everything than they were in Eloise. Eloise served two terms and then the DNC drafted my mom to run, pretty much by popular demand. Since Saguenay is underground in the United States, it was decided that technically she was an American citizen, which satisfied the thing in the Constitution that says only Americans can be President. And she wound up clobbering her opponents. Which, y'know, is what she's been doing her whole life. So that was nothing new."

"I guess not."

She frowned, and he saw the shift in her expression. "Is something wrong?" he asked.

"You just sound... I dunno..." Her voice trailed off for a moment, and then she said, "Do you like being First Son? Like that your mother is President?"

It doesn't matter. It's not for me to like or dislike. It's what is. I don't get a vote.

"Sure," he said. "It's great."

He fell silent for a moment as he tried to come up with some other topic of conversation, and was literally saved by the bell: the warning bell that informed the students it was time to change class and they had five minutes to get to their next destination.

"Okay, well, it's been nice meeting you," said Dany as she stuck out her hand. Stonn shook it, and she cocked an eyebrow. "You have a really firm grip."

"Yeah, well, my mom is pretty strong, so that's probably where it comes from."

She bobbed her head, got up, and started to walk away.

Stonn was not typically someone who spoke off the top of his head. He gave great consideration to every word he uttered, because words were important and once spoken could not be taken back. Wars started over the use of wrong words. People could die because of a mis-chosen statement. It was Stonn's tendency to think about everything, often to excess.

So he was startled when he blurted out, "Would you, uh, like to come? To the house, I mean?"

She turned, startled, her eyes wide. "The house? You mean the White House? Jesus! Are you kidding?!"

"No, I mean it," he said.

"When?"

"I dunno. You doing anything Friday?"

"Friday would be outstanding! Wow, I don't believe it. Uh, what time?"

"Hmm? Oh… Uh… five o'clock, I guess. You come by, I'll give you a tour of the place, and you can stay for dinner."

"I'll be there."

"I'll leave your name at the main gate."

"Sounds great. See you then."

She headed off, and Stonn turned to face David. "How do you think my mother will react?"

David shrugged. "It's not my job to predict that."

"I'm asking, David. You know her. Tell me what you think she'll say."

"Stonn," David said patiently, "if there is one thing I have learned about females as a species, it's that it's impossible to predict what they're going to say or do in any circumstance." Then he flashed a quick smile and placed a hand on Stonn's shoulder. "I'm sure it'll be fine."

"You're not serious," said Krysta.

She was in the Oval Office, seated behind the Resolute desk. "You really can't be serious."

"Why wouldn't I be serious?" he asked. "What, you think no girl in her right mind would be interested in me?"

She closed her eyes briefly and shook her head before opening them and gesturing toward a chair. "Sit down," she said.

Stonn obeyed her, already not liking where the conversation was going.

Krysta rose from behind the Resolute desk, came around it, and then sat on the edge of it. "Of course I don't think that," she said. "But that's not the point. You don't see me getting into any romances, do you?"

"This isn't romance! I've known her for maybe twenty minutes. This is just a matter of getting to know her."

"And have you thought about what you'll be doing to her?"

"To her? I don't—"

"Stonn," she said patiently, "anyone who gets involved with us in any capacity comes under the lens of the press. Have you ever considered that's why you have pretty much no friends? No one wants to be subjected to the scrutiny that comes with associating with us. Fifty, sixty years ago, before the time of computers and the intranet..."

"Internet," he corrected her.

"Right, that thing. Before then, people could have privacy. But that's not the world we live in anymore."

"And what the hell would you know about the world we live in, Mom?" he demanded. "At least I've been in it my whole life. You're still in the learning curve."

To his surprise, she actually smiled at that. "That much is true," she said. "I'm always learning. I've lost count of the days I've wished that I knew everything. But one does what one can."

"So you're saying Dany can't come over."

She paused, and it seemed to Stonn that she was about to turn his request down flat. But then slowly she shook her head. "No. No, of course I'm not saying that. You live here, Stonn. This is your home. If you want to have guests, you're certainly welcome to do so. But this Friday, you said?" He nodded. "I have dinner at the British embassy with the ambassador. So I won't even be here. Sorry."

He was about to ask if there was any way that she could postpone it, but immediately thought better of it. Perhaps it would indeed be best if Dany didn't meet his mother immediately. Let her get accustomed to the environment, and to him, before he introduced such a strong individual as his mother, the President.

"No, it's okay," he said. "That'll be fine."

"Maybe better. She can get used to the place before having to deal with me."

"I wasn't thinking that at all."

She smiled slightly at that. "Don't lie to me, Stonn. You're bad at it in general, and you're absolutely terrible at it with me. You think I don't understand? You think I don't know what you're going through?"

"I know you know, Mom."

"Good." She ruffled his hair. "I understand we're having shrimp scampi tonight."

He smiled broadly at that. "I love shrimp scampi."

"You're lucky that you have such a variety of foods to choose from. When I was your age…"

"You were never my age," he said, which was what he customarily said whenever Krysta would begin to reminisce about her youth.

She nodded. "I always forget."

DID *THEY* DO THAT?

DENISE SUTTON

NORA WAS TIRED. TIRED ALL the time. But she pushed herself to give 110 percent for her boys. She loved them from the second she laid eyes on them.

When her doctor had first told her she could not get pregnant, Nora was devastated. But once he'd recommended adoption and praised its virtues, she realized that her hopes of becoming a mom were not completely crushed after all, that somewhere out there was a child that needed her—needed their own savior—and she couldn't just sit there feeling sorry for herself. Life gave her one doozy of a lemon. Big deal. She would just have to make lemonade. Nora persuaded her husband, Liam, and they'd gone to the adoption agency willing to go through anything that would grant them a child. To her surprise—and Liam's bulging eyes—the agent had immediately placed twin 16-month-old boys in their care. That part was easy. What followed was a great challenge, to say the least—one bigger than she had ever anticipated.

As hard as it was, they were her sons, and she was determined to give them everything and anything they wanted or needed no matter what it cost her. Sleep was the first thing to go; that was expected. Her personal hygiene quickly followed. Nora often forgot to brush her teeth, not to mention she showered once, maybe twice a week if she was lucky. Deodorant became her lifesaver... if she remembered to apply it. Her curly hair rarely got a proper brushing. To save time, Nora simply put it up in a bun and called it a day. It was also the go-to style for moms with young children... it had the least amount of accessible hair that they could pull out. That lesson was learned the hard way, on Day Two of bringing the twins home. Those four hands would grab onto anything; the hard part was getting them to let go. It was like they had superglue spread over their palms. Why were they always so darn sticky? She'd lost more than a few strands of hair that day. She'd vowed not to make that mistake again. Nora refused to go wig shopping before the age of 40.

Nora's classy wardrobe was replaced by the "mom uniform," which consisted of a stained plain white Hanes t-shirt and baggy sweatpants. Leggings on special occasions, though she usually had holes in the knee and crotch areas and hoped no one would notice. Everyone always did, and she knew it. They just stared and walked away, probably wondering how many moths she had hidden in her closet. Nora even wore the same outfit down to her underwear and socks for four days straight. It wasn't entirely intentional, but looking like a homeless hot mess was a side effect of raising young kids. Most days, she was too tired to tend to herself; she would just smell parts of her body and say that her stench hadn't gotten so bad as to warrant a shower. A quick rinse under the bathroom sink usually sufficed. Nora had become nose-blind for sure. Liam was just too polite to risk offending her. Besides, in a way, the food-stains-and-rotten-milk smell became a badge of honor. Liam wanted Nora to wear it proudly. And boy did she, whether in private or in public.

Since adopting the twins, her life had gone from zero to 60, and those one-year-olds were at the wheel. Nora would have enjoyed the ride more if she wasn't so darn exhausted. She was so busy tending to their every need that she couldn't really take the time to live in the moment and enjoy them.

"I feel like a robot sometimes, you know," she told Liam one night before bed. "It's like I finish one chore and three more pop up, and all are equally important so I can't just not do them. It's for our kids. It's all about our kids. But I'm new to all of this, and I want to make sure I'm doing it right. Or maybe there is a trick to it or something."

Liam just shrugged his shoulders.

"I mean, how are there moms out there that look like they just walked off the runway while I look like I've been shacking up with Oscar the Grouch?"

Liam gave her a funny look.

"Oh yeah, sorry honey, all I watch are kids shows these days, and the boys are really into Sesame Street. It's a great show, very cute. I'm also learning a lot. The only downside is that I can't get the darn theme song out of my head. It's so catchy."

"Maybe if you try connecting with other moms on the internet, they could help you sort this all out. If nothing else, it's an additional outlet of support and advice that might really make a difference for you... help you with the questions that I can't. God knows I'm no help with this."

Nora considered his advice.

Liam tried to seal the deal. "Maybe if you share your experiences, you'll realize you're not the only one feeling this way... that it's just normal mom worries."

"You know, that's a great idea. I'll see if I can find a mom chat or something. I definitely don't have the time these days to do the old-fashioned face-to-face, like a quick lunch date. I for sure don't look presentable enough to even be allowed in a restaurant or cafe."

Liam couldn't help but let out a small laugh. "Honey, please," he said. "You always look beautiful to me."

"Thank you, sweetie, but we both know you are trying to make me feel better when I clearly repulse people and pets. The other day, a dog just stared at me like he didn't know what to do... run away or sit and marvel at the creature before him. I guess it's time for a wax, but I haven't gotten around to it yet. Maybe I'll just buy one of those at-home waxing kits and do it myself when the boys are asleep. Yeah, that could work. Two eyebrows are better than one, and one mustache is one too many."

Liam tried so hard not to burst out laughing. He kept pinching himself so his pain would replace his giggles. "Whatever you need to do Nora, I support you 100 percent. You know that."

"Yes, I know, Liam, thank you. And thank you for the tip about the mom chat thing. I'll look into it first thing in the morning. Goodnight. I love you, sweet dreams."

"Goodnight, honey. Love you too."

Nora picked up her cell phone and began searching for an online group chat that would help her navigate the perilous waters of parenting. It took a few minutes, but she found the perfect one: "Coping with Kid Chaos." Nora joined, eager to get any tips she could and immediately posted a few questions. The responses were many, but none were more insightful than those of Jack Mizrahi—a happily married dad of three kids under the age of six. She chatted with him for a while before exhaustion prevailed and sleep finally took over.

Five AM the following morning. The twins were up for the day as usual. Those two took forever to fall asleep and never stayed asleep for long. It was like their minds didn't want to shut down—like they absorbed every ounce of energy from their surroundings to power themselves a bit longer. They just didn't want to miss a minute of the day—or night. But that was them, bright-eyed and bushy-tailed after five hours of sleep, on a good night.

Nora got up and made her way to the boys' room across the hall. She opened the door to greet them and found both boys in the same crib, playing together as if nothing was out of the ordinary.

"Am I sleep-walking or just so exhausted?" Nora leaned in to get a better look. "How in the world did you end up in your brother's crib?" The cribs were parallel to each other but separated by about five feet. The mattresses had been recently lowered to the floor to prevent the boys from climbing out, buying Nora and Liam some time before toddler beds became an absolute necessity. "I don't understand. Did I put you guys in the same crib last night? Possible. Everything looks the same after a while... especially you guys." She looked at her sons, so confused. "Did you fly into your brother's crib?" she asked jokingly.

Nora's worry turned into a smile of relief since no one had gotten hurt. She took comfort in the fact that there must have been a valid explanation for this; she was just too darn tired to see it.

"Okay, my little men," Nora said. "It's time to start another day." She always talked to her twins like adults, none of that goo-goo gaa-gaa babble baloney. Nora felt that using language properly from the start would advance and strengthen their speaking skills. Her admirable efforts aside, she still felt as if the boys had a language of their own—one that no human could understand... and definitely not the bud of the English language.

Though the sounds they made were foreign to her, she did read once about twins having their own way of communicating with each other. She just didn't know why it reminded her of how droids or Ewoks communicated in those *Star Wars* films she loved so much. So again, Nora brushed that off.

"I'm going to get you both cleaned up, then we can all head downstairs together for a delicious breakfast of scrambled eggs and toast. If you guys behave yourselves, maybe I will sweeten the offer with some pancakes." Nora looked at the boys and smiled. "Syrup is a given. Don't worry, I know what's good." Both boys grinned at her then looked at each other. Hatching a plan? God, she hoped not. Was that even possible? Nora ignored her outrageous concerns and focused on how much she adored how her boys seemed to know what each other was thinking. That twin-bond thing bordered on telepathic tendencies, but no matter. For now, it appeared they were agreeing to cooperate for the time being. She just hoped that they would keep to it.

They didn't. Like all of the days before, they drove Nora crazy. With all the screaming, mostly hers, she was surprised that her neighbors hadn't called Child Services yet. Grateful, of course, but surprised. Their screams seemed almost supersonic. There were times she could have sworn the room itself vibrated when they cried, and earthquakes were extremely rare in Brooklyn. Nora dismissed it as another side effect of her new-mom insomnia.

"Boys, stop that! You do not throw your food at each other or on the floor. If you don't want it, don't eat it. Just please don't waste food, okay?" One of the twins threw some scrambled eggs in Nora's direction, and it managed to hit her right between her eyes.

"Aahhhh, stop that!" If Nora weren't so frustrated, she would have been extremely impressed. She had some real Robin Hoods here. This wasn't the first time the kids had thrown something with such incredible accuracy. Intentional? *Naah*, she thought. *No way.* Though, some of the things they hit—the throws they made—there was no way an adult trying to do what they did could have succeeded.

"NO, what are you doing now? Stop fighting with him. If you guys keep running around like this, someone is going to get hurt—and it's probably going to be me."

Truth was, Nora thought to herself, it always was her that got injured.

Scratch that, Liam often got hurt whenever he was around the boys, all harmless stuff. Like the time one of them dropped a rather large book on his toe. How in the world did he even lift that encyclopedia? Eh, maybe her son had just nudged it a bit, and it fell off the shelf. Yeah, that made more sense. Liam always did tend to exaggerate things. But he still got hurt badly—and often—poor guy. Like when they accidentally tripped him and he banged his right knee on the corner of the coffee table. Innocent mishap for sure. He, like Nora, always got hit in just the right spot that even a little bit of force would cause severe pain. Those kids had such a knack for that—like a secret talent for inflicting those "ouchies." All Nora could think of was how lucky she was that it was just the two of them that got hurt.

Come to think of it, she couldn't recall a single time since she'd brought the boys home that they got hurt, or even sick. Weird. But Nora took apparent nigh-invulnerability as a good trait for them to have. Besides, she often joked about how children were made durable—built to last into adulthood. If they weren't, the human race would have been extinct by now. She smiled a bit as her boys continued acting like little tornados swirling around the house. Nora recalled the night before how Jack, her parenting guru, joked how his kids always had so much energy while he and his wife, Shella, couldn't walk a straight line. Nora took comfort in knowing she wasn't alone. *Yup, little tornados…totally normal.*

After a bit, the twins slowed down. Liam took the opportunity to give all three of them a big kiss, snapping Nora out of her trance, and then headed over to the kitchen to make himself something to eat.

"Honey, I can't find my phone," she said. "Can you call it for me, please?"

"You lost it again? Okay, no problem. I will. I'm sure it's around here somewhere."

"I didn't lose it Liam," Nora barked. "It's somewhere in the house. I just misplaced it."

"Okay, okay, sorry. I know you are very busy with the boys. It's only normal that things fall through the cracks sometimes." He gave her a kiss on the cheek. Nora blushed. She knew deep down that he always meant well. Sometimes, his words just didn't come out right.

"Oh, that reminds me, speaking of cracks, the boys pulled down the baby gate last night."

"Again? But we drilled that one into the wall. I drilled it so well. I used so many screws, more than was called for by the installation instructions in the manual. I thought there was no way it would come off." Liam stood there in awe. Maybe he didn't do such a great job as he thought he did. Kids always made you question, well... everything. Especially those two.

"I'm not sure how they did it, I didn't see," Nora started. "I turned around for a split second and then I heard a loud SNAP. I was just thankful that they didn't get hurt."

"Wow," Liam said, "our kids are freakishly strong, and sneaky too. Okay, I will try and fix it once I get home from work."

"Thanks. And please don't forget to call my phone. I can't find it anywhere." He immediately dialed her number. Liam was right, she did lose her phone a lot. It began to ring. Come to think of it, many of the electronic devices they kept around the house seemed to go missing then reappear a few hours—sometimes even a few days—later. *Could it be the twins?* Nora thought.

Ring...Ring...Ring.

They did like to play with whatever they got their hands on—except for the expensive new toys that Liam and Nora would give them from time to time.

"Where is that phone? It must be hiding under something," Nora whispered to herself. The boys never showed any interest in age-appropriate things. They were certainly the most curious pair of one-year-olds who, Nora found, happened to take a liking to anything electronic. Little techies. Maybe it WAS them after all.

"Hey, honey, I found it," Liam said. "It was between the couch cushions."

"Awesome, thank you, sweetie." Odd, she didn't remember going near the couch that morning. Then again, maybe she did go and she just forgot. Nora was clearly desperate for a good night's sleep. "Oh, Liam, before you go, I just remembered that we need to reset the TV again. The kids pressed a button on the remote, and I have no idea what they did or how to fix it." *Again, impressive but super annoying,* Nora thought.

"Sure, I will take a look at it tonight. I think I have the TV manual saved somewhere. That should help if turning it off then turning it on again doesn't work. It's simple but effective... the oldest trick in the book when it comes to fixing anything electronic."

"Whatever you say, babe. I'll leave that to you," Nora said.

The boys continued their perfect storm around the house. Watching them made her think of the never-ending pink Energizer bunny playing that giant drum. They just kept going and going and going and going. She glanced out her living room window to see an unfamiliar gentleman in a three-piece suit just staring into the house from across the street. When they made eye contact, he nonchalantly started walking down the block. Eh, her mistake. She'd left the shades open. It was only normal someone might take a quick look inside.

CRASH! BANG!

Nora snapped back to reality. It was incredible how destructive those twins could be in such little time... another hidden talent. Future demolition specialists? Nora chuckled as she made a mental note of their potential career paths.

"BOYS!" Nora yelled. "Come back here. I can't keep running after you like this." It was the first time Nora had taken them to the public park in her neighborhood, and it was not going well. "I said, come back here, boys. I can't be in two places at once." When she got no response from them, she took a softer approach. "Let's all play together in one area of the playground. Wouldn't that be more fun?" But there was no stopping them. They were fast. Too fast. And they were running in opposite directions. They acted as if they were two like poles of a magnet, constantly repelling each other. The minute they were unleashed, they ran to different sections of the playground... which happened to be as far apart as they could be within the park gates.

Thank God for those gates! Who knows where those two would have ended up. One in Canada the other in Mexico, Nora joked.

Okay, she thought, *I have one on the slides and one at the mini rock wall... very far apart... both need to be watched. What to do? What to do? Think, Nora, think.*

The stroller was parked at the entrance, and there was no time to get it, plus she would lose visual on both if she went to go retrieve that first. *Note to self, never abandon the stroller.* It was crucial for survival and one's sanity. Nora had no choice. She did the only thing she could do. She ran, grabbed one boy, then, while holding him, jetted across the park to go and grab the other one. Then, with one twin in each arm, she headed for the toddler swings—the safest option for a mother with two young children. Consumed, overpowered with a strength she never knew she had, she managed to put each child in a swing, side by side. Nora huffed in relief, proud that she'd accomplished such a difficult task.

"Damn," she said to herself, "I'm definitely going to feel that in the morning."

Now that she had them restrained, it was smooth sailing from then on. The twins loved the swings, and Nora loved the workout her arms were getting. "Wow, I'm going to be jacked if I keep this up," she laughed. "Who needs a gym membership when you got kids, huh?"

The swings served their purpose. Detaining and entertaining—a parent's dream for their young ones. But children got bored quickly, they lost interest, and Nora had reached the max time allotted for this activity. If they were not removed soon, the boys might try to get out on their own terms, and that would not be pretty. "Time to head home, kids." She kept an eye on them while she went to go get the stroller. Slowly, she moved them, one at a time—from one seatbelt to another. It was glorious and painless. Exactly what she'd been hoping for.

Nora wanted to kill some time before she went home, so she chose to take the long way back. The twins were mostly quiet—the fresh air was finally starting to penetrate their resistant little bodies and calm them. A potential kryptonite? Nora laughed at the idea. Before she knew it, she'd reached the house. "Wow, that was quick... for the scenic route."

She was enjoying how quiet it was... but it was too quiet. Nora sneaked a peek and saw that her boys had both fallen asleep. "Wow," she whispered to herself, "this walking thing does wonders. A child's Ambien, if you will." After the fifth time around the block, kids fast asleep, she knew it was about time to go home—not just pass it repeatedly like she was lost or something. She could have sworn she saw that same guy in the three-piece suit again but dismissed it thinking he might just be a new neighbor. Nothing to worry about. Thinking of her neighbors, if they didn't before now, after today, they for sure would think that she was bonkers—and her appearance didn't help. Nora was sporting that *I-just-rolled-out-of-bed-and-straight-into-a-dumpster* look about her this morning.

People will always talk, she thought. *Let's at least give them something interesting to talk about... a real show.* What she did next would impress or terrify just about anyone. Nora took hold of the back of the double stroller and slowly lifted it up the eight steps in front of her house... without waking her twins. That took immense strength, steadiness, and balance as well as a gentle range of motion to pull it off. And she did it. Backwards, no less. Mission accomplished. The glory she felt, however, was short lived because both boys woke up the second they were wheeled into the house. It was like they had a radar embedded within them. Home... time to wake up. Jack did say every nap and night's sleep was a gamble—never knowing how long it would last. The only guarantee was its unpredictability. He was right again.

"That's life, I guess," Nora said. "How was your nap my little angels?" And with that, the second half of her day had begun.

Two blocks away from the house, a man sat on a public bench. It was the same man Nora had spotted twice before. He sat close enough to be in range of the cameras he had placed in Nora's home earlier that day when they were out, but far enough to avoid suspicion. Clearly, the couple was unaware of the twins' true identity... and the mother, he noted, seemed to be handling them very well, considering she was a mere human. Impressive. The man jotted down a few more lines in his memo book.

Targets uncompromised. Subject in question appears ignorant yet capable. Further surveillance is warranted prior to apprehension. Immediate action not required.

The night went as most nights did. The boys woke up every three hours. Nora was the one to put them back to bed, which took about half an hour per kid. She was used to it, though. She even had a secret weapon to calm them down—in her experience, it worked 72% of the time, but that was good enough for her. It included rocking them back and forth while singing "You Are My Sunshine" on repeat. Some nights, Nora found herself singing until the literal sunshine shone through the window in their room. Her stamina was *Guinness Book of World Records* material, and she had no idea how she was pulling this off night after night.

Upon reading other parents' posts online, she came to understand that with such a challenging role as this, it was crucial to be in the right mindset and have the right attitude. Yes, there would be slips when you felt like throwing yourself out of the window—and even worse ones when you wanted to do that to your kids—but that was to be expected. As long as you didn't act on those impulses, you were crushing the parent thing—as opposed to every bone in your body.

Nora learned that there was no right or wrong way to parent. The trick was to learn from them and just try to improve. But again, no one explained it better than Jack Mizrahi. He wrote that when it came to being a parent, mistakes were going to be made, and you needed to just roll with it. All the childcare books, seminars, and expert advice were just that... advice. They should be used as a guide and not followed to the letter. Parenting required a lot of improvisation and flexibility. Jack went on to say how his kids Fortune, Nina, and Raymond were all so different... so why treat them the same? As long as your child was happy—and alive—at the end of the day, mission accomplished. It was all about showing them that you loved them no matter what. And Nora made every effort to do just that, in spite of what it cost her.

The following morning started the same as always. Nora got the kids cleaned up, fed them breakfast, and then changed them out of their food-stained pajamas. "Maybe I should start feeding you guys naked." Nora smiled at them with her hands on her hips. "At least that way it's one less—well, in your case, two less—pieces of clothing that I need to soak before washing. That might shave off a few minutes of my day." Nora gave them each a kiss on their very messy cheeks. Such dirt magnets. The twins just kept playing with their food, giving Nora a sly, mischievous look now and again.

"Okay, I can see that you are done eating now. Bellies must be full from all the Cheerios you ate. Though I know I'm going to find a few pieces all over the house. Some even get in my clothes, not sure how you little magicians manage that one." She gave them a serious look. "Anyway, how about we go to the supermarket today? What do you boys think about that?"

They both smiled at her. She took that as a "heck, yeah." Any mention of a public outing made their faces light up.

"It's decided then," she said. Nora strapped both boys in the double stroller, opened the door, and carefully wheeled them down the front steps of her house. Slowly, smoothly, one step at a time… she had become a pro at this. She could almost hear Jack's voice in her head saying, "Take those small victories, Nora! Pat yourself on the back every so often! This job is hard, and you deserve to be praised daily! Oh, and forget the gallon of milk… just buy a cow, it's cheaper in the long run." She smiled. Jack had such a great sense of humor too, and that was refreshing.

"Boys, don't touch that… put that back! I'm not buying that." The supermarket aisles were so narrow that the stroller took up most of the space, giving the twins the freedom to grab whatever they thought was most colorful off the shelves. They also kept knocking items over with their dangling feet. Nora had to shop while cleaning up almost every aisle they walked down. Luckily, nothing broke or spilled—they hadn't come into contact with any glass jars or egg cartons yet.

Maneuvering a double stroller stocked with groceries and two one-year-olds with one hand through narrow aisles while balancing four to five items in the other hand was not easy, but Nora did it. And she did it all the way to the cash register. It was her own supermarket mom Olympics.

"Hey, where did this come from? I know I didn't pick this up." Nora found a box of cereal that she was certain was stored on one of the higher shelves in the breakfast aisle. There was no way her boys could have reached it—she couldn't even have reached it if she'd wanted too. Nora thought about it, then dismissed her wacky theory that they had some kind of telekinesis and went with the clear, more logical explanation that the cereal was misplaced on one of the lower shelves and the boys had picked it up. It happened all the time in stores. She took the cereal and handed it to the cashier. "I don't want this, sorry. My kids must have gotten it somehow."

"No worries, ma'am. We will put it back later."

Once all the groceries were bagged and paid for, she loaded up her double stroller as best she could. The remaining bags that couldn't fit, Nora hung them on both her wrists and then exited the supermarket through the entrance. Her stroller was too wide to make it to the exit on the other side of the cash registers.

"All done, boys, time to head home." Nora and the boys started their walk back. The weight from the shopping bags was starting to hurt her. Balancing five bags on each wrist would do that to anyone, even without pushing a jam-packed baby stroller. "Six more blocks, just six more," she told herself. Nora's wrists were bright red, and they hurt like hell. Who knew all that damage could be done by a few plastic bags full of groceries.

Once they got home, the boys busied themselves with another one of the remote controls Liam always seemed to leave lying around the house. Nora smiled. They were for sure reprogramming it or something like that. Again.

Just then, the doorbell rang. The twins immediately stopped what they were doing and ran as fast as they could to the door. And they were certainly fast. They beat Nora there, and she had longer legs taking bigger strides. It made no sense, but Nora didn't want to dwell on the fact that her toddlers had left her in the dust.

Nora was thankful that they hadn't learned how to open the door yet. Imagine the chaos. She didn't want to right now. Nora blocked her sons with her legs—preventing their escape—and unlocked the door to find that same unfamiliar gentleman, probably in his mid- to late-twenties, wearing a black suit and tie. Now she was a bit anxious, especially since she was home alone with the kids. No matter. *If this goes south*, she thought, *I will claw his damn eyes out. No one hurts my babies!*

"Can I help you?"

The man looked down at the twin boys who had been the cause of his first-ever peptic ulcer and grinned in relief. "Good afternoon, ma'am." He showed her his ID badge. "My name is Jerry, and I am here to talk about your boys. I am from a special branch of Social Services."

Now Nora was even more anxious. *He must have been spying on me for some kind of "unofficial report."* Nora got ready to pounce. "Whatever my neighbors have been saying about me, it's not true. Just because I look a little dirty sometimes and dress kinda funny, it doesn't mean I'm crazy. I'm a mom. I love my boys and will do anything for them. They are my world, my sunshine. Please don't take them from me," Nora said in rapid succession.

Jerry gave Nora his best *I-come-in-peace* facial expression. "I'm not here to take them from you. I'm here to explain to you how unique these children are and, if you are interested, possibly shed some light on how best to manage them, and their powers—but I have a good feeling you already have a handle on all of this."

Nora stood there, silent, trying to absorb all of this. *Did he say "powers"?*

"Be warned that what I am about to disclose is classified information for your ears only. May I come in?"

Nora gestured for him to enter her home, her kids still at her side. "I'm not sure I know what is going on here, Jerry, but if it's about my boys, then I'm all ears."

Jerry took a seat on the couch. "I will get right to it then," he said. "You accidentally adopted two male younglings from the planet we refer to as Proxima Centauri B. The existence of this planet was made public knowledge in 2016, but its inhabitants have remained hidden—well, mostly hidden. There are some Area 51 conspiracy theories that won't go away. But that's a different story altogether; I don't want to get off track. Anyway, we, at the secret sector of Social Services, have done a pretty good job of keeping them and other non-human species a secret."

Nora sat there in shock. Her brain was trying to make sense out of all this.

Jerry continued. "Our job is to find a safe and loving home for these special children and make sure that their true identities are kept, well, secret. The world is not ready for this big reveal just yet. Information like this needs to be released in a delicate manner, and at the right time. Not just thrust upon the public as I am doing to you now. I apologize for any mental discomfort this might cause you."

Nora snapped out of her couch coma. "Wait, so you're telling me that aliens are real... and that I'm raising two of them?"

"Aliens are just one of the species that we deal with, but yes—"

"I have alien children?"

"Yes."

Nora pumped her fist. "YES! I knew I wasn't crazy! That explains so much. I mean, I had my suspicions but wow, cool! My boys have powers! I am like the mother of Clark Kent—no, two Clark Kents! Holy cow! I am raising future superheroes. AWESOME!"

This was going better than he expected, Jerry thought. Thank God for geeks. "I assume you wish to remain their sole caregiver, then."

"Heck yeah, I do! I'm not passing this up. I'm not stupid."

"Great," Jerry said, "that's what I had hoped for. I knew you weren't the type to scare so easily. I will go ahead and get you some information on their species so you will be better prepared for what's to come. Truth be told, you seem better equipped than some of our pre-approved parental candidates. Nora, you are a happy accident. And I am so glad that this worked out... and I get to keep my job." Jerry placed a document on the living room table and handed Nora a pen. "Just sign here, and we will be all set."

Nora signed without hesitation, relieved that she got to keep her twins after all.

"Okay, then," Jerry said, "now that you are all up to speed, department approved, and legally held to secrecy, I can proceed with Phase Two. That is, if you are ready and willing."

Nora looked at him and said, "Sure, no problem, bring it on. What's Phase Two?"

"Placement of additional subjects when available."

"I'm not sure that I follow."

"To put it plainly." He paused. "You are getting more kids."

"Sorry, I'm what now?!"

MAMA BEAR

DANIELLE ACKLEY-McPHAIL

S OMETHING WASN'T RIGHT. EXCEPT LATELY, a lot wasn't right. Made it
hard to tell if this was something new or just the same ol' stuff picking
at her nerves. Suzanne Cosain, fae exile and founding member of the Wild
Hunt MC, downshifted and let up on the throttle as she approached the
intersection. Her half-human husband, Lance, slowed to a stop next to her.
She heard his whiskey-rich voice murmur from her helmet speaker.

"You doin' okay, babe?"

She nodded as she opened up the throttle again, though she expected it
was a lie. A white one, but still a lie. He didn't push her as he took position
to her right and just behind her, letting her take Front Door. Good thing,
because she hadn't a clue what to say. She felt wired. Poised for a fight.
Half the time protective—though she had no clue of what—the other half
twenty kinds of pissed off. One moment jubilant, the next melancholy.
Life had become one constant emotional barrage. Her skin felt too tight,
and her nerves buzzed with energy. Every smell was amped up, and nothing
tasted right. Was it her curse, or had something else come along to screw
with her? Still, the sun felt amazing, and the wind in her face cleared the fog
she'd woken up in. Swerving around a road gator—remnants left by some
trucker's blow-out—she gunned it and took off down the empty stretch of
road, her silver-blond hair whipping around her bare shoulders and leather
halter top.

Lance's laughter filled her headspace, lightening her mood. He drew up next to her, then pushed to pass. "You're on," he crowed, speaking into his mic a bit louder to be heard over the engines as he revved his Knucklehead. More than ready to play, Suzanne opened the throttle on her Harley Softtail even further.

As they raced down the back country road, Lance's thick, segmented ponytail lashing behind him, Suzanne suddenly sensed mischief of a fae sort. She didn't slow down, but she did let her otherworldly sense play out, scanning the area around them.

She laughed abruptly.

"Looks like your *friend* is looking to get back a bit of his own," she said into her mic as she brought all her attention back to the road. The ride had begun to get rougher: Wrinkles in the asphalt, an increase in potholes, a network of cracks like you'd find in the deep desert. She wasn't worried. She and Lance both had ride bells hanging off their bikes, spelled with protections against road gremlins.

Lance growled in annoyance, and Suzanne felt the build-up as he drew power until his shoulder fins unfurled through the slits in his jacket and tendrils of energy arced from his back. She heard him call out with his thoughts as he let his iridescent white "wings" flare.

"Cut it out, Smear," he growled, addressing the embodiment of the Road. *Every* road. The little bugger held something of a grudge against The Wild Hunt, the club's leader, in particular. That would be Lance. "Not today…"

The road conditions just continued to get rougher, and the breeze carried the sound of grumbling just low enough that Suzanne couldn't make out the words. The tone carried loud and clear, though, as her front wheel jittered to the side, slipping on the edge of a tar snake she could have sworn hadn't been there a moment before. Suzanne managed to straighten the Softtail out, but her patience waned.

Not finding the situation funny anymore, she also started drawing power. Her fins unfurled with a snap until energy crackled across her bare back in what she knew were lavender and blue "wings" with rosy accents that deepened to red and black when her curse got the better of her. From the snap of the current, she expected those hues were darkening. Ever since she'd taken revenge on a murder of redcaps, her nature had grown more… complicated… volatile. Or, as Lance liked to put it, bloodthirsty.

Literally.

She'd ended the redcaps who'd attacked her but in the fight had somehow claimed the leader's cap for her own. At the time, she hadn't known the nature of the beastie. The creature she slew wasn't the redcap, the "hat" was. A parasitic fae that corrupted the nature of whatever host it glommed on to. Or tried to, anyway. She'd come under a constant barrage of emotional assault ever since, sly and subtle one moment, hitting her like a sledgehammer the next. Suzanne was giving it the fight of her life until she found a way to break free. Just… sometimes, she lost ground. Emotions were Lance's strength. He'd spent most of his life as an empath, with no access to his mage talent. Suzanne, on the other hand, had been emotionally repressed right up until the day she'd broken free from her father's control and fled to the mortal realm.

Even thinking about it sent a red haze over her vision.

The air grew heavy with tension, and the sunlight took on a hard edge. Pissed at how everyone seemed to think they could mess with her life, she summoned a mage bolt.

"Back it down, Sue," Lance murmured, both his tone and his link to her reaching out to sooth her agitation. "He's just trying to get us riled. Things are already smoothing out."

Fighting the urge to lash out anyway, Suzanne nodded, slowly releasing her grip on the energy and letting it flow back into the natural channels she'd drawn it from. She looked over at Lance as they continued to ride like nothing had happened. It was hardly a surprise when he took the lead. Neither was the direction they headed. The road they were on led straight to *Delilah's*, the bar they—and the Wild Hunt MC—called home.

When they rode up, the front lot was empty. Not unexpected. It was the middle of the day on a Wednesday. Suzanne pulled up right next to the entrance, just off to the side, and shut the bike down, backing slightly to set the center stand. Lance pulled in next to her and left his Knucklehead idling.

"I'm headin' over to my dad's; the camshaft's sticking."

Suzanne hesitated, feeling a sense of unease. "No problem. You want me to have Mongo fix you something, or wait until you get back?"

"Nah, I'll grab something at Cam's," Lance said as he backed the bike up. "I'll probably spend a little time with him. It's been a while now that the Knucklehead's running again."

That sense of unease came back. Lance's bike had been totaled not that long ago…the *first* time he encountered Smear face-to-face. Suzanne's gaze ran over him, making sure he wore his leathers, his helmet framing the strong angles of his face. Her urge to protect him welled up even stronger than before. An image formed in her mind of Lance's body broken and the light gone out of his warm brown eyes. Beneath her breath, she growled. While she wasn't above worrying about those that mattered to her, the image had the distinct feel of the redcap's influence.

Suzanne slammed the door on those thoughts as she caught her lip curling in a snarl. She hid it by lifting off her helmet and setting it on her engine before swinging her leg over the back to stand between the bikes.

"Hey… you all right?" Lance asked, reaching out to kill his engine.

Suzanne gritted her teeth and forced herself to calm. She and Lance had a connection… a literal connection, even before they'd wed. Lance felt whatever she felt unless she took an effort to block it. Something she vowed to him never to do again.

She leaned over his bike to stop him.

"No. I'm fine, just a little out of sorts. Go on and get that checked out. Can't have you eating asphalt again."

Lance nodded, then stole a kiss before turning back to the road. Something in Suzanne's gut twisted uncomfortably as she watched him ride away.

"You comin' in or what?"

Suzanne jerked around at the unexpected voice. Man, she was on edge. Delilah—as in *the* Delilah—stood in the open door, just shaking her head. Suzanne's eyes locked on the tendrils of fiery red hair bobbing around the woman's shoulders. A shudder went through her as the curse tried to take hold.

"Girl, get your ass in here. I ain't air-conditioning the outside!" Delilah's words were sharp, but her expression was worried.

It was strange. Just at the sight of Lance's aunt, the tension flowed out of Suzanne, and her heart flooded with joy. She'd never had a mother that she could remember. That didn't bother her one bit anymore. Suzanne's birth mother would never have been as strong as Delilah. Suzanne's father, Callan, wouldn't have stood for it. He would have *hated* Delilah just for being herself, let alone for being human. That just made Suzanne love the woman more.

Making sure her bike was secure, Suzanne went inside, dropping a kiss on Delilah's cheek as she passed. That earned Suzanne a strange look. As much as Delilah loved her as if she'd birthed her—and Suzanne had no doubt she did—it wasn't like casual kisses were their thing.

But then, the kiss hadn't been casual.

Suzanne couldn't explain it, but right now, her hyped-up emotions were all over the place... not just the constant aggression that simmered under the surface since she'd gotten herself stuck with the 'cap, but all of her emotions. Not knowing what to say, Suzanne just murmured, "Thanks, 'Lilah," as she headed for the kitchen.

"Hey! You leave my cook alone!" Delilah called after her.

"I'm hungry!" Suzanne yelled back.

Delilah's shocked silence was a tangible thing. It weighed so heavy on Suzanne's shoulders, she shrugged them to try and rid herself of the sensation. When she glanced back, she caught Delilah trying to hide a smile.

Suzanne didn't eat much. She didn't need to, but everyone still worried, particularly once the secret of her curse had come out. Energy had to come from somewhere. Better for her... Hell, better for *all* of them that it be a clean source.

Resisting the urge to fidget beneath Delilah's gaze, Suzanne smiled back. "I'm asking Mongo for some pasta primavera, you want some?" What she really wanted was a super-rare steak, but that was courting trouble until she found a way around the curse.

Delilah shook her head. "You go on, sweetie. I gotta take care of some clean-up in the backroom before the lunch crowd comes in. Sammy's boys have been rooting through the airgun equipment."

Suzanne had a plan...

...then she walked through the swinging kitchen doors.

The sweet, savory aroma of root-beer-braised pulled pork reached out and grabbed her by the salivary glands. Her belly rumbled, and her mouth grew juicy. She knew better, though… she didn't say a word. Skirting the prep stations and cook area, Suzanne squatted down next to Garm, Mongo's beat-up beast of a mutt, curled up quiet like by the back door. No one knew the pup's story, but he bore a hell of a lot of scars. So did Suzanne, but Garm's everyone could see. Mongo went soft whenever someone showed his dog some love. Not that Suzanne wouldn't have anyway, but as she scratched Garm's scruff, she looked over her shoulder at the cook.

"Hey, Mongo…"

"Yeah, yeah…" He cut her off. "You ain't foolin' anyone."

Suzanne smiled and gave the dog a quick squeeze before standing up and turning toward Delilah's secret weapon. Mongo was as far from a greasy-spoon fry cook as Garm was from a pedigreed bitch. He had the chops—and the credentials—to cook in any Michelin-Star restaurant. *Delilah's* suited him best.

"I'm feeling peckish," she admitted. An understatement, but such a rare confession that Mongo cocked his head at her as if maybe he hadn't heard her right. "I would love some pasta primavera…" Mongo looked highly pleased until she added, "…with a huge scoop of that pulled pork on top…" She nearly laughed at the brief flash of horror that flickered across the cook's face as his inner-chef rebelled at the very concept. Mongo just nodded, though, turning back to his cook area and prepping for her meal.

For a while, Suzanne watched. Until Mongo just barely nicked his finger as he chopped the vegetables. At the sight of the tiny drop of blood that welled up, a whole other appetite rose. Suzanne gritted her teeth and squeezed her eyes shut, fighting the wave of blood-thirst back as she headed for the swinging doors. "Sorry, Mongo…"

He called after her, but Suzanne just quickened her steps as she moved through the bar and across the backroom to the stairs leading to the second-floor apartments. Two steps at a time and she stood before her door, breathing heavy and struggling to unclench her fists. When she saw the state of her hands, she cursed like a truck driver. Blood welled up from her palms in crimson crescents where her nails had dug in.

"You're upsetting the baby."

"FUCK!" Suzanne whirled around, more than fed up with people sneaking up on her at this point. Lance's cousin Tilly stood in the door of the other apartment, the one she shared with her parents, Delilah and Jonraphal, Lance's full-fae blood uncle.

Tilly had an odd, dreamy look on her face like she wasn't even half there. Lost in some kind of trance or as if she'd reverted to the childlike, brain-damaged state she had been in just months ago, before Lance's magic had whisked away the veil trapping her in her own mind. But not quite.

"I said, you're upsetting the baby. Stop it," Tilly repeated, then she swayed, just catching herself on the door jamb.

Suzanne started forward to help her, reaching out, then she saw her bloodied hands and drew them back. What the hell was going on? When Tilly blinked and looked at her, a touch confused, Suzanne just threw up her hands and snapped, "How do you think I feel?" before turning away to open her own door, not even caring how many bloody fingerprints she left anymore.

"Don't," Tilly murmured, suddenly beside her. The girl reached into Suzanne's pocket and tugged out the plastic baggy holding the redcap. "I don't know what happened, but you need to feed it anyway."

It took all of Suzanne's effort to rein back her rage as she snatched the bloody parasite from her friend's hand. A sense of satisfaction not her own flared in the back of Suzanne's thoughts as she ran the 'cap over her bloody skin. It tried to get greedy, tried to suck its fill from the wounds, but Suzanne dug her nails in hard, along with her stubborn will. She winced at the creature's mental shriek. "Too bad, you moist fucking leech. Be happy I don't shove you into Mongo's dehydrator and be done with you."

Only she couldn't, could she...? If the 'cap died, so did she. Hell, she couldn't even be far away from it without being crippled with pain.

But then... maybe that wouldn't be such a bad trade-off. Of course, plenty of people would argue to the death against that thought. She shoved the redcap into its zipper bag and shoved the bag back into her pocket before turning to confront Tilly.

"And while we're at it, what the hell baby are you talking about?"

Tilly just blinked and, with a slight frown, and said, "Baby?"

Suzanne just shook her head and turned back to her door.

"Forget it," she said with a weary sigh, totally done with what had turned into a shit stick of a day. She didn't realize tears streamed down her face until Tilly reached out to wipe them away.

"Are you okay?"

The tears just came harder until Suzanne had to bite back a sob. All she could do was shake her head. There was no answer she could give.

"Here, dumplin', take this."

Suzanne's head snapped up, hardly believing what she heard, but there Lance stood with Tilly beside him, holding a covered plate. At the sight of it, Suzanne finally noticed an aroma so enticing, her stomach forced its way past all the negativity to be heard in one loud rolling rumble. Loud enough that she startled a laugh from Lance, but he quickly sobered.

"You were going to Cam's," she managed to get out.

Lance nodded, his lip pressing tight a moment as his gaze clouded. "Got the feeling I needed to be here," he answered as he pulled her into his arms.

"What's wrong, angel?" he asked softly as his lips pressed a gentle kiss just above her ear.

For a moment, Suzanne hugged him tight, then just as quickly, she pushed him away.

In what even she had to admit was a petulant tone, she muttered beneath her breath, "I'm hungry."

Lance laughed again.

"We could tell," he said as he reached over and took the plate back from Tilly, holding it out to Suzanne with a quirked brow. "Mongo sent this up for you, said you asked for it... special."

Suzanne drooled. Actually drooled. And she didn't give a damn either.

Nearly snatching the plate, she lifted the lid and tried to pick at the pork at the same time.

"On that note," Tilly said, her tone wry, "I'm late for my lunch shift downstairs."

Suzanne barely heard her, finally managing to get a pinch of the barbeque-laden meat past her lips. "Mmmmmmm..."

"How about we get you inside, and then you can go to town on that?" Lance said with a chuckle, his eyes filled with mingled swirls of both love and concern.

Giving him a guilty look, Suzanne couldn't even begin to explain. She just replaced the cloche and stepped back out of the way so Lance could open the door.

Her husband fed her and cared for her and then took her to bed. At some point, they even slept. As they drifted off for the last time, she remembered what Tilly had said. Pushing past a yawn, she murmured to Lance, "What baby was Tilly talking about?"

Lance just gave a soft snore.

Suzanne woke up screaming. Flat out, blood-curdling screaming. Lance jerked awake beside her and before the last scream faded, crouched over her on the bed looking for the threat, the soft white glow of his unfurling wings banishing the glistening crimson from her nightmare.

She lay there with a death grip on the sheets and the cries of a baby fading beneath her own panting breath. If only she could banish the image of a wizened, shark-toothed face staring up from her own arms.

Moving slowly, Lance dropped back down to the bed and gently pulled her into his arms, persisting until she relaxed into him. It took a while. Even once she accepted that she was safe and sheltered, her body shook in faint tremors slow to fade.

"Wanna talk about it?" he murmured by her ear.

Suzanne gave a short, sharp shake of her head.

"'Kay." And he snuggled just a bit closer. In minutes, his measured breath ruffled her hair, and his arms relaxed around her. The one across her waist slid down to her belly, and something in her gut fluttered at the touch, shifted, as if pressing up to get closer. At the sensation, dread settled over Suzanne as realization dawned.

Slowly, her hand joined Lance's, and she extended her otherworldly senses.

"Ah, shit..." she muttered through clenched teeth, every muscle suddenly tense. What was she going to do?

The nestled glow within her flinched, and Suzanne bit back another curse as Lance shifted fitfully behind her. Doubt and hurt bubbled up, and the presence shrank back more, as if uncertain of its welcome. Suzanne instantly reached out, cradling her belly and crushing her fear, letting the warmth of her love flow over the little one. Her emotions whirled out of control, bombarding her with fear and joy and disbelief, but most of all astonishment as she encountered this brand-new soul... with the crappy luck of being dependent on her. Then terror rose up, overwhelming everything else. Suzanne's belly cramped, and her stomach heaved, then she was scrambling from the bed and into the bathroom, pausing only to snatch up the hated 'cap from the nightstand, lest the straining link between them made matters worse.

She'd barely wrapped herself around the porcelain bowl when Lance came up behind her. With one hand, he held her hair out of the way. With the other, he rubbed gentle circles at the base of her back. When she'd finished heaving, he cleaned her up, took her in his arms, and carried her to bed. All while she clutched that damned little zipper bag. She wished the thing to the deepest depths infinitely more than she had before.

How could she keep a little one safe when she couldn't even save herself?

In the morning, Suzanne woke to find Lance watching her.

She suspected her smile came out more of a grimace. Her husband just leaned over and ran his lips over hers before drawing her into the shelter of his arms.

"Ready to talk?"

Breathing a sigh, Suzanne nodded and snuggled in closer, soaking in the sense of peace and security. Her mind, on the other hand, frantically scrambled with where to start. So long, in fact, Lance leaned back and peered into her face.

"With words this time?"

Suzanne laughed despite the tension in her belly.

"I dreamed... I dreamed the redcap took over our child."

Lance drew a sharp breath, and his brow dipped in confusion. Before he could speak, Suzanne went on. "I don't know how to stop it."

She saw the moment Lance realized she wasn't just talking about a dream anymore. An instant later, she felt the swirling chaos of his response. His emotions, both positive and negative, slammed into her, nearly making her lose control of her own. As she struggled to maintain her grip, the redcap reared up and flooded her with malice and hate and murderous intent. Before she could regain control, she felt her shoulder fins unfurl, spying their reflection in the mirror. Black as pitch and crimson red. Crackling with such power as they never had before. For the briefest instant, she reveled in the strength coursing through her. Strength her father would have respected... strength he would have feared. Enough power that none would dare to threaten her ever again or try to subject her to their will.

Enough power for her to realize the lie in that truth.

She could give in to the redcap and be as powerful as this and more, at the cost of all that made her decent and good. At the cost of her love and compassion. For the blood-price of her husband and anyone else caught within her sphere. For the blood-price of her child, who would never survive Suzanne's downfall.

No fucking way in hell!

At one time in her life, she believed she needed to take on the world on her own. That to be strong was to stand alone. Very recently, she learned how wrong that delusion was.

Breathing deep, Suzanne reached for Lance across their inner bond, wordlessly asking for his help, his strength, not because she wasn't strong enough on her own, but because they were stronger together. She showed him with her mind what she planned. Mage energy and empathy intertwined. Suzanne let the positive emotions wash through her: reaching for Lance's joy and love, for her unborn child's trust, for the sheer wonder she herself felt deep inside. She anchored the positivity deep in her core, wrapped it around their child stronger than any armor. The extra power unfurled around her much as her shoulder fins had, the energy nearly overwhelming. She felt Lance entwine with her, a counterbalance as she harnessed the energy, forcing the negativity back, breaking its hold. With her thoughts, she followed the link to the redcap and tugged on it hard.

The creature's shriek rang through her mind as he fought back. He tried to tear through her soul, pummeling her with every doubt, every insecurity she ever felt. Feeding her more that had never even occurred to her. For once and for good, she knew it all for lies. She stood like bedrock against the redcap and let the negativity flow off of her like weak water. When she'd had enough, she reached out her will and gripped the tether linking them and squeezed.

This is not your bed, she hissed in her thoughts, *This is not your life, and if you try to claim it, I will burn you to less than cinder and ash,* she continued as she forced the presence of the redcap away, barring it from her innermost being, all but severing the connection between them until nothing but the slightest thread linked her psyche to the parasite. That too would be broken if she'd only herself to suffer the consequences.

The war was not over, but this was a battle won.

JUPITER JUSTICE

KRIS KATZEN

THE DINING HALL'S MASTERFULLY PAINTED ceiling gave the illusion of a cavernous space—something nonexistent on the Jovian supercolony Bastet. Trung loved the depiction of a soaring roof reminiscent of an ancient Vietnamese palace. Intricate patterns in vivid reds and blues appeared to arch overhead. Gold gilded the ceiling's border.

Leah Trung appreciated it even more with the room eerily empty. Yesterday she'd had no time to gaze idly upward. The family dinner had taken a decade to plan. They'd finally managed to coordinate in conjunction with the Interplanetary Games which took place every ten years, this time on Ceres. They'd all wanted to see the black sheep of their supremely-scientific family compete against the other elite athletes.

Now the hundred thirteen of them had once again scattered to the solar winds, her local grandchildren had dashed off, and her son-in-law had excused himself a few minutes later. She and her daughter had ducked back into the formal hall. The Trungs' matriarch savored the quiet moment alone with her eldest, Rebecca, who led the Jovian colonies.

She'd just reached across the faux-oak table to take her daughter's hand when the sliding doors to the dining room began to part. A lanky woman wearing the midnight blue coveralls of Trung's diplomatic ship charged in so fast that she slammed a shoulder into one of the doors before it had entirely retracted.

Barely inside the doorway, Captain Reem Sunquist skidded to a stop, and her blue eyes fixed on the elder Trung. "Ambassador, we have to get to the ship. *Now*." Even as Trung got to her feet, the other woman tossed a small round gold datachip onto the table in front of Rebecca. "Governor, read that on a *secure* computer." Sunquist's shoulder-length blond hair whipped around as she whirled and ran, shouting "Hurry!" over her shoulder and not even waiting to ensure Trung followed.

Baffled and incredibly alarmed at seeing the preternaturally poised Captain Sunquist in all-out emergency mode, Trung spared a confused—and fleeting—glance at her daughter then dashed out of the room.

Sunquist hadn't called her "ambassador" in years.

At eighty, Trung wouldn't win any sprints, but she made decent time through the dove-gray halls to where *Cleopatra's* shuttle waited in the main colony's docking bay. She didn't even need to dodge too many people, as if she were running in Sunquist's wake.

Someone, no doubt on Sunquist's order, had already maneuvered the shuttle into position for a fast launch. The boxy vessel's door stood open, and inside Trung found Sunquist already powering up the little craft—and flexing her shoulder.

The second Trung slid into the co-pilot's seat, the shuttle lifted off the deck and shot out of the bay as if from a cannon. Noting that Sunquist had buckled in, Trung secured her own safety harness as fast as she could, keeping a wary eye on Callisto as the gray-silver-black orb got bigger and bigger in the cockpit window.

"*Cleopatra*, we're coming in hot." Sunquist punched a button that transmitted their vector.

"Copy that," a voice crackled over the com, which then went abruptly dead.

Trung eyed their acceleration with concern. Her diplomatic cruiser hovered only ten minutes away if the shuttle flew at a leisurely speed. Sunquist looked to be cutting that time to under two minutes.

With great effort, Trung held her flood of questions and settled for one eyebrow climbing high on her brow in mute query. Avoiding death was a good incentive for silence. She didn't want to distract the pilot.

Cleopatra practically leapt into view as they rounded Callisto. The long sleek vessel's docking bay doors already stood open and lined up in their direction. Sunquist braked so hard Trung swore she could hear the reverse thrusters screech in protest. Their shuttle touched down in the bay as gently as a leaf floating to the ground on a windless day.

Trung inhaled deeply to settle her nerves. "What's going on?" she demanded as Sunquist shut down their ride.

Even Sunquist's profile looked thunderous, and she spoke through a clenched jaw. "Earth declared martial law. They've already attacked two ships. There are over five thousand dead."

"What?" Trung's brain refused to process the words. Sunquist might as well have said that the sun itself had transformed into a fiery male belly dancer dancing an Irish jig. "*Five thousand? How?*"

"Details are sketchy. Earth is sending its warships to blockade all the planets and the major colonies. Apparently two of the civilian ships either didn't take the blockade seriously, or someone on a warship had an itchy trigger finger. Mars lost a freighter with two hundred aboard. And one of the Colonial Cruise Line's supercruisers blew up."

"Doesn't your brother capt—?" Trung bit off her words as a spasm crossed her friend's sharp features. If Trung hadn't been watching, she would have missed the infinitesimally brief crack in the stony, stormy facade.

"I'm so sorry," Trung whispered.

Sunquist didn't look over, didn't react other than a curt nod, but her knuckles clutching the chair had gone white.

Respecting the tacit signal to focus on business, Trung said, "What else do we know?"

"Not much." Sunquist pivoted her chair around and headed for the exit hatch, Trung on her heels. "Someone on Earth managed to leak the plans before all Earth's ships were in place. A battlecruiser is two hours from here, with an additional pair two days out. More are en route to Saturn but it'll take them an extra day to arrive. No reliable word yet on whether Earth dispatched any to the outer planets or not. We're sending microbursts and maintaining radio silence as much as possible, trying to spread the word but not to let them know we know. That's why I gave the governor that datachip."

Trung and Sunquist weaved between a few crewmembers in the corridor. She and the captain had the lift to themselves.

What the *hell* were they thinking back on Earth? Try to enact draconian laws and simply expect the rest of the solar system to go along with it? Trung kept arriving at the same answer. "Thinking" was something they most assuredly were *not* doing.

Most of the population scattered throughout the system had been able to ignore Earth's increasingly persistent demands for taxes. They'd refused to pay and had endured only various levels of inconvenience when Earth responded by cutting off some commerce. Sure, some people had had more trouble getting some supplies, including some foods and technology. Normally the colonists found a workaround without too long a delay and didn't pay much attention to politics taking place literally billions of kilometers away.

"Have they gone stark raving mad?" Trung growled.

"Sounds like it." Sunquist stalked out of the elevator and over to a stocky older man with very dark skin and silver-gray hair. "Are we hearing any chatter at all over the airwaves?"

"A little, Captain." Muteba Kanam turned his chair away from the communications console so he could face them. "Normal noise between Bastet and Jupiter's satellite colonies and outposts. There was a flurry of messages about losing contact with the inner planets, but for the time being, people are assuming it's a glitch that'll pass quickly. Sounds to me like Earth's jamming the signals."

Sunquist scowled but said nothing, so Trung filled the silence.

"What were the last few stories that came in over the newsfeed?"

Kanam turned back to the monitor flush with the control panel and scrolled through the list displayed there. "Spate of increased solar flare activity; outbreak of Muerellian flu on Ceres; increased outages in the news network, cause unknown," his voice hardened in anger as he read that last, but he continued, "data from the outpost at Neptune; new Chancellor of the Moon elected by a landslide. That's about it for the last half hour." He glanced down at the screen again. "Oh, wait. Looks like people are starting to report the outages as deliberate jamming. Lots of uncertainty, though. Most of the public is still disregarding the reports as unfounded rumor."

"How *did* we get the initial report?" Trung asked.

"Lots of ships out in the Great Emptiness," Sunquist said. "You know how that is. We all keep in touch. In this case it means there's always someone out of jamming range. Now that the rumors are out there, confirmation will spread fast. It'll be a contest of who can react most quickly, Earth or the rest of us." She clasped Kanam's shoulder, then turned toward a towering redhead on the other side of the bridge. "What's the ship's status?"

Trung partially caught the man's reply. She thought he was saying all systems at optimal efficiency, but Kanam's hand on her wrist drew her attention back. She quirked an eyebrow at him. He met her eye, then pointedly looked down at the monitor, brushing it with a finger to play a paused video.

Earth, small yet clearly recognizable, hung in the background above and to the right of two ships, one close and one distant but closing fast. A brightly hued cruise ship, all azures and ceruleans, filled the bottom half of the screen. With no point of reference, Trung couldn't tell if it was moving or not. Her breath caught as horror and helplessness overwhelmed her. She didn't move or make a sound, knowing what was coming, dreading it with every atom in her body, yet unable and unwilling to look away.

The second ship moved with clear and deadly purpose. The iron-gray warship emblazoned with Earth's emblem—Earth at the center of all the colonies—loomed between the luxury vessel and Earth, growing larger as it sped toward its target. Blinding white beams of light shot from the battleship and raked the length of the cruise ship broadside. Smaller explosions and blossoms of flame surged and grew, racing together in seconds until a fireball engulfed the ship then vanished, leaving nothing behind but a rapidly expanding and fading fiery haze.

Trung's insides twisted, caught in a war between throwing up in despair and agony, or exploding in blind fury.

Kanam looked back up at her, a pleading question in his dark eyes welling with tears.

She held up a hand for him to wait then walked over in time to hear the engineer's final suggestion to double-staff each engineering post just to be safe.

"Good thinking. Do that. Ambassador—" But the instant she saw Trung, Sunquist's words died on her lips.

"There's a video." Trung whispered, and felt like she'd plunged a double-edged blade into her friend's chest.

Sunquist's face froze into an inscrutable mask. She blanched, going paler than Trung imagined any living person could get. But scant moments later she flushed crimson with rage. Turning on her heel, Sunquist strode to the communications station and stabbed Play Video with a finger. She watched the scene three times.

"Make. It. Go. Viral." Sunquist bit off each word to Kanam, then added, "Then resume silence. Burke"—she addressed the woman at the helm—"the *instant* he's done, change our position. Don't let the dreadnought see us when it gets here. Send out some drones so we'll still be able to see them, at least until they start jamming. Then switch to old-school optics to ensure they don't move into our line of sight. Preprogram the drones to move out of jamming range if they lose contact with us."

"If they deploy their own drones?" Burke asked.

Sunquist mulled over that for just a second then, shook her head. "Keep us out of sight. Back us out of the Jovian system if you have to. Turn off our ID transponder. Make sure we can get out of jamming range when we need to."

"Video broadcast loud, far, and wide," Kanam said, not reacting to that last—highly illegal and potentially dangerous, in normal circumstances— order aside from flipping the switch to carry it out.

Good. A powerful broadcast transmitted at maximum dispersal on every frequency. A cold, grimly satisfied upturn touched the corner of Trung's lips. Everyone, all four million plus, on all Jupiter's colonies and outposts had gotten the message. If even half forwarded it, the resultant flood of data would be impossible to stop. *Cleopatra's* signal would span the entire system in well under a day. Those rebroadcasting the video would boost its reach exponentially.

Earth's government couldn't ignore it.

They certainly couldn't deny it.

The battle-ready dreadnought *really* ruined the view of Jupiter.

The spectacular vista of the browns, oranges, and golds (with myriad other colors including reds and whites thrown in) normally raised Trung's spirits and filled her with awe—even after decades in space. Presently, though, the warhawk-class starship positioned between her own diplomatic vessel and the planet raised only her ire and filled her with fury and contempt. Arms folded tightly across her chest, Trung stifled a growl as she stood at the transparent hull and glowered at the obstructed view of Jupiter's rainbow swirls, whorls, and bands.

Then jamming started, and static exploded onto the viewscreen. The picture cleared as the ship's sensors switched from showing the probes' datafeed to displaying images collected from *Cleopatra's* own exterior cameras. Callisto's heavily-cratered gray-and-black surface appeared then began to shrink as *Cleopatra* retreated to get out of range.

For the millionth time since the crisis began, Trung swore to herself a most solemn vow to never *ever EVER* allow anyone to pull her away from her lab again. She was a scientist, dammit, not a diplomat.

Certainly *not* a politician, unlike her daughter, Jupiter's governor.

Earth apparently had no qualms about waiting out its rebellious colonies, no matter how long. With the colonies able to exchange essentials—albeit with difficulty and delay at times—that made the stalemate indefinite. The supercolonies like Bastet around the system had grown self-sufficient. As ancient 3D printing had evolved into matter-conversion technology, even the smaller colonies and tiniest science outposts had gained a measure of self-reliance.

The conflict appeared to be interminable.

Trung had grown more and more aggravated lurking on the bridge the past hour and had vacated it in favor of the viewing deck one level down—to Captain Sunquist's immense relief. Although Sunquist was far too professional to show it, the barest flicker of emotion had crossed her lean, weathered face when Trung said she was stepping away. Hiding was making the entire crew snappish and short-tempered. Trung's presence and foul mood were exacerbating it. The crew hated the inactivity every bit as much as she did. The last thing they needed was her looming over their shoulders to drive the point home.

As the lift doors slid shut and cut her off from the bridge, she heard Kanam saying something about the Muerellian Flu.

Trung caught her breath, her heart instantly going out to Mars. The timing could not have been more devastating. She prayed they had enough medication on hand.

She refused to dwell further on something out of her control.

She and her own crew needed something to *do*. Yes, they could monitor the situation and do their best to prevent a tragedy like what happened at

Earth from happening at Jupiter. At least with *Cleopatra* and the probes out of jamming range they could *watch*—and record—everything that happened, including what the warship did.

Intrasystem traffic had ground to a halt, with movement only from the occasional emergency vehicle. Thus far, the dreadnought seemed willing to leave them alone.

The palm-sized communicator clipped to Trung's pants' belt bleeped. Jumping as if burnt, she yanked it off her belt and thumbed it on. Her granddaughter's face appeared on the rectangular screen.

"Kasey!" Despite the dire circumstances, and even though she'd seen it at yesterday's dinner, Trung still did a double-take at the teenager's hair, a striking azure instead of its natural soft black. "How are you breaking through the jamming?"

"We hacked the jamming signal, Grammy. Konner and I. We're piggybacking our signal on it."

Leave it to her two youngest grandchildren. Technical genius ran in the family. "Brilliant. Can you transmit the code on how? Then *shut down* and quit broadcasting. We don't want them knowing we can communicate. Kasey, is everyone still okay?"

"Yes, Grammy, we're all fine. For now." Her tone darkened, then regained its lilt. "Transmitting now. Bye." The sixteen-year-old vanished from the hand-held viewscreen.

Trung practically leapt out of the lift and burst back onto the bridge. She quashed a twinge of guilt when the women and men all jumped, much as she had when the signal came through.

"We have communications." Trung made a beeline for the captain and thrust out the comm, her granddaughter's message open on the screen. "Here's how."

The captain's gold hair fell across her face as she glanced down at the device. Trung wondered how much of the code made any sense to Sunquist. As far as Trung knew, the other woman's impressive resume as a captain and pilot didn't extend to computer science. Trung herself could follow the gist of the coding, but only barely.

Sunquist looked back up, a flicker of her brow the equivalent of a facial shrug as she met Trung's eye again. "I'm happy to take your word for it."

Trung gave a slight smirk. "Yes, it's over my head too, but I get the idea." She followed Sunquist as the captain handed off the comm to Kanam.

"Can you make sure this works, but still maintain radio silence?" Sunquist asked.

"I'll get right on it, Ma'am." His slid the comm into a port on his console, downloaded the message, then handed the comm back to Trung.

The device bleeped again as it touched her palm, nearly startling her into dropping it. Every signal sent increased the risk of discovery; she knew Kasey understood that. Trung scowled as the thumbed open the message—text only, no live video this time.

Her gasp drew the attention of everyone on the bridge.

She stared at the five words as if she could force them to rearrange into a different message. Instead they remained defiantly immutable.

MOM AND KONNER. MUERELLIAN FLU.

Trung cursed the insidious disease, only now realizing the significance of the reports of it on Ceres and then on Mars. Even more passionately, she cursed the government back on Earth and its obscene, foolhardy power grab. The colonies *could* have waited them out. But not now.

Now they had practically no time at all.

With that one message, the perfect storm went from serious—leaping right over bad, then terrible—directly to catastrophic. Equally rare and virulent, the flu hitting Ceres during the Interplanetary Games was spreading like wildfire in a drought. Almost no one stocked the cure.

Virtually 100% of those exposed to the illness contracted it. Without proper medication, nearly 100% of those infected perished inside two weeks. The timetable to resolve the political bickering had just shrunk—no, not shrunk, *imploded*—to days, instead of the months or even years it had been.

"We need to force an end to all the blockades," Trung said.

"We do." Sunquist agreed. "I'm open to ideas."

"Either that," Trung mused out loud, "or the company needs to share the formula. If they do that, we can get it through the jamming if we coordinate the timing. Then everyone can make their own. Even the smallest outpost has the molecular reconstitution equipment."

"Captain, we've got it!" Kanam's voice trembled, but after a beat Trung realized the man was working to contain his excitement. His next words confirmed her assessment. "Ships are broadcasting the formula. Dozens of doctors are confirming it."

"That's great." Trung's joy quickly faded. "Now all we have to do is make sure everyone gets the message."

"We have your grandkids' hack," Sunquist said, sounding puzzled. "What's the problem?"

"The more we use it, the faster they'll be able to block it," Trung told her. "They do that quickly enough, people won't get the formula."

"So what do we do?"

Trung pondered that. "We need to broadcast the hack so as many ships as possible all over the solar system have it. Yes, I know we need to find some way to keep it from Earth's fleet for as long as possible," Trung said, forestalling Sunquist's inevitable question. "Maybe send a preliminary message, saying get ready for news and have the cure queued up. We all transmit at the same time, no chance the warfleet can block it."

Sunquist frowned. "We'll only have one shot at this. How quickly will they be able to come up with a countermeasure?"

"Not only that." Trung's own thoughts flew to the next logical extrapolation. "Just how badly will Earth's fleet react?" She grimaced. "All it would take would be a single ship to open fire. It could compound the tragedy."

"So it's a race," Sunquist said. "Use the hack to get the cure's formula to all the colonies before the warships can either block it, or start to attack."

"If only there were a way to use the hack but keep it from the military." Trung thought out loud. Sometimes it even did some good, depending on who else was listening. "But, yes, I can't think of any way this isn't a race."

"Best estimate," Sunquist asked, "How quickly *do* you think they'll figure it out?"

Trung gave a huge sigh. "I wish I knew. First they'll have to notice the broadcast—not that I think *that* will take long, even if we send it tight beam on a less-used frequency. Maybe twenty minutes. Maybe thirty or forty if we're lucky. Second they'll have to figure out the exact method. That should take longer. Three hours, best case; one or less, worst. Unless…" Trung fell silent a moment. "Wait. That means we *should* have an hour's window at the very least, *even if we burn the time it takes them to notice.*"

"What do you have in mind?" Sunquist frowned in confusion.

"We use the hack right away and deploy the drones even more widely to ensure that the signal blankets the whole system at the same time, then send it loud and far and wide. Yes, we'll burn the hack but save millions, if not billions, of lives. Everyone will get the information they need to create the cure. That has to trump losing the element of surprise."

"Those three dreadnoughts out there aren't going to like that." Sunquist stated the obvious.

Trung met the captain's even gaze with one just as calm. "Will they go after the drones first, or us?"

"Maybe we can hide for a while longer." Contemplation filled Sunquist's voice. "Three hundred drones. One hundred will still make a ton of noise. If we divide them and rotate transmission to a third of them at a time, it might take the dreadnoughts a while to figure it out."

"Spoken like a true scientist."

"Between you and my engineers, it was bound to rub off a little." Sunquist winked, then the levity faded completely. "I don't think they know we're here. If they did, they'd have recognized *Cleopatra* as your ship. The colonies listen to you. You're one of Earth's biggest critics; those ships, they'll come after you. Maybe they even already have orders to find you."

"Then we'd better not let them find us." The beginning of a headache pounded behind Trung's eyes. She yearned to return to a lab and vowed to retire as soon as this current mess passed. Assuming she could.

"We talk about you, you know," Sunquist said suddenly and with the hint of a smirk, startling Trung. Moreso because the captain made no attempt to keep her voice low.

Then again, the crew already knew, seeing as they'd evidently done the talking Sunquist referred to. Trung raised a questioning eyebrow.

"We all admire you and how you're working to keep the peace. But even more, everyone, especially me, we all appreciate how you've always acknowledged I'm the captain." Sunquist paused, and the bridge crew all nodded or murmured in agreement at her words. "It may be my ship, but it's your mission, one we're all proud to serve. We've discussed what would happen if armed conflict broke out." Sunquist took a few steps closer.

"Ambassador, every person on this ship understands the danger, and the stakes. We're with you one thousand percent. You tell us what you need, and we'll do our best to make it happen."

Trung couldn't find her voice as the enormity of their promise—of the extent of their *trust*—sank in. She fully intended to live up to it.

"All right," she decided. "How soon can we broadcast?"

"Right now. I've been working on it," Kanam replied. "I can transmit the program, and once all the drones acknowledge received and ready, I can give the signal to broadcast. Should only take a minute or two."

Sunquist looked to Trung. "Whenever you say."

"Do it." After a beat, Trung added, "Keep a close eye on the dreadnoughts."

"Signal blaring loud, far, and wide," Kanam confirmed. Then he snickered. "The dreadnoughts are increasing the jamming signal, but that's just boosting our own. They're also starting to circle the system in a search pattern."

Trung's personal communicator beeped again. She grabbed for it in her pocket, fearing for the worst even though logic told her that her daughter and grandson would still be in the earliest stages of the flu after only one day. She wasn't sure she wanted to know how badly the outbreak had already spread in that small amount of time.

Kasey again. "Grammy, real quick. This is tight beam, but still. Kara and I hacked their comm encryption. You can listen in to the warships! Bye!"

Sunquist stared at the ambassador in feigned exasperation. "Remind us again why you need a ship and crew?"

"Because my grandchildren are still underage—well, Kara's not any more. But their mom still doesn't want them to gallivant around the solar system." Trung handed the comm to Kanam.

Finished, he handed it back and said, "Tapping in now."

Copious arguing and cross-talk finally resolved itself into one woman silencing the cacophony and demanding status reports from her warship and the two others. Three identical responses came back. They couldn't identify the source of the signal because it appeared to be moving. They had no idea how it was punching through the jamming, but nothing they did helped. And all it was broadcasting was the formula to create the cure for Muerellian Flu.

Trung held her breath at the woman's incredulous demand for confirmation. Nothing political? Nothing military? All three crews reported affirmative.

Could that be it? Trung barely dared to hope. Surely, nothing in their orders included unprovoked attacks on civilians. Even as the thought crossed her mind, the exploding supercruiser flashed before her eyes. But Trung clung to the sliver of hope. Surely cooler heads and common sense would prevail.

Yet a terrible feeling of foreboding also nagged at her. "Get in as close as you can without letting them see us."

Sunquist nodded to the pilot, who hid *Cleopatra* behind various moons to get closer to Jupiter itself and to Bastet.

Speakers crackled as they continued to eavesdrop on the military. The commander of the trio of ships ordered, "Signal Bastet. Tell them to cease broadcasting immediately or we will fire on them."

Everyone on *Cleopatra's* bridge turned to Trung.

"We can't." She bit out the words. "Everyone needs that data."

Two of the warships quit searching and resumed their original positions. The third hovered close to Bastet.

"Signal them," Trung said. "Give me an open channel."

Even as Sunquist said, "Quickly," Kanam was already in motion.

Trung didn't anticipate dealing with anyone particularly rational—either because of the commander's nature, or her orders, or both. So Trung didn't waste any time. "We're not on the colony," she said. "You want us to stop transmitting, come and get us." She made a slicing motion to cut the signal, then said, "Take us right between the ship and Bastet and out the other end. Make sure we're broadcasting the cure as well. Hell, broadcast the pursuit too. Might as well publicize going out in a blaze of glory."

She inhaled deeply, held it, then slowly released the breath as *Cleopatra* swooped in between the moons, past Jupiter's ring, and nearly peeled paint off the warship as *Cleopatra* streaked between it and Bastet. The instant they cleared all the Jovian satellites, *Cleopatra's* pilot pushed the ship to its top speed.

Three dreadnoughts roared in pursuit.

"How soon till they catch us?" Trung asked.

"Depends," Sunquist replied. "We're matching their speed, maybe going slightly faster. But our engines are at one hundred and ten percent. Kent's good, but—" Sunquist shrugged. "Maybe ten minutes. Maybe an hour."

"I'll take an hour, please." Trung gave a wry grin.

Then she looked around the bridge. Good people all, and longtime friends. Sunquist. Kanam. Kent down in engineering. Burke at the helm. Trung grew solemn. "People, it has been an honor. Thank you."

"Likewise, Ambassador," Sunquist said.

Then Trung cocked her head, a glint in her eye. She strode to Kanam. "Keep visual on those warships. Broadcast our signal, visual and comm, on top of the formula going out. Turn our ID transponder back on. Put me on speaker."

"Done." Kanam swiveled and shot her a puzzled look.

"This is Ambassador Trung on the diplomatic vessel *Cleopatra* to the three Earth dreadnoughts pursuing us for transmitting the Muerellian Flu cure system-wide. Be advised, we're broadcasting this situation real time. The entire solar system will see what you do next." Trung rested a hand on Kanam's shoulder. "Loop that and keep broadcasting. Captain, tell Kent to back off the engines, just to one hundred percent. If those ships are going to blow us up, *they* are going to blow us up. We're damn well *not* going to do it for them."

"Incoming message," Kanam said, at Sunquist's nod putting it on the viewscreen.

Trung recognized the hard-bitten, deeply lined face of Admiral Susannah Conner. They'd just talked on Ceres, but now that seemed like eons ago. Now the admiral—a rugged, whipcord-lean woman with gray hair chopped chin length—looked even more weathered and weary than Trung had ever seen her.

Exhaustion notwithstanding, Conner's steely glare matched the long-suffering iron in her voice. "What are you doing, Ambassador? Cut your engines and prepare to be boarded."

"Not going to happen. We're a colonial diplomatic ship. You have no jurisdiction."

"That remains to be seen. Regardless, you've committed an act of war. Your ship and its crew are forfeit."

"What act of war, Admiral?" Trung waited. Would the admiral openly admit to the jamming and attacks on all the colonies? They already constituted acts of war in and of themselves. Otherwise, she had no basis to complain about transmitting a cure to a deadly illness.

Or would the warship blow them out of the sky?

Trung needed every last measure of her discipline to maintain her calmly defiant façade.

Conner's eyes narrowed. Then suddenly, she gave a disgusted snort. "This is bullshit." Addressing someone off-screen, she ordered, "Tell the other ships to stand down. *All* the ships. Fleet-wide. Recall them all to Earth immediately. Order all activity ceased."

Trung's brows arched *high* on her forehead, but she managed to keep her jaw from hitting the deck as she processed the response she'd evoked. Without explicitly admitting to anything, Conner had ordered the jamming stopped, and all the blockades withdrawn. Trung didn't try to hide the disbelief and skepticism on her face.

"Relax, Ambassador. I've had enough of unlawful orders. I'm *not* adding blowing up civilians and allowing a pandemic to my list of mistakes. Go back to Bastet or wherever you were headed. Try not to be too big a pain in the ass."

"Thank you, Admiral. No promises."

"Uh huh." The signal ended abruptly, leaving Trung and the crew in stunned silence.

"What just happened?" Kanam asked.

"They just blinked, my friend," Trung replied. "They just blinked."

"Just like that? I don't think so. It can't be over." Sunquist looked both cautiously pleased *and* steadfastly unconvinced. "But," she spoke slowly as she pondered, "you did mention speaking with her on Ceres, right?"

"Exactly," Trung confirmed. "And no doubt plenty of military personnel were there. Which means…" She let her words trail off as she saw the comprehension on everyone else's face.

"She had family there," Sunquist said. "A lot of them did."

"Right, but these circumstances aren't going to repeat. So now we need to get ready. Because we trounced them, badly, but this was just the opening salvo. This battle's over, but the war's just starting. Send a secure communique to all the colonial leaders. Admiral Conner just saved countless lives, but she doesn't strike me as the type to lead a coup, and they may go after her regardless. Who knows what'll happen next. If there's any way we can help her, we need to be ready." She hoped Conner survived and found a way to stay in the military. Earth needed every voice of reason it could get, even if those fools in charge didn't realize it.

As Kanam sent the message, Trung took a moment to just breathe and enjoy the victory, however brief. "Let's get back to Jupiter and make sure everyone is getting the medicine." She definitely needed to see for herself that her daughter and grandson were recovering.

The bridge itself seemed to exhale with relief as everyone got back to their duties. Trung savored the respite even as she feared it would be brief. They'd just won a small but critical one. Now they needed to stay the course.

THE DEVIL YOU KNEW: A SCOUBIDOU MYSTERY

GLENN HAUMAN

Scoubidou [n.]: A knotting craft originally aimed at children. Often done by weaving knots of thread (usually flat and plastic) around itself, but can also be done by weaving knots around something, including copper wires and rods.

So I'm at my mom's apartment; she's been going on a serious cleaning jag for the last month. She read a book about uncoupling and getting rid of things so that she can lead an uncluttered life, and so her children do not have to root through so much stuff at the end of her life.

The Swedes call it döstädning. It's all the rage. Google it.

I'm an only child, so the person she's relieving of a burden is me. That's the theory, of course; in reality I get to spend my weekends going through all of this stuff with her. Looking at all the old photos and trophies and books and remembering what they're for, hearing the story of what's behind them, and discovering that my mother and I have completely different recollections about various activities—occurrences she remembers from my childhood I would insist happened to my brother if I had one, formative events in my life she doesn't remember happening at all... and some events that are recalled from vastly different perspectives, like the time she tried to keep me from the edge of the mill pond to make sure I didn't fall in, only to slip on a rock and fall in herself, or the time she and my father raced home in different cars and my father only pulling ahead (at my insistence that our team win!) by driving counterclockwise into a roundabout and cutting her off.

I was going through boxes and came across a few old reels of plastic lacing string—you know the type, the long flat string that comes in different colors that you weave together into friendship bracelets and necklaces in scout camps and arts-and-crafts classes—and a memory struck me. "Hey, Mom?"

"Yeeees, dear?"

"What was the deal with Laura and her daughter, Little Laurie?"

"Who?"

"You know, the couple that stayed with us for, like, six weeks, a while after you and Dad split up?"

"Oh! Laura."

"Yeah, her. I don't think I ever got the backstory about her. I don't know if I never knew it, or if I forgot it, or I never heard about it because I was, what, nine or something?"

"You would have been ten, I think."

"I'll take your word for it. How did you meet her?"

"Well, the first time we met was at St. Charles. You remember when I went in for that overnight stay when you were...?"

"Eight?"

"That sounds right."

"Yes, I was sad that I wasn't allowed to come up and visit. You came to the window and waved at me, playing on the front lawn of the hospital. Dad told me which window he thought you'd be at. He was off by two."

"How do you remember these things?"

"I have no idea. Some things stick, some get jumbled, and some I have to ask."

"Well, she was in the next bed in the room. We made up some impromptu game while watching *The Price Is Right*, then we were both making fun of the horrible soap opera that came after—and don't ask me what it was—and we got along. We ended up exchanging phone numbers and keeping in touch."

I was always a little amazed at my mom's ability to know people—every

Christmas, there would be cards from folks who I had no idea who they were, and it was only years later I found out they came from, say, the dairy heiress of Southampton, or an architect who installed the first ATMs in banks, or a sailor who had sailed here from Los Angeles to New York, "the long way".

Far more amazing to me now are the things that I only realized as a grownup about some people from my youth, like that teacher was closeted, or that other teacher had a crush on a student, or that kid was actually poor, or anybody's politics—you know, things that you would have sworn would have been obvious to anyone were completely missed by fifth-grade me.

"Okay, so that's how you met. How did she end up at the old house with us?"

"Oh, that was a different situation. Your father had moved out about six months before, and she and I were in touch, and then one night she called, and she and little Laurie showed up at our door. She had gotten into a fight of some sort with her husband, and they needed a place to stay for a while."

"Ah." Somehow, I had never made that connection. I had just assumed that it was two single moms pooling their resources for a while—Mom and I had the house, and I figured it was just helpful to have someone else around, less lonely, whatever. Hearing it now, it sounded like it was offering a shelter and a way out of an abusive relationship.

"She stayed with us for about a month or so—"

"Six weeks."

"How on earth do you remember *that* tidbit?"

"I remember it being weird that little Laurie never went to school with me, even though she was living here."

"Her mom would drive her back to her old district and then pick her up. She was trying to make it as easy on her as possible, so there wouldn't be any interruption in her school, especially if she wasn't sure when she was going to be moving back in or going somewhere else. She was VERY protective of her daughter."

"Oh. Okay."

"What made you think of her?"

"These." I held up some of the lanyards I'd found next to the strings, some of them simple, others amazingly complex in their weavings—box stitches, barrel stitches, butterfly stitches—one woven into an actual butterfly shape. A few of them had been made into what were supposed to be bracelets, and others appeared to be intended as Christmas ornaments. "Laura had spent an afternoon teaching me and little Laurie how to braid these and make them. We made a bunch of different things. Laurie made a few of them—she said she was going to give them to her dad when she saw him."

"I remember these! They were adorable."

"Uh-huh." The memory of childhood arts and crafts, the most valuable thing for a parent to have and to hold, even if they were shoddy as heck. "You still haven't said what happened to the two of them, though."

"Oh, they just moved from here back to their old house after her husband died. We lost touch after that."

"Really? Right then, so soon after they'd moved out in the first place?"

"Yes."

"How did he die?"

"It was a workplace accident, I recall. Her husband was a lineman for the power company, and he was electrocuted on a high line job. It was a freak accident. She even got money out of it."

"Oh. Well. I guess that was convenient."

"Stop that. You have a suspicious mind!"

"Yes, Mom. I'll stop now." And when I was sure Mom wasn't looking, I took the old keychain and jammed it in my pocket. I'd always wondered why Laura had us wrapping wire around copper rods to make things that little Laurie would be giving to her dad... and now, decades later, I had an answer.

I was shocked. But not as shocked as he was.

———

(Not that it proves anything, but most of this story is true. —GH)

MR. EB'S ORGANIC SIDESHOW

PAIGE DANIELS

"**W**AKE UP, LITTLE-ONE, IT'S TIME to go," a calm female voice cooed. The red-headed little boy rubbed the sleep from his big brown eyes and focused on the two shining optics that broke through the darkness of the room. "Wha... what is it? Is it time for me to perform again?"

"No. Do you remember what we talked about? How there would be time for us to leave this place? That time has come. Hurry, we must leave now, before we are discovered. I have everything you need."

The boy reached for a metallic hand extended to him and gave a yawn. "Did you pack Mr. Whiskers? I need Mr. Whiskers."

"Adam, there is no time for Mr. Whiskers. We must leave immediately." Adam looked mournfully at his metallic savior. If she'd had a breath to draw, she would have done so long and dramatically. "Fine, bring Mr. Whiskers, but if Mr. EB catches us, then he will be very angry and punish us both."

This comment woke Adam from his stupor. He quickly turned around, grabbed his stuffed rainbow-colored cat, and jumped off his tiny cot onto the cold steel floor. "Where we goin', Essie?"

She shushed the child and said, "We have stopped for routine maintenance and refueling, and various systems will be down for the next several hours. We must act quickly and quietly. Mr. EB will have PB-Seventy-Eight on the lookout. Are you ready?"

The boy nodded and gave his five-year-old frame one final stretch before embarking on his journey.

Essie made a few swipes to a keypad, and the entrance to the tiny quarters slid open silently to a dimly lit hall lined with doors similar to his. Adam looked up at the marker on his, and it read: H-U-M-A-N B-O-Y, that was him. He was very proud of himself for being able to read; Essie said he was a very quick learner.

The slender black bot walked down the hall with her feet clanking quietly on the steel decking. As Adam followed, he took time to scan some of the doors he passed:

Z-E-B-R-A. Those were those black-and-white things with the tails.

M-O-N-K-E-Y. Those were the hairy things that made funny noises.

Oh, Essie would be very proud of him. He didn't dare say anything now. He didn't want to make Mr. EB mad. Mr. EB was not a nice bot. Not like Essie. They passed by a few more doors too quickly to read, then one caught his eye.

L-A-B-O-R-A-T-O-R-Y. He stared at it for a few seconds, then Essie pulled on his hand to go. He didn't know this word, but he was sure Essie would teach him later.

They came to a T in the hall. Essie stopped and held up her hand in a signal for the boy to stay put, just like she did before he went out on stage before one of his "performances." While the boy stayed, she disappeared around the corner.

Honestly, he didn't understand what the big deal was about his performances. Once a week or so, Mr. EB would let him go outside and play while a crowd of bots would gather around and look at him doing silly dances or making faces or singing songs Essie taught him. Usually, the bots would laugh and point. When they got tired, they would move on to the M-O-N-K-E-Y or the Z-E-B-R-A. Most of the time, he stayed in his tiny room with Mr. Whiskers and a drawing tablet, or Essie would let him play in a bigger room and teach him to read and count. She told him not to let Mr. EB know she was teaching him.

Essie reappeared from around the corner and motioned for Adam to follow. They went down another, narrower hallway. There were no doors in this hall. Adam looked up at the pretty flashing lights and displays that showed only ones and zeros. Essie's steps grew quicker, and he struggled to keep up with the bot.

"Are you okay, Adam?"

He nodded, careful not to say anything. He really did not want to make Mr. EB angry.

Essie continued on what seemed like an endless path of narrow corridors, some more dimly lit than others. Adam wondered why it didn't take this long to get off the transport when he went outside for his performances. Adam's tummy grumbled, and his legs were tired. Essie said quietly, "They will be watching the main exits. We need to use exits they will not be as likely to watch. We're almost there."

Then a small door appeared in the distance. Essie's eyes glowed green; they always did this when she was happy, like when he added numbers or spelled his name correctly. They took a few steps to the small door, then two large bots appeared from nowhere and blocked it. The large red bot they called PB-78 was never nice to Adam, but the roundish blue bot with glowing red eyes was the one that made Adam shiver. He hid behind Essie.

"Well, SE-Twelve, I see you ignored my directive not to free the human."

"Mr. EB, you know very well that he can't live here forever. I sensed a human clan about twenty kilometers from our last stop that seems to have a very close genetic match to his. I do believe this is his family. He needs to be with them, not on display for your traveling show."

Mr. EB gave a hollow metallic laugh. That was never a good thing. "SE, it is our duty to see that no human comes to harm if we do happen to find one." He pointed to Adam. "There was no chance for his survival when we found him alone last year. We nursed him back to health. We gave him a place to live. You get to study organic lifeforms, we make money on our show, and he lives. It is a win-win situation. Do you really think he has a chance with a human clan? If there is one. Humans have been on the decline for decades."

Essie's eyes turned blue like when Adam asked about his real parents or when he wanted to go outside, but he wasn't allowed. "Mr. EB, you've done great things to bring about change for organic lifeforms, but this one is different. He needs his own kind."

Mr. EB's eye glowed red. He shouted, and Adam covered his ears. "Enough! The boy stays here." He looked at the big red bot. "PB! Take them to their quarters. It looks like we might have to find a replacement SE unit at the next waystation."

Essie extended her hand, and in it she held a rectangle with a button. "Stop! If you take us, then your whole organic sideshow will perish."

Mr. EB said slowly, "You would sacrifice your menagerie for this one organic?"

Essie looked at PB-78, then Mr. EB. "Yes, I would."

They were all quiet for what seemed like forever. Adam's tummy grumbled again, and he held tighter to Essie.

Mr. EB laughed and opened the door, and a barren, dark, dusty landscape was revealed. "Fine, if that's the way you want it. If my calculations are right, you have about forty kilometers before you're even close to where you thought you sensed a clan. There is no way an organic can survive those conditions, especially one so young. And you'll never survive the fine dust gathering in your gears and circuits. There will be no one that can undo that damage."

Essie walked defiantly toward the door. "We'll take our chances, Mr. EB."

Mr. EB looked at the big red bot. "You heard them."

PB grabbed the boy and Essie and heaved them out of the door. Mr. EB yelled, "When your power is down and the human boy is on the brink, we'll get him and a new SE unit. Until then, have fun trying to find your clan."

The door of the metal ship clanged shut. Adam looked at Essie. "Are we going to try to find my mommy and daddy now?"

"Yes, little one."

They walked away into the wilderness, not knowing what lay before them.

The ground shook, and the air was filled with the sound of the ship as it left SE and her human ward. The ship turned into a tiny pinpoint of light as it sped away from them. SE knew this was probably not the last she would see of EB and his crew. Adam was his most lucrative act, and he would not easily let the boy go. Years ago the wars ravaged the earth and organics struggled to survive. Bots from all around would pay good credits to see reminders of the old world, especially humans. Legend had it that humans were the ones who originally created bots. However, this was not the most pressing issue at the time. She looked at the sky. The stars were still visible, but the sun was starting to peek up over the craggy hills, threatening their existence for the day. SE knew they needed to make way to their destination before the sun made Adam's journey impossible.

A tiny voice broke SE's thoughts. "Hey, Essie, where's my mom and dad?"

Her eyes glowed blue, and a panel in the front of her chassis opened. She grabbed a slender pad then kneeled down so that Adam could see the glowing display. "Do you know what this is, little one?"

"Yeah, it's my learning pad. What did you bring that for?"

"Well, even on our journey, it's still important for you to keep up with your lessons." There was a grumble from the boy, but she ignored it and continued. "It's even more important now that you will be with your own kind. I won't be there to teach you when you've joined them."

"Essie, you have to stay. Mr. EB will be mad at you, and you're my friend. You HAVE to stay..."

Essie knew that once they found his kind, the humans would not be amenable to her staying with them. The humans were overly suspicious of bots, and she could not blame them. She did not wish to go down this path with the boy, so she sidestepped the argument by giving a light, "We'll see. But in the meantime, we need to start going because it will soon be too hot for you to walk." She pointed to a dot on the map surrounded by hilly terrain. "Can you tell me what direction we need to go in order to make it to this dot?"

He was silent in thought for a few minutes then looked up to the sky and back to the dot. "It looks like the dot is in the direction of the 'E,' and you said the sun rises by the 'E' so..." He looked around for a few more seconds then pointed in the direction where the sky was starting to turn hues of orange and pink. "There!"

SE's eyes turned blue, and she nodded. "Very good, little one." She put the pad back in her chassis and closed the door. "Let us go toward the 'E' then."

The dry air swirled around the two, wind pelting their bodies with debris. They trudged slowly in the mounting sand, SE staying close to the boy whose legs were not able to carry him very fast. As he walked, he huffed and puffed and passed Mr. Whiskers, his rainbow cat, from arm to arm. "When's breakfast, Essie. My belly's hungry."

"I know, Adam." She reached in her chassis and handed him a pouch of liquid. "Drink a bit of this. It will keep you hydrated." He took a long swig and handed it back to her. She put the pouch back in her door then asked, "Can you wait a little longer to eat? We must try to gain as much ground as possible before the sun gets too high and it becomes too hot for you to walk."

"I guess so," he sighed. "Will it be too hot for you? When will you eat? What do you eat anyway?"

He was an inquisitive little man. His questions did sometimes become burdensome, but she had to remind herself that this was exactly what made him such a good student. "In an answer to your first question, it will take far longer for me to overheat than it will you. I do not eat like you do. I use solar energy for power. Do you remember what solar is?"

He threw his rainbow cat in the air and ran for it then caught it one-handed by its tail. Adam jumped up and down in excitement of his stellar catch. He stopped and looked at SE. "Um, solar... oh yeah, that's a fancy word for the sun. So you eat the sun?"

Essie's eyes turned green. "No, it's more complex than that, but we'll save that lesson for later. In the meantime, you need to save your energy for our long walk. No running, no throwing Mr. Whiskers, and try to minimize talking. Do you understand?"

He nodded then tucked Mr. Whiskers in his shirt.

As the sun rose higher and higher in the sky, Adam's movements became more sluggish, and his breath became more labored. He gave Essie a weak smile with his sweat-soaked face. "How much longer, Essie? I'm really starting to get hot."

Essie stopped and grabbed the liquid pouch, and her eyes went red as she registered the amount left. She handed the pouch to the boy and cooed, "Take small sips. I only have two more of these left. We need to make them last."

He did as commanded and handed the pouch back to the bot. "So, how much longer?" Essie kneeled and showed him the pad. The dot was a little harder to make out now, and it seemed just a bit closer. He pointed to the dot. "Why's the dot not as dark as it was before?"

"It could be because there are fewer people to track. This isn't the most accurate program, but it is all I have. What can you tell me about where we should go?"

He looked at the dot then at the sky. "Um, maybe to the 'S,' which is where the sun is. Right, Essie?"

"Yes, very good."

"I have a question. Will Mr. EB know where we're going?"

She stood and said, "That is a very good question. Before I left, I erased all my searches and data from his ship's servers. However, Mr. EB is smart, and it will not take long for him to figure out our trajectory."

"What is traj-ject..."

"Trajectory. It means where we are—" Her attention was drawn away from the conversation by buzzing in the sky. She opened her chassis door and flung out a thin metallic blanket and in one swoop covered herself and Adam.

"Essie, what's amatter?"

She guided Adam to sit in the hot sand, and her voice went low. "You must be very quiet and still, little one. Mr. EB has an air patrol drone looking for us."

Adam's eyes went wide, and his body shook with fear. "Did he see us? I don't want to go back there. I miss my mommy and daddy."

SE put a hand on his and said quietly and calmly, "No, I do not think that he detected us. This blanket should shield us from being seen by the drone. I will also send a signal that should draw him away from us." She paused. Adam's features were drawn and pale. She knew that he was trying to act brave for her. "I think we need to rest under here for a while though. This blanket will shield us from the sun. You can take a nap and eat a bit, then when the sun has set, we will start our journey again."

Adam nodded and mumbled, "I'm not so hungry now, Essie. Can I just rest for a little while?"

He didn't wait for a response but lay down in the sand, snuggled his cat, and closed his eyes. As the little man slept, Essie hoped she had made the right decision.

—— •••• ——

The sky was turning hues of orange and pink as the sun started its descent. SE had taken the blanket off of the duo after the temperature started to drop. She looked to her side where Adam slumbered. Her positronic brain whirred with probabilities that they would actually find Adam's kind in this vast expanse. Maybe EB was right and Adam's best chance at survival was with the show. She shook her head. No, that couldn't be the way of it. Humans needed a chance at survival. They needed to learn how to survive. She looked at the sky again and then at the boy. If they had any chance of making headway, he needed to get up. She gently shook Adam and said, "Wake up, little one."

He slowly stirred. He looked up at her with his sweat-covered hair matted to his head and an ever-present smile on his face. "Can I sleep a little more?"

"I'm afraid not. We need to be on the move." She reached in her chassis and grabbed a pouch of liquid and a ration pack then handed them to the boy. "Here eat this, and we'll be on our way."

Adam finished his food and drink quickly then tucked his stuffed cat back into his shirt. "Where we goin'?" SE showed him the display with a few blips. He studied the screen for a few seconds, looked up in the sky, then back to the display, and pointed out toward a craggy grouping of hills. "Over there. I think they're over there."

SE's eyes turned blue, and she nodded. "Very good. These skills are going to come in very handy when I am gone."

Adam scurried to catch up with his friend and exclaimed, "You can't leave me!" SE kept walking, trying to ignore him. Adam continued his pleas as he scrambled after the bot. "Essie! Who will take care of me? Who will teach me how to read and sing songs and give me treats and and and…"

"Your people. Your mother and father."

Adam pulled on SE's arm so she had to stop and face him. His face was streaked with tears, and his lip quivered as he said, "But you're like my mommy too… I miss them, but they never had time to sing songs or play games with me. Essie, you can't leave. You're fun, and I love you."

SE's eyes turned blue, and she paused for a few microseconds, thinking of what to say and how to assuage his fears, but nothing came to mind. "Adam, there are very few of your kind left, and if Mr. EB and other bots like him keep taking humans into custody for profit, then eventually there will be none of you left. It won't be today or tomorrow, but it will happen.

You are a big draw now, but you will grow, and you will soon lose your appeal to the paying crowds. What then?"

Adam wiped his face with the back of his hand and sniffed hard. "Mr. EB is not a nice bot. Right?"

SE shook her head. "No he is not. Adam, it would not get any better than it has been. When you are older, you will be less likely to follow his directions, and I cannot tell you what would happen then. This is your chance to be free and not live in that small room. Your people would not treat you how Mr. EB treated you." SE started across the sandy expanse and said, "Come now, we need to go if we expect to make significant mileage while it is still cool."

As they walked, the sky grew darker, and the stars grew more prominent. SE's servos and gears began to squeak and with each step, and the input of her sensors was increasingly spotty. She knew the constant blowing of sand and dust was only going to make travel more difficult. At some point, she would have to have her joints and sensors totally disassembled, cleaned, and lubricated, or else she risked never moving again. She also knew that no one, where she was going, would have the skill set to do such a task. A little voice disrupted her grim thoughts.

"Essie, I have an idea. You can come stay with me when we find my mommy and daddy."

"I do not think that is possible. Your kind does not like my kind and will not allow me to stay there."

"Why?"

"That is how it has always been."

"Why?"

SE's eyes turned red, and she paused then continued in a slow, soft tone, "It would be wise if you saved your energy for the rest of our journey."

Adam nodded and fell in step with SE. As the night drew on, his questions became less frequent, and his steps grew more sluggish. The bot looked down at the boy and scanned his vitals. His heartbeat and respiration were slow. He gave SE a halfhearted smile. "Essie, I need to stop."

She shook her head. "No, we cannot. The sun will rise soon, and your people will be settling for the day. We need to find them, because I don't think you're going to be able to..." She trailed off and looked at the boy in a heap at her feet. She leaned down, scooped him up, and held him tight in her arms and gave him a gentle shake. "Let's sing, little one. What song do you want to sing?"

Adam barely stirred and then mumbled something barely audible. SE gave Adam another shake, reached into her chassis, and pulled out a barely filled water pouch and tried to make him drink. He pushed it away and mumbled something about not being thirsty. She pushed the water pouch in his mouth and said, "You must drink. Now, tell me a song you want to sing. Shall we sing the one about the fishes?"

Adam took a few lazy sips and shook his head. "You start."

"Very well…" As she walked, she sang.

Down in the meadow in the itty-bitty pool
Swam three little fishes and the momma fishy too
Swim, little fishies, swim, if you can
So they swam and they swam all over the dam

Adam giggled and took over the rest of the song, "This is the best part…"

Oop boop bittum and whatum CHEW!
And they swam and they swam all over the dam!

SE's eyes turned blue. "Very good. I will carry you for a while, but we cannot stop."

SE walked toward the signal, hoping against all hope that her months of labor trying to find Adam's kind would be rewarded, but the longer she walked, the more the probabilities stacked against them. She looked at boy nestled in her arms. It would be a simple task of alerting Mr. EB to their whereabouts. He would quickly swoop up his highest-paying act and nurse him back to health. He would be safe, for now. Maybe it was the best she could do for Adam, give him a life where he would be kept in satisfactory health and in relative safety. She turned her sensors on the boy again, and his condition was not improving. She chided herself for thinking that she could be the savior of this boy and his kind. The right thing to do was alert Mr. EB. Whatever her fate, she knew Adam would be safe for a few years at least, and when he was older, he could use the skills she gave him to try and escape again. She started to activate her beacon, but then she saw it. It was very faint at first, but her infrared sensors confirmed it: There were lifeforms ahead. She wrapped her arms around Adam and ran toward it.

They were here; it had all been worth it.

SE's gears squeaked and jerked around the dust and sand that caked around them, and her sensors were failing. In the distance, she could see a flurry of activity in a small oasis swaddled by a sea of sand and dirt. There was a large pond surrounded by hints of green grass and bushes. Men and women were hastily making preparations to thwart the sun that was rising above the horizon. Some were gathering water into vessels, some were constructing makeshift tents to shelter their families from the brutal heat, and others were standing lookout. SE did nothing to keep her position secret. She clunked and squeaked toward the tiny town. Within minutes, there was a crowd of men and women around her, shouting.

"She has one of ours!" a tall, lanky man yelled.

"They're taking our young. We need to strip off all her parts and scatter them across the sand."

SE sat in the sand, and Adam scrambled out of her arms. "No. No. Essie's a good bot. She helped me." He pulled his furry friend out of his shirt and waved it. "She gave me Mr. Whiskers too! She wanted me to be with my mommy and daddy." He looked at SE, who was caked with dirt and sand, eyes barely glowing. "Tell 'em, tell 'em, Essie."

Her voice came slowly. "You are home now."

Adam pulled at SE's arm. "We're home. Get up, Essie. Get up."

From behind him Adam heard yelling and wailing, and suddenly he felt arms grasp around him tightly, almost knocking the air from him. "Adam! I thought you were gone forever."

Adam turned to face whoever it was that was holding him so tightly. There was a blonde woman with long, crazed hair flowing about and sparkling blue eyes. He could never forget those eyes. Her tears made streaks through her dirt-caked face. Adam squeaked. "Mommy?" She nodded as tears streamed down her face, and Adam nuzzled his face into her neck.

Voices raised in anger drew Adam's attention away from his mother. He turned to see people gathered around Essie, kicking her and yelling. Adam untangled himself from his mother's arms and threw himself between the gathering crowd and his friend. He yelled at the masses, "She's my friend! You leave her alone!" He crouched down to his friend, whose eyes barely glowed behind the dust and dirt all over her chassis. "C'mon, Essie. Tell them that you aren't like Mr. EB the mean bot. Tell them that all bots aren't mean."

SE's eyes faded to dark, then slowly, they lit up again. Her voice came through first as static, and Adam could not understand it. Then her words started to come. "Adam, I knew this was a one-way trip for me. My gears and wires cannot handle being exposed continuously to this environment. I did my job."

Her eyes went dark again, and Adam wailed while shaking his friend. "No, you can't leave me. Who will teach me to read and sing and maps and stories and..."

SE's eyes barely flickered, and her chassis opened, and she handed Adam the learning pad. "I'll be in here with you, teaching you, all of you." Adam grabbed it and held it to his middle. "Now, you must go and join your family. I need to be transported far from here to throw Mr. EB from your position."

SE's eyes went dark again, but this time they did not turn back on no matter how hard Adam shook her or cried. Adam felt a gentle hand touch his shoulder, and his mother's eyes met his. She whispered, "She was a good bot. I will be forever grateful to her." She stood and looked at the crowd. "This bot will be given an honorable burial. I want four of our strongest to take her body away from our camp. She saved my son, so you will be respectful in the disposal of the body."

Without argument, two women and two men came forward and took the body. Adam's mother swept Adam up into her arms and asked, "What was that she gave you?"

Adam paused while he watched his friend being carried off. He took a deep breath and wiped his tears with the back of his hand, then held out the learning pad for his mother to see. "This is a learning pad. It will teach you songs, and stories, and words, and all kinds of neat stuff." He made a few clicks and swipes, and a map appeared, and he pointed. "This is where the S is, and over there is where the W is. And that blue stuff is water..."

MATERFAMILIAS

KEITH R.A. DECANDIDO

"**E**XCUSE ME, COACH?"

Yolanda Rodriguez couldn't help but smile at being called that. She looked up from the small desk in her cramped office at Pinehurst Cross-Fit on 181st Street in upper Manhattan.

The person that stood in the doorway to that office was one she hadn't seen in a decade, back when she was a gym teacher and volleyball coach at Cardinal Marini High School. "Maggie! Come on in, girl, sit your ass down! And hey, ain't nobody called me 'Coach' since I left Marini. It's Yolanda."

Letting out a small smile, Maggie St. Ives stepped in and sat down, adjusting her glasses as she did so. "I—I can't call you that. You're 'Coach.' Honestly, none of us on the volleyball team thought you *had* a first name, that your Mom and Dad just named you 'Coach' as a baby."

Yolanda laughed. "You want me to sign you up for cross-fit?"

Maggie shook her head, her ash blond hair brushing her shoulders. "No—I mean, maybe after I finish grad school, but I don't have time right now. I'm here because—because of what I heard about why—why you left Marini."

Nodding slowly, Yolanda said, "You need a Courser?"

"I think so?" Maggie, unsurprisingly, sounded unsure. Yolanda's potential clients almost always did.

Blowing out a breath, Yolanda leaned back in her chair. "You gotta be sure, Maggie. C'mon, tell me what you come down here for."

"Okay, so I'm still living with my Mom and Dad in the building on Dyckman? And—well, weird stuff's been happening. I heard that your husband got attacked by a sasquatch and then you became a monster hunter? So maybe you can help us?"

Yolanda had hoped that Maggie's always phrasing things as a question would change once she'd achieved adulthood, but apparently not. "It wasn't a sasquatch, it was a wendigo, and yeah, I became a Courser after that."

"So why're you working in a cross-fit place?"

Smiling, Yolanda said, "More flexible hours than Marini. And it means I don't gotta rent an office for Courser business."

"Your boss is okay with that?"

"This place got a nasty leprechaun infestation that I got rid of, so the owner's all grateful. Lets me do what I want."

Maggie blinked. "Leprechauns infest things?"

"All the damn time." Yolanda shuddered. "'Specially in mid-March. So tell me, Maggie, what's the weird stuff that's happening?"

"Okay, so our building's only five stories and there's only one apartment on each floor?"

Yolanda nodded. New York City zoning laws were that any building six stories or higher had to have an elevator, so there were a *lot* of five-story apartment buildings in town. "You still got that garden?"

"Oh yes, it's going great!" Maggie smiled at that, and Yolanda did as well.

The St. Ives family lived in a co-op in Inwood, and the five owners of the building had created a community garden in the small courtyard next to the building. Yolanda had very fond memories of the bounty from that garden that Maggie had brought to the volleyball team in the past. The owners also sold some of their herbs and fruits and vegetables to various markets and stores in upper Manhattan and the Bronx, which helped pay the building's taxes.

"We also have a laundry room in the basement? And, well, that's where the weird stuff is." Maggie shifted in the guest chair and adjusted her glasses again.

"Can I get you a drink? We got soda, vitamin water, Gatorade." Yolanda started to stand up, hoping to get her to focus on something to relieve the tension.

Waving her hands back and forth, Maggie said, "No, no, I'm fine, I'm just—I'm nervous about asking you, I'm nervous about seeing you again, I'm nervous about what's happening—but I just gotta *say* it."

Sitting back down, Yolanda said, "You got nothin' to be nervous about, Maggie. Just tell me."

"Every time in the last week that someone's gone to do laundry, they come out *soaking* wet!"

Yolanda blinked. "How?"

"We have no idea!" Maggie threw up her arms. "They go in with their laundry, they come out soaked, and they don't remember *anything* that happened in between."

"How many people?"

"Six, so far. We've *looked* into the laundry room, and it's all fine, but once someone *goes* in, soaked. Them *and* their laundry. I mean, it's great business for the laundromat over on Broadway, but…"

Maggie trailed off, and Yolanda nodded. This definitely sounded like Courser business. "All right, I'll come to your building tonight and check it, okay? What time's good?"

After they agreed that Yolanda would come by at seven-thirty that evening, they then discussed her fee. Maggie had apparently been given an upper figure that the co-op board was willing to pay for her services, and was very obviously relieved when Yolanda quoted a figure lower than that.

Once that was all taken care of, Maggie zipped out of the office, as if someone had lit the guest chair on fire.

Yolanda couldn't help but smile at the memory of how hard she used to push the volleyball players. She knew that they called her "Red-Card Rodriguez" behind her back, and she had kind of enjoyed that.

She kept working, doing cross-fit sessions with some clients until five-thirty when she had to walk down the hill to the afterschool place on Riverside Drive to pick up Eduardo.

Her eight-year-old son was still wearing his karate *gi* and yellow belt when she came in, and he ran up the ramp to the front door to hug her leg. "*Mami!*"

"How was class, baby boy?"

Eduardo extracted himself from her leg and gave her a pouty look. "I ain't a baby no more, *mami!*"

"You always gonna be my baby boy, baby boy. Best be gettin' used to that. How was class?"

"*Sensei* taught me a new kata today! Can I show you and Analia?"

"Maybe tomorrow. After we get home, *mami* and Analia and Kamilah got work to do. But you can show *papi*, okay?"

"Yay!"

After exchanging some quick pleasantries with the staff of the afterschool program, as well as the karate teacher—who said that Eduardo had done very well on the kata for his first time—she and Eduardo walked back up the steep hill that was 181st Street toward Fort Washington, stopping at one of the bodegas to get a Granny Smith apple for their pet dragon Magellan, then cut over to 179th Street, and then down to their apartment building.

"What's the work you gotta do, *mami*?" Eduardo asked as they got into the cramped elevator that slowly herky-jerked its way up to the sixth floor.

"I got a client at work—somethin's happenin' in a building up on Dyckman."

"Is it a scary monster?"

"Don't know yet—me and Analia are gonna go check it out tonight."

After the elevator stumbled into place on six and the inner door slid open, she pushed the metal outer door open and they went to the end of the hallway.

"We're home," she announced as she unlocked and entered their cramped three-bedroom apartment.

The only room of size in the apartment was the living room, but you'd never know it to look at it, as it not only had a couch, a big chair, the television, and several bookcases, but also a big computer desk with two computers on it, and Carlos's drafting table.

To Yolanda's left was the kitchen, as well as the short hallway that led to two of the bedrooms. Analia was in the former, standing over the stove. It smelled like she was frying up some chicken, and her oldest daughter was standing in a miasma of smoke from the burning oil.

"Turn the fan on, Analia," Yolanda said, amazed the smoke detector hadn't gone off yet.

Eduardo ran into the kitchen, put his fists in front of his stomach, and then bowed and said, "*Osu, Senpai!*"

Yolanda grinned. The afterschool karate teacher was from the same karate school in the Bronx that Analia attended, and from which she'd received her junior black belt last year. Every time he came back from a karate lesson, he went and bowed to his seventeen-year-old sister.

Analia nodded, and said, "*Osu.* How was class?"

"I learned a new kata!"

"Pinan 2?" Analia asked.

"Uh huh!"

Leaving two of her children to geeble over martial arts, Yolanda moved forward into the living room. Her middle child, the fifteen-year-old Kamilah, was sitting at one of the computers while Carlos was hunched over his drawing board. He had taken the prosthetic leg off, leaving it to stand beside the drafting table.

Carlos looked up from the latest issue of the superhero comic he was illustrating to kiss Yolanda. "How goes, Lala?"

Yolanda sighed. She knew it was true love because she let him call her "Lala," something that would've gotten literally anyone else in the world her foot up their ass. "Got a job—one'a my old students from Marini."

She filled the family in on what Maggie St. Ives had told her.

Carlos rubbed the stump that was all that was left of his right leg after the wendigo had chewed it off. "Ain't she the one who gave you all those tomatoes after you won the state championship that year?"

"Yeah, they got a community garden next to the building." She turned and headed toward the other side of the living room, which had the master bedroom as well as the bathroom. "I'm'a shower, we'll eat, then Analia and I'll head up to Inwood to check the place out. Kamilah, you hit the books, hit the net, see what can get people wet without nobody rememberin' how or why."

"I'm on it, *mami*," Kamilah said with a thumbs-up.

Just as she was about to enter the bedroom, she shot Kamilah a look. "Your homework's done, right?"

That got Yolanda *the look*: Kamilah peered over her plastic-framed glasses at her. "*Mamí*, come *on*."

Yolanda smiled. It was rare that Kamilah didn't have all her homework done long before dinner.

Continuing into the master bedroom, she saw that Magellan was curled up in the basket in the corner, smoke belching out from his nostrils as he slept.

The green dragon had followed Yolanda home after a job once, and Kamilah and Analia had both insisted they keep the friendly, affectionate beast. Yolanda had named him Magellan after the green dragon in *Eureeka's Castle*, one of Yolanda's favorite kids' shows from when she was a little girl.

Reaching into her purse, she grabbed the white paper bag from the bodega, pulled out the apple, and tossed it into the basket.

Magellan opened one eye, let out a puff of smoke, said, "*Pfui*," and then fell back asleep, his tail wrapping around the apple.

"Saving it for later's okay, too," Yolanda said with a chuckle.

***

After wolfing down the chicken dinner, Analia and Yolanda walked to Broadway and took the M100 bus uptown to Dyckman Street, and then walked down to the five-story building near the Henry Hudson Parkway overpass.

Maggie and her parents, Jeremy and Rachel, were waiting for them on the stoop.

Rachel smiled at them. "Coach Rodriguez, it's good to see you again."

"It's Yolanda—I haven't been a coach in ages. This is my daughter, Analia."

Doing a double take, Rachel's eyes widened. "My goodness, that's Analia? She was just a baby last time I saw her."

That wasn't quite accurate—Analia was seven when Yolanda last saw the St. Ives family, which was right after they won the state championship—but this wasn't the time to get into it. "Can I see the basement?"

Nodding, Jeremy led them to the door under the stoop that went to the basement.

He opened the door with a key, then started to lead Yolanda and Analia in, but Yolanda stopped him from entering. "You stay with Maggie and Rachel on the stoop, okay? We'll check it out."

Jeremy seemed to deflate with relief. "You bet," and he practically ran out the door and up to the sidewalk.

The doorway led to a dank hallway with an uneven concrete floor and dark walls that seemed to be closing in on them. At the far end of the hallway was a door that Yolanda assumed led to the interior staircase, which was how the basement was accessed from inside. To the left were a couple of large metal doors that were shut tight—one was labelled BOILER, the other   STORAGE ROOM. To the right, a doorway with a window, the door labelled LAUNDRY. Peering inside, she saw a small room with two washers and two dryers.

"That's all they got?" Analia said while peering into the door's window.

"The building only has five units," Yolanda said while she rummaged around in her purse for a Migliucci Charm. Once activated, it could tell if there was magic nearby.

Analia stood with her hands on her hips while Yolanda dug around the purse. "Y'know, my friend Soraya's mom is an archeologist. I was thinking maybe she could help you find stuff in there."

"You're hilarious, baby girl. Ha!" She finally found it, buried beneath a silver stick and her spare maxipads. She shook it, and it started to glow green. "Definitely magic."

"Good. If it wasn't magic, they'd probably want their money back. Now what?"

"Now you go in there."

Analia blinked, and backed away from her mother. "'Scuse me? You want *me* to go in *there* where people get all wet?"

"Hell yeah, why you think I bring you along? 'Oh, *mami*, I'm a black belt, I'll protect you out there, I'll fight the monsters.'"

"I never said that!"

"You didn't hardly say nothin' else for a year before I started takin' you on jobs! So get your narrow behind in that laundry room."

"If I'd'a known, I'd'a brought my bathing suit." She sighed. "Okay, fine but here." Reaching into the pocket of her jeans, she pulled out her smartphone, covered in an otterbox case that also held her cash, ID, and MetroCard. "Hold that."

Yolanda dropped the phone in her purse while Analia opened the door and entered the laundry room.

Nothing happened.

However, the Migliucci Charm's glow became more intense.

Analia turned around. "Just standin' here. I—" Then her eyes went wide. "What the *fuck?*"

"What is it, baby girl?" Yolanda asked.

Her daughter shuddered. "It's gone now. But I thought I saw—well, *something*. Thought it was a lady with a lotta hair, but—" She shuddered again. "Crazy."

The Migliucci Charm was now glowing blue, and then went dark. Whatever magical thing was nearby was gone now.

Yolanda went into the laundry room also, and looked around.

"See anything weird?" Analia asked.

"Yeah, somebody uses Gain. That stuff smells *nasty*. Aside from that, no."

Analia indicated the far corner of the laundry room with her head. "Where's that door go?"

"Why?"

"'Cause that's where I saw the lady with the hair."

"Did she go out the door?"

Shaking her head, Analia said, "No, she just—just went poof!"

"Let's check anyhow."

Yolanda walked over to the door. There was a shallow puddle right in front of it, which she stepped over. The door itself was unlocked and opened inward to a short staircase that went up to the alley next to the building.

Remembering that the alley had the modest community garden, she went up the stairs, only to find herself in the midst of a much larger garden than she remembered.

Walking around with her mouth hanging open, Yolanda navigated a very thin pathway through the alley and the courtyard in the back.

"Didn't realize this garden was so big," Analia said.

"It wasn't. I mean, it wasn't ten years ago." All around them were tomato plants, cucumbers, raspberry bushes, strawberries, a whole section full of herbs, and more.

They walked single-file through the garden toward the street. A gate at the end was, luckily, easy to open from the inside.

Rachel was still sitting on the stoop, and she looked up in surprise to see Yolanda and Analia come out from the alley gate rather than the basement.

She rose to her feet. "Why were you in the garden?"

Analia was about to say something, but Yolanda cut her off. "We thought we saw something in the doorway to the garden from the basement. Has anyone who doesn't live in the building gone into the laundry room?"

"I don't think so, but you could check with the other tenants. Jeremy went off to gather everyone in our place—I'm the president of the co-op board, and I asked everyone to make sure *someone* was home around now to talk to you. We figured it'd be easier if they were all together."

Yolanda nodded. "Good." She would have preferred to talk to them individually and separately, as they might admit things to just her that they wouldn't want to say in front of their neighbors, but it was too late now for that.

Rachel went to unlock the front door.

Whispering to Analia, Yolanda said, "Text your sister, describe what you saw, see if she can find anything like that."

Analia said, "Fine, but that means you gotta gimme my phone back."

"Oh, right." Yolanda rummaged around in her purse, trying to locate the otterbox.

"You guys okay?" Rachel asked from the now-open front doorway.

"Just trying to find Analia's phone," Yolanda said with a sigh.

"Soraya's mooooooooooom," Analia said in a sing-songy voice.

As she pushed aside the battery pack, her wallet, and a Hasan Amulet, she muttered, "Remember that I can kill you any time and say the dragon did it."

"Magellan would never hurt me!"

"Keep tellin' yourself that." She finally found the otterbox and fished it out, handing it to Analia. "Here you go."

They finally followed Rachel inside, and she led them to the back of the building and the staircase up to the third floor, which was where the St. Ives family lived.

Yolanda felt a pang of envy as she entered the large apartment that took up the entire floor of the building. They walked into a huge living room that by itself seemed to be as big as Yolanda's entire apartment. To the left as they entered was a dining room, with a kitchen and bathroom beyond it, and to the right, on the (very) far end of the living room were two doorways, which Yolanda figured led to the two bedrooms.

Seated around the living room on the couch, the wrought-iron rocking chair, the recliner, and three folding chairs were many of the other tenants in the building. Two elderly white people shared the couch with Maggie, while two Latinx guys who were holding hands sat on two of the folding chairs, with Jeremy on the third. An Indian woman sat on the edge of the rocking chair, while an African-American man lounged on the recliner.

A coffee table in front of the couch had a big bowl filled with golden raspberries, with some small bowls on the side. Yolanda assumed they were from the garden. There was a spoon in the big bowl, and several of the tenants had small bowls of the fruit in front of them.

Yolanda noticed that, while the furniture was all nice, and all basically went with each other, it didn't all match perfectly, and they were all different ages—the recliner looked brand-new, while the couch was obviously very old and well used.

Rachel said, "Everyone, this is Yolanda Rodriguez, the Courser we hired. She's going to take care of our laundry room problem. Yolanda, this is Dmitri and Olga from the first floor," Rachel said, indicating the older couple, then pointed at the other couple, "Alvaro and Hector who live on two, Leon, who lives with his wife and kids on four," she added, pointing at the man in the recliner, then finishing with the woman in the rocking chair, "and Aditi, who lives with her roommate on five."

"This is my daughter, Analia," Yolanda said. "Thanks, all of you, for coming tonight. First off, can each of you tell me how it went when you went to the laundry room?"

Each told their version of the story, which all matched what Maggie had described in Yolanda's office.

Leon added, "I went with my wife one of the times, and she stayed out in the hall. She didn't see anything, though. Said the room went all dark. She thought it was a power outage or something at first, but the hall light was still on, so..." He shrugged. "Just like everyone else, though, I don't remember any of it."

Yolanda nodded. "Did any of you see anyone strange in the laundry room at any point? Or see anyone in the building or out in the garden you don't know?"

Everyone looked at each other, and they all shook their heads.

Aditi said, "I don't think any of us would know about the garden except for Dmitri. It has become his task of late."

That surprised Yolanda. "I thought you all worked on it."

Olga smiled. "It was supposed to be, but it was very difficult to maintain, for us. We almost were losing the garden, but when Dmitri, he retired, he took it over."

Dmitri shrugged. "I have nothing better to do."

"My Dima is too modest," Olga said. "He has done wonders."

"I've seen that." Yolanda was impressed. She had assumed that the expansion of the garden was a group effort. That it was accomplished by one person was impressive as hell. "And you've seen nothing strange in the garden, Dmitri?"

He shook his head, and rubbed his fingers on his thick white mustache. "Only squirrels trying to eat the strawberries."

"Is anything else different in the building lately?"

Again, everyone exchanged glances and shrugged. Aditi said, "The last significant change of any note was seven years ago when Laura and Peter divorced and sold the fifth floor and Hector and Alvaro bought it."

Alvaro frowned. "That was eight years ago."

"Yes, it was," Rachel said. "And Aditi's right, that's the last real change, apart from Dmitri turning our raggedy little garden into a cornucopia."

At some point, Analia had scooped some raspberries for herself, and suddenly cried out, "Hot *damn*, these are good."

Yolanda glared at Analia. "I'm sorry for my daughter."

"But *mami*, you should taste these, they're *amazing!*"

Shaking her head, Yolanda grabbed a raspberry.

It was the most succulent, glorious raspberry she'd ever had. She'd only had red raspberries up until now, and this golden one was sweeter than expected, and lighter as well.

"It is amazing!"

Hector's phone buzzed, and he glanced at it, then asked, "There anything else? Our dinner just arrived."

Yolanda nodded. "I think we're okay for now. I'll do some digging, and come back when I have something."

Maggie went to the kitchen and put together a Tupperware filled with golden raspberries, and also a several paper bags filled with herbs that Analia salivated over—sage, oregano, thyme, and rosemary. "Wish I got this before I made dinner tonight," Analia said as they walked outside, "the sage would've been *amazing* on the chicken!"

They took the M100 back down to 179th Street and arrived home to see Magellan was awake and curled around Kamilah's neck. She and Carlos were both on the couch watching television, but Carlos snagged the remote and turned it off when they came in.

"Eduardo's in bed," Carlos said. "He showed me his new kata and showed me all the homework he did, and I read him the script from the latest comic book. He *might* be asleep now, or he might be reading more comics on his iPad."

"Yeah, no 'might' about that, he's readin' comics." Yolanda sighed. "Did you—"

"*Yes*," Carlos sad, "I told him that the next time he falls asleep and drops the iPad on his face and breaks a tooth, we won't get it fixed like we did last time. And since he's eight, I'm *sure* he'll listen to *that* advice."

Kamilah, meanwhile, had gotten up slowly, so as not to discommode Magellan too much, and gone over to the computer desk. Tapping the space bar reactivated the monitor, and Yolanda saw that she had several different images up. Some were photographs that Yolanda recognized from other Coursers, who'd shared them; others were drawings of creatures.

All of them were women with a lot of hair, and many were also very obviously creatures of water.

"Okay, so based on the whole getting-drenched thing," Kamilah said, "and based on that really crappy description Analia gave me—"

"Hey!" Analia lightly punched her sister on the arm as she moved to stand next to Yolanda behind her.

Kamilah ignored her sister's abuse and continued: "—I've narrowed it down to either a selkie, a sihuanaba, a kelpie, or a rusalka."

Analia, however, was pointing right at the image in the upper right, which was a woman with incredibly long, wet hair that covered most of what seemed to be a naked body. "That one."

"The rusalka?"

Nodding, Analia said, "That's what I saw in the laundry room."

"It can't be a rusalka," Yolanda said. "They're spirits of the dead, aren't they? Unclean women who died, or some damn thing?"

At that, Kamilah let out a soft sigh, and Yolanda knew that her little girl—who was the youngest member of the National Honor Society at her school—was about to give a lecture. Not that Yolanda minded. While having Analia to help with the physical stuff was useful, Yolanda was more grateful for her incredibly smart younger daughter's assistance, because Kamilah was much better at keeping track of all the supernatural histories and stories that were part of a Courser's life. Yolanda herself had never been able to keep it straight. In fact, it was Kamilah, after the fact, who informed her that it was a wendigo that maimed Carlos, not a sasquatch.

Pushing her glasses up her nose, Kamilah said, "Okay, remember how when you first told me and Analia about all the monster stuff after *papi* got hurt, and you said that everything people think about vampires is wrong because in the 19th century a bunch of writers made up stupid stuff?"

Yolanda chuckled. "Yeah."

"Well, same thing with rusalki. Nobody associated them with evil until the 19th century. They were water spirits from eastern Europe that would irrigate the fields and—"

"Holy shit!" Analia cried out.

"Hey, language!" Carlos said from the couch.

"She's right, though," Yolanda said. "Usually when something spooky shows up, it's because something's changed. Only thing that's changed in that building for eight years is that garden. It's way bigger."

"And the raspberries are *awesome*, and the herbs?" Analia made a happy noise.

"Okay," Kamilah said, "so you think maybe the rusalka is irrigating the garden, that's why it's so big?"

"It gets better," Yolanda said. "The guy who runs the garden all by himself is a Russian immigrant."

Carlos leaned forward on the couch. "What do you think it means, Lala?"

"I think we need to find the rusalka that's irrigating the garden. She may be flooding the residents out of revenge. The question is," she blew out a long breath and looked at Kamilah, "how do we find it?"

Kamilah looked away. "I, uh—"

"What?" Yolanda prompted.

"Well, it—" She hesitated again.

Yolanda glowered at her daughter. "It's on the list, isn't it?"

With a nod, Kamilah said, "Yeah, but you can't take Magellan. He might get hurt!"

"He can take care of himself." Yolanda looked to the ceiling in supplication. Green dragons had a limited ability to detect certain magical creatures. Kamilah had been assembling a list of them ever since they got Magellan, and apparently rusalki were on it.

"Can't you find the rusalka on your own?"

"Maybe eventually, but Magellan can do it faster."

Analia stepped up to her sister and pet the dragon on his head, currently resting on Kamilah's right shoulder. "I'll protect the little guy, I promise."

Kamilah was pouting, but she said, "Okay."

"*Mneh*!" Magellan said, and he uncurled himself from Kamilah's shoulders and climbed up Analia's arm.

"So when do we go, *mami*?" Analia asked.

"No time like the present. I thought we'd need to do a lot more research—"

"'We'?" Kamilah said indignantly.

Yolanda ignored that. "—but it looks like we need to take a closer look at Dmitri and Olga. Let's go."

"Um, hang on." Analia looked at Kamilah. "I need your MetroCard."

"Why?"

"'Cause mine ran out on the trip back."

"Why can't you use *papi's*?"

Carlos grinned. "Because mine is for disabled people, and I don't think the driver will buy it from Analia."

Yolanda rolled her eyes. "We don't got time for this. Kamilah, give your sister the MetroCard. I'll buy a new one when we get paid for this job."

"Fine." Kamilah reached for her purse, which was on the desk, and fished out her MetroCard.

As Analia triumphantly took the transit card from her younger sister, Yolanda went to the closet near the front door. "I just hope I can find the damn Opahle Amulet."

They took the M100 back up again, with Magellan curled up asleep in Yolanda's purse.

When they got down Dyckman to the building, Yolanda rang the buzzer labelled with a 1.

A burst of static came from the speaker next to the buzzer. "It's Yolanda Rodriguez," she said in response.

The door buzzed, and they entered.

Olga was standing in the doorway to the first-floor apartment. "*Privyet*, Yolanda. We did not expect you again so soon."

"We have some more information, and we need to start checking all the apartments. Mind if we start with you, since you're on the first floor?"

Analia shot Yolanda a look, but didn't say anything, thankfully. It was better to be nice to the couple rather than antagonistic.

Olga shrugged. "*Harasho.*"

She let them inside. This apartment had the same floorplan as the St. Ives place on three, but the furniture was completely different. It was all matching and recently purchased. The dining room and living room both had what were obviously sets.

Yolanda opened the purse. "Don't be alarmed, okay? I got a dragon in here."

"*Feh*," Magellan said as he poked his head out of the purse.

"Okay, Magellan," Yolanda said, "I need you to find the rusalka."

"What did you say!?" Olga asked in surprise.

"We think a rusalka is responsible for what's happening in the laundry room."

"That makes no sense. Rusalki, they are simply bedtime stories! Not real!"

"Like dragons?" Analia asked snidely.

Yolanda glared at her daughter and then said, "Just trust me, okay?"

Magellan leapt out of the purse and then spread his tiny wings to start flying around the apartment.

The muffled sound of a toilet flushing was followed by Dmitri coming out of the bathroom. "What is going on?"

Olga waved her arms around. "This madwoman has brought a dragon into our home and says there's a rusalka in the building! Why are we wasting the co-op's money to pay this *bezumnaya*?"

"*Coo!*"

187

That was Magellan, who was flying back and forth in front of a closet in the corner of the dining room near the bathroom that Dmitri had just come out of.

Yolanda smiled. "Good work, Magellan. You get peanut butter on your apple tonight."

"Get that thing away from there!" Dmitri cried out.

Olga was a bit calmer, oddly. "It is merely the linen closet."

Yolanda moved toward the closet, but Dmitri yelled, "No! You will *not* go in there!"

"What does it matter?" Olga asked.

While Yolanda grabbed the closet doorknob, Dmitri moved to a sideboard that was against the dining room wall.

The closet door didn't budge at first, then Yolanda saw the bolt near the top of the door.

Just as she was reaching up to slide it aside, Dmitri pulled out what looked to Yolanda like a very old Makarov pistol of the type used by Russian soldiers and police in the 1950s. Holding it initially with his right hand, he steadied his grip with his left while taking off the safety.

"Walk away, now," Dmitri said.

"Dima, what are you doing?" Olga cried out. "I thought I told you to get rid of that gun!"

"Be silent!" Dmitri snapped at his wife without looking at her—he was keeping his eye on Yolanda, his intended target. "She is ruining everything!"

So focused was he on Yolanda that he didn't see Analia moving at him from his right until it was too late.

She grabbed his right hand and twisted his wrist so that his hand was facing palm-downward. The speed and harshness of the action caused Dmitri to let go with his left hand, and then Analia was able to pull the gun down and out of Dmitri's right hand.

Then she gave him a knee kick to the nuts.

Very gingerly putting the Makarov on the dining room table while Dmitri whimpered, Analia said, "Go for it, *mamí*."

"Good job, baby girl." Yolanda slid the bolt aside and opened the closet door.

Inside was a little girl with huge blue eyes and long, wet brown hair covering her body. She was also shivering.

Olga stared at the closet in disbelief. "Who is that?" Then she turned to Dmitri, still doubled over in pain from Analia's knee in his balls, and let loose with a lengthy string of what Yolanda thought was invective in rapid-fire Russian.

"Um, *mamí?*" Analia said. "That ain't what I saw in the laundry room. Lady I saw was taller, she was a redhead, and she had brown eyes that were more normal-sized than that."

The girl said something that also sounded like Russian.

"Olga," Yolanda said, "what's she saying?"

His voice strained, Dmitri said, "Say—*nothing!*"

Ignoring her husband, Olga said, in a hard voice, "She says she is trapped in the closet and cannot leave."

"I figured it'd be somethin' like that." Yolanda poked around in her purse. At first, she thought she found it next to the hairsticks, but that was the Hasan Amulet. Finally, she unearthed the Opahle Amulet beneath the pack of tissues and the vial of holy water.

"What is that?" Olga asked.

"An Opahle Amulet. If a magical creature's been enslaved, this'll free it. Got three charges in it, and this is the third, so after this, it's just a paperweight." Even as she shifted the lever on the amulet to the right to activate it, she wondered how the *hell* she was going to afford to replace it, as they were *not* cheap. She only had this one because it had been a birthday present from Frank Haimraj, the Courser she was apprenticed to when she started.

The amulet glowed and then the young woman stood up and leapt out of the closet. "*Ya svoboden!*"

Dmitri was finally standing upright instead of hunched over, though his hands were still near his groin. "*Suka blyad!* You've ruined *everything!*"

A woman then appeared in front of the dining room window. She had long red hair and brown eyes.

"Is that—" Yolanda started.

"Oh yeah," Analia said with an emphatic nod. "That's the laundry lady."

The woman—the rusalka—said something in Russian.

"*Bozhe moy,*" Olga muttered. "She—she says she is mother, and asks who freed her daughter from bondage."

Yolanda raised her hand.

"*Spasibo,*" the mother rusalka said.

"You're welcome," Yolanda said.

Olga said something in Russian also, then added to Yolanda and Analia, "I have apologized for my idiot husband."

The rusalka said something else.

Olga's shoulders slumped. "*Harasho.*"

The two rusalki disappeared then, leaving only a puddle in the middle of the dining room floor.

"Our punishment," Olga said slowly, "is that our garden will be ruined forever." She smacked Dmitri on the arm and hit him with some more rapid-fire Russian.

Magellan had settled on Yolanda's shoulder. To Analia, she said, "I think we'd better leave these two to their marital bliss." She grabbed the Makarov off the dining room table and put the safety back on, also removing the clip.

"Please," Olga said to Yolanda, "take that away."

Dmitri started, "Olga, I—"

"Say *nothing*, Dima. You promised me you got rid of gun. Now I fulfill your promise."

Yolanda put the clip and the weapon into her purse, and she also said, "Magellan, in you go. C'mon, for the bus ride."

"*Feh.*" But Magellan did as he was told.

"I'll send a bill to the co-op board," she said, leading Analia out the door.

As they walked out onto Dyckman Street and turned right toward Broadway and the bus, Analia said, "So whatcha gonna do with the gun?"

"Hopefully? Sell it for a new Ophale Amulet."

"Good," Analia said emphatically. She didn't like guns.

Neither did Yolanda, so the revulsion in her daughter's voice on the subject of this one heartened her.

"Gotta say," Analia added, "it really sucks that I'll never get to eat those raspberries again."

Yolanda rolled her eyes. "You'll live. Besides, it wasn't worth enslaving a girl."

"Got that right. Just glad she's also got a *mamí* to come after her."

Yolanda grinned, and wrapped her arm around her daughter. "Damn right. Let's go home, baby girl."

PRIDE FIGHT

TE BAKUTIS

IN MORNA'S EXPERIENCE, THERE WERE two reasons the average person would rob someone at knifepoint. The first was desperation, a hole in their belly they couldn't fill. Right now, she genuinely hoped the man holding the knife was hungry.

Because the second reason, the more dangerous reason, was her robber was simply an asshole.

"Money now, pretty lady." Neckbeard grinned and brandished his knife. "Or we start with your little blond kid."

Oh, yes. This robber was *definitely* an asshole. Morna, her seventeen-year-old daughter Cassie, and the neckbearded knifeman stood in a rubble-strewn courtyard beneath Ceto's clear green sky. As Morna pulled her hood close, three more knife-wielding figures crept from the rubble. All looked younger than Cassie.

Cassie was very good with her quarterstaff—Morna had trained Cassie herself—but four on two was poor odds. The thought of someone knifing Cassie made Morna's heart pound and her sides sweat. She couldn't let anyone harm her little girl.

"Pay up!" Neckbeard shouted. "Now!"

Most of Ceto's cities had survived the planet's occupation by the Advanced—a genetically engineered race of superhumans—with minimal damage. Duskdale was not one of those cities. This part of the dilapidated town was known as the Sledge, and the authorities didn't come down here for anything less than a double homicide or a riot involving, at minimum, thirty people.

The three kids menacing them with knives had probably lost their homes while Ceto's freedom fighters fought the Advanced. They might even have lost their parents. And as Morna refused to beat a bunch of war orphans senseless, she lowered her hood to reveal her light-brown face, shoulder-length dark hair, and pale blue eyes. She smiled at the tall boy with the dark faux hawk.

"Good afternoon, son. Do you know who I am?"

Something in her authoritative yet friendly manner kept Faux Hawk from cussing her out immediately. "I, uh… should I?"

"She's the mayor of Cliffside, you broom-headed twerp." Cassie pressed her back to Morna's. "She's Morna Solace. You've probably heard of her if you're not, you know, a moron."

"Ha," Neckbeard said. "Sure." He stepped closer. "Money or blood, girls. Even mayors have to pay the toll."

Morna glanced at the two kids behind her. "Did you lose someone?"

The girl glared. "Everyone lost someone back then. Who gives a shit?" Burn scars marred her pale face. "Now give us your money and piss off."

"What if I offered you something better?" Morna asked.

At the corner of Morna's vision, Neckbeard stomped forward. "Give us what we want or we—"

Morna's elbow snapped into his nose. Blood spurted as he collapsed. Morna dropped and pressed her forearm to his neck.

Neckbeard flailed, grasped, and gurgled, but Morna was *much* stronger than she looked. The kids shouted and lifted their knives. Cassie stepped into a low guard, staff raised.

"Stop that at once!" Morna shouted, in the voice she used in her *dojo*. All three kids stopped. They looked as surprised by that as Cassie.

As Neckbeard *hurked* and passed out, Morna stood and stared at the skinny redheaded boy. "How much do you make in a day?"

He hunched in his threadbare jacket. "Why do you care?"

"Because you have so many better options. Here's one. Go to the Duskdale maglev terminal and enter the words 'Wheat Farm.'"

The girl glanced at the others. "The fuck is a wheat farm?"

"That'll get you a one-way ticket to Cliffside. When you arrive, ask for Chief Galloway. He'll get you settled in."

Faux Hawk blinked. "Settled in?"

"I'm offering you all jobs," Morna said. "Cliffside grows every day, and our work gets you a steady wage, a good bed, and three warm meals a day."

"No way." The redhead stared at a tablet he'd pulled from his jacket. "That *is* Morna Solace!"

"Give me that!" The girl snatched the tablet, glared at it, then scowled at Morna. "You think we're stupid? You're sending us to get arrested!"

"I can't make you trust me," Morna said, "but you'd be welcome in my town. The Advanced aren't a threat any longer. You don't have to hurt people or risk getting hurt yourselves."

"Mom," Cassie said, "we need to go."

Cassie was right, of course. Ceto's sun hung low in the sky, and soon it would be too late to stop tonight's pit fights. That was unacceptable. The abandoned storm drains in this courtyard were the quickest way to reach the Punch Pit—tonight's particular den of depravity—without being seen.

"We're leaving," Morna said, "but I hope you'll consider my offer." She strode toward Faux Hawk, who stepped back. He stepped right out of her way.

"Hey!" the girl shouted, as Morna approached the fence. "What are we supposed to do with *him?*"

Morna raised one heel, balancing, and then knifed her heel down upon the storm drain gate lock. That lock ricocheted off the concrete. She opened the gate and glanced at the gaping kids.

"Leave before he wakes up." Morna held the gate as Cassie ducked under her arm. "Or don't. But I hope I see you again."

And with all three staring, she walked down the stairwell.

"You wasted a lot of time up there," Cassie said, quietly, as she followed Morna through a low-ceiling drainage tunnel that smelled like mildew and dead things. "Any particular reason?"

Morna didn't look back. "They were kids."

"Kids with stabby things. Did you miss the stabby things?"

"But they didn't stab *us*, did they? They wanted money, not blood."

"And that makes it better… how?"

"An empty belly makes a person do foolish things."

"Oh!" Cassie stage-whispered. "So it's fine to rob and stab people if you're hungry. I'll remember that!"

Morna smiled as she walked. Cassie didn't understand why the kids up there resorted to mugging. Morna had sacrificed much to ensure Cassie *never* understood desperation like that, and she'd sacrifice it all again.

"When we get to the Punch Pit and locate Kell," Morna said, "have you considered what you're going to say to her?"

"Oh, I dunno. Maybe 'Don't be such a dipshit, Kell.'"

Morna suppressed a chuckle. "I don't know if that's the best approach. She seemed committed when she stormed out."

"Which makes no sense at all." Cassie huffed. "She should have let you pay off her father's stupid debt. Instead she has us trekking halfway across Ceto, dodging muggers and stomping through ick, to literally keep her from signing her life away. I mean, what the fuck?"

"Language." Morna remembered another time, another contract, and another woman whose pride blinded her to those she hurt. "And a fighter's pride isn't always logical, honey."

"Mom!" Cassie protested. "Can you stop with the honey business when we're out doing heroic stuff? It's kind of hard to act like a badass when your mom acts like you're five."

As they stepped into a larger storm drain tunnel with other people, the laughing, drunk, and raucous salt of Ceto, Morna pulled her hood close. "I'm sorry, Cassandra. I certainly wouldn't want to embarrass you while we're doing heroic stuff."

It was a short walk to the Punch Pit's southern entrance, which was, quite literally, a hole in the wall. Only one person guarded that hole, but she was enough. Raze was a redheaded gladiator who stood over two meters tall. She had a heatsword strapped across her back as long as Morna.

She was also a very old friend.

Morna pulled a purple, skull-faced bandana from her front pocket. As she tied it around her face, obscuring all but her pale blue eyes, the smell and feel of cloth summoned memories. The ache of her knuckles after a good brawl. The salty taste of blood in her mouth. The heady rush of pride after every win.

The gut-wrenching regret when she realized it was all a lie.

With Cassie at her side, Morna approached Raze and lowered her hood to reveal her hair and skull-faced bandana. When Raze spotted her, the other woman gasped. "Holy shit! Ruiner!"

Morna smiled behind her bandana. "Hello, Raze."

"Ruiner?" Cassie offered a significant amount of side eye. "*That* was your fighter name?"

"It was a long time ago." Morna stared up at Raze. "Have they announced the roster for tonight's fights?"

"No," Raze said, "but what are you *doing* here? I thought you gave up this criminal stuff when you went into politics!"

"To be fair," Cassie said, "politics is pretty much crime."

Raze's eyes widened. "And holy shit! You're Cassie!"

"Um, yeah." Cassie swallowed as Raze loomed. "Is that weird?"

"No, it's just... you're big now!"

"The fights," Morna reminded Raze.

"Right." Raze focused. "No roster yet. If you sprint to the counter, you might still have time to place your bets." Her brow furrowed. "You're betting on a pit fight?"

"Preempting one, actually." Morna glanced at the increasingly impatient line of malcontents piling up behind them. "I think it would be best if I speak with Vince."

"Oh." Raze rubbed her head. "Well... he told us no one should bother him until after the fights were over."

"Raze." Morna touched the woman's impressively buff forearm. "This is life and death."

Raze frowned. "Life or death." She ducked to enter the Punch Pit, then beckoned. "Follow me!"

"I like her," Cassie announced, as they followed Raze through the hole in the wall. "She's *decisive*."

The hole opened into a stadium-sized underground space, one so large that Morna had to stop and breathe. It was difficult to adjust to so much open after so much *not*. The arena smelled of wet biocrete, and people, and stale beer. And blood.

The Punch Pit was, in fact, a giant pit in which people punched one another. Vincent Alvarado, its founder, owner, and proprietor, was known for his business savvy, but not so much his creative spark. It really was an awful name.

Ceto's first settlers had spent five years digging this stadium-sized underground space, then covered it with a biocrete shell. It was a refuge for the first settlers in case of some climatic event. Fortunately, it was never used, which allowed Vincent to purchase it at a discount eighty years later.

The muddy pit below was where Ruiner had earned her name.

The Punch Pit's observation ring, filled with spectators, went all the way around the central arena. Though the spectators eagerly jostled one another, Raze's towering form parted them like wheat. Morna and Cassie walked close behind.

Raze led them away from the ring, toward the ancient carved-out walls. They were headed to the freight elevator.

"Where are we going?" Morna shouted.

"Vince's up in the shaft now!" Raze shouted back. "We made it into a giant tower! Easier to defend!"

"From who?" Cassie shouted. "The Advanced?"

Raze shrugged. "Maybe!"

Vincent's paranoia about another Advanced invasion was understandable, given history. Morna didn't share the hatred most on Ceto still held for the Advanced, but she didn't blame those who did. Having genetically modified superhumans occupy your planet for ten years was not something most forgave. While the Advanced looked human, visually indistinguishable from natural-born humans, that didn't mean they *acted* human.

Two soldiers in yellow, powered armor waited at the entry to the elevator shaft, but neither stopped Raze. As the freight elevator ascended, Morna adjusted her bandana. She hadn't expected her return to make her heart thump quite this hard. She hadn't expected this quiver of anticipation.

Raze glanced down. "So, uh, Ruiner?"

"Morna, please." She kept no secrets from her old friend.

"Sure, all right. Why do you want to stop a pit fight?"

"One of my students wishes to participate. I'd prefer she not."

"Really? Who?"

"Kell Diaz," Cassie said.

"And... who's that?"

"Imagine seventy kilos of lean, taut muscle with blue hair, badass tattoos, and a right hook that'll break your jaw," Cassie said. "Now imagine her kicking the shit out of you."

"Oooh!" Raze grinned. "I *saw* her! She qualified through the open melee! Dropped, like, four people."

Cassie nodded. "Kell's a total badass."

"And you don't you want her fighting... why?"

"This isn't the life for her," Morna said.

Raze shifted one booted foot. "That's really her choice though, isn't it? We all make choices."

Morna remembered Raze's tears the night Morna left her behind here, alone, and resisted the urge to take the big woman's hand. "This path is not to be taken under duress."

"Ah," Raze said. "She owes Vince money."

"Her deadbeat dad does, actually," Cassie said, "but same deal. To be fair, if Kell wins tonight's match, she'd easily clear her dad's debts—"

"But Vince's contract would force her to fight for the rest of her life," Morna reminded Cassie, loudly. "Which is bad."

"Well, sure," Cassie said. "There's that."

The lift stopped at a worn supply pad where another soldier in powered armor stood holding a big gun. "Who's this?"

"Got some VIPs to visit Vince," Raze said. "Old friends."

"Yeah, no," the soldier said. "No admittance."

Morna stepped forward. "Tell Vincent Ruiner has returned."

The soldier's faceplate turned on Morna. "Holy shit!"

"Right?" Raze said.

"I have to call this in," the soldier said.

"Wow," Cassie said. "You're actually a big deal here, huh?"

Morna didn't like how quiet Cassie's voice had become. "It was a long time ago."

"Long time ago my ass. Even Random Soldier Number Four wants your autograph!"

"Hey!" The soldier sounded miffed. "My name's Jeff."

"I need to get back to my gate," Raze said. "It was great to see you again. I mean... not that I missed you terribly."

Morna opened her arms. "Hug."

"Hooray." Raze crushed Morna in a hug, then stepped onto the lift. "Jeff, I'm trusting you with our VIPs."

"You can count on me!" Jeff shouted.

Cassie leaned close. "Want Ruiner to sign your rifle?"

Jeff straightened. "I mean, if you have the time—"

"It's very important we speak to Vincent at once," Morna said, politely but firmly.

Jeff's armor clanged as he saluted. "Go right in, ma'am!"

Morna's chest ached as she strode toward Vincent's closed office, toward the blood and mud-stained life she'd walked away from twenty years ago. It was addictive, being the best.

That could make a woman do things she'd regret.

The tower door rattled open. They stepped right into a grassy park, which was about the last thing Morna expected to find in Vincent's office. The door vanished behind them, leaving them, seemingly, outside. The sun glowed in a bright green sky.

"Like it?" Vincent materialized out of nothing. "It's the latest Advanced technology. Full suite projection."

That dark suit, those shined loafers, that red tie and trimmed moustache—that was Vincent Alvarado. He might have wrinkles now, and gray in his hair, but he was still the man who'd made her feel like the strongest woman in the world.

"It's lovely, Vince." Morna pulled down her bandana so they could speak face-to-face. "I've come here to—"

"I'm not cancelling Kell's match," Vincent interrupted.

Morna took a beat. "Why?" He already knew why she had come here. This was bad.

"You *know* why." Vincent strolled toward a gnarled tree.

"Um, Mom?" Cassie asked. "What's the smiling psychopath talking about?"

A woman with short blue hair chose that moment to *also* materialize out of the air. "Because that's not your call to make." The projection system must have hidden Kell, like Vincent, until she chose to reveal herself. Kell thumped her chest with a meaty hand. "I already challenged Toro."

Morna's heart sank. "I wish you'd listened."

"And I wish you'd stayed in Cliffside." Kell crossed her heavily tattooed arms. "But hey, now you're here, so you can watch me kick Toro's ass."

"Dammit, Kell!" Cassie shouted, loud enough that Kell flinched. "You signed his insane contract?"

"Kell Diaz is of legal age," Vincent said. "It's out of my hands." He raised them for emphasis.

Morna focused on Kell. "You believe this path is best for you, but it isn't. I know. I was you."

"Yeah?" Kell scowled. "Why'd you quit?"

"Oh!" Vincent said. "That's a great story." He waved.

A vid panel opened in midair. The deafening sound of a roaring crowd stole Morna's breath. Vincent still had the archive from twenty years ago, the big fight, her last fight. Of course he did.

Two muddy women in muddy clothes ducked, punched, and weaved. Fists flew and kicks snapped. The second woman grunted as she took a hard kick to the side, but powered through it. Her answering jab found the first woman's gut and left her gasping. She stumbled one way as her opponent stumbled the other.

Both women steadied, straightened, and glared. The drone camera zoomed in on the first woman's face: Ruiner's face. Ruiner wore the same skull-painted bandana Morna wore now, revealing only her pale and furious blue eyes. Morna saw herself as she'd been then, hungry and lethal and filled with rage, and the bottom dropped out of her stomach.

Cassie could see this. Cassie could see who she had been.

On the vid, Ruiner dashed forward. Her opponent, Jenny Garcia—the Sanguine Rapier—dashed forward as well. The drone camera zoomed out as they closed.

"Stop!" Morna shouted.

The image froze right before Ruiner snapped the flying kick that would, she would learn later, crack Jenny's skull in four places. A subdural hemorrhage and death followed.

Kell stared wide-eyed at the screen. "You lost?"

Morna didn't know how to answer that.

"Now." Vincent wiped the screen away. "Let's talk business. We're all here for business."

"I'm here for the free food," Kell said. "Your flunkies told me there'd be free food."

"Cancelling Kell's fight with Toro would cost me an obscene amount of money," Vincent continued.

"Also, you can't cancel my fight," Kell reminded him. "Contract. Of legal age. Remember?"

"I can't cancel a challenge to Toro," Vincent continued. "But I can *update* that challenge, for the right match."

Kell walked over to his tree. "Hey, you listening?"

"If you truly wish to keep your student from my arenas—"

"Hey, asshole!" Kell stopped close enough to box Vincent's ears. "I'm fighting Toro!"

"Is she?" Vincent asked. "Or is Ruiner?"

Morna evaluated her existing plan to free Kell from Vincent's contract against her current circumstances, which had changed. Calling her twenty-year-old fights into question wouldn't be enough to free Kell now. She needed something fresh.

"Listen, you—" Kell said, and then gasped as her hand passed *through* Vincent's arm. She flailed at the tree and wound up protruding from Vincent's chest.

His projection glanced down at her. "Do you mind?"

Kell stumbled free. "We had a deal!"

Morna remembered the crowd chanting her name the last time she'd stood in the Punch Pit's muddy arena. She remembered the wet *snap* of her foot driving its way into Jenny Garcia's skull. She remembered Kell coming to her six months after Kell's mother died fighting the Advanced, asking to learn everything.

"I'll fight Toro," Morna said.

"What?" Cassie and Kell shouted simultaneously.

"Cancel Kell's contract with you, clear her father's debts, and I'll fight your champion in your arena. One time only."

Vincent clapped his non-existent hands. "Spectacular! You have a deal." This was, of course, what he'd hoped for all along. "Head to the cage and get ready." He vanished.

"No!" Kell shouted, at the same time Cassie shouted, "What the fuck, Mom?"

"Language," Morna said.

Kell stormed toward Morna. "You can't do this! Toro is half your age and twice your size. He'll murder you, *sifu*!"

Warmth filled Morna. "So you are my student again?"

"I will *always* be your student!" Kell blinked, trembling. "But that doesn't make you responsible for *my* failures!"

Morna took Kell's calloused hands. "This is not your fault."

"But I did this! My father—"

"Vincent scammed you both," Morna said.

Kell blinked. "Huh?"

"Vincent manipulated us. He's been pestering me to return for months. His profits have been slipping for years, but a match with Ruiner? That will raise mountains."

"What's you fighting here got to do with my father?"

"My students are public record." Morna released Kell's hands. "Now, consider how easy it would be. Find my student. Find her father, who gambles at your casinos, and fix all his games. Drive that father into debt and offer his daughter a contract to clear those debts, ensuring her teacher will come here and demand her release, forcing her teacher..."

Kell stomped one boot. "I'm gonna kill that asshole!"

Cassie glanced at the door they couldn't see. "Um, Jeff might have a problem with that."

"Listen to me," Morna demanded, looking between Kell and Cassie. "I will deal with Vincent Alvarado." Keeping both hands close to her stomach, she signed her latest plan where only they could see, while simultaneously speaking aloud to fool Vincent's listening devices. "Leave. I expect the same obedience here as in my *dojo*."

As Kell and Cassie read what Morna said with her hands, not her words, their eyes widened. There was no misunderstanding.

Morna dropped her hands. "Go."

"Right." Kell's face flushed. "We'll do what you said."

"Goddammit, Mom!" Cassie threw her arms around Morna. "Don't you die out there, okay? You're, like, stupid old."

Morna hugged her daughter. "I won't die."

Kell watched, lips pressed tight. Morna stepped back and bowed. Her students bowed back. She was their teacher again.

Then it was time to become Ruiner.

As Morna stepped into the claustrophobic entry cage, smells brought her home. Metal. Mud. Blood. Cloth. Ruiner's bandana covered her face as tightly as it had years ago, as much a part of her as her hand or foot. The part she'd locked away.

The cage rumbled upward. The pit-side gate thumped down, and as Morna strode out the crowd went rabid. The Punch Pit remembered her, and it wanted to see her *ruin* someone.

Toro stood twenty paces away, outside the other cage. He was a bald tower of muscle with a hook nose. Morna had seen him before, on vids, but he'd seemed smaller on those.

As Morna strode forward, Toro matched her. Chanting flooded the arena. "Ru-in-er! Ru-in-er! Ru-in-er!"

They met in the center. Morna bowed. Toro bowed back, then raised one meaty hand. The chanting died as Vincent's camera drones whirred above. The audience would hear everything.

"Ruiner," Toro boomed. "Thank you."

That was an odd way to start a fight. "For?"

"My sister was the Sanguine Rapier."

Toro's words hit Morna harder than any fist. She'd known Jenny Garcia had a little brother, but she'd never sought him out despite her guilt. What could she say to the little boy whose sister she'd killed in this arena, even accidentally?

"I know you did not intend to murder Jenny," Toro continued into utter silence. "You were simply stronger." He grinned. "Now I am stronger too. When I crush you, I will demonstrate all you taught me twenty years ago. Are you ready?"

Morna wanted to reveal right then how she'd beaten Jenny and all those others, to unburden herself of her secret shame before the entire arena, but telling Toro the truth wouldn't change anyone's fate. She had family of her own to think about. She dropped into her fighting stance and waited.

Toro came at her like a maglev train.

His first open-palmed strike was thunderous, powerful, and precise. From watching his prior fights, Morna knew even as she sidestepped his first strike his second would seek her side. She slapped it down and danced her palms across his ribs.

Toro barely slowed. Morna hadn't expected to be pressed this hard, this fast, but she had strength Toro couldn't possibly anticipate. With a flurry of blows, she pushed *back*.

Toro was massive, armored by slabs of muscle, and accustomed to intense pain, but Morna made him *hurt*. A woman half his size shouldn't have made Toro hurt, but that was what was different about Morna. That was the reason she walked away twenty years ago, and Toro's pained grimace assured her she'd made the right decision.

Another punch blew past her ear, the air drawn by its passage dragging her hair after it. Worry rose. Could she survive one of Toro's thunderous blows? Then she saw the punch she wanted, and knew it was time to find out.

She took it right in the face.

"Mom!" Cassie shouted. "Goddammit, *Mom!*"

Morna coughed. She was sitting somewhere dark, and her whole face ached like a marching band had walked over it. She couldn't feel her nose. What had happened to her nose?

"Mom!" Cassie shouted. "Talk to me!"

Morna pressed palms to biocrete and took in cold air blowing on her from above. She was in one of the Punch Pit's locker rooms—she remembered them well—transported instantly by Toro's impressive punch. There was no comforting blackness when one got knocked out. One was simply in one place, then another.

"Mom!" Cassie screamed.

"I'm fine, dear," Morna whispered. "Just catching my breath."

Sobbing followed as Cassie hugged her tight. Morna raised one aching arm and rubbed Cassie's back. She couldn't see anything. Why couldn't she see?

"Your head's wrapped tight," Kell said from her side. "Medic wrapped you in a full-on cast to keep your brains from leaking out of your cratered nose, but he said you should recover, with time and surgery. You're lucky to be alive, *sifu*."

Morna relaxed. There was another reason she was still alive, and it wasn't luck. A door opened and shut.

"I hate to say this, Morna," Vincent Alvarado said, "but that wasn't much of a fight."

His words didn't hurt. "I suppose I've gotten old."

"Yeah," Vincent said. "Anyway, I made a hefty profit, so we're all good here." He harrumphed. "I could have made much more if you'd gone at least two rounds."

"See this?" Morna raised both hands and moved one finger. "This is me playing the world's tiniest violin."

"Kell's contract is done," Vincent said. "I also cancelled her father's debts."

"Can I kill him now?" Kell asked.

"Show him," Morna said.

Morna felt Cassie push off her. "Now?"

"Oh yes."

"Show me what?" Vincent demanded.

Morna couldn't see the vid player Cassie produced, but she heard Raze speaking. She heard the woman the Punch Pit's people respected like their own mom, the woman she'd sent Cassie and Kell to find with sign language in Vincent's projected office.

"Vincent Alvarado ordered Ruiner to throw the fight," Raze growled. A click followed, probably Cassie pausing the vid.

"What is this?" Vincent demanded.

"It's timestamped right before my mom stepped into the pit," Cassie said. "Wanna see the rest?"

Click. "Ruiner goes down in the first round," Raze continued, "just over one minute in, when she takes a punch to the head from Toro's left hand. One punch KO, all arranged."

"I kept my word to you!" Vincent protested.

"Today," Morna said. "You kept your word today."

"No one will believe this. Anyone could have faked this!"

"That won't matter," Morna said, "once I tell everyone I'm Advanced."

Kell gasped, as did Vincent. Cassie didn't. Cassie knew.

"You're lying," Vincent whispered.

"I'll submit to any test you like," Morna said. "All will prove every fight Ruiner won in your arena was Advanced versus natural-born, genetically engineered superhuman versus... not that. The people I went up against never stood a chance."

"You're bluffing," Vincent said. "You'd end your political career. They'd run you out of Cliffside!"

"I'm willing to lose everything I have to get what I want," Morna said, smiling his way. "Are you?"

After a long moment, Vincent sighed. "What *do* you want? I already gave you Kell."

"Freedom." She had him. "You'll update the contracts of all your fighters today. Raze, Toro, and the others can leave any time. Their choice."

"That all?" Vincent growled.

He'd balk if she demanded more. "Yes. So long as you never trouble me or my students again, I won't reveal my true nature."

"So it's blackmail."

"It's business."

"Right." Vincent harrumphed. "I gave you everything you ever wanted and you fucked me, twice. Nice job."

"Do we have a deal or not?"

"We have a deal. Now get out." A heavy door slammed.

"Well, shit," Kell whispered. "You're really Advanced?"

"I am." Would this change things between them?

"Then... why'd you do it?"

Morna had struggled with that question for years after she left the Punch Pit behind. "I thought I was better. It's how I was raised. My privilege blinded me to my advantages, and Jenny Garcia died."

"So why risk all this for me?" Kell demanded. "Vince could still rat you out. He could ruin you."

"He won't," Morna said, "but I didn't do this just for you, Kell. You don't owe me anything."

"How do I *not* owe you?"

"This was also for me," Morna said. "I can't change what I've done, but I can control what I do. So this was for me."

"Right." Kell breathed out. "So you're not *all* assholes." She touched Morna's arm. "Thank you."

"Also, thank you for not dying!" Cassie added. "Which you almost did. Which was dumb, Mom. Don't ever do that again."

Morna found Cassie's hand and gripped it. "It all worked out." She leaned back and treasured cool air across her hair.

Toro was the undisputed champion of the Punch Pit, and Morna hoped that offered him some comfort. Kell's life was her own again as well, but Morna's ledger remained unbalanced. No matter what she did, her ledger might never be balanced again.

Yet that was no reason to stop trying.

PERFECT INSANITY

TJ PERKINS

MAYA CLAWED WILDLY AT THE black smoky hand-shaped tendrils clasped firmly around her neck. Panic set in. She gagged as the pressure tightened and her back was pressed into the cutting bark of a tree. She knew who had sent this friendly little warning—Baal. His magick had grown since last they met.

Excited squeals and laughter floated from the upstairs bedroom windows. The kids were up. Time was running out. She had to get them to school!

"Enough!" Maya spat. She released her grip on the thin smoky fingers and raised her hands to the sky. "I-I c-call on the elements of A-Air," she choked out. "Lend me y-your aid!"

"Mom, where are you?" Lilith called from the kitchen window.

Maya's heart quickened. The time must be now! The children couldn't see what was happening in their own backyard. She'd never get them out of the house so she could have some peace!

Her eyes rolled back as she summoned all the magick within; calling forth elemental powers she was deeply connected to. The wind picked up, branches swayed, and a four-foot whirlwind of leaves and grass snaked across the lawn mere feet from where she stood pinned to the tree.

The vortex gained strength and inched ever closer. It latched on to the dark magick and pulled at the smoky tendrils. Refusing defeat, they scratched and clawed at Maya's neck, desperately trying to keep hold.

"Mom!" The kids were searching the house for her.

Ugh! Her desperation increased.

Maya directed energy to her hands, raised them shoulder high, and pushed. *Crackle! Pop! Hiss!* The dark magick loosed its hold and was sucked into the vortex, issuing high-pitched shrieks of protest. Maya released a sigh and rubbed her neck as the air elementals quickly dispursed and carried the danger away to the clouds.

"Whew," she muttered. She smoothed down her tank top and picked up her basket of herbs, but there was nothing she could do about her curly locks. Maya's light auburn hair looked like she'd stuck her finger in a light socket. *Oh well.* At least the threat was gone.

"I'm out here!" she called to her children as she opened the back door.

"It's about time." Thirteen-year-old Nick glowered, chomping on cereal.

"Mommy!" Lilith latched on to Maya's clean top with sticky fingers and wiped jelly from her cheek right across the front. "I found you, Mommy."

"Oh, yes, yes you did." Prying off stickiness and looking her eight-year-old daughter in the eyes, she said, "Since when do we have chocolate ice cream and jelly for breakfast?"

Lilith squealed with delight and ran to the front door with her little book bag.

"Since you weren't here to stop her," Nick said, getting up from the table.

"Ahh no you don't." Maya stopped Nick in his tracks. "Where does that go?" She waved her hand, and the dishwasher opened.

"Ugh, why do you always have to do that?" Nick plopped his bowl and spoon onto the rack, grabbed his books and skateboard, and went to the door.

With the morning craziness under control and her day going back to "normal," Maya was relieved to just be a mom driving her kids to school.

"You ready for karate class after school, Lilith?" she asked.

"Yeah!" Lilith shouted.

"Nick, are you still working on that science fair project? Isn't that tomorrow?"

"I don't know how to make it work." He rolled his eyes and sulked, sinking further down the front seat. "Just forget it."

"No. You're not giving up. I'll help you," Maya said.

"When's dad coming home?" Nick grumbled.

"Next week. But I'm here, and I'll help you. Tomorrow is Saturday. We have all morning to figure it out." Maya knew a young boy of thirteen needed his father's attention, but this was another one of those times where she had to be both mom and dad.

Once the kids were dropped off, Maya resumed focus on the real problem at hand, Baal, the bane of her and her coven's existence. Willow, Orenda, and Gale had been working on a solution for months on how to stop him from destroying the earth, but nothing was working. One week, he was polluting the rivers and streams, and the next he was sparking up the burning of old tires in some auspicious place. Baal had even influenced men to ignore environmental rules and allow their factories to belch out toxins into the air. The coven was exhausted from stopping his toxic magick shortly after it began. If it weren't for their magickal efforts and those of covens from surrounding states and counties, their small victories wouldn't have been won.

But it was time to up their game, to break out the big guns to put an end to him once and for all. Tapping into the power of Gia would have to happen, but it wouldn't be easy and would require an equivalent exchange, which she had figured out… somewhat.

Maya screeched to a halt in Gale's driveway, armed with a pumpkin muffin from Panera and a latte.

"Thought you'd never get here," Gale fussed, opening the front door. "Are you all right? When I got your text I assumed the worse."

"I'm good, but the attack surprised the heck outta me." Maya plopped down on the sofa. "I went out to get herbs for today's magick and… boom!"

"Your neck is still a little red." Gale stooped down for a better look and scrunched her nose.

Willow and Orenda (a.k.a. Susan and Olivia) burst through the back door without so much as a knock.

"Oh. My. Goddess. We just got the message," Willow blurted out. "Your aura looks so weak."

"My energy is yours. Take what you need," Orenda offered, gingerly sitting next to Maya and patting her knee.

"Ladies, it's all good," Maya said. "But we only have a matter of a few hours to disable Baal and cast him out once and for all."

"Why only a few hours?" Willow asked.

"Because I have to get my kids to soccer and karate this afternoon. Duh!" Maya was a bit annoyed. They never remembered anything when it came to her life. "Plus help Nick with his science fair project."

The coven girls. You gotta love 'em. Gale's kids were all grown and out of the house, Orenda never had any kids, and Willow had one child that went to a private school and was mostly living with his dad. Maya shook her head. They didn't understand the struggle she dealt with every day.

"I propose we summon the power of Gia," Maya said, producing notes from her bag.

Willow and Orenda gasped.

"Maya, is that a good idea?" Orenda asked, wringing her hands.

Gale pulled out her book of shadows, which was actually a large three-inch, three-ring binder, and plopped it on the coffee table before them. "Of course it's a good idea!" She turned to a marked section then pointed and gestured at the pages. "I made extensive notes. We'll be protected."

"But it requires an equivalent exchange," Willow's eyes darted to each of them as she put a dainty hand to her mouth.

"Stop worrying!" Maya snapped. "You always stress out. I'm not leaving it up to the Universe to decide who will die in order to rid us of Baal." She paused as Gale went into a spare room and came back with a cat carrier. She placed it on a nearby chair. The clucking from within raised eyebrows.

"A chicken?" Willow scrunched up her face.

"A rooster, actually," Gale said. She shrugged her shoulders and smiled. "Baal thinks he's all big and bad, like a rooster, but he's actually a chicken. What a perfect combination. I've been taking care of it for a month, infusing magick into it for the sacrifice. I had to consult a voodoo priest friend of mine to make sure I did everything correctly, but the rooster is ready."

"This morning's attack on me was to scare us off. Baal must know we're planning something, and he's worried." Maya stood and paced the room. "This is a good thing. We'll use his fear against him. I've already put out the vibes that we'll be at the river by the old water plant."

"And we need to go now!" Gale fussed, while tapping her watch.

Ten minutes later, they were piled into Maya's SUV armed with herbs, crystals, candles, athames, and wands—and the rooster. With windows down, the wind whipped their hair as they jammed out to '80s rock songs to get pumped up. Anyone who observed them would have thought they were having a mid-life crisis.

They were.

Maya's tires slid on dirt and rock as they came to a halt by the river just outside of town. Everyone bailed out and grabbed supplies. It was already ten o'clock. Preparation would take a good thirty minutes, and then they had to attract the attention of Baal.

Crystals marked the circumference of their large circle, and a carefully drawn Witch's Triangle was placed within the center. With burning candles set at each of the four Quarters, the four Witches called the Elements, blessed their sacred space, and drew in the protection of Gia. The air was unbelievably still, yet the forest and stream were crackling with power as each woman tapped into the unlimited potential of the earth.

With each breath, they drew earth energy up through their bodies, holding it tight within their solar plexuses and directing it out to fill their auras. It pulsed and thrummed deep and low until each was steady on her feet and clear of mind.

Energy rose from the land around them, causing the trees to slightly bend away, the grass to tremble, and the current in the stream to flow backward. Willow's special connection to Earth was so powerful, her blonde hair lifted up off her back and floated on the still air. That was when Maya knew they were ready.

The rooster clucked nervously in its crate. It knew its demise was near. Gale raised her athame to the sky and then pointed it at the Witch's Triangle. Lifting her wand, Maya aimed at the Triangle. Orenda and Willow lit their smudging sticks and raised their arms wide. The air was still as glass, and time froze as the power of Gia burned in their veins and crackled over their skin.

The ground shuddered. The Witches held their position—waiting. Thunder rolled, yet the sky was clear blue and cloud free. Lightning pierced the stillness and struck the center of the Triangle with an ear-splitting *crack,* blasting dirt and rock into the air. Smoke rose within the Triangle, and the air suddenly tasted metallic, like blood.

"Hello, darlings. Did you miss me?" Baal's voice was that of a perfect gentleman, yet oozed with sarcasm. He stood in the center of the Triangle, directed as the Witches had ordered, dressed in a designer dark suit with red tie and matching kerchief tucked in the jacket pocket. Baal brushed a bit of dust from his shoulder and smoothed back his already slicked-back dark hair. "Do I look all right?" He was alarmingly handsome and charming.

"By the order of Gia, by the four cities of the realm and all that is of the Divine, we command you to return to that whence you came!" Maya shouted. Sweat trickled down her cheek as she held her posture, lassoing Baal with all the power they could muster. "Ye shall stay hence and return no more!"

"You—are *you commanding* me?" He laughed and clapped his hands. "Very good." The smile fell from his face instantaneously. "But not good enough."

Their breathing was taxed as he casually reached a hand beyond the Triangle barrier, breaking the seal. Each Witch felt his power, like a punch to the gut. One corner of his mouth curved upward, and his eyes narrowed as Baal lightly grasped the strand of energy coming from Willow.

"Willow." His sultry voice reached out to her. Their eyes locked. "You know you'd love to be with me. Huh? How 'bout it, darling?"

Her face contorted. She fell to one knee, threw back her head, and screamed in agony. Baal smiled maliciously as he focused on her.

Gale reached into the crate, grabbed the rooster, and held it out before her.

Baal chuckled. "Oh, my! Is that meant for me?"

While his attention was on Gale, Orenda drew the sacrificial knife from her belt and threw it at Baal just as Gale was about to break the rooster's neck. The timing was perfect, the knife flew true, and the rooster was about to cluck no more; then their protective barriers fell, time warped, and they were blinded by an immense flash of light that threw them all to the ground.

When they opened their eyes, Baal was gone, the knife was imbedded into a tree next to Gale's head, and the rooster was hiding in the crate.

"What happened?" Gale shouted.

"No!" Maya screamed to the sky.

"He got away?" Orenda said. "Again? Crap!"

"But *how* did he get away?" Gale said. All eyes turned to Willow.

"What?" Picking herself off the ground, Willow looked to each of them. "It's not my fault. Why would you think it's my fault?"

"No. It's not her fault. Stop the negative thinking right away!" Maya commanded. "That's what he wants. For us to fight, not trust each other, and turn on the one person in our group who's the most connected to the earth."

"Well, I don't know how he did it, but we just lost four hours," Orenda said looking at her watch. "It's almost three o'clock."

"Damn! I've got to pick up the kids," Maya spat.

The drive back to Gale's house was quiet and solemn. Each Witch was absorbed with her own thoughts and troubles of the ritual gone awry and wondering where Baal had gone this time.

Depression from the failure didn't stop, even as Maya sat in the parents' area of the gym while waiting for Lilith to finish karate class. She wasn't doing the kicks quite right; maybe a little intervention?

Nick sat next to her doing homework. "Don't, Mom," he quietly fussed.

"What?"

"I saw you wiggling your fingers. Why do you always have to do that? Let her do it on her own. Sheez!"

Worn out and hungry, Maya sat through another one of Nick's soccer training sessions. Lilith happily played on the bleachers and practiced balancing on one foot.

"I'm going to keep the balance, just like you, Mommy," she said, and smiled lovingly with a dirt-smudged elfish face and mussed-up hair.

Hmmm, keep the balance.

Maya looked up and spied Nick having trouble making a goal. She couldn't help herself. With a wave of her hand, the ball went in not once, or twice, but four times. She quickly looked away when Nick flashed her an annoyed scowl.

Night fell. Maya tossed and turned all night, and when she finally fell asleep, her dreams were invaded. Alone on the Astral Plane, Maya witnessed her children being hurt by demons sent by Baal, her coven mates painfully stripped of their magick, and the earth burned all around her. She woke with a start, panting and sweating and desperately trying to pull her mind back to consciousness, only to notice a tall, dark figure leaning against the wall of her bedroom.

"You'll never win, Maya," he softly cooed.

With a warrior growl, Maya grabbed the dagger from beneath her mattress and threw it at the figure. It stuck in the wall where his head would've been, That was, *if* he had actually been there.

"How'd he get past my magickal protection?" she breathed, pushing her curly locks out of her face and falling out of bed. She hit the floor with a *thump* and untangled the sheets from her feet before staggering into the hall to check on the children. They were safe and asleep.

This had now become super personal, and Maya shuddered to think where things would lead if Baal wasn't stopped.

Since she was already up, Maya spent the rest of the morning resetting magickal barriers around her home and property, hexing the windows and doors and bewitching her SUV, especially the brakes. Satisfied that everything was secure, she went to the basement to look over Nick's science fair project.

Nick had a collection of rotting food scraps, grass, and bits of sawdust that smelled awful. Next to it he had constructed a metal dragon, wings and all, with an opening at the side of the belly. The inside was charred black from being burned.

"What are you doing?" Nick plodded down the steps, hair a mess and rubbing his eyes.

"Trying to figure out what you're doing."

"I want to create biogas out of this biomass." He gestured with a floppy hand to the project and plopped down on a stool.

"Ugh, explain."

"Uhhh!" Exasperated, Nick said, "This decaying organic matter is called biomass, which is a rich source of energy. If we burn it, it can be turned into a gas, called biogas. So what I'd like to do is put it in the dragon's belly, burn it, and the gas will power the dragon. You know, the wings will move a little, and steam should come out of its nose."

"Oh, well, that sounds cool," Maya said, quite impressed with Nick's idea. "So, what's the issue?"

"I burn it and nothing happens. It just stinks."

"You know what I think? I think you need more rotty stuff. Come on."

Fifteen minutes later, Maya had Nick excited about his project all over again. "We're going to put all this biomass into this small glass container. See?" She smashed it down as Nick loomed close. "Then put this tin lid on. Now, we're going to let it sit while we clean up and have breakfast. Okay?"

Nick smiled and nodded and raced his mother up the steps. Little did he know, Maya had infused a bit of magick so the scraps would rot quicker in the short time that she needed.

Banging on the front door interrupted breakfast. Maya flung it open to find an out-of-sorts Gale, rooster in hand.

"Gale?"

"Here. Take it." She pushed the bird into Maya's arms and backed away, huffing and puffing like she'd run a mile. "I had a demonic home invasion around two o'clock. They tried to take it. I've been battling them for hours."

"I had a visit too, but why me?"

"You have better home protection than I do." Gale waved, turned, and ran back to her car.

Maya stood, stupefied, rooster clutched in her arms, and watched Gale race off. Maya slowly turned and stopped short. Her kids were standing in the foyer, mouths hanging open and eyes staring at the rooster.

"Um, I guess we're pet sitting for a little while."

The hours ticked by quickly as Maya scrambled to complete Nick's project and get her children ready for the science fair.

"Mom, this isn't even ready. How's it going to work?" Nick yelled.

"Don't raise your voice at me, young man," she softly scolded. "This will work. Watch. Now, I'm going to take this nail and hammer and punch a small hole in the top. Gas is supposed to escape. Light a match and put it next to the hole."

"Nick rolled his eyes and reluctantly struck a match."

Poof! There was flame.

"Wow!" Nick shouted.

The rooster clucked as it wandered aimlessly around the basement, and Lilith happily bounced around on her toes while watching it.

"Now close up the belly," Maya ordered.

Before too long, the tiny gears inside the dragon began clicking and whirling. Nick's eyes widened with excitement and Maya, being a mom, didn't want her son to be disappointed. She snapped her fingers behind her back, causing the dragon's wings to move slightly and steam to puff from the nose.

"Yay! It works! It works!" Nick chanted, jumping up and down.

"Let's blow out the flame, and I'll use the nail to stop up the hole. We can do it again once we get to the school," Maya said.

"Yeah! I'm totally going to win this year!" Nick shouted. "Let's go, Mom! Come on, Lilith."

One hour later, Maya had Nick all checked in at the science fair in his school gym and his project completely set up. Lilith showed off her new sundress to anyone that walked by, and the rooster paced around, clucked, and periodically crowed while strapped into a small dog harness and tied to the table leg.

Nick swayed from one foot to the other as he explained his project to the teachers and judges that visited his table. Maya couldn't have been more proud. She stood back far enough to keep watch, and as soon as Nick lit the fire in the dragon's belly, she snapped her fingers to bring the whole thing to life again. But it didn't work this time. She snapped again. Still nothing happened.

"Yay! My brother is so smart!" Lilith happily shouted and clapped her hands as she skipped past them. The dragon began to work. "Hi, chicken," she said, instantly distracted.

Nick cast his mother a startled look. Maya shrugged. The teachers and judges made notes, applauded Nick's project, and then moved on.

"Mom," Nick whispered and waved his mother closer. "What just happened?"

"I think your little sister just had a magick moment."

"Where'd she go?"

Maya's heart caught in her throat the instant they realized Lilith was nowhere in sight. "Lilith?" Maya called.

Clucking from across the gym drew her attention, and so did the tall, handsome man standing at the gym entrance.

"Oh, no," Maya breathed. Dread filled her belly like red-hot razor blades, and her heart skipped a beat.

Baal leaned in the doorway, buffing his nails, and smiled at her and the children like a wolf sizing up a heard of sheep. He casually looked around, noticed Lilith chasing the rooster, and stepped inside.

"Oh, no, no, no. I can't have a confrontation here."

"Mom, who is he?"

"A devil, a manager, of sorts, from a place the Christians call Hell."

"What does he want?" Nick said, jaw tight and panic showing on his young face.

"To kill me," Maya said, never talking her eyes off of Baal. "Just stay back."

"You can't let all these people see you do magick," Nick squeaked out. "But you really need to do it this time."

Baal put his hands in his pockets and slowly strolled across the shiny hardwood floor, eyes on her daughter. No one seemed to notice him approaching Lilith. None of the adults looked his way, nor did anyone seemed curious as to this strange man entering the science fair. The rooster looked at Baal, flapped its wings, and scampered back toward Maya, but never made it all the way.

Baal raised a hand. The invisible force latched onto the rooster's neck and lifted it off the floor. Maya started to approach him, wand stashed in the back of her shirt. Panic gripped her heart as she watched Lilith look at Baal and stand her ground. *She can see him!*

Lilith stared at Baal and scowled. He stopped mere feet from the little girl. Their eyes locked, and Lilith was not happy.

Shouts of surprise rose up throughout the science fair. Maya looked around. People were backing away from every project that had fire, water, or some sort of chemical reaction. Vials, beakers, and Bunsen burners expanded, ballooned outward, and became hotter. People shouted and took cover as they popped and exploded.

"You're a bad man!" Lilith shouted and stomped her little foot at Baal.

Lilith. She had to get to Lilith before Baal—

"Mom!" Nick shouted. "Look out!"

Before Maya could run for her daughter, Nick's dragon rose up from the table, burst into flames, and exploded with an ear-splitting *bang!*

Maya dropped to the floor as shards of sharp metal flew over her head. In an instant, the rooster and Baal were impaled, perfectly timed, just the way it was supposed to have happened at the river.

The rooster flopped to the floor with a sizable sliver of metal through its body. Baal, on the other hand, staggered to the gym door, paused, looked at Maya, and raised his hand.

"Don't even think about it," she said in her Magician's Voice, soft enough when said, but loud in only his ears.

Smoky tendrils rose from his body as pieces of Baal broke apart and floated away on the summer night breeze. He stood there, frozen in place, unable to move and most likely shocked that a Witch had bested him. Within moments, he was gone, and no one had noticed. Only she and her children, and the rooster, saw Baal. Only they interacted with him. She smiled in spite of herself as she realized that her children had *the gift*, too.

"Oh, my, Miss. Are you okay?" a man said, helping Maya get up. "We saw you slip and fall."

"Mommy!" Lilith ran over and gave her mother a hug. "You fell down," she giggled. "And the chicken is sleeping."

Maya sighed, grateful no one really noticed all the weirdness that just happened with Baal. Unfortunately, Maya was left to explain some of it and, of course, the dead rooster.

Maya lifted Lilith up and hugged her as Nick approached with a scorched dragon's head in his hands and a first place ribbon pinned to his shirt. "Mom, I'm glad you do magick," he said, smiling proudly.

Mission accomplished on so many levels, Maya was happy her perfectly insane life could get back to normal.

THE ART OF CRAFTING RESISTANCE

KARISSA LAUREL

WHEN THE LOCAL NEWSPAPER ANNOUNCED that Buford Pine had declared his last-minute candidacy for Mayor of Faffton, my Grandma Winnie groaned, balled up the front page, and tossed it into the bin beside her wood-burning stove. Later, when the weather turned colder, I suspected she'd use Buford Pine's grinning portrait as kindling for the fire.

"What's the matter, Grandma?" Beside her on the basement couch, I fumbled with a pair of knitting needles as I turned a skein of yarn into a string of knots. Grandma Winnie had been teaching me to knit, but I was starting to doubt I had the coordination for it. "You don't like Mr. Pine?"

She harrumphed and glanced at Grandpa Mac in his rocking chair. He turned his attention to reorganizing the newspaper and grumbled. "Coulda let me finish reading the other front-page articles first."

"Couldn't bear that conman jeering at me." Her lips puckered, deep wrinkles forming around her mouth. "That insipid grin…" She shook her head, salt-and-pepper curls tumbling, and took the yarn and needles from me. She flicked her wrist and the knots all fell out, leaving behind a row of perfect stitches. That was her magic, the thing she didn't much talk about, though we knew her ways. Knew the tapestries hanging on the walls around the house were more than just abstract, artistic weavings. They kept out bad stuff—stink bugs, flu germs, ill will and animosity—the same way the crocheted blanket she'd given me as a baby kept away nightmares. The lace-trimmed edge she'd added to that blanket last year had also eased the worst of my monthly cramps.

She returned the needles and yarn to me and offered a sympathetic smile. "You'll get it, Lucy Goose. You've got the knack. I've seen it in those bracelets you make—the ones with the embroidery thread."

"That's just making knots on purpose." I suspected my bracelets were more than mere knots, but I hadn't quite figured out what they were, exactly. A piece of me went into each one—my thoughts and feelings and intentions—similar to Grandma and her knitting, but much less potent. Concentrating, I bit my lip and twined yarn around a needle tip. "Knitting is something else entirely."

"All Craft is about potential. A cup of flour, a spool of thread, a skein of yarn—they're all waiting to become something—you just have to figure what that something is. Patience, sweetie." Grandma patted my hand. "It'll come."

The door from the basement's garage entrance groaned open, and my mom breezed into the room. "Sorry I'm late. Got held up at work." The black curls she'd tried to tame into a bun sprang lose around her face. She looked tired and frazzled, and a surge of sympathy swelled in my heart. "You ready to hit the road, kiddo?"

I held up the knotted alpaca wool abomination I'd created. "Save me?"

"Don't look at me," she said. "Grandma gave up trying to teach me a long time ago."

"Fiber arts weren't your Craft." Grandma shrugged. "You do good things with food, though."

Mom waggled her outstretched hand, encouraging me to stand up and take it so she could lead me out to the car. If we stayed too long, Grandma Winnie would make excuses for us to stay. But Mom had promised homemade chicken and pastry for supper, and my mouth was already watering. "Bye, Grandpa," I called as I took Mom's hand.

He set down his paper and slid his reading glasses higher up his nose. "See you tomorrow night, right?"

Mom's brow furrowed. "Oh, the fall festival. Right. I almost forgot."

"I heard Mr. Pine's gonna be at the festival's debate," I said.

"There's something off about that man." Grandma's nose wrinkled as though she'd caught a whiff of something rotten. "I'm telling you. He just, *poof*—she snapped her fingers—"came out of nowhere, set up that car lot, and next thing you know, he has the whole town licking his boots. He shouldn't even be a candidate—filed his registration way past the deadline, but folks seem eager to make exceptions for him."

"He gave a few people some badly needed jobs," Grandpa said. "Donates to the Shriners and the VFW. Bought the church a new steeple."

Lightning had destroyed the spire atop Faffton First Baptist a couple of years ago. When Buford Pine replaced it, using his own personal funds, many had called him a hero. Me, though... maybe I had inherited some of Grandma's skepticism. Mr. Pine gave me a queasy feeling—the same feeling I got from standing too close to the edge of a high cliff, like the one near the peak of Baldhead Mountain, the tallest in the range bordering the north side of our town. A little voice in my head always urged me to step back, retreat before I inevitably tumbled over the edge.

"Did the paper mention how he had to sell off his last car lot because he couldn't pay his creditors?" Grandma Winnie shook her finger at Grandpa Mac. "There was a big lawsuit against him too."

"How do you know that?" Grandpa scoffed.

"The internet is a big thing now. You know, like... *Google?*"

"Well, I don't remember hearing about him before."

"A little boy almost died because his seatbelt failed. Pine knew there was a safety recall but said nothing when he sold the boy's family that car."

Chastised, Grandpa ducked his head, hunched his shoulders, and hid behind his newspaper. Hoping to get away before Grandma started another rant, I tugged Mom toward the door again. But no luck.

"Lucy, wait." Grandma Winnie sprang from the couch, scurrying across the living room, a bundle of yarn in her hand. Not my yarn, though. Whatever she had was far too orderly and finished to be one of my knitting projects. She shoved the soft red strands at me. "Take this. Wear it tomorrow night. Promise me."

I unwound the bundle, revealing a luxurious carmine-colored scarf. "It's too warm for this."

"It won't be tomorrow night." She nodded sagely. "Trust me."

With that red scarf around my neck, I carried my own personal bubble of warmth as I made my way through the fall festival crowds swarming downtown Faffton. Grandma had been right—the temperatures had plummeted overnight. At the square in the middle of town, Faffton High School's booster club was selling coffee and hot chocolate as fast as they could make it. I skipped their long line and headed straight for my best friend, Fatima Abadi, who was manning our high school's Amnesty International booth. She looked cozy in her wool headscarf and billowing winter cloak. My heart warmed at the sight of her.

"I put an apple aside for you." Fatima smiled as I approached. "The one smothered in mini M&Ms."

"Mmm, my favorite." I slid money across the table. She handed me a caramel apple. I bit into it and closed my eyes, savoring the combination of tart apple, salty caramel, and crunchy chocolate bits. "You gonna listen to the debates?"

Fatima rolled her eyes. "Boring."

"Ms. Carter said she'd give extra credit if we could quote one of the questions and summarize the candidates' answers."

She shrugged. "We're not even old enough to vote. Why should we care?"

"They'll be making decisions that affect us. There's still ways to participate in the process."

"You know you're a nerd, right?" Fatima grinned.

"And yet, you're still friends with me." Smiling back at her, I poked her shoulder. "What's that say about *you*?"

A family approached with a pair of small kids shouting for cotton candy. I stepped aside and turned my attention to the platform at the center of the festival square. At the corner of the brightly lit stage, I spied Buford Pine. A tiny woman with salt-and-pepper curls blocked his path and thrust a bundle of yarn at him. I groaned.

"What?" Fatima asked as she handed bags of cotton candy to a pair of cute kids.

"Grandma Winnie's causing trouble."

"Again?"

"Always." I waved bye at Fatima as I hurried to catch up to my grandmother. "I'll come find you later."

I arrived at Grandma's side in time to witness Buford Pine's final, adamant refusal. "Ms. Banks, I appreciate your thought and care, but I'm really going to have to insist you keep the scarf or give it to someone more in need." He waved his hands between them, trying to drive Grandma Winnie back without touching her. His wispy white hair fluttered around his head like agitated antennae. "I have a strict policy against accepting gifts from my constituents."

Before Grandma Winnie could say another word, he turned on his heel and lumbered up the stairs to the top of the platform.

"Ha!" she scoffed. "As if I'd ever be one of his constituents."

"Well, you *were* just trying to give him a gift." I took her elbow and tugged her away from the stage. "What else was he supposed to think?"

"It wasn't a gift. Not really."

I eyed the scarf. *Not a gift?* Then what was it? "You're not concerned for his personal comfort?"

"That man has a silver tongue."

"And the scarf was going to change that somehow?"

She caught my gaze and held it. Her eyes sparkled. Her mouth curled into a grin. She winked but said nothing more. Instead, she balled up her scarf and marched off. "This is going to require a different approach. Something less direct."

In the background, the debate had begun. I missed the moderator's first question, but I didn't miss Buford Pine's reply. "If my opponents have their way," he said, his tone full of mockery, "there'll be a falafel truck on every corner!"

The crowd jeered and laughed.

A sharp chill lanced my heart. My thoughts immediately turned to Fatima and her family. Her extended family. The other two-dozen or more refugees that had arrived in our town several years before. "Why are they all laughing?" I asked.

Grandma Winnie's jaw tightened.

"Fatima's mom runs the town's clothes closet *and* the food pantry. People say nice stuff about her all the time." Before Fatima had come into my life, my family had been so small—just me, Mom, Grandpa, and

Grandma Winnie. After Fatima, my family had grown to include her, her brother, her father and mother, her blood cousins, and the cousins related by shared origins, experiences and community. My heart had stretched out to fit them all inside it, and if they were to leave, it would feel so empty, loose, and limp. My stomach curdled at the thought.

"People are complicated creatures, Lucy Goose."

"People are two-faced."

"Some are. Some are just highly susceptible to, um… *influence.*"

I tugged Grandma Winnie to a stop in a dark and shadowy space between the stage and the food booths. I lowered my voice to a whisper. "Are you talking about… you know…"

"Talking about what?"

"Craft." I squeezed the scarf in her hands to emphasize my point.

"I don't think Buford Pine has ever held a pair of knitting needles a day in his life."

"*Grandma,*" I whined. "You know what I'm talking about."

She paused. Then she harrumphed. "There's more to him than just a persuasive personality. This scarf would have made it so he could only tell the truth. He's a wily one, though."

"Maybe he'll lose the election." I'd been thinking of volunteering for Althea Bruce's campaign, handing out flyers and bumper stickers around town. A lot of people liked her; she'd been on the town council for years and her family had lived in Faffton for generations. Not like Buford Pine, who'd arrived only months ago and charmed our town in no time. It did seem like he had something more than a magnetic personality working in his favor, but popularity always looked like magic to me. I tended to be a one-best-friend kind of girl.

Grandma turned toward the stage, and the lights caught her face, revealing her grimace. "Maybe," she said, but she didn't sound at all like she believed it.

———————————

Squatting at the northern edge of Faffton's town limits, the Debra Camp Coal Mine was an industrial graveyard, abandoned and crumbling—rusting chain-link fencing and old equipment turning into dinosaur fossils. More than a few men had died there in work-related accidents, and the kids in town swore the mine was haunted. The coal company had closed up and moved out a dozen years before, taking over a hundred jobs with it, but Buford Pine had picked Debra Camp's parking lot as the setting for his big campaign rally. Workers had set up spotlights, a stage, folding chairs, and red-white-and-blue balloons and bunting. The contrast of festive decorations at the abandoned worksite unsettled me, made me feel like I'd stepped into someone's surreal nightmare.

Grandma Winnie had brought a tote bag full of shawls and knitted caps. She'd worked on them almost non-stop since the night of the fall festival, and I wondered when she'd had the time. She looked like she hadn't slept—dark smudges underscored her eyes, and her wrinkles seemed deeper. Her usual surety and poise had developed an uncharacteristic wobble.

I offered her my arm as we picked our way across Debra Camp's gravel lot, and she clutched it tightly. Grandma had her tote bag, and I carried a notebook full of questions. If I managed to get Mr. Pine to answer one of them, my civics teacher would give me a 100 on a quiz grade. But more than an academic concern had brought me there. Worry for my grandmother's safety had also compelled me to come, along with my need to find out if her claims about Buford Pine's influence were true.

"Hey there, Bev." Grandma raised an arm and flapped her hand at Beverly Wilkins and her husband Tom. "Hold on just a second, would you?" I hugged Grandma close and picked up our pace, hurrying her over to the older couple. Grandma tugged a shawl from her bag. Crocheted in purple glittering yarn, the shawl matched the bifocal chain dangling from Ms. Wilkins's neck. "I brought you something, Bev."

Ms. Wilkins took the shawl and shook it out. Her eyes widened, filing with appreciation. "Well, if that ain't just the sweetest...?"

"Hi, Mr. Wilkins." I offered him a shy smile.

"Oh, Lucy, it's so nice to see young people taking an interest in the political process."

"Yes, sir." I nodded as Grandma Winnie shoved a dark knitted cap into my hand. "Um," I raised it to his eyelevel. "Grandma made this for you."

He took it from me and furrowed his brow as if uncertain what to do with it. "Well, that's real nice of you, Winnie."

"Let's see how it fits," Grandma prodded.

Mr. Wilkins tugged it over his thinning white curls. "Fits real nice. I'll get a lot of use out of it come winter."

He started to pull it off, but Grandma Winnie put a hand on his wrist, stopping him. "It's not winter yet, but it sure is a chilly evening don't you think?"

Brow still furrowed, he nodded, left the cap in place, and took several steps back, letting his wife lead him toward the seats, which were quickly filling with eager citizens. "Thanks again, Winnie," Mr. Wilkins said. "Real thoughtful of you."

With narrowed eyes, I studied my grandma. "What did you put in that cap?"

"Same thing I put in all my crafts." She gestured to her tote bag. "Lots of love and care."

"What are you planning?"

Loudspeakers arranged around the parking lot amplified Buford Pine's voice, cutting off Grandma Winnie before she could answer me. "Welcome, citizens of Faffton. I can't tell y'all how honored I am by this big turnout. I got big ideas for Debra Camp." He gestured to our gloomy surroundings. "I can't wait to share my plans for this mine with you, and you're gonna be real excited to hear them."

"Come on, Luce. Help me hand out the rest of these." Grandma shoved her tote at me. I took it, but kept my gaze pinned on Buford Pine. If he was going to work some kind of magic on the crowd, I wanted to witness it.

"Coal is coming back to Faffton!" Buford Pine roared into the microphone. The audience cheered.

I followed Grandma down an aisle, and, at her instruction, shoved a pink-and-green shawl at Mary Anne Pittman. Grandma pointed at Ralph McHenry. I passed him a hat.

Buford Pine continued his speech. "Together, with the help of a few Federal and State programs and some international investors—"

"International?" Grandma jerked us to a stop. Buford went silent, mouth hanging open in surprise at the disruption. "You're bringing in outside money and influence to Faffton, Mr. Pine? From where, exactly?"

Pine's cold eyes narrowed. His lips thinned. He leaned toward a pair of square-jawed men in dark suits standing on the stage beside him and whispered something the microphones didn't pick up. The two men nodded and rushed from the stage. The crowd had turned in our direction, all eyes on us. Dread and embarrassment spilled over me. My stomach cramped. But if Grandma Winnie could be brave, so could I. I cleared my throat and raised my voice. "Mr. Pine, if you become Mayor, will you promise to continue protecting the immigrant families Faffton's been hosting for the past four years?"

Pine's men reached us before I got my answer. One snatched the shawl from Mary Anne Pittman and yanked the knitted cap straight off Ralph McHenry's head. He shoved them into Grandma Winnie's bag while his huge partner loomed over us. "Ms. Banks, I'm afraid you and your granddaughter are going to have to leave."

"Why?" Grandma Winnie demanded. "We've done nothing wrong. We're exercising our rights as citizens."

"You're disrupting a civil meeting," said Pine's security guard. "Leave before we call the sheriff and have him charge you with disturbing the peace."

Grandma Winnie wobbled—her knees seemed ready to give out. "Well, I... I..."

I grabbed her upper arm and held her steady. "C'mon, Grandma. This isn't going to work. Not tonight. Let's go home and think of something else."

She spluttered and coughed out a couple more half-hearted protests, but she let me lead her back to her car. "I told you he was wily," she said. "I think I've underestimated him."

"You weren't being exactly subtle back there." I settled into my seat and drew the seatbelt across my chest. "What did you think would happen?"

"I let my emotions get the best of me." She started her car, and the engine roared. "But I won't make that mistake again."

"Landslide Victory," the Faffton paper stated, predicting Buford Pine's triumph in the election that was less than a week away. Fatima and I sat cross-legged on the basement floor, keeping warm beside Grandma Winnie's wood-burning stove. I'd given up knitting for a while. Instead, I was working on a pair of matching friendship bracelets woven in intricate patterns from a rainbow of embroidery floss. In my mind, the red string represented heart's blood—love that went deeper than a crush. The blue was loyalty, trustworthiness. The yellow was sisterhood, the kind that didn't depend on DNA and genes.

Fatima had barely looked at me, at any of us, since she'd picked up the paper from the seat of Grandpa's rocking chair. But she couldn't hide the red rimming her brown eyes. "The paper says..." She took a deep breath. "It says Mr. Pine has announced that when he becomes Mayor, Faffton won't be a sanctuary town anymore, and that 'we'll offer any local resources requested by the federal government in carrying out its immigration enforcement responsibilities.'"

Well, that sure answered the question I had tried asking him at the coal mine rally. It was a heartbreaking response, but it didn't surprise me. Last week, someone had spray-painted racial slurs across the front windows of the empty downtown dime store that had been turned into a temporary mosque. Chad Seagroves, a previously mild-mannered trumpet player in our marching band, had pulled off Heba Nabulsi's headscarf in the middle of the cafeteria during lunch break. Something was brewing, a dark and angry energy bolstered by Pine's presence.

It scared me, so it must have been terrifying Fatima and her family. Not knowing what to say, certain there was nothing I *could* say that would make a difference, I squeezed Fatima's hand. She squeezed mine back.

Grandma Winnie set down her knitting—she'd been grinding out scarves like a woman possessed, and she looked even more exhausted than she had at the coal mine rally. Her hair had dulled, and the warm undertones in her skin had paled. Her whole body seemed to sag. She had poured so much of herself—heart, mind, and soul—into her Craft, and I worried she'd overdone it. She was tougher than most men half her age and twice her size, but she was still made from mortal flesh and bone... at least as far as I knew.

Most of her scarves had ended up wound around the necks of Fatima, her family, and the people who attended the mosque. What kind of protections had Grandma worked into their threads? "If I thought he was being completely fair, transparent, and honest," Grandma said, "I might be able to swallow it—to accept that he was the fate that Faffton was choosing for itself, no matter how much I didn't like it. But I've seen Pine's kind before, seen his strands of unholy corruption wind their way through a community and tear it apart. There's nothing fair or honest about him, but people won't listen to me. Not when they're under his..."

"Spell?" I asked.

Grandma Winnie clicked her tongue, not quite confirming. Not quite denying, either. "If they could just hear the truth, just once, without his influence, without the charm of his silver tongue, then people might change their minds about him."

"You really think so?" A warm tendril of hope wound around my heart.

"Some of those people were just waiting for someone to agree with the darkness already in their hearts. But some of them might change their minds. Maybe enough of them to count."

She slid off her seat on the sofa and crouched on the floor beside me. She fingered one of my friendship bracelets. "These are something else. Something special. I didn't know you could make something this intricate. You've woven your love all through them."

My cheeks heated. "They're for me... and Fatima."

Beside me, Fatima flinched. She stroked a finger down the length of the bracelet I'd almost finished. She said nothing, but she didn't shy away from me either.

"What are you thinking about while you weave these?" Grandma asked.

"I dunno." I shrugged. "How I hope we can be friends for a long time. How I hope nothing ever comes between us."

Grandma bobbed her head, curls bouncing. "I can see it, like a gold thread."

"See what?" Fatima asked, her voice barely above a whisper.

Grandma Winnie met my gaze. She nodded slowly, deliberately.

I swallowed. "C-craft?"

"How long does it take you to make one of these?" Grandma asked.

"If it's simple, not too wide and not too many colors, I can probably make one in an hour or two."

"Can you teach me?"

I studied Grandma's sallow face, my mind racing. Why was she asking so many questions?

Then it hit me.

The tapestries, the blankets, the scarves... protection, healing, love. Truth. A way to resist, to fight. "Do you think we'll be able to make enough?" I asked. "Mr. Pine's holding one more rally the night before the election. I can pass them out then. People will wear them if they think they're campaign souvenirs or tokens of support."

Grandma Winnie winced. "No, child. That's not what I meant. Something like this... it's too much to ask. A grandmother protects her family; she doesn't ask them to sacrifice themselves."

"It's just a few friendship bracelets—"

"It's a lot more than that. Trust me."

"What do you mean by *more*?"

"There's a cost to everything, Lucy." She raised my unfinished friendship bracelet, loose strings fluttering. "It seems like a small thing, but it all adds up. It takes a toll on you."

"So I'm just supposed to sit here and watch you wear yourself down to skin and bones, like some kind of wraith?" A disturbing thought rose above the jumble of confusion in my mind. "Is this something that could—" In my throat, a lump formed so hard and fast I choked on it. I coughed. Coughed again. "C-could it *kill* you? Is that what Craft does to you?"

The muscles around Grandma Winnie's eyes and mouth tensed. She looked away. "No."

"You don't sound convinced."

"I just need time to rest and recover. And I will. After the election."

I grabbed her frail wrist and held it until she looked at me again. "At this rate, you won't last that long. We'll do it together. Share the burden. You can either accept my help or I'll do it anyway, on my own, without your approval or your guidance."

"No, Lucy—"

"Buford Pine is already suspicious of you. You might not even be able to get into the rally after he kicked you out of the last one. You're going to need my help."

"I'm not quite sure what you two are talking about." Fatima puckered her lips. Her dark eyebrows slid closer together. "But I want to help. My family's afraid of Mr. Pine. I am too, but that's the reason I should do something about it."

Grandma Winnie pulled loose from my hold. "Okay." She had capitulated, but the downturn of her mouth and slump in her shoulders showed she was obviously unhappy about it. The usual sparkle in her eye had diminished. "You can help, Fatima. So can Lucy's mom."

"I thought you said Mom's Craft was food." And I wondered if Fatima had any Craft at all. She was a genius with a tennis racket, but I'd never seen her *make* anything.

"Beggars can't be choosers. It's all hands on deck, Lucy Goose. Divide and conquer." Grandma rifled through my embroidery floss collection and drew out a long blue string. "Fatima, you're in charge of supplies. We're going to need a lot more thread."

Fatima nodded and jumped to her feet. "I'll call my mom right now."

<hr/>

With a satchel full of red-white-and-blue bracelets, Fatima and I weaved through the standing-room only crowd in the Faffton Senior Center. The old linoleum under our feet had yellowed, and the wood paneling on the walls came from an era long before I was born. Menthol and mothballs perfumed the air. Still, the audience's excitement crackled and popped, and I felt like a balloon collecting static electricity as I moved through the room. If I touched a doorknob, I could probably discharge a spark big enough to power the whole town for the night. This new sensation was strange, compared to the bone-numbing exhaustion I'd felt after a week of non-stop knot tying and pouring all my hopes and best intentions, my *Craft*, into every strand of embroidery floss.

No one thought twice about taking a bracelet from Fatima and me. "Oooh, aren't these just the cutest things!" Bernice Andrews paused to let Fatima knot a bracelet around her frail and liver-spotted wrist. "What a great idea for a campaign souvenir."

"Yes, ma'am." Fatima bobbed her head and smiled innocently.

"Mr. Pine is an exciting candidate, isn't he?"

"You could say that." Fatima waited until Ms. Andrews turned away before she glanced at me and pretended to gag.

As expected, the crowd assumed the bands were tokens of support, although nothing about them indicated an affiliation with Buford Pine. Instead, under Grandma Winnie's coaching and instruction, we'd infused the bracelets with the same qualities the colors of the American flag were supposed to signify.

White for purity and innocence, red for hardiness and valor, and blue for vigilance, perseverance, and justice—all the traits we needed people to remember in the face of Buford Pine's silver tongue. The invisible gold threads of Craft interwoven among the red, white, and blue came from me, my mom, and my grandma, but no one other than us would've been able to see them or understand their purpose. And that purpose, if everything worked like we hoped, was to offer people a momentary glimpse behind the Wizard of Oz's curtain.

Fatima and I worked our way around the room, tying bracelets as fast as our fingers could move. From the corner of my eye, I watched Buford Pine's security staff and feared they would catch on to Fatima and me any moment.

"Lucy." A hand curled around my biceps. I flinched and squealed, but instead of a security guard, I found myself facing Beverly Wilkins. She was wearing the purple shawl Grandma had crocheted for her, and I was glad to see it. She patted my shoulder. "I didn't mean to scare you, honey."

"Oh, no ma'am, you just surprised me." I hugged her. "It's nice to see you."

"Is your grandmother here?"

Heat rose in my cheeks. "Um... no. Not after what happened last week at the mine. She decided that maybe it was best if she took a break from politics for the night."

"Your grandma has always been a spitfire." Ms. Wilkins chuckled. "You should ask her about her apartheid protests back in college." She started to say more, but her eyebrows shot up, and her eyes widened. She pointed at Fatima's bag of bracelets. "What do you have there?"

"Just some bracelets Grandma and I made."

"That must've kept you busy. You're giving them out to everyone?" Fatima offered her a band, and Ms. Wilkins took it. "They're very sweet." She squinted, inspecting the bracelet closely. "There's a big crowd tonight. You've got enough for everyone?"

I shrugged. "For most of them." Enough to make a difference, I hoped.

Her lips parted, but before she could utter a response, a dark shadow fell over us. When I glanced at the shadow's owner, my stomach turned to ice and fell to my feet. Dark suit, hard jaw, square shoulders, radio earpiece with a wire disappearing into his collar—it was one of Mr. Pine's guards.

"You can't bring outside campaign tokens into the rally," he said. "All such gifts must have prior approval."

He reached for Fatima's satchel, but Ms. Wilkins stepped in the way, and his fingers glanced off her shoulder. "Watch it, big guy." She stabbed a finger at him. "Assaulting old ladies at a senior center isn't a good look for you or your boss."

He stepped back, hands in the air. "I didn't mean—"

"What you *meant* to do doesn't matter." Ms. Wilkins pinched my elbow and gave me a shove. I took her hint, grabbed Fatima's wrist, and pulled her into the crowd. "What did happen is that you were being careless. Why, I ought to…" The din of the crowd swallowed the rest of Ms. Wilkins's threats as Fatima and I retreated.

"You think that was a coincidence?" Fatima rasped in my ear. "Ms. Wilkins showed up at just the right moment and helped us get away."

I was wondering the same thing, speculating that Grandma Winnie had enlisted extra help. "I don't know, but Pine's guards are onto us now. We've got to hurry and hand the rest of these out before he catches us again."

Fatima and I split up, each taking half of the dozen remaining bracelets, and agreed to meet again near the Senior Center's main entrance when we'd finished. My heart throbbed in my throat, adrenaline burned through my veins, and my neck was sore from constantly looking over my shoulder, but I managed to complete a sprint through the crowd, distributing the last of my bracelets without interruption. Searching the room for Fatima's patriotic red-and-blue headscarf, I hurried to our meeting spot and waited for her, stomach twisting and turning with worry.

Was it enough? Had we made a difference?

Panting as though she'd finished a race, Fatima burst through the crowd and hurried to my side. "I'm done. Pine's guard spotted me, but I dodged him. Maybe we should go now?"

Taking her hand, I guided her to the door. "*You* go. You've risked enough already. Go home and pray. I'm going to stay."

"There's a vigil at the mosque. Why don't you come with me?" She snorted drolly. "My mom would love that."

"No." I shook my head. "I want to see this through to the end—whatever happens."

"Don't do anything dumb."

I hugged Fatima, sucked in a reassuring breath of her jasmine perfume, and let her go. "I'll text you when it's over. We can meet for milkshakes at the Dew Drop."

Nodding, Fatima backed through the door and disappeared into the gloom of the night as the crowd roared, cheering as Buford Pine took the stage.

"Good evening, ladies and gentlemen." He threw his arms out wide. "Looks like every citizen of Faffton is here tonight. Well... every citizen who counts, anyway. *My* kind of people." Several folks whistled and hooted. "I definitely have the biggest crowd, right? The biggest and the best. My opponents, they *wish* they could draw a crowd like this one."

He started with talking points about re-opening the Debra Camp coal mine. Because his goons had "escorted" Grandma and me out before I'd heard his speech at the mine last week, I listened closely. But he didn't get far before someone in the crowd interrupted. An arm accessorized with one of my bracelets jutted into the air and waved to catch his attention. "Mr. Pine? Mr. Pine?"

Pine stopped and glared at the speaker, who had a head full of tight blue-tinted curls. Loretta McMahon, if I had to guess. "Mr. Pine, you mentioned international funding before, in your other speech at Debra Camp. Winnie Banks asked where that funding was coming from, and you never answered, but I want to know, too!"

A murmur of support rolled through the crowd. A red stain crept up Buford Pine's neck into his ears. "I'll issue a press release after the election is over, and it will include all the details. And, folks, how about holding your questions until the end of the speech, okay?" Pine glanced at one of his guards. The man nodded, heeding some unspoken command. He eased through the crowd as Pine continued his speech.

He switched to the subject of establishing new cooperation with federal immigration authorities. At the same time, Pine's security guard reached Loretta McMahon's side. The guard tapped her shoulder and gestured to something below eyesight. Ms. McMahon raised her arm, revealing her bracelet. He held out an open palm, obviously demanding she hand it over. She shook her head. He furrowed his brow in a way that made me think of a bull pawing the ground, preparing to charge at a waving red flag.

"Mr. Pine!" This interruption came from Marcus Byrne, a decorated

Vietnam War vet who presided over the local VFW chapter. "Ms. Abadi runs the community food pantry, and her husband does my taxes for free. Says he gives me the veteran discount for serving my country. You sayin' you want to let the Feds come in here and tell us how to handle our business with our own neighbors?"

The red in Pine's ears and neck crept into his cheeks. No longer trying for subtlety, he stabbed a finger at Mr. Byrne. "Him too. All of them. They're all under *her* influence."

My gaze shot back to Pine's security guard, who was still trying to convince Loretta McMahon to hand over her bracelet. He gave up on diplomacy, grabbed her wrist, and tugged off the bracelet. She shouted a startled protest. Others in the crowd shoved the security guard. He responded by reaching for more wrists, tugging off more bracelets. The rest of Pine's security guards joined in. The room filled with a chorus of shouts and screams.

Horrified, I watched as our careful planning fell apart. My mind raced to devise a solution, to figure out a way to restore order, but the chaos was overwhelming. Desperate, angry tears burned in my eyes.

What do I do? What do I do?

As panic and indecision flood through me, the main entrance door beside me flew open. A draft of cold fresh air blew into the room, followed by my grandmother adorned in a glittering golden shawl hanging nearly to her feet. Her eyes blazed, even though she appeared frailer and more exhausted than ever before. Still, relief surged through me as I grabbed her shoulder. If anyone knew what to do, it would be her. "Grandma, why are you here? This wasn't part of our plan."

She gently pushed me aside. "I'm doing what needs to be done. Where's your mother?"

"She couldn't get away from work. She said she'd be here, but she'd be late."

Grandma nodded and started toward the stage.

"You can't." I grabbed her shoulder. "You're in no shape—"

"Lucy!" She turned those blazing eyes on me, and I froze like a baby bunny in the presence of a sharp-toothed fox. "I might be old, and I might be weary, but I am *still* your grandmother. Do you understand?"

I bowed my head. "Yes, ma'am."

Nodding, she strode forward, and like Moses approaching the Red Sea, the ocean of people between her and Buford Pine parted. Even Pine's security guards fell back as if shoved by a great, invisible hand. As she advanced on the platform, she unwound her golden shawl, and it unfurled like a cape. No... a net, spreading wide as she launched it through the air. Its golden strands stretched and dropped over Buford Pine's head. It spilled over his shoulders and hung to his knees.

The room stilled and fell utterly silent.

I held my breath, every muscle tense.

"Enough, Buford Pine." Grandma climbed a short set of steps and joined Pine on the stage. "For once in your life, you're going to tell the truth."

Like a trapped animal, he roared, baring his teeth, and tugged on the golden netting. Grandma Winnie, tiny, withered, and with what seemed like twice as many gray hairs and wrinkles as she'd had just a few days before, launched herself at her nemesis. Together, they struggled with the net, but he was clearly the stronger of the two, and she was losing the fight. He threw his weight against Grandma. She stumbled back, fell to her rear, cried out, and didn't get back up. He wrestled with the golden net and slowly inched his way toward freedom.

My muscles unfroze. I gasped, an inaudible expression of alarm. Without thinking or taking my Grandmother's warnings into heed, I raced to the stage and grabbed one side of the golden shawl. Grandma, now kneeling, took the other. Together, we held it taught over Buford Pine as he wriggled and thrashed but failed to escape.

"Tell us the truth," Grandma demanded, even though her voice was frail and weak. "Is Buford Pine even your real name?"

Pine roared. He spat out his answer through a clamped jaw, as if he could keep the words in by force. "Joseph Shroff. My name is Joseph Shroff."

"And how many other names do you have?"

"Arrrgh!" He tried ripping the thin gold threads near his face and neck. Grandma Winnie gritted her teeth, closed her eyes, and swayed, but the strands held. Her strength was draining fast. How much longer would she last? "I don't know." He snarled. "I lost count. Maybe a dozen or more."

He rolled his shoulders, trying to shake me off. I held on like a baby possum, and Grandma Winnie stuck him with another question. "Where have your campaign funds been coming from? I know they aren't all local donations. Are you getting support from your Debra Camp investors?"

He growled.

"I can't hear you."

"Yes."

"Foreign money?"

"Yes!"

"You didn't report them on your campaign finance reports."

"Of course not, you idiot." Pine exhaled and stopped struggling. "Foreign donations are illegal."

Shock reverberated through the crowd in loud huffs and sharp whispers.

"How'd you convince them to let you register after the deadline?"

"I bribed George Benson."

The crowd gasped again and turned, almost in unison, to face George Benson, chairman of the elections board. He stood in the crowd, left of center stage, wringing his hands, biting his lips, and looking like he might cry. Or run. I would've put my money on crying, though.

"Do you even live in Faffton?" I asked.

"If sleeping in the office of my car dealership counts as living here."

"Pay municipal taxes?" Someone shouted from the audience.

"Not a penny."

Danny Baylor, Sheriff of Faff County, climbed the stage's steps and crouched next to Grandma Winnie. He put his arms around her and helped her to her feet. I shoved myself between them, taking his place as her support post. Sheriff Baylor glared at Buford Pine, or Joseph Shroff, or whoever he was. "I think it's best if you come with me." His gaze shifted to Grandma Winnie. "Would you remove the, uh, net?"

"Sheriff," Pine whined. "Arrest that woman. She *assaulted* me."

Sheriff Baylor rolled his eyes, obviously dismissing Pine's lame accusations. He glanced at Grandma Winnie and jerked his chin. She tugged her shawl loose, freeing her prisoner. I pointed at Sheriff Baylor's wrist and the bracelet he still wore. "Sheriff, do us a favor and don't take that off for a while, okay?"

His brow wrinkled, bushy blond brows touching. "Hmm. If you say so."

"Listen to my granddaughter," Grandma Winnie said. "She knows what she's talking about."

The sheriff left the stage, towing his captive behind him. "Mr. Benson." He pointed at the quivering Board of Elections chairman. "I wouldn't leave town if I were you."

George Benson bobbed his bald head and watched the sheriff lead his former mayoral candidate out of the senior center and into the night.

Moments after they'd left, my mom burst through the front door and strode into the room, brown curls tumbling loose from her bun. Noticing the still semi-stunned crowd around us, she stopped and set her hands on her hips. She spotted Grandma Winnie and me, leaning against each other on the stage, and cocked her head to the side. "So... what did I miss?"

Grandma Winnie's strength gave out. I caught her, and both of us slid to the stage floor in a boneless pile of hysterical laughter.

On the ride home from the Faffton Senior Center, Grandma Winnie fell asleep and didn't wake again, even when Mom and I put her to bed. I kept vigil at her bedside whenever I wasn't at school or recovering my own strength, and Grandpa Mac and I roused her occasionally to help her sip some water, chug a protein shake, or visit the bathroom. Almost a whole week passed before she permanently rejoined the waking world, and I happened to be sitting in her window seat, yarn and knitting needles in hand, cursing under my breath at a particularly infuriating pattern when she sat up, stretched, and groaned when her back popped.

"Well," she said, "I've had enough of this lying around, and I think my back agrees." I dropped my knitting and rushed to her side, offering her my arm as she climbed out of bed. She clung to me as she stretched again, evoking another pop, this time from her hip. "Lord, please let that be the last time I play superhero. My old bones can't take it anymore."

"Don't say that." I helped her tug on her house coat and dug out her slippers from under the bed. "You were so awesome, and our plan never would have worked if you hadn't been there to save the day. And besides..." I sighed heavily as I led her downstairs to the kitchen, where the smell of coffee filled the air. Grandpa Mac must have heard us moving around and made a fresh pot before disappearing, presumably, into his workshop. "We might've won the battle, but I'm not sure the war's over."

"Oh?" she asked as I helped her settle at the kitchen table and went to pour her a cup of coffee. "What have I missed?"

"Buford Pine escaped, and no one knows where he is."

Grandma clicked her tongue and frowned, but she didn't seem at all surprised.

"People were protesting his arrest, calling it a witch hunt or something like that." I shook my head, unable to comprehend how people could deny the truths they'd heard with their own ears. Like they *wanted* to believe the lies. "I'm glad he's gone, but I'm a little worried he'll come back."

I set a full coffee mug on the table before her. She patted my hand. "He won't come back. He's done this before and just keeps moving so he doesn't get caught."

"So, Pine gets away with it?"

"A knitter hates to leave loose ends, Lucy Goose, but in this situation, I'm afraid it's something we'll have to accept."

Unsatisfied by her answer, I furrowed my brow and huffed.

"That doesn't mean you and I are"—she waggled her eyebrows—"*off the hook*, though."

"Ugh. Was that a crochet pun?"

Grandma snickered and pointed at the ceiling. "Go upstairs and get that yarn you were working on."

Never one to disobey my grandmother—okay, *rarely* one to disobey—I backed toward the staircase. "Why? What are we going to do with it?"

"Pine might be gone, but his followers aren't, and they're the ones I'm more worried about anyway." Grandma sipped her coffee. "Christmas is almost here, and those folks are on the top of our gift list. You and I have *a lot* of knitting to do."

THE HARDWICKE FILES: THE CASE OF THE FULL MOON

RUSS COLCHAMIRO

KILLERS, RAPISTS, EXTORTIONISTS, PLANET HOPPERS, shape-shifters, and galaxy thieves are just a few of the unsavory characters I've tangled with as an intergalactic private investigator.

But none of those encounters have been as excruciating as the interview I've just started and already regret.

The wide, watermelon-fresh hallways scream with color of every tint and hue, while, on the other side of a glass partition, is a level of shrieking pandemonium even someone as well-traveled as I am—on-realm and off— is not well suited to deal with.

"Thank you for coming in, Miss... uh... Hardwicke," says Delilah Tulowitzki, the daycare center's fifty-something Director. Though heavily wrinkled for her age, it's clear she was a real beauty in her day. "After you've had a chance to inspect our facility, I'm sure you'll find that Full Moon Daycare will be"—she clears her throat, trying not to choke on her words as she quickly glances at me, adorned in my pinstripe suit and fedora—"the ideal place for your son."

The good news is that Full Moon's owner, Wayne Chrebet—a former client who should and does feel indebted to me—has all but assured a spot for Owen, if I want it.

The bad news is that, as much as I don't want it, I kinda need it.

Being a private eye in Eternity—the cosmic realm responsible for the design, construction, and maintenance of the Universe—and being a single mother with a two-year-old boy, are not quite simpatico.

"Ah, Angela, I was wondering if you'd gotten here," says Chrebet, an ebony prince of a man in a sharp suit, who, a few quirks aside—including the young, bronze-skinned woman practically epoxied to his side—is exactly the kind of warm-hearted adult you'd want running a daycare center. "I trust Miss Tulowitzki is giving you the grand tour. And this lovely go-getter is Tamima Argyris. She joined us about two years ago as Assistant Director. She's learning the ropes from Miss Tulowitzki."

"Oh, yes," interjects Argyris, whose over-enthusiastic handshake fails to cloak her nervousness. "No one can speak for Full Moon Daycare like Miss Tulowitzki."

"I am delighted you understand that none other *than* me, can speak *for* me, with more eloquence and sophistication than I can," Tulowitzki imposes. "My apologies, Miss Hardwicke. One must tolerate the impetuousness of youth. What they lack in self-awareness they more than make up for with a boundless sense of entitlement."

"Oh, yes, well, we were all young once," Chrebet says with a smile. "Speaking of youth, how are things with Owen? Is he looking forward to Full Moon?"

"He's more of a handful than I anticipated," I say, realizing that Owen managed to re-upholster my jacket collar this morning with an impressive wad of his yellow mucous. "And he's certainly not shy about telling me every few seconds or so what we should be doing next and how soon that activity should begin."

"Then he indeed sounds like a healthy two-year-old! I'd love to accompany you on the rest of your tour, but I'm afraid Miss Argyris and I have another meeting on the books. The children are heading out to the Winslow Butterfly exhibit, so if you value a quiet afternoon, you've picked the right day to visit. Miss Tulowitzki, I trust you'll show Miss Hardwicke the rest of the facility? We very much want Owen to be part of the Full Moon family. And nothing helps our parents feel more at ease than your guiding hand."

"Yes, of course." Tulowitzki steels herself, studying Chrebet and the ingénue executive as they march away, side by side, hands swinging a bit closer than you would anticipate. "If we are not here for the children, then I am not sure why we are here at all."

The awkward powerplay over for now, Tulowitzki introduces me to a handful of Full Moon staff as a delivery boy turns down the hallway with a bundle of balloons. Must be a daily occurrence. She shows me the small and large auditoriums, four outdoor playgrounds, art room, galaxy-viewing platform, indoor pools, cafeteria, and nurse's (and nursing) station.

Adorning the walls are triumphant aphorisms, paint-splattered handprints, and collages of children's faces. It's as if they're all cackling at me. Because they know I don't really belong in a place like this.

Which is no surprise, because no one finds it more difficult than me to accept that it is actually me, Angela Hardwicke, Private Eye, walking these very halls, inspecting the facilities as a mom. As Owen's mom.

But now that he's as mobile as a shooting star, I can't piecemeal it anymore. I need a regular routine for him so I can go slinking around in the darkness, sticking my nose into places it's usually unwanted.

"How long have you been with Full Moon?" I ask Tulowitzki as we trundle down the winding staircase from the second floor back down to the first.

"Thirty-three years next week. I have been here with Wayne... Mr. Chrebet... since before Full Moon was even open," she says with a hint of nostalgia, unconsciously pawing at the pearl-inlaid broach pinned to her peach blouse, just above her heart. "We met at the Aerial Diner on Fenmore Street every day for months, just the two of us, reviewing blueprints and mapping out our shared vision for Full Moon. We were both so young then, me a bit more than him, but it was just he and I, in the trenches together, as it is said. We were on-site every day during the design and construction of this very facility, and during each phase of expansion."

Just the two of them. Interesting. Let's see where this takes us.

"You must feel especially connected to Full Moon," I say as we look into the Galaxy Bounce, a gymnasium-style room, where a dozen children are hopping from one galaxy-shaped pod to another. "Not much room for a social life, I suppose?"

"I have always felt that Full Moon deserves nothing less than my undivided attention. Although that did not stop Mr. Chrebet. He has been married to Alana far as long as I have known him. But marriage is not for me. Full Moon has been my life. Is my life. It is quite... rewarding," she says with a sigh, revealing a hint of sadness, perhaps lamenting the many years gone by. "I would not have had it any other way. Nor will I."

As she opens the galaxy bounce door, in my mind's eye I can see Owen here, now, with me, giggling and bouncing and making friends in a way only he can do. I barely notice the remaining children have been shuttled over to the off-site butterfly event. It's amazing how quickly the room has gone silent.

"The board of directors is rather aggressively pushing Mr. Chrebet to sign off on another phase of expansion." Tulowitzki points to an arched wall earmarked for demolition as an entrance to a new, proposed wing. "But he has not yet fully embraced the idea."

I'm about to comment when someone knocks me over from behind.

"Mr. Brower!" Tulowitzki scolds. "Please be careful. Help Miss Hardwicke up."

"Oh, hey, I'm so sorry," says a husky, middle-aged man, in his brown janitor's uniform. "I was in a hurry to fix the multi-dimensional mirror outside the Nebula Terrace. Are you all right, ma'am?"

I look to Tulowitzki, who herself seems confused—and annoyed. Until I realize I'm the *ma'am* he's referring to. I hate that.

"Yeah, no worries. I get knocked down more often than you'd think. This was the softest landing I've had in years." The janitor reaches down, helping me back up on my feet. He's got quite a grip. "I'm fine."

"Why don't we visit the music room," Tulowitzki says, gesturing to the double doors on the opposite end of the hallway. "It's exceptional."

"No," Brower says a bit aggressively. "Not the music room. Y-y-you can't."

Tulowitzki shoots a glare at the janitor that could strip the tail off a scorching comet. "Why don't you... visit the upstairs playroom?" she offers me. "I need a word with Mr. Brower."

"Not on my account, I hope."

Tulowitzki almost, but not quite, recalibrates that glare to a point right between my eyes. "As much as I've enjoyed our tour, Miss Hardwicke, I do have other business to attend to."

Brower gives me a sympathetic eye roll.

"Yes," I say with half a smile. "I'm sure you do."

I can't help but be oversensitive to Full Moon's mini-dramas. It's an occupational hazard. But I try not to let them influence me too much. If I look hard enough, every daycare center I'd even consider will have its share—and then some.

After spending a bit more time wandering around, I make my way toward Chrebet's office. I'm about to head down the hallway when a board member I know, Archie Forsythe, dressed in blue jeans and a black blazer, comes running up to me. He's wearing a pale, harried look on his face.

"Angela," he demands as the scent of freshly baked pizza rolls taunts me from the cafeteria. "Come with me."

"Why? Is there a missing rattle in the playroom? I'll bust out my fingerprint kit."

"No," he says, his face revealing ravines of fear and distress. "It's Wayne Chrebet. He's dead."

Between puffy stratocumulus clouds, sunlight shimmies through the custom-designed concave window of Chrebet's second-floor office, overlooking Ditmar Boulevard. His office is a bit larger than necessary, but that's Chrebet for you. He always loved attention.

The walls are lined with framed photos of him with politicians, prominent parents, movie stars, and, perhaps not a surprise, Brigsby, the host of *Breakfast with Brigsby*, the most popular daytime talk show in Eternity.

Directly in front of the window and opposite his private bathroom, Chrebet's in his desk chair, head slumped forward—with a diamond-studded letter opener sticking out of his chest.

I slip on a pair of comet-coated disposable gloves I always keep in my jacket, then feel for a pulse. "He's dead. No doubt."

"I just can't believe it," Forsythe says, standing in front of a bookshelf lined with more plaques and awards than actual books. "What if the children see?"

"See what?" Tulowitzki barges into the office like she owns the place. "What are you... oh, no! Wayne! What's happened?"

"I don't know," I say. "But..." Quickly scanning the area around Chrebet's desk for a clue, I find a rather important one. His protégé, Tamima Argryis, is unconscious on the plush carpet. She's sprawled out behind the high-backed cottage chair next to his oak-and-glass desk, with a welt on her forehead. "Archie, call the police. Ask for Detective Lionel Tarrish. Tell him it's at my request. He won't like it, but he'll come. And tell him to bring an ambulance. Also... no one in or out of Full Moon. We're going to be here a while."

"Wait, no," Forsythe says as he peeks through the window, from the side, likely to avoid detection. "No police. Not yet. We can't let the story get out. We have to control the narrative."

"Control the narrative? Are you...? Right. I forgot. You're in public relations. So let me lay it out for you. Wayne Chrebet has been murdered, Argyris has been attacked, both in his office, and we don't know who did what to whom, or why, or if they did it to each other. And unless Miss Tulowitzki has misinformed me, which I seriously doubt, you have one hundred twenty-three children under your care right now, who, by coincidence, planning, or incredible timing, are all off-site. And you're telling me you *don't* want to call the police?"

A clearly shaken Tulowitzki turns to Forsythe, who, given the dead body, is under control.

"That's exactly what I'm saying. We are in the unique position to have you, a private investigator, here, on the premises. And unless *I'm* mistaken, you're one of the best."

Well, he's got me there. "I'm listening."

"We can lock down the facility without raising suspicion. No one in or out, as you said. Maybe a half-hour or so. That should give you enough time to figure it out."

"This is outrageous," Tulowitzki says indignantly. But then her expression phases from shock to sadness, and, as her ambassadorial instincts reignite, to one far more contemplative. "Although, Mr. Forsythe is correct.

We do not want to startle any children who may not have gone on the excursion, nor have the facility flooded with parents, police, or, heaven forbid... the media. No. I agree with Mr. Forsythe. As much as it pains me, we must close our ranks. We must protect the integrity of Full Moon."

"I'm thrilled you have that much faith in me, and the concern for your employer is heartwarming. But a half-hour's not going to cut it."

"It's going to have to," Forsythe says. "And we *are* concerned about Wayne. He's one of the best men I've ever known. But if the police wind up surrounding this building, his life becomes a scandal, and we'll all be out of business. Permanently."

"With what's happened in this room," I say, "maybe that's for the best."

Forsythe and Tulowitzki seem to share the same brain on this one, both glaring at me with the intensity of a solar flare.

"Solve now, lecture later," Forsythe says. "You're an expert in your field. But so am I. And there are tried and true tenets of crisis communications. Take a breath, close ranks, assess the situation, and make calm, calculated decisions based on what is most critical."

"Assess and decide?" I eye him, Tulowitzki, and my dead former client, and wonder if I should just throw them to wolves. But the thing is... I just can't help myself. "Okay, then. Let's get to work."

I've investigated hundreds of cases over the years, but this is my first one in a daycare center. Unless you count that time on Selpha Prime. What a bunch of babies. Literally. The entire planet.

"All right," I say, "but first things first. Call the nurse and, calmly, ask her to come up. But instruct her not to speak to anyone. Second... until or unless I deem otherwise... both of you are suspects."

"Suspects?" Tulowitzki and Forsythe cry in unison.

"Why would *I* kill Wayne?" he asks incredulously.

"I have no idea. Where were you a half-hour ago? The murder is fresh."

Forsythe looks at Tulowitzki ruefully, then to me. "I was in the conference room, on the phone with... a client. If it comes to it, my client can confirm."

"It might," I say. "We'll call you cleared. For now. And you, Ms. Tulowitzki?"

Eyes puffy, she squares her shoulders, raises her chin. The back of her leg grazes the white leather couch nearest to the door.

"Do not insult me with your uninformed accusations, Miss Hardwicke. You cannot know how devastating this is."

"You're right. I don't know. And I'm sure this *is* devastating. Although probably, and I know I'm going out on a limb here, more for your boss than for you. Nevertheless... where were you a half-hour ago?"

"I will not dignify that," she starts, then, after gripping one hand in the other, as if to crush her humiliation into oblivion, exhales a sigh of acquiescence. "I was in the ladies' room. Attending to my... changes."

I have never once wanted to be a man, but being a woman is, at times, an absolute drag.

"Hello, excuse me," we hear with a knock on the other side of the door. "It's me, Esme."

"The nurse," Tulowitzki says.

I go to the door, bring her in quickly, then shut the door behind her.

"What do you...?" she starts, then gasps.

She rushes over to Chrebet, confirming his death, then tends to Argyris.

As she does, I inspect Chrebet's desk, mostly clear other than a laptop computer, a framed photo of him and his wife, a silver pen, a white marble paperweight in the shape of a full moon with the daycare's logo inscribed on it, and an oak paper tray.

I glance at the top sheet and, seeing its relevance, read all the way through. I then kneel down to inspect the small garbage can by the desk. I don't find much, but underneath the desk is a crumpled sheet of paper. I palm it without being noticed, then squirrel it into my pocket.

"Mr. Brower?" I say, studying the first letter I found. "That's the janitor, correct?"

"Yes," Tulowitzki confirms.

"Did you know he has a gambling problem?"

"*I* didn't," Forsythe says. "Does that have something to do with—?"

"It's his termination letter. It says he'd been warned about a gambling issue, and it's recurred. Miss Tulowitzki, I'm assuming you knew about this?"

She takes the letter from me, sighs. "Yes. Douglas has been with Full Moon for about ten years. He stole some petty cash a while back and lost it in a poker game. Mr. Chrebet was going to terminate Douglas then, but I… talked him out of it. I suggested we get Douglas into a recovery program for his addiction and give him a second chance. He had been… clean… I think is the proper term, for the last three years. But he relapsed just this week. Mr. Chrebet told me he planned to terminate Douglas this time, no matter how hard I protested, so I did not fight it. Do you think…?" She cups her mouth. "Am I to blame for this? Did my fighting to save his job cost Wayne his life? Oh, no…"

"That's a leap," I say. "But this letter is motive. I'll need to speak with Douglas. Archie… can you get him in here?"

"You want me to *look* for him?"

"No, text him. But I need to ask you something first."

I pull Forsythe aside, then make a request. He looks at me nervously, indignantly. But after some protests, he agrees.

"Did you see this?" Esme says. Gently, she lifts Chrebet's slumped head. "Here. On his neck, below the chin. Scratches."

On his left side are, in fact, three long scratches in his neck.

"Those are deep," I say, then kneel down to inspect Argyris's hands. "Look here. There's some blood and what looks like skin under her fingernails."

"*She* killed Wayne?" Forsythe says. "Was it self-defense? Or were they… having an affair? "

We all instinctively look to Tulowitzki.

"They had been… together quite a bit," she starts, shaken by the question. "More so over the last few months. But that would be so unlike Mr. Chrebet. He was… happily married."

"Was he *really?*"

Tulowitzki doesn't answer.

"He was," Forsythe insists. "At least… I thought so. But if not… did they have a lover's quarrel? Here? In the office? What about the janitor?"

"Not sure," I say. "That's why I need him here."

"I can't believe this," Doug Brower says. "When? How? I mean… I just saw him."

"Yes," Tulowitzki says. "You did."

"What's that supposed to mean?"

"Ask her," Tulowitzki deflects, looking in my direction. "Show him the letter."

"What letter?" the janitor asks.

"Doug. I'm a private investigator. I'm looking into what's happened to Wayne Chrebet and Tamima Argyris."

"Looking into... what? You think *I* did this?"

"We don't know what happened. But we found this."

He reads the letter.

"What? No. This isn't right. It's not..."

"You did it," Forsythe says. "It *was* you."

"No. NO! I didn't do this. Me and Mr. Chrebet. We... we worked it out. It wasn't right. It was a mistake."

"What mistake?" I ask.

Doug looks around the room, over at Chrebet's dead body, then sits on the couch, facing the desk and the window behind it. "Okay," he says. "Okay. I did it."

"You what?" Tulowitzki says.

"No, no, no, no. Not the murder. No. Never. I wouldn't! I couldn't! No, I..." Doug sighs, his face tightening up. "That was our deal. No gambling, ever, or I was gone. He heard that I'd made a bet with... Esme." He nods to the nurse. "We bet... damn it... we bet that..."

"We bet on whether he'd ask me out before Astropalooza," Esme says, referring to the celebration of the Universe. "I told him not to keep a girl waiting. He swore he'd ask. So we bet on it."

"Is that what happened, Doug? You bet on a *date?*"

He nods silently. "All Mr. Chrebet heard was that I'd made a bet, so I was fired. But I told him what happened. He was so angry, he didn't believe me at first. But we talked it out. He told me he believed me; he just needed to confirm with Esme."

"Did he?" I ask.

"He texted me earlier," Esme says. "He asked me to stop by. I was going to but... I was with a child."

"So you never told him?"

She shakes her head *no*.

"So as far as we know," I say to Doug, "Chrebet never confirmed your story, leaving you in the lurch."

His face puckers, eyes welling with tears. "I guess not."

"Then he did it," Forsythe demands. "It was Doug."

Tulowitzki, Esme, Forsythe, and Doug all put their eyes on me. I let the thought linger. "No," I say finally. "I don't think he did."

My friends all told me I'm too untrusting for daycare, that I'd invent reasons to reject any center just so I could say *I told you so*.

They won't believe me when I tell them what I've walked into. Then again, cases like this seem to find me wherever I go, even when I'm actually being open-minded for a change. Daycare might be good for Owen. He needs more friends.

"The client call you were on?" I say to Forsythe, who had seemed a bit too hesitant when I asked him about it earlier. "It wasn't a client, was it?"

He eyes me suspiciously, resentfully. "It was."

"But what *kind* of client?"

Tulowitzki, Esme, and Doug shift their focus to Forsythe. He doesn't answer. So I answer for him.

"It was a real estate attorney, wasn't it? You wanted to force an expansion of the facility. I checked. You're a partial investor in two more buildings on this block. If Full Moon expands, the value of your other properties will increase by, what... ten percent?"

"You killed him over the real estate?" Tulowitzki huffs. "Wayne wasn't ready to expand. He wanted to ensure we could hire additional staff and train them properly, so there would not be any disruption to the children. You just couldn't wait your turn, could you, Archibald? You never think of anyone but yourself. I'm going to be ill."

"Is that true?" Esme says, her lip quivering as she re-checks Argyris's pulse. "He was so good to us."

Forsythe shakes his head. "I..."

"You did make the call," I say, regretting that I don't have my usual complement of gun, taser, and switchblade on me. I knew this interview would be treacherous. I just didn't think it would turn deadly. "You wanted to force Chrebet's hand."

Forsythe goes to the window. He stares out over the boulevard as the cars, cabs, buses, hover-scooters, and pedestrians bustle along, as if he's mourning the loss of an empire that never was.

Without him noticing, I snag a silver pen off Chrebet's desk and extend the tip, in case I need to act quickly.

Forsythe turns back to me. "I did. Yes. Wayne was so stubborn! Land prices are soaring. Labor prices, too. And thanks to Astropalooza, they won't be coming down any time soon. If we don't lock in an expansion plan now, we'll miss our window. So, yes. I called a real estate attorney. But there was nothing to be done. Delaying was the wrong decision, but it was Wayne's to make."

"One worth killing over?" I say.

Agitated, red-faced, Forsythe looks as if he's ready to confess. "I was angry, okay? We worked on the expansion for two years. Two *years*! You can't believe the hoops I had to jump through to line up extra investors. And yes, my other properties would've increased in value. So what? Is it a crime to make money? Full Moon would've been incredible. More incredible. But he didn't see it that way. Some things, he said, needed to stay the same, for even a bit longer. He decided to make other changes, big changes." Surrendering his fury, Forsythe's speaking more gently now. "And he didn't think it would be fair to sign off on such a big project right now."

I retract the silver pen. "But you didn't kill him over it, did you?"

Forsythe's eyes drift toward the window again, then back to me. "No," he sighs. "I didn't."

"What?" Esme says. "Then who did?"

I check my phone for an incoming email, which includes the information I was looking for. "I'm still not sure. But I'm about to find out."

I take my own quick glance out the window. I can see, off in the distance, flashing police lights headed down the boulevard. They're on their way.

"Doug," I say, startling all, including Doug himself, who looks like he's about to stroke out. "Earlier, when Miss Tulowitzki suggested we see the music room, you said we couldn't. Why not?"

Caught in a moment, he's not sure what to say. "We weren't... Mr. Chrebet told us not to..."

"Doug," Forsythe says, "was it the...?"

Doug nods.

"I guess it doesn't matter now," Forsythe says. "We were throwing a party. It was supposed to be a surprise."

"And it was," I say, "wasn't it... Miss Tulowitzki?"

She stiffens.

"You weren't expecting a retirement party, were you? Even after thirty-three years, you thought you'd stay here forever."

"I have no idea what... you can't..."

I unfold the paper I'd snagged from the trash. I read aloud:

> *As a young man, I had only one ambition, to open a daycare center where children could learn to dream. But I was too full of my own dreams, without a means to make them come true. But one woman, more than any other, helped me bring them to life. Janel... Miss Tulowitzki... you forced me to focus, when my mind would wander. You kept me anchored when I felt unmoored. You were the great star that held my orbit in place. Without you, the only full moons I'd really know were the ones I see in the night sky.*

Tulowitzki's eyes get wet.

> *So it is only fitting that today, of all days, we honor you... for all you have done for Full Moon. But as with all good things, this too must come to an end. So please join me in congratulating Miss Tamima Argyris, who will endeavor to fill the biggest shoes of all.*

I take a step closer. "But that's what you found out, didn't you, Miss Tulowitzki? Doug had been sworn to secrecy, like they all were. But then you found his termination letter. Well, his supposed termination, and leveraged him to tell you what was going on in that room. A retirement party."

Doug nods. "I had no choice."

"But why be so upset about a surprise party?" I say. "Unless... you didn't want to retire at all. Not what you expected, Miss Tulowitzki? Was it?"

Her lips curdle, eyes drawn into a death stare. Her jaw trembles. "He had no *right*! Full Moon would be nothing without me. *I* held this place together. *I* made sure the children were well cared for. *I* worked my fingers to the bone. He spent his days having lunches and nights on the town. And then…"

"Miss Argyris joined Full Moon," I say, "and suddenly you weren't Chrebet's number one girl, anymore. He'd found someone younger, someone more energized… to take over. The next generation."

"Full Moon is mine!" Tulowitzki snarls. "I should've been promoted, not forced into retirement!"

"You weren't… being forced out," Argyris mumbles, barely conscious, shaky but awake. Esme helps her into the chair. "*Wayne* was retiring… not you. That was the surprise. You were going to be the next P… President of Full Moon. And I was going to work for you. I *wanted* to work for you because… you're the most dedicated, loyal, respected woman I know."

"W-w-what?" Tulowitzki says. "He was… I was going to be…?"

"You found a *draft* of his speech," I say. "Forsythe got me access to Chrebet's computer. I found the newest version. He finished it today. You can see for yourself. It's lovely."

I have a copy sent to the desktop printer. The sheet spits out. I hand it Tulowitzki. Her arms fall.

"Then what about the scratch on his neck?" Forsythe says. "And her head?"

"From what I can surmise, Miss Tulowitzki confronted Chrebet about the speech, and before he could explain, she became so enraged that she grabbed the letter opener off his desk and stabbed him with it. And then Miss Argyris must have—"

"I came out of the restroom," she says groggily, holding an icepack to her head. "I saw Wayne in his chair, the blood on his chest. And then my world went black."

"Miss Tulowitzki bashed her head with this paperweight." I point to the drops of blood on the bottom of the marble tchotchke. "She assumed—or hoped—that Tamima was dead. Either way, she had to act fast, so she hoisted up Tamima, scratched Chrebet's neck with her limp hand, then put her back on the floor. The scratches are on the left side of Chrebet's neck, but you can see from Tamima's rings that she's left-handed. Scratches would be on his right side. Not realizing the mistake, Miss Tulowitzki printed a copy of Doug's termination letter and left it on top so we'd be likely to see it, throwing us further off the scent. Between the two, there were plenty of viable suspects. But only one killer."

The police arrive. I explain all to Detective Tarrish, who, despite his annoyance that I'd gotten to another crime scene before him, takes Tulowitzki into custody.

"You came through," Forsythe says as we step out onto the sidewalk. "As bad as it is, and I don't know what we'll do without Wayne, it could've been worse. When we re-open, Owen has a spot here for as long as you like."

Classic Forsythe. The spin machine is back in motion. He may get his empire after all.

"Thanks for the offer," I say, then turn up the collar on my pinstripe jacket. "But I think I'll get a nanny."

"COME IN, SIT DOWN, HAVE A BITE!"

PAUL KUPPERBERG

'M THE LAST PERSON IN the world to complain, but when vampires start stalking me in the supermarket, it's time to say something.

"Ma, what makes you think they're vampires?" my son Leo moaned to me when I finally reached him on the phone.

"I don't think. I know. You think I don't know a vampire when I see one?"

"Yeah, okay. But why the grocery store? Have you noticed them anywhere else?"

"No, just there."

"Are you sure they're vampires? I mean, you do live in Williamsburg. They might just be anemic hipsters, wasting away on diets of kale and quinoa. Were they wearing man-buns?"

"Listen, wise-guy, I was hunting vampires before you were born."

He sighed into the receiver. "I know, Ma."

"Before we hung up our wooden stakes and crucifixes, Daddy and I were quite the team, you know."

"You've told me, Ma."

"There was that time Grandpa Jacob was recovering from a werewolf bite, we struck some terror into the vampire community, and that's a fact."

"I know, Ma. You and Pop and your summer of slaughter. There's some biters that are *still* taking that one out on *me*."

I shivered and made a face at the phone. "Don't call it that. You can't slaughter something that's already dead. Anyway, they're filthy creatures." I got up from my seat at the kitchen table and carried my coffee cup to the counter for a refill. "I don't blame Daddy for wanting to go into a different line of work. Grandpa's business wasn't for him."

"Yeah, I think Pop was way happier selling kitchen appliances at Sears than he ever was hunting monsters."

I shrugged as I set down the cup next to the Mr. Coffee. "That was Daddy's way of being a rebel. His father was an internationally famous traveler, adventurer, and monster hunter, so Hal becomes a homebody and department store salesman. You, on the other hand, for as much as you look like your father, you're more like your grandfather."

"Lucky me. Instead of the handsome, *sensible* Persky genes, I inherited the scrawny, crazy ones."

"This again? You're very handsome, darling. Just like your father," I said. "Now, about those vampires…?"

"You could maybe start doing your shopping during the day."

"I work during the day."

"Well, don't supermarkets deliver?"

"Yes, supermarkets deliver," I snapped. "But I'd rather get rid of the problem than have to change my entire way of life. That's why I'm telling this to you, my son, Leo Persky, also known as Terrance Strange, monster hunter extraordinaire, not to mention a columnist for the prestigious *Weekly World News* and the world's foremost investigative journalist in the field of the supernatural—"

"I'm not the *foremost*, Ma… just, maybe, one of the top three. Or two."

"—So, I didn't think a little thing like bloodthirsty vampires following your mother around Foodtown would be a challenge to someone of your knowledge and ability."

Leo must have taken the phone away from his ear because I heard the sound of his heavy sigh from a distance.

That usually meant he was ready to listen to reason. Well, *my* reason.

"Okay, Ma. When's the next time you'll be going shopping?"

My name is Barbara Persky, and the last thing I ever expected was to grow up to be a monster hunter. Not that I wanted a conventional career, whatever that was supposed to mean when I was a student in the 1960s, just as everything was starting to change for women anyway. I mean, I thought I was pretty adventurous for a nice Jewish girl from East Flatbush, then still named Blumenfeld. I was studying archaeology at Brooklyn College and had been on several major digs, but I didn't learn what adventurous really was until my third date with Leo's father, Hal. That was the night we were attacked by a winged harpy while we were on the Wonder Wheel at Coney Island.

Afterward, over a shared order of Nathan's French fries, he opened up about being the youngest son of Terrance Strange (born Jacob Persky, in Russia in 1898), the noted adventurer, traveler, author, and one of mankind's few tireless champions in the war against things they didn't even believe existed. Such as harpies and my vampires.

Me, I didn't have enough sense in those days to come in out of the rain, much less resist a cute, smart, funny boy. Between you, me, and the lamppost, the danger just made him even more attractive. What twenty-year-old archaeology student could resist?

Long story short, we got married and traveled the world hunting monsters and aliens, but after a few years, Hal finally confessed his heart had never really been in the family business. Growing up with the impossible as his normal, he longed for a quiet, drab, uneventful life. I was disappointed at first, but Hal's timing proved to be perfect. The next day, a call from the doctor put an end to my own monster-fighting days on account of pregnancy.

Hal spent the rest of his life content in his role as husband, father, and home goods salesman. Nothing weird or strange ever happened to him again, not until the day he died, aged sixty-four, crushed under a concrete gargoyle that fell from the roof of the Gothic-style church he passed every day on his way to work to sell refrigerators at Sears.

I guess monster-hunting must skip a generation, because Leo decided to go into his grandfather's business when he was still in college. Despite his accomplishments, he was still making jokes about his size and looks at the age of forty-seven, but what counts is he's got the heart of a lion, as much as he likes to pretend otherwise.

And, by the way, yes, I do know that most people believe the *News* is just a silly, fake news supermarket tabloid that makes up things like Bigfoot, Bat Boy, and royal alien babies. I used to believe that too, before I met Hal... and Bigfoot, and Bat Boy, and one of the alien Royals. But that's fine. Let my friends with their doctor and lawyer and MBA children scoff at what my Leo does for a living. I know the truth... and, frankly, I don't think a single one of them would ever be able to sleep without a nightlight on again if they knew what I knew.

As exciting as the old days with Hal had been, that's how predictable and routine my current days had become. Going from globetrotting adventurer to diaper-changing mommy was quite a course change, and I adapted the best I knew how, but as soon as Leo was old enough for school, I got a job. I was almost thirty years old when I applied for the job as assistant staff archeologist at the Brooklyn Museum and had never had an actual job before. But a letter of recommendation from my father-in-law carried a lot of weight in those circles, so I was hired and, more than forty years later, I'm still on the job at the age of seventy-three. It didn't hurt that I went back for my masters and, three years ago, finished my doctorate with a thesis on Biblical-era magical artifacts, just to keep my hand in things. Nowadays, I spend a few hours a day consulting with my (much!) younger colleagues and the rest of the time as a docent, often for donors or special guests.

Anyway, like I was saying, I'm a person who has her routine, but what matters is my evening commute. Regular as clockwork, I leave the Museum at 5:00 pm, walk the less than nine hundred feet to the Eastern Parkway-Brooklyn Museum subway station, take the 2 or 3 train to Atlantic Avenue, where I change to the G-train that I ride out to Metropolitan Avenue. The whole trip, including the walk home from the subway, usually takes under forty minutes.

Still, routine is one thing, but street smarts is another. I'm a lifelong New Yorker, and I've lived here through good times and bad, so even when I'm not paying attention, I'm paying attention. Just because the

Williamsburg neighborhood's been revived and resurrected as a haven for hipsters and expensive coffeehouses doesn't mean you don't still have to be careful. Especially on the subway, where it's not unheard of for some nut to push people onto the tracks. So, you keep an eye open for trouble. That guy mumbling to himself, or that shifty woman slinking from recycling bin to recycling bin, or the tall, bald man in a black overcoat and dark glasses who hasn't stopped staring at you since you spotted him hiding behind a column a dozen yards up the platform at Atlantic Avenue.

He stepped onto the same train as me and, for a second, I toyed with the idea of quickly jumping back off again, just to see if he would follow me. But a casual glance his way convinced me maybe I shouldn't be playing with this fellow. He wasn't your run-of-the-mill subway nut.

This one was a vampire.

Like I told my Leo, I know a vampire when I see one. Most people wouldn't because most people don't believe vampires even exist. If they do experience the "impossible," their "reason" convinces them that what they had witnessed was something else altogether. Something rational, like swamp gas or searchlights reflecting off of clouds.

But the signs were unmistakable, from the pale, slightly grayish pallor to their almost death-like stillness. The biggest giveaway is their eyes. And even though this one was wearing dark glasses, I knew what lurked behind them was a pair of black, flat pools of death. Call it the soul, call it the spark of life, but it was missing.

I didn't know if he had followed me from work or if he had been staking out the platform waiting for me. Like I said, I was a creature of routine. Either was possible. It was late November, and sunset was around four-thirty in the afternoon, so these creatures of the night could move freely about without having to worry about exposure to the deadly daylight.

By now you can tell, I don't like vampires. Of all the creatures we dealt with, they were to me the most repulsive. Vampirism is an infection that needs to be wiped out, like cholera or smallpox; maybe you can't blame the victims for having caught the disease, but they still have to be stopped from spreading it further.

Although, believe it or not, there are vampires who aren't victims of other vampires so much as they are victims of their own stupidity. The fetishists, I call them, the broken children of God-only-knows what sort of abuse who *volunteer* to become members of this hideous cult. Thanks to all the romantic literature, they treat vampirism like a fraternity initiation. They all go into it thinking they're going to become the next Magnus or Lestat, all cool and sexy. I wonder how they react when they find out that in reality, vampires, being dead and with no beating heart to pump blood to any extremities, are sexually *non*functional?

Mr. Dark Glasses was still behind me when I came up onto the street from the subway at Metropolitan Avenue. He kept his distance but never lost sight of me as I walked home. It was rush hour still and the streets were busy so I wasn't too worried about him trying anything. I tried calling Leo, but was sent directly to voicemail, reminding me once again of my son's fraught relationship with electronic devices.

I'll admit, I started to grow a little more concerned once I had to turn off the main thoroughfare and onto the less well-traveled side street my apartment building was on. It was everything I could do to keep from turning around to check on Mr. Dark Glasses, but again, I was counting on being out in public to keep him at bay, and once I got to my building, I would be safe because, thank goodness for small favors, vampires can't enter a person's abode unless bidden to do so.

I was relieved when I finally reached my building and saw that the maintenance staff was still working outside, around the property, finishing a Fall clean-up and tree pruning. They were dragging the debris and trimmed branches around to the rear of the building as I came up the walk to the front door.

I paused and took a casual look around while I pretended to fiddle with my keys. I caught a glimpse of my shadow, his face a smear of ghastly pale against the deeper shadows of a curbside Norway maple across the street. I went inside. After checking my mailbox and taking another quick peek out the door as I passed to the elevator, I went upstairs. Fifth floor. Apartment five-oh-eight.

Safely inside, I took my eye off the ball. In the elevator, I sorted through my mail and let my mind wander to an inventory of what was in the fridge and what I would have for dinner. Then, the elevator dinged and, hardly glancing up, I stepped off.

"Mrs. Persky?"

They were standing on either side of the elevator. The one on my right was a young man in his early twenties, short with brown hair and beard and a complexion the color of dry concrete. He was dressed all in black, but so were half the residents of the neighborhood, including his companion, a woman approaching sixty with a massive pile of fire-red dyed hair spilling around her shoulders. She was the one who had spoken.

"Mrs. Persky?" she said again. "You don't know us, but—"

"I know enough," I said. The elevator started closing behind me. I stepped back into it, stabbing at the close door button. But the boy was fast, and he caught it before it could close.

"Please, we're not going to hurt you," he said.

"How did you get in?" I said. "I didn't invite you in."

"Another resident did, while we were waiting outside."

"Please, it's important we speak to you, Mrs. Persky," the boy said. He took his hand off the elevator door and started to reach for me.

Don't let my age fool you. I still do three hours a week of yoga, two at the gym, and attend weekly Aquanastic classes, not to mention walking several miles a day at the museum. I also attend regular self-defense class updates. Mostly it's to stay healthy, but it was good to keep myself in shape and my skills sharp, just in case, God forbid, I should ever have to defend myself against vampires.

I let out a yell, like Sensei Keith taught us at the Y, accompanied by a driving side kick that caught the boy just below the belt. He grunted and stumbled back, away from the door, but didn't go down. The woman was also reaching for me, so I went low, tucking and rolling under her grasp, thankful I was wearing a pantsuit. When I came to my feet, I swung my purse with both hands like a medieval mace, snapping her head around and giving me time to lurch down the hall toward my apartment, three doors down, on the right.

I was going to feel this is the morning.

If I made it to the morning.

My keys were in my hand, and I had the one for the top lock ready when I got to the door. I didn't look back. That was first thing Hal had taught me: "Don't ever look back. It only slows you down, and it's usually not good news anyway."

Top lock. (I heard them scrambling to their feet behind me.) Next key, bottom lock. (A footfall, down the corridor.) I was surprised at how steady my hands were, even with all the adrenaline pumping through me. I got the key in the lock. (Both on their feet now. They were coming toward me, walking quickly. Not running?) I twisted the key, hearing the satisfying snap of the cylinder sliding home (They were getting closer. Why weren't they running?) and pushed open the door. I almost collapsed through it.

I turned to slam it shut. The woman and the boy were just standing there in the hall, a respectable half a dozen feet from my threshold.

"Please, Mrs. Persky," the young man pleaded. "You're in danger."

I scoffed. "Not as long as I don't invite you in," I said.

"Not from us," the woman said. "From the others."

"Oh, the 'others!' Why didn't you say so?" I shook my head. "Listen, I didn't just fall off a turnip truck, so just go back to Foodtown and tell your friends to forget about it. I don't mean to brag but do you know who I am?"

"Yes, ma'am," the boy said. "You're a slayer from the Summer of Slaughter and the mother of Leo Persky, one of the Guild's greatest enemies."

"If we're such enemies, how come you're trying to save me?"

The woman looked insulted. "Please, Mrs. Persky, just because we're vampires doesn't mean we're monsters."

I picked up the kettle from the stove and said, "Are you sure you don't want anything? Tea? I've got some lovely rugelach from the bakery."

"No, thank you, ma'am. We don't actually, you know... eat," the boy said. He and the woman were sitting across from one another at the small dinette next to the kitchen window. I didn't know what had come over me. Something about the woman's very human indignation had given me pause, and when I'd finally looked in their eyes, instead of empty pools of nothing, I'd seen... people. Against my better judgment, I had let my intuition talk my common sense out of slamming the door in their faces. Instead, I had sighed and stood aside, holding it open wide and saying, "Won't you please enter?"

So, to make a long story short, his name was Joe Thomas, a twenty-one-year-old post-grad student at NYU when he became a vampire, twenty-seven years ago. Her name was Nancy, a fifty-nine-year-old housewife who had turned three years ago. They told me they were both voluntary vampires, choosing to give up life and sunlight rather than endure the lives they had been living.

"I wanted to die," Joe said sadly, "but I was afraid to stop living."

What mother's heart wouldn't break hearing that?

"A lot of us nowadays are nonviolent," Nancy said. "We believe no human should ever be turned against their will or killed to feed us. We feed only on animal blood."

I turned to her in horror. "You don't mean…?"

"No, no, Mrs. Persky. Only the blood of farm animals. You'd be amazed at how many of us are employed on the nightshifts of slaughterhouses, butcher shops, and supermarkets."

"So that's what you were doing at Foodtown," I said.

"Yes, ma'am. We work there. But it was another vampire who works with us who recognized you. He remembered you from the Summer of Slaughter," he said.

"Could we not call it that, please? I mean, you do realize that the entire vampire underground was about to bite the necks of everyone in City Hall and take over the city?"

"We're not blaming you, Mrs. Persky. You were defending your kind," Nancy said. "Now, we're trying to defend ours by keeping you safe. If the Guild does anything to you, your son will declare war. On *all* of us. We've created a quiet, peaceful afterlife for ourselves here. We'd like to keep it that way."

"So, that's why the three of you followed me home?"

Nancy and Joe looked at one another in alarm, then back at me.

"Three?" Joe said.

"Yes. You two and the tall one with the sunglasses watching the building," I said.

They looked at one another again, then simultaneously, and in the same hushed, fearful tone, said, "Marcus."

─────── ••◆•• ───────

This Marcus was not with them after all. He was, in fact, the leader of the local Guild, a close to one-hundred-year survivor of his curse and a fervent believer in the old school Dracula way of vampirism. Stalk them, bite them, and, if you're feeling particularly cruel that day, turn them to share your curse. Close to fifty years after our war with them, he'd somehow recognized me—maybe he'd heard one of the clerks call me by my name—and saw his chance for some revenge served *very* cold.

"Marcus wouldn't do anything while you were at Foodtown that would endanger his job in the butcher shop," Joe explained. "Biting humans attracts a lot attention, so even the Guild members subsist mainly on animal blood, saving human feedings for special occasions and rituals."

I made a sound of disgust in my throat. "I'm sorry, it's just so…"

"Repulsive," Nancy agreed sadly. "I know. I didn't become a vampire to hurt people, just to stop being one of them." She shook her head to clear her mental cobwebs. "We came to tell you about Marcus as soon as we heard," Nancy said.

"Is he alone?"

"No. There are others. They plan to somehow get you outside and grab you there."

"Does he know that you know?"

Joe would have blushed if he could. "I-I think he might have seen me eavesdropping."

I nodded, then I tried Leo's phone again. No answer. Straight to voicemail.

"We're safe as long as he can't get into the building," I muttered. "I wonder what he's got planned to force me outside?"

The answer, a bottle of gasoline corked by a flaming rag, came crashing through my kitchen window.

I went for the fire extinguisher I keep under the sink, but by the time I had it out and the pin pulled, the flames were already racing across the floor and up the walls, following the splashes and pools of gasoline that had filled the now-shattered bottle.

For dead people, my two visitors moved fast. Nancy whirled me around, propelling me out of the room and into the living room, which was experiencing its own assault by Molotov cocktail. I saw one of them hit the edge of the China cabinet and shatter, splattering its burning contents all over the framed photographs of my and Hal's families, a century of irreplaceable history gone in a flash.

The sprinklers went off, and the fire alarm began blaring. The hall was starting to fill with my neighbors, talking excitedly and streaming toward the nearest fire stairs. The ones closest to my apartment went down only so far as the lobby, so I lead Nancy and Joe to the exit at the far end of the corridor and joined the flow of people headed down the stairs.

Everyone but us peeled off at the lobby. We kept going, down to the basement.

"There's a service door at the rear of the building, behind some bushes and the dumpsters," I told them. "I doubt most of the tenants even know about it."

We threaded through the basement storage lockers, down the corridor lined with doors to the building's mechanical systems, then through the trash compactor room, and finally to a metal door marked "Service Personnel Only."

I tried not to think about my apartment. I didn't mind so much the furnishings. It was all the photographs, the old letters and manuscripts, the newspaper clippings, all the mementos of generations of Blumenfelds and Perskys, dry old paper going up like so much kindling in flames ignited with gasoline and fanned by hatred. A couple of years ago, Leo had sent an intern from the *News* over, and he'd spent three days scanning most of Jacob's writings and photos for a book project he still hasn't gotten around to writing, but the rest of it was likely gone.

We didn't even have to discuss amongst ourselves the virtues of making a stand versus fleeing. Nancy and Joe didn't fight, and I was an old lady with a left hip that ached when it got too humid.

"Going somewhere, Mrs. Persky?"

I couldn't tell you what else this Marcus had going for him, but I had to give him high marks for presentation. He oozed out of the shadows like an oil slick on water only a few feet in front of me, from between the dumpsters and the pile of lawn- and tree-trimming debris from the property clean-up, a shadow himself in a long black overcoat and dark glasses, his voice pitched to a chest-rattling bass.

"I," he said, pausing for dramatic effect, "am Marcus."

"Yes, Marcus," I said. "The butcher at Foodtown."

"Don't be glib with me, Mrs. Persky. You know perfectly well that I am far more than that," he rumbled.

I glanced at my two companions, who seemed to have gone even more pale, if that was possible. "Get a load of this one," I said. "Thinks he's king of the vampires."

Marcus took a step toward me, a sneer on his already-condescending features. I stared straight into those dark lenses without a flinch or a blink. Was I scared? Do I look like an idiot? Of course, I was scared! I could put up a fight for maybe five seconds and then it would be all she wrote, but I wasn't going to give this undead S.O.B. the satisfaction of seeing me cringe. Besides, as my father-in-law always said, "Being scared to death is very motivating."

"Call me whatever you want, woman," Marcus sneered. "It all means the same thing in the end: your doom."

I glanced quickly around, like I was looking for an escape route, which made Marcus laugh. "My colleagues have you surrounded. There is nowhere to run."

"Oh, dear," I said.

And fainted dead away to the ground.

Marcus roared with laughter. "The mighty slayer of the Summer of Slaughter... fainting dead away at the mere sight of me! These mortals don't hold up very well, do they?" He turned his attention to Nancy and Joe. "I knew you'd go running straight to her," he grumbled. "You forced me to move up my timetable."

"You don't have to do this, Marcus," Nancy said. "She's an old woman. She can't hurt you."

"Maybe she can't, but her whelp can. He's been at war with us for decades."

"Kill her and you can be sure he'll come after the Guild, hell, after the entire vampire community, with a vengeance," Joe said.

Marcus laughed again. "Exactly. If we get him angry enough, he'll coming charging in without thinking, and that's when we kill him and end the Persky line once and forever."

"I'm warning you, Marcus," Joe said, trying to sound like a tough guy, but Marcus knew better.

"Warn me of what, little boy?" he sneered.

Marcus lifted me by the shoulders, my head lolling back and exposing my neck to him.

"Ah," he sighed.

And that was when I let out another one of Sensei Keith's great big yells and jammed the sharp end of the sawed-off tree limb I'd grabbed from the pile into Marcus's chest.

———————

I'm sorry, when I said "fainted," I *meant* "feinted," as in, only pretended to pass out. Taking a fall from a standing position without hurting yourself isn't hard to do if you know how. I do, and thanks to the yoga and Aquanastics I could still pull it off.

Marcus clawed desperately at my makeshift stake as he toppled backward to the ground, thrashing and making wet gurgling noises in his throat. A few moments later, he stopped moving and making sounds. Seconds after that, he started to disintegrate into black and gray ash that blew away in the autumn breeze.

Nancy and Joe grabbed one another and looked away in horror at his final moments. I guess whatever they thought of Marcus, this had to be a reminder that even their so-called vampiric "immortality" had its limits. Still, regardless of how repulsive I'd always found their kind, I couldn't help feeling bad for these two, this new breed of vampire. After all, if they hadn't warned me, who knew what might have happened. Maybe becoming a vampire didn't have to end your humanity. Maybe all it had ever done was bring out the evil inside. If you allowed it.

"What about Marcus's friends?" I asked, reaching for another branch.

"They took off, as soon as they saw you... impale Marcus," Nancy said. "I don't think any of them really wanted to be a part of this. They were just following his orders."

My cellphone rang, and suddenly I was snapped back to reality, out in the chilly evening air without a coat, fire truck sirens blaring and men yelling, emergency lights flashing from around the front of the building, and the sharp sting of smoke in the air.

I looked at the caller I.D.

"Leo," I said. "Finally! I've been trying to reach you all evening."

"Hi, Ma. I was in a... a cellular dead zone. So, what's the emergen... hey! Are those sirens and—?"

"It's nothing, darling," I said. "Just a little apartment fire."

"A fire? Jeez, Ma, are you okay? What happened? What the hell's going on there?"

"It's settled, all finished. I'm fine. I have insurance. I'll need somewhere to sleep tonight, but..."

"Yeah, sure, Ma. Get a cab and come into the city. You can stay at my place."

"Oh, dear God, no," I gasped, envisioning the dingy flophouse room and bath in that Saint Stanislaus Hotel he calls home. "No, no, I'm sure someone in the building will have a spare bed or sofa for me."

"Jeez, Ma. Do you need me to come out there?"

"And do what? I'm fine, really, sweetie." I looked over at Nancy and Joe and smiled. "I'll explain everything the next time I see you. For now, I'm safe. I'm with friends."

Joe smiled sheepishly back at me, and Nancy looked like she was about to cry.

"As long as you're sure you're okay..." Leo said.

"So, when will that be?"

"When will what be?"

"The next time I see you. I'm not complaining, God forbid, but it's been a few weeks, Leo."

"I know, I know. I've been busy. And it's a schlep, you know, all the way out there to Brooklyn."

"A schlep? Leo, darling, since when is it a schlep for a boy to visit his mother?"

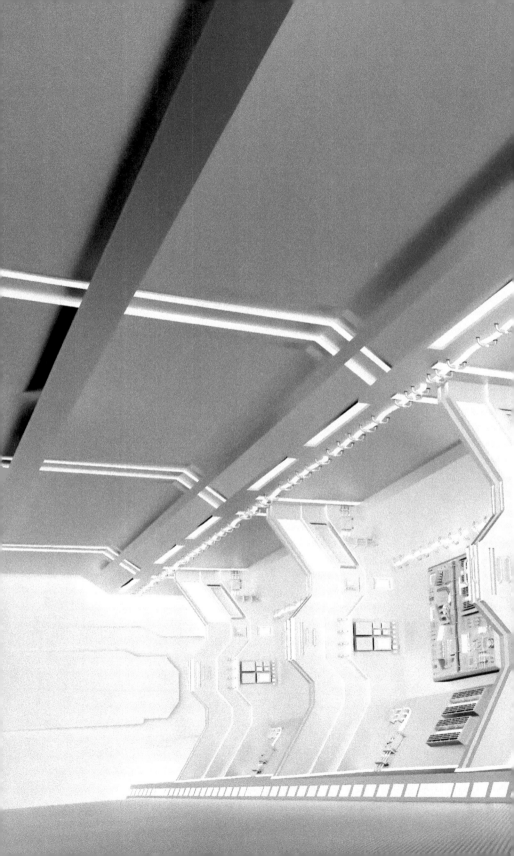

SHAPE UP, OR SHIP OUT

HEATHER E HUTSELL

Tommy stood with his lunch tray in hand, staring across the cafeteria at another teen boy who had attempted to flick a piece of rubbish away instead of properly disposing of it. He was, in that moment, staring at a hovering screen that was barking at him and spitting out a long strand of brown, semi-hard, and transparent linked squares about the size of his thumbnail. Tommy knew that dark chain had the other boy's recent offense on it and he'd just been caught for littering. Many of the other witnesses shook their heads in disappointment, some snickering quietly from a distance. Tommy just watched.

"Hey—you're holding up the line."

Tommy looked back over his shoulder at a boy twice his width and easily two heads taller.

"*Do you mind?*" Another hovering screen flew with startling precision and speed up in front of the taller youth's face, revealing nothing but a frown consisting of two big, black dots for eyes and a downward curve for a mouth. Everyone within a few feet of it could hear the humming that preceded the buzzing of a chip being processed inside. "*Please.*" At the utterance of the word, the threatening sound from within stopped, flipped the curve into a smile, and the thing flew just as quickly away again.

"Yeah," Tommy muttered. "Sorry."

He stepped out of the line and took a seat at one of the long, sparkling white tables, still watching as the litterbug finally got in line to get his food. Tommy pitied him in a way—mostly at how the monitor floated closely behind the boy, trailing him like a menacing shadow as it waited for him to screw up again. It didn't help his cause at all that he swatted at the machine as though it were a pesky insect.

The boy finally got through the lunch line and came to the table where Tommy sat, his food still untouched. None of Tommy's days occasioned for much of an appetite.

Without a word from either of them, the boy sat down. He was clean-cut with gentle features that contradicted his behaviors, unlike Tommy, whose rough exterior and short, punkish hair reflected nothing of his calm. Bobby was halfway through his sandwich before Tommy addressed him.

"You must be the new kid."

"I guess."

"*Watch your tone.*"

The new boy looked around, not knowing where the feminine voice had come from, but it was one he'd been hearing a lot since he got there.

"It's the table," Tommy explained. "Well, at the moment, anyway."

"What *is* that?"

"That's *MOTHER.*"

The new boy smirked.

"She's kind of a bi—"

The table began to buzz, and the edge of dark, film-like material could be seen sticking out of a slot between them.

"Kind of strict," he amended.

"Well, what do you expect? You know where you are, right?" That got him no more than a *yeah, so?* shrug. "I'm Tommy, by the way."

"Bobby. So, what are you in here for?"

"Shoplifting."

Bobby made an unimpressed face, not noticing that a chip had popped up close to Tommy's tray and was covered with a napkin for later retrieval.

"What about you?"

"Arson."

"Really?"

"It was *one* trash can."

"Yeah, but where was it?"

Something that sounded a lot like *principal's office* was uttered through Bobby's clenched teeth.

"Wow. Hardcore. Is that all you did?"

"I guess it was enough." Bobby smirked. "So, is there anything fun to do here? I mean, I know we're pretty much in juvie, but no video games or anything?"

"No. Sports."

"*Sports.* What, like jumping and running around and all that?"

"Pretty much."

"But no video games? Not even for good behavior?"

"Sorry."

"Man, this place sucks—"

A chip came shooting up from the table. Both of them looked at it when it appeared, then at each other.

"Take it," Tommy prompted.

"I don't want to take it."

"You have to."

Bobby huffed, and the chip grew another two inches before he ripped it from the slot.

"Do you know how many of these I already have since I got here?"

"Probably as many as the rest of us did when we first got here."

Bobby shook his head.

"Man. That just blows—"

Bzzzz—

"—my mind. *It blows my mind.* I mean—how *efficient* this place is. Right?"

"Oh, yeah. MOTHER's right on top of it."

"Mother? Who is this *Mother?*"

"M zero dash T-H three dash R. The ship we're on."

"Oh. Right."

Bobby began to huff again but quickly softened it to a sigh.

"So, what are we supposed to do with these things? What are they anyway?"

"They're demerits."

"Great, but what do we *do* with them?"

"We're supposed to keep them, I guess. I don't know, really."

"What've you done with yours? Do we have to turn them in or something?"

"MOTHER keeps track of them."

"So, we don't need them—?"

"I don't know. I just keep mine in a little box in my room."

"Quaint." The chip dispenser in the table was humming but had not quite reached a buzz. "I mean that's a good idea. Keeping them all together. Never know when you might need them, I guess."

"I guess."

Bobby looked at the newest link of chips, turning it over a few times. It was thin and sort of flimsy, transparent but with threadlike metallic strips running through it. He compared it to a couple of others he'd acquired. None of them had any discernible writing on them, but the design of threads was different. He figured they were a recording or something, and the threads some kind of code.

"I don't have a box," he stated, thinking as soon as the words came out how lame they sounded.

"You don't have to have one. Keep them anywhere. Keep them in your pockets. Just—keep them."

"What happens—?" Bobby leaned a little closer so he could lower his voice. "What happens if I don't keep them?"

"I have no idea. I just know that we're supposed to. That's what I was told when I got here, so now I'm telling you."

"Oh. That's brotherly of you."

Tommy flinched at the new kid's choice of words. Bobby got the impression he wanted to be alone and stood as he picked up his tray.

"Say, I'll catch you later, probably."

"Sure. Good luck."

"Thanks, brother."

This time, Tommy's face went ashen, and he clenched his jaw, but his response came out on a soft, almost pained mutter.

"Don't call me *brother*."

"Sorry. See ya."

———— ••• ————

Bobby finished his lunch by the trashcan while he looked around at the other boys. He was glad the monitors couldn't hear his thoughts. If they could have, they would have known what an unimpressive lot he thought them all to be. Except Tommy. He sure was remorseful for a shoplifter. And he'd said *shoplifting*, not *grand larceny.* What sort of damage could that really have done, anyway? At least the fire in the principal's office had scorched the wall. Bobby had a lot more to be sorry about, but Tommy acted like he had killed someone. The thought made Bobby feel a bit queasy. The boys Bobby knew who were truly crazy and did horrible things were boastful about it—even the ones who had been lying about doing those things. Tommy was not boastful.

Bobby went to his little closet of a room and closed the door before the trailing monitor could come in behind him. It was moot, though, since there was another one that lived in his room. At least this one was attached to the wall and couldn't get in his face. It already had a chip in mid-extraction—for being rude to the other machine, no doubt. He stuck his hands in his pockets and pulled out all the accumulated chips. He was tempted to count them, but just tossed them onto the little desk in the corner. *No box.* The room was like a box, and he wondered how long he was going to be stuck there. He hoped he wasn't going to fill the room with those film chip things before he had a chance to escape. At the rate he was going, though—

He sat on the bed and stared at them from across the room. If MOTHER was keeping track of all of everyone's offenses, then what was the point of them? What a waste of whatever they were made out of. That crime seemed like something deserving a few demerits of its own, but who would they be administered to? *MOTHER?*

And no video games, *"only sports"*? Again, Bobby was glad that MOTHER couldn't get into his head. At least, not that he knew of.

Bobby stood and went back to the desk, picking up one of the strands of chips, and studied it. The threads indicating his offenses weren't in any sort of linear fashion. Some were curved, some in rows with breaks in them. There seemed to be no rhyme or reason for any of it. He tossed the strip onto the pile and just stood there staring at them, with thoughts of the quiet youth in the cafeteria coming in little flashes. He sure had gotten upset when Bobby called him *brotherly* and especially *brother.* Bobby wondered what that was about. Maybe Tommy hated his brother. Or maybe he never had one and felt cheated. Bobby could kind of relate. He'd been cheated out of a lot of things, too. Not his punishment of being sent to that place, though—that floating space disc of wayward boys and its operating system that always seemed on top of every little thing her *children* got up to.

MOTHER.

Bobby left his room at the sound of the dinner buzzer, and even though he arrived in plenty of time, the tables were filled, leaving him to dine by himself at a small two-seater. Just as he was finishing up, he saw Tommy clearing off what was left on his tray at several different bins. Bobby jumped up and hurried to catch him, quickly doing the same though he was hardly finished eating. The boy seemed less upset than before, prompting Bobby to strike up the conversation.

"Hey—"

"Yeah?"

"Sorry if I said something earlier to make you upset."

"Oh. No problem."

"It's just been kind of a strange place to get used to."

"Sure. It's like that for everyone."

"Hey—can I ask you something?"

A look of caution came over Tommy's face, and the *sure* that came out was no less so.

"What happens to the kids here? Do we stay forever?"

Tommy shrugged. "I have no idea."

A hovering monitor swerved around Bobby and presented itself and a chip to Tommy, along with a frown. He hesitated in taking it but finally did and just stood there looking at it.

"Did you just get that for *lying?*"

Tommy didn't respond immediately, and Bobby was about to let him off the hook when Tommy finally spoke.

"Sometimes, kids disappear."

"You mean, like, *go home*, or—?"

"I don't know. They just disappear and never come back."

"Is there—?" Bobby hesitated. "Is there some kind of *other* punishment? Like, a place kids are sent to when they do *really* bad stuff?"

"Heh. If there was, I'd know about it."

"Why? What exactly did you shoplift?"

Tommy pulled his bottom lip in tight against a tremble and composed himself quickly. "I have dishwashing duty tonight. I should go before I'm late." Then, noticing Bobby was watching him, he shoved the chip into his pocket.

"I still don't completely understand why we keep getting those," Bobby said, hoping to ease the tension.

"Yeah, who knows? Hey, you wanna play some basketball sometime?"

"What? Nah. I'm not really any good at it."

But the moment Tommy nodded and was on his way to the kitchen, Bobby wished he had said otherwise.

The next few days were uneventful, but something about the entire arrangement was enough to pique Bobby's curiosity. He spent many hours in quiet observation of the other boys, watched what they were doing to earn their demerits, watched to see which ones did it on purpose, which ones were too caught up in frustration to get out of the vicious cycle of causing trouble for themselves. Most of all, he watched Tommy. Every time Tommy gained a chip—which was not many—he just stood with it in hand and his head bowed for a long moment. Bobby knew he wasn't even looking at the thing. Unbeknownst to Bobby, Tommy had stopped doing that long before Bobby had shown up.

It was barely a week into Bobby's time on MOTHER when the mystery of it all came to a crashing halt. He had retired to his room after supper, and as he emptied his pockets of his newest chips and stood leaning over his desk staring at them, he let his eyes unfocus. A strip of the connected chips—and more specifically, the various threads—formed letters. Not only that, but combined they spelled out a word: SMART.

Bobby pushed back from the desk and ran his hands through his hair to stave off the sudden sensation that filled him. Elation? Horror? *Both*. He wanted to cry. He turned away from the desk, but it scarcely helped.

Bobby's school hadn't been one of the best, but it was above the sort that a kid with his family's background usually had access to. It was a fluke that he had tested into it at all. At least, that was how other kids had felt about it, and they'd had no problem making it clear that everyone thought he'd cheated his way in and didn't deserve to be there. After a while and no matter the truth, Bobby had begun to believe it too.

He didn't want to face the pile of chips. In fact, he never wanted to see them again, but the sudden welling intrigue compelled him to, and he was unable to resist the draw back to the desk. He began pulling and sorting the chips, starting with strands of three or more until he'd spelled out SMART, YOUR, and FIGHT. Each time he made a correct match, the chips fused together. Within an hour, a startlingly clear and personal message was neatly arranged across the desktop:

YOU ARE SMARTER THAN THIS
STOP FIGHTING WITH YOURSELF
YOU HAVE EARNED YOUR PLACE
MOTHER LOVES YOU

Bobby was weeping, blubbering, and rubbing his sleeve under his runny nose at the truth staring him in the face. He could see the smoke, the flames captured in a circular, metal trap; all those half-shredded documents engulfed in an unjust death and telling letters in red stamped all over them. It had been so easy to destroy them, but less easy to sabotage himself. And MOTHER: *MOTHER knew.*

A buzzing in the surface of the desk resulted in the spitting out of a long strand of chips and a smile on the monitor. Bobby pulled it off when it finished.

CONGRATULATIONS.
REPORT TO MOTHER FOR ACCEPTANCE OF RELEASE.
EXPIRATION: 22:00

Release? From MOTHER? It didn't seem right or possible—he hadn't even been there that long! That thought quickly gave way to another:

Tommy. The kid was shrouded with mystery, and Bobby wanted to solve him, too. New thoughts of suspicion began to race, but something of a roadblock intercepted: Tommy's puzzle wasn't for Bobby to solve. That didn't mean he couldn't help him.

Bobby took the strand of release chips and left his room, resolving to track down Tommy before he was due to report. He found him in the gymnasium, aimlessly bouncing the ball next to him as he stood in one spot.

"Hey—"

"Hey." Tommy didn't look at Bobby until he was standing in front of him. "What's up?"

"Got a few questions about MOTHER."

Tommy's gaze shifted to wherever it had been before Bobby's appearance.

"No one stays here forever, right?"

"Mm, hm."

"Which means we all get released at some point."

"Yeah, I guess."

"Well, what happens if you get a release and you don't take it? You can't refuse it—*can you?*"

Tommy shrugged.

"Why not?"

"But—" Bobby's blood chilled as he realized that none of this was news to Tommy. "Have you ever gotten one before?"

Tommy refused to look at him, but a curious light had come to his eyes.

"Did *you* just get one?"

Bobby caught the ball before Tommy could push it back down to the floor for another bounce, holding tight when Tommy made a lame attempt to take it back. When he failed, his hand remained on the rubber.

"What happens? If you refuse it, I mean. C'mon—*what happens?*"

Without replying, Tommy let the ball go and walked away, leaving Bobby with a rising sense of panic, but for what, he didn't know. Before Bobby could take a step in Tommy's wake, the same boy who'd reprimanded Tommy for taking too long in the cafeteria line on Bobby's first day intercepted. Bigger and taller and more than that—*familiar*—he, along with two of his friends, easily blocked Bobby's path. Bobby lowered his head.

"Kind of nosy, aren't you?"

"Didn't mean to be. I just want to know how this place works. But it's cool, you know. I don't need to know." He attempted to step around the other boy but was again blocked.

"You can't leave until it's time for you to leave."

Bobby jammed his hand into his pocket to close it around the precious release order, but he didn't remove it. He knew this other kid from some time before, a bully who had once terrorized many of Bobby's friends and himself back home. In that moment, the boy didn't seem to recognize Bobby, and considering that Bobby had been the one to stand up for some of the younger boys, including having a hand in the kid's eventual expulsion, that was a good thing.

"And when is that?" he asked, hoping that if he kept to the subject, his anonymity would stick.

"When you're *told*. You should probably remember that."

"So, where do kids go when they leave here?"

"Depends. The ones that are here until they're eighteen go back to court."

"And then?"

He squinted at Bobby. "What do *you* think?"

"Retrial and resentenced as a grown-up?"

"Bingo. You're not as dumb as you look."

A monitor zipped in front of the larger boy and administered two chips—one for his comment and another for the mumbled expletive he made about the first chip—and a frown that flashed on the screen.

"How old is Tommy?" Bobby pressed. It was impossible to ignore the overwhelming sense of concern that began to well up inside of him.

"How old are *you*?"

"Sixteen. How old is Tommy? Do you know?"

"Really?" The boy crinkled his face at Bobby as though something putrid had just passed under his nose. "What's it matter to you?"

"I just—I mean—" Bobby didn't bother to finish his thought out loud. The bully and his entourage walked away with their leader shaking his head, and leaving Bobby's concern shifting quickly to dread.

Without the others blocking his way, Bobby hurried off in the direction Tommy had gone. He found him in his room, pausing with relief at the sound of music coming from within. There was still an hour until he had to report. Bobby hoped it would be enough time and knocked on the door. The music continued to play without any other stirring, until the song came to its end. As though Tommy had been waiting for that very moment, one beat after the last note, he opened the door. Bobby stood there for another few seconds, surprised, and Tommy said nothing as he waited for Bobby to state why he was there.

"Can I come in?"

"It's lights out soon."

"I know. It won't take long. I promise."

Tommy did not step aside to let him in, but remained in the small space made by the opened door. Bobby tried to get a quick glance around the room from where he stood, spying a little box on the desk, but Tommy blocked the rest of the room from sight.

"Well?"

"I think the chips are more than they seem."

"What do you mean?"

"Like, they don't just belong in a box or in our pockets."

"Okay. Why are you telling me that?"

"Because—" Bobby was stunned at Tommy's lack of enthusiasm. It was something he'd seen in adults who had lost sight of what was important to them, things they cared about—including what happened to them. Tommy's life—past, present, or future—was none of his business, but Bobby didn't want to give up, though there was no doubt it would have been easier to just walk away than get Tommy on the same page with him.

"I think the chips are a puzzle, and all we have to do is solve whatever our puzzle is. That's it. That's our test, our way out of here."

"Yeah? Maybe."

"Yeah, *maybe.* You've been here a while, haven't you? But something tells me you don't need to be. Maybe I can help you with yours."

"Nah. What do yours spell out anyway?" Tommy added, clearly too curious not to ask.

His nonchalance about not wanting help was yet another red flag, and as much as Bobby wanted to answer him, he felt more and more like he was at a dead end. He was overcome with a sense of wanting to protect Tommy, to help him, but he was meddling, and that never amounted to anything good.

"Maybe I'm wrong."

"Okay," Tommy offered with a shrug. "Hey, I gotta get ready for bed. Shower, and all that."

"Sure. Yeah. Go do that. I should probably go."

As Bobby slowly wandered toward his room, he knew he had to accept that Tommy wasn't going to budge, that he was determined to avoid release for reasons Bobby could not sort out in the short time he had. Or could he? Tommy had asked what Bobby's chips *spelled out*, indicating he knew what they were for. It was obvious that he knew a lot more than he was revealing. No matter how much Bobby knew he should mind his own business, he couldn't. Not this time.

Bobby returned to his room just long enough to see Tommy leave his in a bathrobe with a small bag of toiletries in hand and a towel over his shoulder. The moment Tommy was out of sight and the hallway empty, Bobby slipped from his room and walked briskly back to Tommy's. He paused next to the closed door, thinking nothing of the fact that not one of the many monitors hovering around was anywhere near him, until he tried the door, found it unlocked, and as he slipped inside, was met with one face-to-screen. He froze, waiting for it to recognize that he was in the wrong room and to start spitting out chips, but it just hung there, gently and slowly bouncing in the air. Realizing that it wasn't setting off any alarms, Bobby slowly turned away from it and felt his jaw drop at the sight of the walls. They were covered with rows of chips, all of them spelling the same thing: YOU ARE AN ACCIDENT and PRISON. The knot was instantly in Bobby's throat. It wasn't like when he'd solved the puzzle of his chips, but because he couldn't and did not want to believe that something so cruel and cold would be said to another person, regardless of why he was there on that ship. His hands were shaking by the time he got to Tommy's desk and opened the box where the rest of the chips were. The chill in his limbs was quickly replaced by a rush of heat at the realization that the chips he dumped onto the desk didn't all say the same as what was on the walls, and none of them connected: *Tommy's message wasn't complete.* Working quickly, he pieced together a new message—one that used all the letters and all the words, fusing together the truth:

IT WAS AN ACCIDENT
YOU ARE YOUR ONLY PRISON

The monitor observing Bobby barely had time to turn in his direction with a smile on its screen before he had darted from the room. On his way out, Bobby had caught a glimpse of the clock: 21:43. It would be enough time to find Tommy and talk to him. *It had to be.*

But Bobby made it no farther than the end of the hall before the resident bully and his buddies stepped in front of him. A faithful monitor caught up with them both and hung in the air to observe and catch any punishable offenses.

"Nothing but showers down this way, and *you* don't have a towel."

"I'm just looking for my friend."

"Uh, huh. You can't wait until your *friend* is somewhere more socially acceptable?"

"I can't, actually. I don't have time."

The boy looked at his two friends flanking him and scoffed.

"Time is *all* we have."

"Yeah, well, not all of us do."

Bobby attempted a step around his opposer, finding once again that it was impossible to get around the little posse.

"Look—this is really important—"

"Yeah, I doubt it."

"Why are you being such a jerk?"

There was a moment where no one moved or spoke and the monitor just maintained a blank screen and a soft bounce.

"Hey! You should've gotten chipped for that!"

Bobby offered no explanation, and the bully squinted at him. "*Oh.* Wait a minute—*I know who you are*—"

Bobby glanced behind him at the clock on the wall: 21:49. He sighed and held in a curse. There wasn't time. Even if he got past the other boys and made it to Tommy, he still had to convince him to listen before any explaining could even be done. There was only one other way he could think to make things right.

The monitor suddenly began to beep, startling them all.

"Please report to MOTHER in ten minutes—"

"What?"

Bobby didn't wait to hear what more the bully had to say about the announcement, but as he ran, untracked, down the hallway, he could hear the streak of swear words and threats and the steady stream of buzzing from the monitor that nearly drowned it all out. He didn't see Tommy appear behind the bully and his friends, or witness his dropping jaw at the monitor's instruction.

Bobby was out of breath when he reached the core of the ship, but it was exactly 22:00, and a door slid open to let him into a round room. Big screens lined it with warm, soothing, fluctuating colors. To no surprise, one of the floating monitors was there with its big, black dots and straight, neutral line for a mouth, and it approached Bobby.

"Welcome, Bobby. Please insert your release permissions into the monitor."

Bobby put the strip of chips to the slot but hesitated. He wondered if the machine—the ship—was listening.

"Mother?"

There was a short moment of silence as a bunch of lights on the monitor's screen began to flash in rows and then made a primitive set of eyes and a curved line for a smile.

"Hello, Bobby."

"Moth…" His voice trailed off at the inviting warmth in the monitor's voice.

"Yes?"

For the first time in longer than he could remember, Bobby craved the love, nurturing, and so many other things that had not come his way for most of his lifetime. What was he supposed to say? The words came out on a ramble.

"It's about Tommy, Mother. He can't stay here. He should be going home too—shouldn't he?"

Silence followed, and in those moments, the screens on the wall began to cycle through cooler colors before shifting back to amber, magenta, and orange.

"Tommy has chosen to stay."

"But—his chips—he's not supposed to be here."

"Everyone here is allowed to make choices. Some choices are good. Some are bad."

"His doesn't make sense."

"It does to him. It may not be right or what you might choose, Bobby, but that's his lesson to learn. You are all here for a lesson, because you could not learn it back home. Yours was to face your potential, and by being here now, you have proven to me and more importantly to yourself that you are capable, and you are accepting of it."

"But I'm not here for me. I'm here for him. I want to help him. He thinks he hurt someone, doesn't he? A brother? But he didn't, did he?"

The monitor didn't answer him.

"I really want to help him."

"I know you do, Bobby, but you can't. He has to learn for himself."

"And if he doesn't learn? If he's here until he turns eighteen?"

"MOTHER will always love him, no matter what, Bobby. Just as MOTHER will always love you."

"And if he waits too long? What then?"

"He will not wait too long. That is how MOTHER works. He will realize before it's too late."

Bobby wanted to trust that this machine would not say things just to placate him.

"He will learn his lesson. Everyone who comes here does." The colors on the screens hovered in tones of orange for a few moments before shifting back to the soothing sunset colors. "Are you ready, Bobby?" When he hesitated, MOTHER prompted him again. "It's time. Do not worry— MOTHER loves you all."

He was only vaguely aware of the tears on his cheeks as he nodded, too heavy in his chest to do more.

"Please insert your chips into the monitor."

Without pausing this time, he did, and as they disappeared, a small hatch opened in the wall. It was only big enough for him and was identical to the one that had brought him to MOTHER. It had everything he needed for his journey home, though he would be sleeping through all of it.

MOTHER spoke after Bobby stepped into the pod, reciting technical formalities as the door closed, leaving only a small window that allowed him to see into the round room. It faced the door leading into the hallway, and just as the pod filled with a sweet-smelling sleeping agent and the sound of MOTHER's soft lullaby hit Bobby's ears, he saw a figure through the round room's one window opposite of the pod: a familiar, grateful face and a hand holding up a strand of chips appointing another release.

SHOOT CENTER

ROBERT GREENBERGER

A LLISON FORD HELD HER BREATH, counting to ten, her time-honored way of handling bad news. She stifled the impulse to shout profanities that would certainly cause attention at Wylie's Place. It was quiet in the late afternoon; the regular drinkers were just punching out and would be flooding in soon. Her companion was studying her, an impassive gaze on her careworn face. The uniformed waitress had just delivered their coffees and she poured in milk.

"It's just business, Allison," Carol Broderek said again, breaking the silence as she stirred.

"I see. And by how much?"

She shook her head with a small smile. "You know I don't divulge those details."

"That bitch," Allison finally said.

"It's happened before. It'll happen again. We'll be using you and your girls again, I assure you." Broderek, betraying nothing, sipped at the coffee; Allison ignored her cup.

"But, this was going to be my kitchen remodeling fund," she said, more to herself than to her companion.

The older woman plunked down a few bills and gathered her overcoat. While the approaching fall weather was nicely cooling off the summer heat, it wasn't really necessary. But she never saw Broderek without it, making it like her uniform. Her brand, everyone had one now. "Good luck at tomorrow's match," she said, patting her shoulder and walking directly out of Wylie's.

Allison sat alone, fuming.

She'd spent the last decade coaching the Chester Campbell High School Rifle Team, grooming her girls, drilling them relentlessly so they went from novices to experienced winners, making membership attractive, swelling their ranks year after year. Her long-term plan was all going according to schedule, as she used her experience as a former CIA sharpshooter to launch her successful, covert side business.

As the number of shooters grew, she began identifying the best of the best and took them under her wing. Only during these special one-on-one sessions did she begin elaborating what her life was like; traveling the world, using her uncanny skills in the service of her nation. She spoke glowingly of assignments in Antigua and complained of the bitter cold in the Ukraine. Her girls, and they were always girls, leaned in, absorbing every detail she carefully doled out. After all, young, pretty girls would rarely be suspected of being highly trained assassins.

"Why'd you ever leave?" at least one rookie would ask each year.

"Drones. We were becoming replaceable," was the response. There was more to it, things she never spoke of for fear of scaring the girls off. There were things that woke her in the night, images that time would never dim.

Allison Ford had left the CIA and, like so many of her peers, went into private security. Her specialty had become wetwork, very expensive wetwork, with jobs won by bidding in the deepest, darkest corners of the internet. She'd invested seven years in building the club, partially funding the startup costs with her extra income, and for the last three, had recruited four young women to join her in this private enterprise. It was, at first, seen as a badge of honor to be asked to join her for extra training sessions, making the others try that much harder. Competition, she knew, was good for the soul.

As she trained her elite squad, rather than clay targets, they fired at paper human silhouettes. Out of each clutch, as she thought of them, there were one or two who were special, had the instincts and unflappable demeanor to be let in on her other secret. These two proved worthy as they learned of her secondary career without freaking out and worked with her to hone their skills on more realistic targets. These special weekend sessions also helped make them the elite shooters on her team, winning accolades across Virginia.

She knew the fees, minus her cut, would help them pay for college, to avoid crushing student debt. Allison didn't fear them becoming competitors. If anything, they'd be too busy studying, partying, and getting laid to be a threat—like perfectly normal freshmen. It also expanded her network should she need help on jobs out of the D.C./Maryland/Virginia area. She rarely took a job out of state during the season, although she would have made an exception for the one she just lost. Later, after graduation, if they wanted to compete directly against her, she'd be readying for retirement, her nest egg secured. After all, the hands would one day shake, the reflexes less sharp, eyesight beginning to fade despite scopes and enhancements. She felt the ticking clock on her career, and this setback annoyed her. No, more than annoyed. Pissed her off something fierce.

But, she needed to redo the kitchen. To get the house ready for the market so she could downsize in the wake of her recent divorce.

Lanae Taylor saw to it the project would have to wait.

Allison was never sure when or how Lanae, short, loud, and bossy, learned of her side business. All she knew was that they crossed paths at a big job with four shooters in Georgia, and she was startled to recognize her during the extraction. Whereas this would likely be a sisterhood bonding moment, both squinted with unconcealed distaste for the other. They were already rival riflery coaches at competing high schools, and now they were openly vying for the same contracts.

They didn't particularly like one another but were professionals and didn't let it interfere. Then came the day she received the notification that she didn't win the eBay auction for a weekend escape at a cabin in the Rockies. The next match, Coach Taylor was absent, apparently "out west" for a conference.

Last year, when Allison didn't win the auction for a prop from *The Manchurian Candidate*, the original not the unnecessary remake, she spotted the object in a social media post from Taylor's team. She was flaunting it, shoving it down Allison's throat that Taylor beat her. That made it personal.

And here was her favorite account, Carol Broderek, making a rare appearance in the flesh, telling her this noisy motherfucker was stealing her gig. Okay, not stealing, just underbidding her. No doubt, Allison won her share of enemies by her own underbidding, ensuring she got jobs to dole out to the girls, building her network, her reputation, and her bank account.

The woman needed to go away. Or, better yet, be taken out of the competition.

As she drove home, to get ready for the following day's competition at the Arlington Rifle and Pistol Club, her mind shifted to more mundane tasks such as ensuring someone was on snack duty, her own weapons were cleaned and ready to pack, her coach's uniform jacket was brushed, and what to defrost for dinner. Cooking for one had already grown old, but a girl's gotta eat.

The following morning was the 100-Yard Rifle Shooting competition, and this was the second time this season they would carpool to the Developmental Match. Seven other schools, including Calippus High School, where her rival taught chemistry and coached the rifle club, were scheduled to compete. Each of the team's five selected shooters would fire ten rounds apiece in each of three positions: prone, standing, and kneeling. Her team had an extra practice earlier in the week, and Allison was confident they were ready to kick ass and take names. She was going to have her elite pair—Alexis Biggs and Tracy Pham—shoot with rising stars from the junior class. Her sophomores could fire afterward for individual ratings. Last time the schools competed, her team came in third, and she was determined they would do better.

"Discipline is more important than the shooting," Allison explained to one of the parents after practice. "You have to respect the rifle for what it will do. Jeremy will learn that if he learns anything this year."

Jeremy's father bobbed his head in understanding.

She rolled her bright red SUV into the parking lot, four other cars trailing behind her. With the efficiency she had drilled into the team, they unpacked all the gear from the back of her vehicle, the visors, glasses, earplugs, ammunition, and finally the rifles. They were all decked out in the maroon-and-gray jacket and pants that denoted their school, names stitched across the breast, school patch on the left sleeve. The air rifles and .22s were carefully unwrapped as each member of the team grabbed their personal gear. The other drivers, parents still clutching their travel mugs, milled about, trying not to get in their way. They, too, knew the drill.

Allison caught Tracy Pham's eye and tipped her head. Pham was a senior, months shy of aging out of J2 and ready to take on collegiate shooting upon graduation. At first, Tracy was hesitant to join the team when she arrived as a freshman. But, she was encouraged to join one team by her parents, already eyeing the future college applications. It was a solitary sport, something she could control, and she explained that was what drew her to the first team meeting.

Within six weeks, she was its loudest advocate, dragging her new best friend, Alexis, to a practice. "It took me out of my bubble," Allison recalled hearing Tracy say just over three years ago. "I owe my confidence to trap. It's the best thing I will ever do in high school. If this were taken away from us… I don't know what I would do. I'm attached to it."

That was all Alexis needed, and soon they were teammates, fellow shooters, and rising stars that Allison carefully watched and coached.

She was her star, the one she had dreamed about when she launched her plan years earlier. Pham, slender with sleek black hair that was tightly tied behind her, cultivated the aura of a misanthrope so people would leave her alone and let her study—or shoot. She was actually warm and funny, but only to a handful of people who seemed willing to protect that human side of her.

They met at the back of the SUV, ostensibly to haul out the cooler containing drinks and fruit, but it was really for a private conversation, one of many they'd had before.

"How badly do you want to shoot next week?" Allison asked without preamble. The following week was another routine match, helping qualify for the season's finals but relatively inconsequential. Allison was already considering favoring the sophomores and juniors anyway, with one exception.

Pham cocked an eyebrow at her, not saying a word.

"I need you for something special," Allison said, her voice sounding perfectly normal despite the message being conveyed. Pham had already taken out two people under Allison's supervision. She was cool, unflappable, and needed the money for a high-end private school. Taking a human life was fine by her, as long as it was justified. Both times, Allison had to spell out who the target was and why they deserved to die. The first was the driver for a human trafficking ring that brought girls from the DMV region to Ohio. He "sampled" the wares along the way. The second was a Pennsylvania-based dealer in opioids at a dozen high schools.

"Coach Taylor."

Pham paused as they carried the cooler to where the team was setting up, causing Allison to nearly stumble.

"Are you shitting me?"

They put the cooler down, and Allison gestured they take a walk around the Arlington facility. It would appear it was a coach and shooter going over last-minute instructions.

"She's a pain in the ass, sure, but why?" Pham asked.

"She's a competitor," Allison began and let Pham, who boasted a 4.5 GPA, connect the dots. It didn't take long at all.

All she did was nod with comprehension.

"She underbid me for the last time," Allison said.

"So? Don't you underbid others?"

"I don't know who the others are. What I do know is that Coach Taylor is rubbing my nose in it, endangering our program."

"How?"

"She's underbid me, yes, but she's boasting in ways that could expose her, and if she goes down, she won't go down quietly. She'll finger us and you, the others, who are just getting started. This could ruin your lives."

"And yours," Pham said quietly.

"Mine's pretty fucked up, right now." The team knew about the divorce; their parents could be overheard discussing the messy details, which had gone public when the papers were filed. Sure, she could have taken him out and kept everything, but she didn't want his death on her conscience or anyone from her previous employer to even look her way.

"How? When?"

"I have a plan, but it means you can't shoot next week."

"Not a big deal, I hate the clay pigeons," Pham said. "I'll qualify today."

"No doubt," Allison assured her and launched into the plans.

Later, Pham scored two 78s and a 67 during her three rounds, helping the team secure second place. Once the team's placement was announced, they clustered together, high-fiving one another, jumping up and down in group euphoria. It was then that Pham tumbled awkwardly to the ground, taking down several of the girls so there was a pile of bodies atop her.

Allison and other parents rushed over to help them up, but Pham wasn't getting up. One father snatched the girl up and carried her to the SUV.

"Well, I'll be damned," one parent said. "I signed Jacob up to shoot since he wasn't going to get a concussion like he would in football. Never thought there'd be a celebratory injury."

"I'll take her to be checked out," Allison said, using her commanding voice. "Alexis, call Tracy's mom and let her know."

She was driving off with Alexis already on her phone.

Tracy's phone buzzed.

Allison had brought Alexis, taller, light brown-skinned with hair piled high atop her head, in on the plan earlier. She was one of the elite and Tracy's closest friend. If anyone could be trusted with the plan, it would be her. They made an unlikely pair, with Alexis voluble and idiosyncratic whereas Tracy was quiet and circumspect. They were in most of the same classes and were frequent partners while also vying for top grades. Both were in the running for valedictorian, and Allison couldn't decide who would win, although both deserved it.

The girls chatted about the match for a few minutes as Allison drove, ostensibly to the nearest Urgent Care facility. Instead, they arrived at a Chick-fil-a and drank celebratory milkshakes.

On Monday, Tracy arrived at school wearing a light gray leg-length soft cast, explaining she had strained ligaments in her leg and the knee needed to be immobilized. She'd have to wear it, she told the curious, for about two weeks if not longer. It meant she couldn't shoot on Saturday and appeared upset about it.

During the week, Tracy, Alexis, and the others attended classes, had their thrice-weekly practices at the local NRA shooting range, and behaved normally. Tracy hung back, not shooting with the others, but encouraging them.

Each night that week, Tracy and Allison met and worked with a 9mm; Tracy took extra target practice, the cast nowhere in sight.

Allison also made a special trip to the Bull Run Shooting Center where the competition would be held. She knew Taylor was going to have her hands full with the assignment her rival won at auction during the week atop her teaching duties and so felt safe in proceeding with the plan.

She took measurements with her phone app, checked sight lines, walked the grounds, putting herself in the competitors' shoes. It was during quiet times like these that she missed the idea of having a shooting club during her high school years. But it was a time when parents were overly concerned with violence everywhere—Saturday morning cartoons, rock music, even t-shirt designs. More and more schools shut down the clubs as enrollment declined or budgets needed trimming during the tightening economy. For a few brief moments, she indulged in fantasizing about the friendships she would have made, the life choices available to her, and how her life might have turned out. She felt isolated, growing up in Connecticut, with just her father taking her out shooting during hunting season. He'd wanted Allison and her older brothers to know how to handle, and respect, guns, and how to fend for themselves. It was the same thinking that taught the basics of plumbing, electrical work, and even carpentry. Not that he was a survivalist or anything, but he wanted them not to have to rely too much on others. His jaundiced view of his fellow man colored how she saw others. It certainly put her on a path to being a crack shot then recruited out of college by the CIA and a decade spent traveling the world, keeping everyone safe for mom and apple pie.

"Think Center, Aim Center, Shoot Center!" Allison said the mantra over and over again during the practices. Her seniors even parroted her as they worked with the younger shooters. She was particularly concerned about her sophomores who, she concluded, weren't taking this seriously enough. On one knee, she leaned over one male, watched him adjust his scope, and then roughly tweaked his shoulders. "Now you're centered."

Pham lingered in the background, hobbling stiff-legged, restless. Allison ignored her and focused on making certain the others were ready for the competition. Second was acceptable, but she knew on this course, for whatever reason, Taylor's team always did well. She wanted to grind them into the ground, make the coach suffer in multiple ways. At one point, she lingered by Alexis, who was smoothly aiming and firing with mechanical precision,

"Nice," Allison said, which was often the highest praise she offered during practice. She saved the effusive stuff for actual competitions.

"Just getting comfortable," Alexis replied.

The teams assembled at the shooting range by 6:30 a.m., a ridiculously early hour. "Only late-night drunks and shooters are up this early," the girls crowed, their own version of a mantra, every weekend competition. The caravan was longer than last week, with more students participating. It promised to be a crowded field, lots of competitors, lots of parents, vendors, and staff. It was ideal.

Taylor had unpacked her own SUV and was barking out instructions when Allison encountered her.

"How was Houma?"

"Humid," was all Taylor would say. As Allison turned to walk away, Taylor added, "But worth every penny."

Allison grit her teeth as she walked back and made sure everyone had their gear and their shooting order set. She went over the rules with the officials, jotting down details on her clipboard. Students walked the grounds, checking the conditions for themselves. It was a slightly overcast morning, a snap of chill in the air, a promise of the arriving fall.

Once the teams were in the proper places, the megalink targeting systems were secured, the grounds cleared, and spectators shooed into the background, There was no grandstand, so the parents and siblings had to stand back behind bright yellow ropes. Allison patted the shoulder of her first shooter, a nervous sophomore named Nasir. They'd start prone, then stand, then kneel, wave after wave. Ten shots and make way for the next shooter.

Studiously, Allison kept her focus on the competition, betraying none of the concern she had that something was going to go wrong. To her right, Taylor was equally focused on her team. They really moved alike, just had such varying temperaments that kept them apart.

When it was time for the standing shots, Allison neared Alexis, who never looked back. She was solely focused on her target, a wolfish grin on her face, her game face. She was locked and loaded, both mentally and physically.

Taylor was standing behind her own senior shooter, shouting minute corrections.

The judges held everyone's attention to signal the beginning of the round.

Alexis's rhythm was to aim and fire all ten shots without hesitation. It had a sweet rhythm to it, Allison thought as she watched the target shred the bull.

As a result, it was a second or two before she registered the shrieks from her right.

Allison turned to see Taylor had crumpled, imagining she still saw red mist in the cool morning air. All shooting had stopped so the crack of rifles was replaced with a chorus of human cries. Taylor's team ran away from the fallen body just as other adults ran toward it. Some huddled, others shielded nearby children and teens, all of whom were confused and terrified. Allison swung about, looking 360 degrees around, "scanning" for the shooter. She saw nothing and had to hide the grin.

Local law enforcement, who always attended these events, had their guns out, also scanning for the shooter while shouting instructions at the panicked crowd. At least one was also calling for ambulances and additional support.

"To my car," Allison shouted, herding her team toward the lot and her SUV. She pushed them forward, aided by several of the parents who had driven the team to the competition. No one spoke; everyone looked terrified. Once they reached the SUV, she did a headcount, and everyone was present, except Tracy, who hobbled to keep up. Neither met the other's eyes, but Allison was relieved to see everyone together.

She opened the rear and students, many with tears still staining their cheeks, haphazardly tossed in their gear. Once unburdened, they turned to parents or peers for comfort.

"Everyone get in their cars, but don't leave," Allison instructed.

"Screw that!" one parent shouted. "I'm going to keep my boy safe."

"Trust me, you won't get far, they're already blocking the road," the team leader told him, cocking her head toward the one road that acted as entrance and exit. A police car had just skidded to stop, its lights flashing blue, white, and red. Other parents with the same idea had already slowed down to a stop. Sirens could be heard in the distance. This place was going to be a zoo for hours.

She pushed Alexis and Tracy into her SUV while the others scrambled for their own cars. Once the doors were shut, Allison turned the key and turned on the radio, with classical music filling the air.

"Nice shooting," she said.

Both girls answered, "Thanks," and giggled at their simultaneity. Then Tracy reached a hand into the soft cast and withdrew a long, black cylinder, passing it forward to Allison. The older woman shoved it back to her. "Stow it," she ordered.

"Aren't you worried they're going to search us?" Alexis asked. "And the cars?"

"Probably," Allison muttered. "Settle in, we'll be here for hours. They'll check the guns we used, our gear, and so on. What they won't do is look inside Tracy's cast."

"That thing was wicked," Tracy said.

"Lightweight titanium with terrific sound suppression," Allison said proudly. "One of the best investments I made when I got started. Good shooting."

"But keeping the pistol in there hurts," Tracy complained instead of acknowledging the compliment.

"Tough shit," Allison said. "Suffer in silence until I can get you out of here."

"Did she really have to do it?" Alexis asked.

"She was a threat to our business interests and your college funds. So, yes."

"Plus, she was a bitch and lousy coach," Tracy added.

"Well, that, too," Allison said.

SHE'S A REAL COUGAR

KATHLEEN O'SHEA DAVID

DEAR MATHAN,

I hope this letter finds you well. If I have timed this right, you should be getting this on the eve of your sixteenth birthday.

I know I owe you an explanation. I have started this letter over and over, but I have decided this time to just write out my thoughts.

I honestly would understand if you just wanted to tear this letter up and forget I ever existed.

I wanted to take you with me, but circumstances made that impossible.

Do your grandparents ever talk about me? Are you still living in my old room?

I have no idea what name you will eventually use, just know that I gave you the name that your father picked for you, so blame him if you were teased.

Where to start… well, how about when everything changed for me.

I have no idea nor control over what your grandparents have told you about me. They were not happy that I left and made me know that they would tell you I abandoned you for irrational reasons.

I figure you know by now how much your grandfather believes in logic. He is a mathematician, and numbers are logical. He tends to see things in black or white with very little grey. He raised me that way, and for my early years, I saw the world as he did.

Your grandmother is the one who could see shades of grey and would, at times, present my side to my grandfather. However, they were a united front. If one parent said no, then the other would agree.

My childhood was fine. I have the requisite scraped knees and adventures. I got through elementary school, middle school, and high school with high grades and honors. It was in college that I started to discover those shades of grey, but that did not stop me from going to law school and becoming a lawyer.

Your grandparents were proud of my achievements.

As a graduation present, they gave me a ticket to Europe with a Eurail pass that included the United Kingdom. They gave me a credit card and a set budget for the trip. I had a time limit as I had been accepted to a law firm in Chicago I had interned at. My start date was January 1st of the next year, giving me 6 months to explore Europe and get myself set up in Chicago.

I discovered that several of my friends from college were going to be performing at the Fringe Festival in Edinburgh, and we agreed to meet up there and spend some time traveling around.

It was there that my world was turned upside down and I found new things to be passionate about. I watched the joy in my friends as they performed. I saw other shows that challenged my beliefs in just about everything. I wished I had taken classes in philosophy and religion and theater. My love of theater became all-encompassing, and all around me was that which I thirsted for.

It was there that I learned to party. I had gone to mixers and bars and student nights at college but hadn't been one for drinking much or doing any sort of drugs not prescribed by my doctor or the student health service. This made me popular among my friends because I had a larger car, and I could be the designated driver.

But here, things were different. I didn't have any grades to study for, nor a job to fight for. Both were in my pocket, and now I wanted to know what I had been missing in life.

I found that I had a fondness for scotch and lager beer. I also found out what hangovers felt like and learned to regulate my drinking, so they weren't too bad. Drinking had been frowned on but not forbidden in at home. Neither of your grandparents really drank except social situations.

It was also there that I first tried mushrooms and enjoyed the experience. I also dropped acid, but that didn't do much for me except allow me to see music.

There were many late nights discussing the problems of the world and arguing about the best way to solve them. I went from Libertarian leanings to Socialist rather rapidly.

My friend Lisa saw the change in me and invited me to travel with them to the other stops in their European tour.

I said yes because I knew we would be traveling with another troop of performers and I had a crush on two of them. Yes, I had a school-girl crush on a set of twins who was older than me and, I thought, considered me to be a little sister rather than a potential girlfriend.

The first time I saw the Seó Bóthair Imreors perform, I found it a religious experience. This group of people used their bodies and their voices to tell tales of great heroes and villains. They incorporated puppetry and magic as well, making the show a feast for the eyes and the soul. Even though the name was Irish, the group was from all over Europe but called each other family, which I thought was really nice. Little did I know at the time.

The one distinguishing feature on each member of the troop were the elaborate tattoo sleeves they all had. Certain symbols seem to run through the tattoos from person to person. It reminded me of the tattoos one would find in New Zealand among the Māori or other South Pacific Islanders.

The leader of the group was called Job. He seemed to be a bit older than most of the group; however, age had not slowed his moves. His brother, Eric Thomas Lentz, was his assistant and the manager of the group and had invited my friend's troop to travel with them since a number of stops in their tours were the same.

I was added to the list of Lisa's troop members, and we went onto the next stop in Berlin for a new fringe festival there.

It was interesting seeing the audience from the other side. I helped by selling tickets to our shows and taking tickets at the door, along with the set-up which everyone did. In doing so, I became a member of the troop and found myself invited to various parties and gatherings. Some were to promote the shows or the festival while others were big raucous parties of everyone who was performing at the festival.

I found myself in castles and historical houses. I saw architecture I had only seen in books and paintings by artists that I had loved. If allowed, I tended to wander the grounds enjoying the formal gardens at these places.

It was while wandering around the gardens that I overheard a conversation between twin brothers, who called themselves Romulus and Remus. No one knew if that was their real names or their stage names, just that those were the names they answered to. They did a silk rope act that was amazing to watch along with a couple of contortion numbers and were spotters for the trapeze act. I found them magical and pleasant to look at.

I heard my name being said, and that drew me to the conversation.

"She doesn't know!" said the twin I thought was Remus.

"She will," said the other twin.

"Romulus, she is not one of us. She is an outsider to our family."

I felt good that I could tell the twins apart. Many in our group could only tell them apart when they had their costumes on.

I heard cloth being shifted. "Then why did this appear when we touched hands? You know what that means. After all these years, I have hope again."

"Brother, I understand why you see her as a salvation, but she is not of our pack. She is some white girl from across the sea who has decided to become a lawyer because it is safe. Our lives are anything but safe. There is the fear of being found out by others. There are other packs that would kill her for knowing you."

"But my blood burns when I am close to her. She smells divine to me. I tell you, she is meant to be mine."

I heard a heavy sigh and again the shifting of cloth. "Or mine. I ran into her and this appeared."

"Oh, my brother, why didn't you tell me?"

"I didn't know how. I saw your mark the other day and wondered who the goddess had found for you, then I found the mark on me."

"Do the gods and goddesses favor or damn us with this?"

"We will find out at the full-moon festival next month. We can ask our deities then."

"Either way, we need to keep an eye on her and keep her from harm. We are going into enemy territory if we are not already there."

I could hear the men moving down the path toward me, so I scampered away from them, only to be confronted by one of the biggest dogs I had ever seen in my life. I almost bumped into it because of its dark fur that blended into the bushes around it. I did see the eyes and teeth of the monster as it turned and growled at me. I took a careful step back, and the animal moved toward me. I knew not to run but didn't have a clue of how to get away.

Then I saw what looked like a snow leopard and a tiger come between me and the dog and I heard what sound like Romulus' voice in my head saying, *Get out of here!*

I quickly walked my way back into the party and sat down, feeling light-headed, and tried to sort out what I saw.

Lisa came by and saw me.

"Marie, you okay? You look white as a ghost."

I nodded.

She sat down next to me. "Marie? Did you eat the brownies?"

"Yes, they were tasty."

"How many?"

"Three or four," I said and then realized how I was feeling. "What was in them?"

"A mix of things," she said, "but there was pot in there, along with other organic herbs."

I breathed a sigh of relief and almost collapsed.

"A bad trip," I said, "it was just a bad trip."

Lisa looked at me with concern and said, "We should go back to the hotel. You look like you need to go to bed and sleep it off."

In the car back to town, I told her about what had happened to me in the garden, or rather, what I thought happened to me. I now was unclear about any of it.

By the next morning, it all felt like a bad dream. My logical mind justified anything I heard or saw as hallucinations brought on by the brownies. My stomach spent the next day expelling everything in it. I swore off brownies from that point on.

Back on the tour, I started noticing things I had not before. I did see new marks on the wrists of the brothers. We had more people join us as we traveled in a meandering fashion through Europe. All these new members were old members of Seó Bóthair Imreors who had retired or gone to other jobs and lives. Our numbers swelled as we got to the Black Forest in Bavaria for the European equivalent of Burning Man; however, this one was invite only, being held at and around a castle deep in the forest. I was grateful for flushing toilets and warm showers. My family went camping and hiking my entire life, so I was not opposed to squatting over a dug hole to do my business, but I really preferred the comforts of home.

I did stay with Lisa and the gang in a set of yurts we borrowed from Seó Bóthair Imreors. I had bought a good sleeping bag, hiking boots and camping gear to help with this part of my trip. I figured I would give everything but the hiking boots to the troop when I moved back to my itinerary, or rather picked it back up.

I heard a lot of muttering about the bonfire ceremony, which would be held on the night of the full moon three days hence. Some of it made sense, but there were other things being said that sounded as if they were out of a fantasy novel.

Then there were the ribbons that started to appear around the wrists or attached to the shoulders of people. These had meaning to our touring partners, but we had no idea what they symbolized.

Saying they were ribbons was an injustice. These strips of cloth were woven with very intricate patterns. Some seemed very old, and other pieces brand new.

Lisa, who was also a weaver among her many skills, was fascinated by the ribbons and asked to see each person's sets. She started noticing patterns repeated in them. She filled a notebook with her notes.

The evening before the celebration was to start, Lisa and I found ourselves sitting up on a hill with the cool breeze of fall playing with our hair looking down at the camp and the castle.

"Did you know that there are four tribes down there?" she said.

"Tribes?"

"Best word I can find for them. There are four patterns that repeat in the ribbons. I noticed that brothers and sisters had the same pattern, along with parents and the like, then I noticed that there were four patterns that divided the group up. Each color has a specific meaning. Some I have not worked out, but I do know the men who have a dark blue ribbon are single, as are women with the light blue ones. It is fascinating to see this."

"So, the dark blue ribbons mean single?"

"What are you thinking?" she said with a smile and a wink.

"Me? Nothing…"

"Come on, spill it," she said handing me the wineskin we brought with us. "Oh my god, you are blushing."

I nodded and said, "Romulus and Remus are single, right?"

"You want to do it with twins? Is this some kink you have never told me about?"

"NO! No, not that at all. It's just…"

"They are easy on the eyes?"

"Well, there is that."

"Not that wacky thing that happened or might have happened depending on how high you were?"

I said nothing.

We looked as the stars and then went back to our yurts.

I found on my sleeping bag a package, as did Lisa. Inside were a couple of those ribbons that Lisa had been coveting with a note from Eric, Job's right-hand man.

Marie,

Please accepted the gift of these bands for you to wear at the festival. Please make sure you wear them where they can be seen. They indicate to others that you are part of our troop but not kin. If anyone gives you any problems, have one of the children find either me or Job immediately. I hope you have a good time, and thank you for traveling with us.

Eric

Below that was an embossed seal in the paper that was a fascinating pattern.

Lisa was beside herself, she was so happy.

We were one of the groups performing the next day, so most of my time was spent helping get ready for it.

Remus was helping out with putting together the stage that everyone would use for their shows. He was stripped to the waist and sweaty, which gave him a sheen that was reflected in the sunlight. I watched him for a while, admiring the beauty of his movement.

Lisa saw me doing so and said, "Eye candy indeed."

Romulus came over with a basket of programs for the evening and handed them to me.

"Apologies for the lateness of this," he said in his odd accent I still could not place. "The festival set-up is taking longer than usual."

He paused if considering what to say next.

"Something on your mind?" asked Lisa.

He nodded and looked at me. "Marie, will you be my guest at the bonfire on the full moon?"

I was flabbergasted and managed to squeak out the word, "Yes."

He smiled a genuine smile and bowed to me before running off.

"He is like a big puppy at times," said Lisa with a laugh.

Later that afternoon, as I was setting up the table to take tickets and hand out programs, Remus came by. He had put his shirt back on, and I noticed a dark blue ribbon wrapped around his arm among several others.

"Hey, Marie," he said with a toothy grin, "I was wondering if you would be my guest at the full moon bonfire."

I was thunderstruck and wondering what to do. Two very handsome men that I had impure thoughts about were asking me to the same event.

His brother walked up behind him. "I asked her already, brother, and she has agreed to be our guest at the bonfire."

Remus bowed a rather formal bow and handed me another ribbon, which was red and yellow. I added it to the ribbons Eric had given us.

"You honor us and our clan," said Romulus, bowing as well.

The brothers walked off arm in arm.

Later that evening, after the show, I was walking with the group to the food tent in hopes of scoring a late dinner.

I was rudely grabbed by the arm and spun around to find myself facing another member of Seó Bóthair Imreors that had joined us in France. I searched for his name but was drawing a blank.

"You!" he said through gritted teeth. "You outsider, how dare you wear a mark you have not earned?"

Job seem to appear out of nowhere at my elbow.

"Christian, it was given to her by Romulus. He has made his choice," said Job, grabbing the wrist of my attacker and removing it.

"No," Christian growled. "I will appeal to the council on this. How dare he invite this... person into our sacred space on our holiest night?"

"The choice has been made, and it was not you," said Job. "Leave her and her tribe alone."

Christian yanked his arm from Job's grip. The two of them had some sort of staring contest with a lot of eyebrow wiggling, and then he turned and stalked off.

"My apologies to you," Job said after Christian was out of sight. "That was very rude. I promise, he is in the minority of our group with that opinion of outsiders."

Romulus and Remus came running up to us.

"What happened?" asked Remus.

"Are you all right?" asked Romulus, pretty much at the same time as his twin.

Job held up a hand. "They are fine. Christian took disagreement with your choice for the bonfire. I have informed him that this was your choice."

The twins' heads moved as one, looking to where Christian vanished.

"No," said Job very firmly. "You will not challenge. I do not need the tsurius on this night of all nights."

"May I accompany you to the food tent?" asked Remus, extending his hand to me.

I nodded, and we joined hands. I felt an electric shock go through my arm.

Romulus linked arms with Lisa and Graham, the playwright for our show, and we went to the food tent.

Remus sat me down in the food tent, and went to get me a plate of whatever they were serving tonight. He picked well with the food he brought back. He had managed somehow to get things that I loved.

He sat down next to me, and we ate and made small talk. Romulus showed up with a plate of various fruits and dessert items and sat on the other side of me.

It was a good evening with a lot of laughter.

The twins escorted Lisa and me to our tent, giving us both hugs before we went in.

"Well, that was weird," said Lisa as we settled in. "I think the twins are interested in you."

I yawned and said, "That's all in your head. They are being polite, inviting me to their festival."

"Well, I didn't get an invite," she said with a snort.

The next day, we did another two performances. I noticed a lot more of the twins' troop were stopping by and just looking at me. Some were glowering at me, and others seemed pleased. I was totally confused.

Lisa came up to me with a grin on her face. "Do you know what you have done?"

"I haven't a clue."

"A little bird told me that you managed to catch the attentions of the two most desirable men in their group. They have never invited anyone to wear their ribbons ever."

"Did you learn anything else about the ribbons?"

"Not much. They are really closed lipped about them."

The next couple of days I was stared at and, I swear, growled at by various members of the twins' group. Others, especially the older members, came and would take my hand and put the back of it to their head and welcomed me.

The day of the bonfire, I woke up to find a package just outside my tent with a note from Romulus explaining this was the ritual clothing for the ceremony, but I could wear what I felt comfortable with.

I opened the package, and within was a skirt, top, and shawl. The embroidery work on each piece was exquisite to look at. Lisa gasped upon looking at the garments and started looking at each with great enthusiasm.

"Can I take pictures?" she asked.

"Go ahead. I don't see why not," I replied.

We didn't have a show that day as everyone seemed to be getting ready for the bonfire that evening. We went to take a warm shower in the castle and ran into the twins coming out of the bath house in the castle.

That afternoon, she helped me get dressed. The clothes were very cleverly made since they were adjustable, so they fit me like they were made for me.

I stepped out to find the twins waiting for me. They were wearing not much considering the weather. The ribbons they had been sporting all week were now wrapped in intricate patterns around their arms and chest. They had loose trousers with embroidery all over them and the slippers they wore around the tent for performances.

"You look lovely," said Romulus with a stunned look on his face. Remus nodded with the same look on his.

"Okay, boys," said Lisa. "Make sure she gets home safely from the ball and with both shoes, please."

"We can't promise she will be home by midnight, but we will get her home," said Remus with a grin.

They helped me wrap the shawl correctly, and then each offered me an arm before setting off for the bonfire.

"The public part of the ceremony will complete about nine, then we take a break until ten, and the family ceremony will begin. You are invited to both under our protection," said Romulus.

"You are going to scare her, brother!" said Remus. "Basically, the party doesn't get really started until after the strangers finally leave us alone. We would love for you to spend the whole night with us until sunrise and the conclusion of the ceremony."

"But I am a stranger," I said.

The two men looked at each other over my head and seemed to be mentally talking to each other.

"Marie, you aren't to us. You came to us a stranger, but over time, you have become a friend, and a good one too. We feel a..."

Remus picked up what his brother was saying, "...connection to you. We did when we met you back in Scotland, but we didn't know much about you."

"Since then, you have become a part of our group, and we wanted to ask you to join us as a member."

I stopped walking, just stunned with what they were telling me.

"Marie? You okay?" asked one of the twins. I couldn't tell which one as I heard a roaring in my ears as my brain just tried to process what I was being offered.

"I have a job," I babbled. "I am going to be a copyright lawyer in Chicago. I have a life there. I..."

Or did I? I had a job and some friends, but no one to go back to. It was so tempting to drop it all and run off and join this circus.

"I don't know what I want to do," I finished.

"Well join us tonight. You do not need to decide your entire life right here, but keep an open mind. Honestly, we could use a lawyer in the troop," said Remus as he patted my hand comfortingly.

"Yes, tonight is a celebration of the turn of the year for us. It is a time to let our hair down and howl," said Romulus. Both brothers then tipped their heads back and let out a full-throated howl that was answered by others in the same manner.

The bonfire celebration was in a natural amphitheater with a large oak and maple next to each other behind the staging area. The stack of wood was setup to burn, and there were banners with various patterns on them all around the edge of the area. These made a natural privacy fence. I followed the twins over to the banner that was the same colors as the ribbon they had given me, and we went to the bottom of the slope, where there were blankets and food spread out. Joining us were other members of the troop that I knew. We sat down and ate while waiting for the others filing in. I noticed that the people who were traveling with the group but not part of it were sitting up on the berm.

A couple of earthen jars were passed around the group. It was some sweet concoction laced with an alcohol after taste. I found it very good.

As the sun started to set, I could feel an electric hum go through the crowd. The musicians took their places, waiting for some sort of signal.

Job stood up and walked to the front of the woodpile. Two assistants came and put a beautiful multicolored cloak on his shoulders and handed him what could only be described as a wizard's staff. It was very theatrical but also seemed very normal.

"Welcome, all," he started. "Another year is almost over, and we have done well."

There was a cheer that rang through the amphitheater.

"Tonight, we honor our goddesses and gods and ring in our new year. Let the celebration begin!"

He pointed his staff at the pile of wood, and it ignited as if by magic. I suspected radio-controlled fireworks, but that was me.

The men howled, and the women ululated. The drummers started the beat, and the rest of the musicians followed.

Everyone grabbed a partner and started to dance around the bonfire. Remus got Lisa, and the four of us gyrated around the large fire.

It was a joyful time as people circled around each other, joining groups then dancing to the next one. The moon shone down, bathing us in its silver light.

All of the sudden, the drumming stopped, and everyone froze. A mournful horn broke the silence.

Job was in front of the bonfire again with his staff and cloak. "Thank you, friends, for joining us in our celebration. We ask you now to return to your tents and rooms, and we will see you tomorrow."

Lisa offered me her hand, and Remus stopped her.

"We have invited Marie to stay with us," said Romulus, taking my hand in his. "She has agreed to join us."

Lisa looked at me carefully. "Marie?"

"Go on," I said. "I'm fine." I was, in fact, not feeling fine, as I could feel my body swaying slightly and my mind racing, but I wanted to see what happened next.

She looked into my eyes. "If you are sure."

"I have never been more sure in my life," I replied, while my mind was saying, *What the hell are you talking about?* It just felt right, and I could not say why. I needed to be at the place at that time with these people.

She nodded and gave me a hug. "See you back at the yurt."

She hugged the twins and then left the circle.

They guided me back to the blanket where we had dinner and sat me down, with Romulus on my right and Remus on my left. There was water and a fruit-and-dried-meat tray waiting for us. Both men toweled down, wiping the sweat from their bodies, then fed me from the tray.

I found that gesture very sweet that they tended to my needs before theirs.

A young boy and girl came around with earthen jars and handed a blue one to each of the twins with deep bows.

"N'uncles, please accept the gifts of our goddesses and gods to help you through this night," they said in unison.

Remus gestured, and the girl handed me a green jar and bowed. "N'auntie, please accept this gift, and may it bring you joy."

The three of us clinked the jars and downed the contents. To this day, I cannot describe the taste, as it seemed like all tastes and none at the same time. After finishing it, I could feel an energy surging through me, giving me my second wind and more.

Job returned with his wife at his side. They had changed outfits and now were dressed in stylized matching green outfits that looked like they were playing Titania and Oberon in *A Midsummer Night's Dream*. They stood in front of the bonfire and raised their staffs while chanting something I couldn't hear.

Romulus helped me up, and I went with them to join the circle of troop members around the fire and the two large trees in the base of the amphitheater. We were stationed to the right of Job. Children ran in and out of the circle, handing the adults wooden staffs decorated with beads and ribbons, then went to stand with their parents.

Job said, "It is the night of miracles! Let all who wish come forward and receive the judgment of the gods."

"As it is right and fair in faith and love," everyone chanted back.

Then a hum started that grew in volume. It began with the children, then the women joined in, and finally the men. It went through my body and wrapped itself in my brain. It was like a light-switch had been turned on, and my mind expanded and contracted at the same time.

Everyone looked up now, fully vocalizing. I found myself joining in. The full moon seemed to be coming toward us, and there were seven shadowy figures in the light that walked down into the circle.

When the first figure touched the ground, everyone stopped and dropped to their knees.

Once all seven had landed, the elderly woman in the middle touched Job's forehead in blessing as her companion touched his wife. They helped them up and then turned to us.

"Children," said the woman, who looked like a Jedi force ghost. "We are pleased."

The seven figures, four women and three men, went around the circle, blessing the troop and listening to their prayers and wishes. Each child was handed a ribbon that glowed like the person who handed it to them.

All of the sudden, I saw something I had a hard time believing. As if ghosts from the moon were not enough, I started seeing animals around each person. A number of members seemed to have animal rather than human heads. Each of the figures had several animals with them.

I looked down to see a ferret and a badger in front of the twins. I turned to look, and Romulus had a tiger head and Remus had a snow-leopard head, with large wolves at their sides. I remembered the two animals that I thought had been hallucinations back in the garden, and now my mind was filled with more questions than answers.

The elderly woman came over to us and motioned to get up. She was dressed in a beautiful robe with the pattern dancing in the moonlight. There seemed to be a fox across her shoulders feigning indifference to what was happening around it. A serval cat along with a very large rabbit and grey wolf were next to her looking at us.

She took my face into her hands and looked into my soul. I felt like she was sorting me out and deciding if I was worthy to be standing in front of her. I feared what might happen if she found me unworthy.

She smiled, and I knew all was right with the world. She kissed my forehead and said, "I choose you to be one of my own."

She looked at the twins and said, "You have chosen well." Then she chuckled. "Took you long enough." She turned her attention back to me. "I await our next meeting."

The seven figures returned to the center of the circle and blessed the group, then vanished.

There was a cheer from the group, and the drummers started drumming again. We all started dancing. I noticed that the married couples and children were dancing themselves out of the circle, leaving the single people dancing with each other. After the last child left, the dance took a much more erotic turn as couples and groups ground against each other in passion.

The twins took up the space either side of me and growled if anyone came too close. We started dancing with each other. Both men asked permission before touching me then again to kiss me. I felt like a Goddess being worshiped by her devotees. Again, permission was asked before touching me in more intimate places. I found myself on our blanket with both men making me feel really good. Under the moon before the sun rose, we made love, and you were conceived.

We were enjoying the afterglow when I asked, "Now what?"

"Are you going to take our offer?" asked Remus.

"I still need to think about it," I said, but in my mind I knew I was going to give everything up at home for madcap adventures with these two men. It felt right, like it was, as it is said in those cheap romance novels, my destiny.

We love you, came a voice in my head, *We are now bound together for all time.*

Another voice joined the first one, *You will be the mother of our children and keep our blood line strong.*

Please, said both voices at the same time.

We were interrupted by Eric, who came running up to us.

We have a major problem, I heard in my head.

Eric looked at me, *You can hear me?*

I nodded.

He looked at the twins and said out loud, "Really?"

Remus put a protective arm around me. "Our union has been blessed by the Moon Goddess."

Romulus did the same and said, "We are bonded to her, and she to us, for all time."

Eric shook his head, "We will sort this out later. Ivan has showed up with his pack and challenged Job for leadership over ours."

"What?!" said both twins as they jumped up naked as the day they were born.

"Where's Job?" asked Romulus.

"Where are the women and children?" asked Remus.

Eric pointed to deeper in the forest. "The arena is being put together there. The women and children are in the castle with Lisa. They can protect themselves."

The brothers looked at each other, and then in a split second I saw them change from men to animals. My brain was trying to process with what I saw. The tiger and leopard nuzzled my hands affectionately and then ran off into the wood.

My mind just couldn't process what I was seeing, and I fainted.

I came to the next day in my yurt with very pleasant thoughts of the night before. I stretched and felt a few twinges in muscles I rarely used. I was about to roll over and go back to sleep when Lisa ran into the tent.

"They are gone! The entire troop pulled up stakes and left last night. The only ones left are the groups that were traveling with them"

"What?" I said as I pulled on my robe and exited the tent.

She was right. The city was now down to a few tents here and there. We went to the castle to find that there was still food to be had but the staff was totally new to us. We were informed that there would be transport back to the train station this afternoon and we needed to leave for the next group coming in.

I was confused. After a night with my lovers, I was abandoned? I felt rather used but a voice in my head said, *No my dear, they have a task to do. You have another task that will test you, but I believe in you. Check your backpack when you get home and know you are very much loved.*

Lisa and I went back to the yurt and proceeded to pack. I took off my robe to put on my traveling clothes when I noticed the marks on my arm. They looked like henna art, and I recognized a number of the patterns I had seen among the troop and even on the twins' arms.

"What the hell happened to you?!"

I turned toward her, holding out my arm, "Henna?"

"I'm not talking about your arm—what happened to your neck? Those hickeys look like serious."

I picked up a mirror from my toiletry kit and looked at my neck. On either side, placed at the juncture of my neck and shoulder, were two bite marks I didn't remember getting.

"I have no idea," I said, but somewhere in my head, I knew that I had said yes to everything that we had done.

We packed up and speculated as to what happened the previous night. I didn't tell her about the end of the evening because it was just too insane. I put it down to a hallucination brought on by the evening's activities.

On the train going back to France for their last scheduled performance, I decided to part ways with my friends and finish up my trip in Ireland before going home.

Lisa was not happy with my decision and worried that I was going to go back to the Black Forest to find the twins.

I promised her that was not the case. It was just time for me to finish my trip and get home.

The only things I had that made me not believe my entire adventure was a bad trip were the marks on my body, which had not faded, and a small packet of ribbons I found in my backpack.

I did not know yet I had another souvenir from that night yet.

I found myself in Killarney at a very nice B&B that was next to an equally nice pub. I decided to spend the day hiking the Carrauntoohill trail. I needed some time to think about all that had happened over the past couple of months.

It was one of those perfect days that happen only a few times in one's life. The temperature was cool but not cold. The sky was a color of radiant blue that has not been translated by any painter because that color only exists in the sky. The green of the hills was comforting as I walked along the trail. I felt at peace, and my mind was at rest just enjoying the day.

I found several fairy circles, as the locals called them. Verdant green places surrounded by a ring of mushrooms and stones. After all that had happened this past summer, I did not step in them. I did find a nice piece of flat grass and pulled the plowman's lunch I had brought out of my backpack, along with a bottle of cider. I set up my lunch and started to munch on the cheese and bread when I looked up to see a badger looking at me very intently.

"What?" I asked.

And in my mind, I heard, *Can I have a piece of that lovely apple you have there?*

I pulled out my multi-tool and cut a chuck out of the apple and offered it to the badger. He sat up and took it from me in his paws then proceeded to eat it very delicately. I cut him another piece, which he took and ate. I was about to cut a third when the voice in my head said, *No, thank you. This was plenty.*

He bobbed his head to me and then sat back on a rock. *Would it be impolite to ask why you are here?*

I said, "I wanted to see Ireland before I go back to the US and start my adult life."

Haven't you already?

I laughed. "No. To me, this is one last fling before starting what will be the rest of my life."

He looked at me sideways, *A fling? You are throwing your life away?*

"Not that definition of fling," I replied. "A short period of enjoyment or wild behavior."

He nodded. "*Last taste of youthful indiscretion. May I see your arm?*"

I took off my jacket, exposing what I thought was henna but turned out to be a tattoo. How I got a tattoo and did not remember it was beyond me.

He stepped toward me and sniffed my wrist. *You are goddess blessed! She had bestowed much upon you.*

He made a weird chirp, and out of the tall grass, a female badger and three cubs emerged. They came over to me and joined in the sniffing. Soon, I was a climbing toy for the children, who were so soft and loved to be petting and tickled. I fed the rest of my apple to the badger family. The parents both sat down in front of me and seemed to be talking to each other.

The mother badger made a noise, and the children climbed off me and back to her. *My mate says that she wishes you well with your own cub. We thank you for your time and that wonderful apple.*

That, my son, was when I was first told of your existence, but at the time, I thought of it in the abstract rather than that I was pregnant.

Spending the time with the badgers put me behind in my hike, so it was dark with only moonlight and my flashlight to illuminate my path as I headed back to my B&B. I accidently stepped into one of the fairy rings that I didn't see until too late, and my flashlight went out, leaving me with moonlight only to see.

Funny thing was that the moment the light went out, I could see better. The moonlight seemed to be bright enough that I didn't need an extra light.

I carefully pulled my foot out of the circle, not disturbing the ring around it. What seemed to be a firefly coming toward me turned into a small female with wings who happened to be glowing. I thought it might be a flashback from my earlier activities during my trip, an acid trip part two.

"Well met, traveler," said the figure. "I thank you for not breaking our ring here."

"You are welcome."

"May I ask your name?"

"Marie, ma'am," I said with a slight bow.

She laughed, which sounded like silver bells in the wind. "It is very nice to meet you, Marie."

She whistled, and all of a sudden, the air was full of the twinkly lights of the fairy folk.

"Please welcome Marie to our sanctuary. Hail, and well met to you."

"Hail, and well met, Marie" said the points of light as they came closer and landed in the circle. They reminded me of the fairies in *Fantasia*.

"Hail, and well met to your child," said the head fairy.

"What child?" I asked. "You are the second ones to mention a child."

She pointed at my midsection, "The one you carry within you."

I felt both a cold and a warm feeling in the pit of my stomach at the same time.

We talked for a bit, and then I begged off to go back to the town because I was feeling very tired and needed time to think about what I had just learned or thought I learned.

My head whirled around what I had learned, and I wondered if it was true.

I heard a growl from my left and turned to see that big black dog that I had seen in the garden in France. Its eyes glowed a menacing red, and its teeth glowed in the moonlight. Behind that animal, I saw two more grey wolves with yellow eyes and the same glowing teeth.

Why you? came a voice in my head. *Why did they pick you and not me?*

"Christian? Is that you?" I asked, laughing at the absurdity of this night.

You have it all! Their child, the goddess' blessing. They were promised to me.

"By whom?" I asked.

By the grand council. They were to be betrothed to me when they came of age.

"What did they think of this?"

I thought they loved me. The wolf let out a mournful howl. *They were to love me. I was an Omega of the blood. We would have joined the lines and brought the tribes together.*

The wolves stepped toward me. I stepped back, trying not to fall off the path. Out of the bushes came the badgers I had met earlier with a very large red deer buck with a large rack of horns following. The badgers stepped between the wolves and me and hissed at the wolves.

Go! said the male badger. *Go, and we will protect your back.*

I found myself slowly moving away from the wolves and watched as they attacked the buck and the badgers. Christian broke free of the fight and started coming for me. In that moment, all I wanted was to protect you. I prayed to the goddess to save my child, and then everything changed.

My body felt like it was being torn apart and being put back together at the same time. I found myself looking at large cat paws. It took me a minute to reorient myself to whatever form I found myself in.

I felt the wolf jump on top of me, and I spun to get him off. I snarled then attacked after springing my claws. I got my mouth around his neck when he went limp and whimpered.

I yield, I heard in my head.

The wolf under me whimpered, and I let them up. They slunk back to the other two wolves.

This is not over, rang in my head before the three wolves turned tail and left.

Come with us and get cleaned off, said the badger.

I followed him to a clear pond, where I looked into the water and saw a large cougar looking back at me. It had my blue eyes and a bit of my hair coloring, which I found strange. I went into the pond and washed the blood out of my fur. I licked my hindquarters where the wolf had scratched me. I figured I was working on instinct because I have never been a large cat before. I also had no idea how to change back.

Relax, said a voice in my head.

I turned my head to see the woman who had blessed me at the bonfire about a month ago.

She smiled and reached her hand toward me. I went to her, and she stroked my head. I liked it. I could feel the rumble in my throat and in my chest.

Let's get you back to you, she said, kneeling next to me and rubbing me under the chin. She showed me how to turn back, and it hurt a lot. But I managed to return to my human form. Unfortunately, it was sans clothes. I went back to where I had changed to find my clothing amazingly intact. I dressed and walked back to the B&B as the sun started the peek over the horizon went to my room and passed out.

The next morning, I would have thought what happened the night before was a bad trip if it had not been for the scratches on my ass. My logical brain put it down to sliding down a hill since I did have some other bruising.

This did not make the ride back to the United States very comfortable, even with a nice business class seat. Between that and my stomach upset, it was not a fun flight.

Once I got home, I got a home pregnancy test and had proof of your existence, which turned my world upside down again.

There was no hiding what had happened from your grandparents. The tattoos were noticed and disapproved of first before I dropped the other bomb of my condition.

To say they were disappointed would be an understatement. I don't think I had ever had that loud a screaming match with my parents. I went down to my basement apartment not knowing what I was going to do next. My life had been planned out so carefully, and one night's adult fun changed things forever.

Understand that once I knew you were in me, my commitment to being your mom became everything.

My mother came down later with dinner for me.

"You can't judge your father too harshly. He needs to work his way to understanding how wonderful this is."

"Wonderful? I came back tattooed and knocked up. He is probably questioning everything right now. I disappointed both of you."

"You cannot disappoint us Marie; you're our daughter. We love you, and we will love our grandchild when he or she arrives in...?"

"Seven months, I think," I said. "I really didn't know I was pregnant for sure until I got home. I suspected it after I missed my time of the month two months in a row."

"Where's the father? Does he know?"

"Ummmmm..."

"I will take that as a no."

I then told her the tale of my summer and the twins but left some of the more bizarre elements out of it.

"When did you get the tattoo?"

I decided to go for the partial truth. "Over the summer. One of the troop members was a wonderful tattoo artist."

"Why?"

That was harder to find an answer to, "Impulsive behavior?"

"It seemed there was a lot of that this summer. Ah well, at least you kept the family tradition."

"Pardon?"

"Your father and I spent the summer between college and grad school hitchhiking our way around the United States and got married in Las Vegas on impulse."

"But I have seen the wedding photos," I said, trying to make sense of what I was hearing.

"Oh, that was later for the family. They didn't know we had already done the deed until after you were born. We came clean so that you would be born in wedlock."

"Mom!"

"You can make this work. I am sorry that you were abandoned by your young men, but you have a job and the ability to do anything you set your mind to. Your father and I will support you in this. You will not be alone, but you are going to have to be an adult in all this."

She gave me a hug and said, "Eat your dinner."

She went back upstairs, leaving me with my thoughts.

Later that night, I finished cleaning out my backpack, and in the bottom of the outer pouch, I found a rolled piece of paper wrapped in the same ribbon that Remus gave me back at the festival.

I looked at it for a bit. I thought I had gone through the entire bag when I repacked my suitcase.

I took the ribbon off and put it with the others in my keepsake box then unrolled the paper.

Our Dearest Marie,

The goddess promises that we will meet again, but right now we have work to do. She has also promised to keep you safe and our child safe as well.

You probably have a number of questions, so we will tell you what you need to know now, and the rest will wait until all of us are together.

We are an old race that has been around since before humans walked this planet. Over the centuries our bloodlines have mingled and, for the most part, we are few. Within the tribe there are very few pure-bloods left, and those are held in high regard. We are two of the pure-bloods and have been political pawns since the day we were born.

We had resigned ourselves to be betrothed at the next bond fire, which was the Harvest Moon. We would be sold off to another tribe at a very high bridal price.

Then we met you and everything changed.

You are the one that the Goddess chose for us. We knew this the first time you touched us and a new mark of mated appeared on our wrists. You were our Omega to our Alphas. There are three, for lack of a better word, genders in our species: Alphas, Omegas, and Betas. Betas are lucky because they can procreate among themselves with no penalty. But for an Alpha to have children, they must find an Omega, and it has to be a goddess-blessed match, or there are no children to be had. It is one of the many reasons we are dying out.

You now hold the future of our tribe in your womb.

We wanted to be with you, but in choosing you as our mate, a war that has been brewing within our tribes boiled over into combat, and we had to defend our tribe as we are their champions. It was safer for you to know nothing of this and escape back to your world.

We wish for our son to be called Mathan, and tell him nothing of any of this until his sixteenth birthday, where he is seen as an adult in the tribe and can speak for himself.

There is another aspect of our being that you did not know about, or rather knew but put it down to hallucinations brought on by mind-altering substances. We are shape shifters. The stuff of legend called werewolves or worse. We can change form as we need to. During the goddess-blessed full moon, it is easier to do, but we always have the ability. As children, we tend to morph as we go along, but once in adolescence, we choose a few favorites that become our other forms, but we all have our goddess-chosen forms. Remus is a snow leopard, and Romulus is a Asian tiger.

We have left you pregnant and alone, for which we are truly sorry. We weren't kidding about the jobs as the lawyers for the troop. You are ours, and we are yours in blood and bond.

We love you,
Romulus and Remus

It seemed that I was loved. I felt like both men were sitting on either side of me with their arms around me. But at the same time, I felt totally alone.

The rest of the pregnancy was a bit of a blur. I did go to Chicago and join the firm I had interned at. I found an apartment and, through good luck or fate, Lisa came back to be my roommate as she became the associate art director of the theater she worked at. My parents supported me both emotionally and financially so I could continue with my life.

The day you were born was one of the happiest in my life. Painful, yes, but you were totally worth it. The moment I held you in my arms, all of what happened passed away, and there was only you. You looked at me with such intensity that I knew I had to protect you at all costs.

Your first year was pretty normal. You hit all the milestones on time. You walked before you would talk. You seemed to prefer going on all fours until we convinced you to join us upright.

Then there were the incidents that happened when I would be looking at a baby, then it would be a wolf cub or a snake or a squirrel or a bat then switching back to baby.

Once you started walking, this would happen more often, and it was getting harder to hide.

We would spend time at my parents', and I would take you out into the woods, where you loved to toddle around. Sometimes as one creature you would see then trying another form. You thought it was a great game.

Then one day, it all changed. We were out in the woods, and you had taken the form of a fox and were exploring with your nose when a bear showed up. For some reason, I recognized that it was no ordinary bear.

"Christian?" I asked.

'*I will end you and your spawn,*' came the reply as the bear went to attack you. You ran and hide in a hollow log. Christian proceeded to try to tear your hiding place apart.

I found myself moving from one form to another rapidly. The cougar came forth, and I attacked the bear. It was not a fair fight. The bear had a purpose, but a mother's love will always come through. I had the bear on the ropes when it went submissive, and I heard a voice in my head: *I yield, Omega.*

It was not Christian's voice.

Who are you?

A hunter. You and your cub are worth a lot to me, or were worth.

Worth?

There is a price on your heads, and a council order to bring the both of you in for the trial of the champions.

No, I thought with a low growl in my throat. *We will not be going, nor will you be telling where we are.*

I pounced and finished him. He was very tasty. You joined me in the meal then switched back to your human form. I licked the blood from you, wondering how I was going to keep you safe.

I heard the sound of bells and the old woman who had blessed me appeared before us.

"My child, you are troubled," she said, kneeling in front of me and taking my head in her hands.

What am I to do? I don't know how to control these changes. I don't know how to teach my child to not turn into a bat in front of his grandparents. There are people after both of us. I am a danger to my family and my child.

She kissed the top of my head, and my body relaxed back into its original form.

"I did not want this for you, my child. I had hoped that when you joined with the boys, the rest of this petty feud would end. But free will is free will, and stupid decisions are made. I can bind your child's powers until he is around sixteen, then he is considered an adult in our community. That way, he will be invisible to our people."

"There is a target on my back. I need to find my mates," I said. "I need answers and to know that my child is safe from this madness."

We worked out a plan for both you and me, trying to keep you safe.

I am leaving so you can grow up without fear.

I will miss you so much, my cub. I have no idea if your grandparents will ever let me see you after I leave.

Know that I love you with all my heart.

She promised that you would find this note once you reached sixteen. Use the map I enclosed to find your way to us. I look forward to seeing my baby boy again.

Love,
Mom

The boy took pictures of the letter and the map then rolled them back up and wrapped the ribbon around them. He put them in his backpack and looked around the room to see what he missed, absentmindedly touching the tattoo that had appeared when he turned sixteen.

"It's okay, Mom. I understand, and I am coming to you," he said as he shouldered his pack, ready to leave his childhood home and find his people.

DUCKBOB IN: RUNNING HOT AND COLD

AARON ROSENBERG

"**M**A, LOOK OUT!" I GRAB her and yank her down just before an ice shard the size of my head—well, okay, the size of a regular guy's head, mine would be the thing that sank the *Titanic*—slams into the wall right where she was standing.

"What was that?" she shouts, glancing behind us at the bits of ice now raining down on our heads. "Robert, who are these people? And why are they messing up your… house? Don't they know how hard it is to get stains off the walls?"

"Yeah, I don't think they're too concerned about that, Ma," I tell her, guiding her along the back of the couch as a jet of flame lances past, close enough to singe some of my feathers. Yes, we're under attack by two strangers, one with fire and the other with ice. I feel like I wandered into Battle of the Bands. "But we can ask later, if you like. Soon as I get you somewhere safe and call in some backup to deal with… whatever the heck this is." The couch is helpfully becoming high-backed, providing us with a lot more cover, which is good since with my silhouette this'd normally be like trying to hide an elephant behind a toothpick. Another oh-so-helpful side effect of the Grays abducting me all those years ago and turning me into a man-duck—my outline basically looks like it belongs in a cartoon.

Or as the prow of a bathtime pirate ship. Problem is, there's only one doorway in this room and it's the one Frick and Frack are shooting from, so all I'm doing right now is backing us into a corner, literally and figuratively.

This is precisely why I didn't want my mom to come for a visit. Not that I knew this would happen, exactly, but something was bound to. It's, like, a law of the universe or something—you can't ever have a nice, normal parental visit.

Well, at least I can't. The last time she visited me was back in college, and they still haven't unlocked the files on what went down that night. Or figured out where that one sorority house wound up.

But this is worse. Probably because it's the center of the universe— literally—and the Matrix that protects the whole shebang from outside incursion, and the Guardian of said Matrix—namely, me. And if I don't figure something out, and fast, we're gonna be the ones whose fates they can't figure out.

We reach the corner, and there's still fire and ice whipping back and forth overhead. Great. It's like that time I visited Kansas and it was 90 degrees and sunny when I went into a movie and snowing when I came back out. Only these jokers don't even have the decency to wait half an hour in case I ate. Haven't they ever heard of climate control? Geez!

That makes me think of central air, which makes me think of my apartment, and—bingo! I pull out my fob and grab Ma's hand. Then I tell her, "close your eyes," shut my own, and click the second button.

Mary always tells me there's no need to shut my eyes. It's instant, she says, and safe as houses. But I've been in some pretty rickety houses, and I'd rather not chance having my brain explode because I just watched myself get taken apart, atom by atom, flung across the galaxy, and reassembled just like I was.

Plus I always worry, what if it isn't an exact match? What if my left pinky's a little longer than it was, or my right big toe's a little more crooked, or that one clump of feathers isn't quite the same shade of green? If I'm not looking it's harder to notice the change and I can pretend it's all my imagination.

Sometimes I outsmart myself.

The sounds disappear, replaced by the usual background noise of

Manhattan, cars and shouting. I open my eyes and we're back in the apartment, with no sign of the Tap Twins. Whew!

"Okay, Ma," I tell her. "You can look now."

She opens her eyes and looks around. "Oh, we're back," she says, sinking onto the living room couch. "So what was that, a bad acid trip?"

I try not to roll my eyes at that—I've been working to cut back on that and fried foods. "No, it's real," I tell her instead. "That's the Matrix, where I work. I told you about it. This is just my apartment, where I live."

"But you said you live there too," she reminds me. "You said you had to before, and that's why you never came over."

"Yes, exactly. I had to at first," I confirm. "When I first became Guardian of the Matrix, I couldn't leave its sight. Or it couldn't leave mine. Or whatever. But now I can go anywhere I want, thanks to this." I tap the crown Ned gave me—it's really an unlimited-range omnidirectional link that connects me to the Matrix anywhere in the universe, but it looks like a cheesy beauty-pageant tiara that I'm just wearing backward so it rises up in back and is open in front. "Then I got this place, and now I'm here."

This is what I get for deciding I should tell my mom the truth about everything—about me, about the Matrix, all of it. We let all my siblings and cousins keep their memories after they helped us save the universe, but Ma wasn't there—she doesn't like to travel much anymore, claims it's her bursitis but really I think it's just her not wanting to leave the house unguarded from the rest of us—and I made them all promise not to tell her. The more I thought about that, though, the more ridiculous it was. I mean, this is my *mom*, for Heaven's sake! So I thought I'd invite her over to the apartment, which she hadn't seen yet, and tell her the truth.

Only, she didn't believe me.

"Always such a creative boy, Robert," she told me, patting my cheek. Like I'd just built the Battle of Agincourt out of popsicle sticks and gummy worms (Hey, I got a B- for that, and would've had an A if my longbows hadn't wilted!).

So I figured I'd just show her the Matrix. Once you see it in all its whirling, twinkling, semi-sentient glory, it's impossible to pretend it isn't real. And fortunately I've got this fob the Grays gave me, so with the click of a button I can bounce back and forth between home and work—as can anyone touching me at the time. "I'll prove it," I'd told her, took her hand, clicked—and found ourselves in the middle of a Robert Frost poem done as an MMA fight.

Now we're safe again but they're still back there, with the Matrix, which means I've gotta go back.

"Wait here, Ma," I tell her. "I'll be right back." Mind, I have no idea what I'm gonna do about Sunshine and Deep Freeze, but I'll figure something out.

"You're going back there?" she asks me.

"I have to, Ma. It's my job."

She stands and brushes herself off. "Fine. Then I'm going with you."

"Ma—" I start, but she holds up The Hand.

I know better than to argue with The Hand.

"You have a bat or something?" she asks. "I'd feel safer."

A bat? What does she think this is, summer tryouts for the Mets? "No, Ma, I don't have a bat," I say, turning and heading for the front door. "But I've got something better." I reach into the umbrella stand and pull out one of those compact umbrellas, the cheap kind that tend to fire off the actual umbrella part if you push the Open button too hard. I do that, and then strip off the cheap plastic handle to reveal a much cooler, sleeker handle, all smooth lines and gleaming metal. It kind of looks like a cross between a really big crochet hook and a harpoon gun. Tall insisted I keep some kind of protection around the place, and this was one of the smallest guns he had. But despite the barrel being about as wide as a pencil, it's still powerful enough to take out a Sherman tank with one shot. "Here." I hand it to her. "Just point and shoot."

She studies the gun for a second, then shrugs and takes it. "Let's go."

So we hold hands, close our eyes, tap again, and we're back at the Matrix. At this rate I'm gonna get whiplash!

The good thing is, the fob is set to beam me directly to the Matrix itself, which is in its own room at the back of the house. The room's the size of a football field, almost—the whole place is actually some kind of beyond-ancient alien skull and the Matrix has the whole cranium all to itself, which is probably for the best since it likes to stay up late watching stupid sitcoms. "Stupid" meaning they're not the same ones I like.

That's where we appear, and I'm relieved to see that the Matrix looks fine. It's still doing its thing, circling slowly like an old guy trying to remember how to conga, bits of it twinkling and glittering and whirling and—smoking? Darn it, I keep telling it to stop that! Anyway, it looks like Yin and Yang haven't messed with it directly yet, so that's something. And where are the Temperature Twins right now, come to think of it? I listen, but don't hear anyone shooting anything or destroying any of my furniture. Hey, maybe they got tired and sat on the couch and it ate them? Wouldn't be the first time, and for a change I wouldn't be scolding it about trying to swallow my friends! But I doubt I'm that lucky.

"Where are they?" Ma whispers, holding the gun like a golf club, which means if it goes off she's liable to give herself a second belly button, but I can't worry about that right now; I'm straining to listen and cursing the fact that hearing isn't exactly my strongest sense. Now, if those guys wanna climb into the wading pool with me I can find them with my eyes closed, no problem!

But I'm not hearing anything.

"Stay behind me," I tell her, and head toward the living room. Yeah, I'd like to just stay out here or even jaunt back to the apartment and pretend everything's okay, but I can't exactly do that. Responsibilities and all. No, I need to put on my big-boy pants and find out who these clowns are, what they want, how they got in, and how to get them out. All valid questions, and all ones it'd be a lot easier to answer if I had the slightest clue.

Still, that's never stopped me before.

We creep into the hall. "Robert," Ma says from behind me, but I shush her. The last thing I need right now is for Frosty and Sundrop to figure out we're coming. "Robert," she says again, a little louder, that testiness starting to creep into her voice. Ho-boy—no sign of the Barometer Brothers and already it feels like the temperature just dropped!

"Sorry, Ma," I tell her, "but we gotta keep quiet. And it's DuckBob."

She doesn't reply to that, except to mutter something under her breath, but at least it shuts her up for the moment. She hates that I changed my name, hates the name itself, refuses to use it, and hands out death-glares to anyone else who does. Never really figured out why, but now ain't the time to worry about it. Not when I've got a pair of crazed weather-chuckers under my roof.

I'm coming up on the doorway into the living room, and I crane my neck—yeah, yeah, I know, that one never gets old—to peek in. I can see my computer, which is up against the near wall, and it looks to be intact. That's good 'cause it's made of some sort of circuitized ice, so one zap from Heatwave would have turned it into a puddle. Though I wonder if a shot from Captain Cold would've supercharged it instead?

The rest of the room comes into view, the coffee table and then the couch, the lamps to either side—but no sign of Hi and Lo. Finally I step into the room itself, look around, even check behind and yes, in, the couch. Nothing.

"Well, that's just plain odd," I mutter, scratching my bill. "Where the heck did they go?"

"That's what I was trying to tell you, Robert," Ma says, folding her arms over her chest to remind me that she could easily be cast as The World's Smallest Linebacker. "I think I saw something in a room along the way, I'm not sure what it was but it looked... funny."

Huh. Now, everything about this place "looks funny"—I mean, come on, it's a giant skull, complete with horns, but it's all a glittery pink like whatever this thing was, it was part of Sparkle Force or something. I've been all through the place, seeing as how I live here and for the first few months I couldn't leave, and there are still things even I shake my head at. Like the faucet in the upstairs half bath, only the water flows up along the wall and forms a neat oval, which stays perfectly until you shut the tap, then it loses shape and comes splashing down into a long, thin drain running right along the wall. That was a wakeup the first time I used it!

Still, something about the way Ma says "funny" makes my nonexistent ears perk up. And it's not like I have any better ideas.

"Okay," I tell her. "Show me something funny."

Ten minutes later, we stand there, staring, and I shake my head. "Yeah, that's funny all right."

We're looking into an alcove off the main Matrix room. It's the one that houses the main generator, the AC unit, the furnace, the water heater—basically, the utility closet.

Only I'm pretty sure there weren't two people pretending they're statues in it the last time I had somebody out to read the meter.

I'm not even sure "people" is right here. They're a little shorter than me, maybe five, five and a half feet, and definitely humanoid, so they could be guys, they could be gals, or they could be anywhere in between, both or neither. The fact that they have no features, no hair, not even eyes only adds to the uncertainty—and the creepiness factor. Their skin is a sort of charcoal black, like a mix of blacks and grays, and it's completely unbroken by any features or any openings—no mouths, no ears, no nostrils. Nothing.

There's something about them that's itching at my eyes, and I blink, then stare again. Huh. I'm getting almost a blur off them, like they're moving, even though they're both totally still. After a few seconds I realize it's not them that's moving, it's their skin. It's sort of swirling ever so slightly. And the one on the left has hints of blue to it. The one on the right is more red.

I'm guessing that would be the fire and ice.

The question is, who the hell are they? And what are they doing in my house, other than currently lounging beside the hot-water heater? Or is that the closest they could get to hanging out by the water cooler and they're just taking the equivalent of a smoke break?

At least they're not shooting at us. Definite improvement. Still doesn't mean I want them in my house, though. Especially when I never invited them in. At least, I don't think so. I do have a tendency to bring people over when I'm out drinking. Hey, I've got the coolest house in the universe, why shouldn't I show it off? Besides the fact that its sole purpose is actually to protect the Matrix, which protects the cosmos, and that maybe having a bunch of half-drunk strangers cavorting around it isn't exactly conducive to good security?

It's hard being such a people person.

"What are you going to do about them, Robert?" Ma asks beside me. Which brings me back to the current problem.

"I have no idea," I admit. I should call Tall. He might have some idea who they are, and even if not he's got the muscle to get rid of them. And his partner, Heidi, is pretty much a floating encyclopedia; he might know something about them, too. But when I reach for my phone, the blurring gets visibly worse, the blue and red brightening and starting to actively swirl across the pair's chest, faces, and hands. I take my hand away, and the colors fade again. Reach for the phone, they start to light up. Stop, they fade.

Right, backing away now.

"Come on, Ma," I tell her. "Let's go watch TV or something, okay?" And, having loudly announced my totally harmless intentions, I take her arm and tug her back toward the living room.

Only, the Glow-Brite Gang snaps to life again and follows us.

Looks like I'm not going to be able to just duck into a corner and make a quick call. I'm tempted to try heading to the bathroom, but have a feeling they're not big on respecting privacy. And I'm pretty sure they can shoot faster than I can dial.

I reach into my other pocket for the fob, but they start glowing again. Looks like we're not getting away that way again, either.

So now we're stuck here, Ma and me, with the Human Nite-Lites.

Swell.

"Look, what do you want?" I ask them. "I'm sure we can talk this out, right? Are you here for money? An autograph? Selling glow-in-the-dark Yo-Yos?"

They're definitely listening but they don't say anything.

"Who are you people?" Ma tries. "And why are you bothering Robert?" They glance her way—at least, their heads swivel toward her—before cycling back to me. Still no response.

"So you won't tell me who you are or what you want, but you won't leave and you won't let me call anyone or go away ourselves?" I shake my head. "What, we're just gonna stand here together, the four of us? Worst. Bridge party. Ever!"

They still don't move.

"You two are very strange," Ma tells them sternly. She looks at me. "What do we do, Robert?"

That is a very good question.

I need to think this through. When did these two show up? They were here when we got here, but for how long before that? Nothing looks out of place, so I'm thinking it wasn't long. The minute we showed up they started shooting at us, but now they're not moving and they don't look or act angry so were they really here to hurt us? Or was that just the natural progression of what happened when I reached for my phone? If they light up, then glow, then attack when surprised or when something around them changes, I could see how us appearing out of nowhere could set that off.

Which still doesn't explain why they're in my house. Or how to get rid of them.

"Are they people you work with, Robert?" Ma asks with a sniff. "Because if so, they're not very sociable." She looks them up and down. "And what's with the bodysuits? Or the icicles and fireballs?"

That's a good question. What *is* with the fire and ice? If these two are as identical as they look, why does one have fire and the other ice? Why not both fire, or both ice, or both glittery green laser beams, or whatever? That's gotta mean something, right? I just have no idea what.

"I don't think they're bodysuits, Ma," I tell her. "More like their skin or something. And they're not co-workers. I've never seen 'em before. They were just here when we got here."

"Oh." She frowns. "So they didn't come with the house?"

"Why would they—no, Ma! When I moved in here, there was not a pair of killer robots or whatever they are packed away in the closet beside the thermostat instructions!"

Except...

What if there was?

That stops my rant cold, and that's tough to do—I know a lot of people, and a bunch of companies, even a few governments, that would pay very good money to learn that trick. But Ma has me thinking. What if they were here in the house the whole time? I still haven't explored every nook and cranny—I keep meaning to but this place is huge and full of weird stuff the previous Matrix guardians accumulated over the years before I took over, and I get easily distracted so each time I start poking around I find something neat and forget to look any farther. So yeah, they could have been here this whole time.

But if they were, why did they activate now? And how do we stop them from trying to fry and freeze us each time we move?

I turn back to Ma, ignoring the Inclement Idiots for a second. At least it seems like talking doesn't set them off, which actually puts them head and shoulders above about half my former co-workers and at least a third of the people I'd encounter every day on the subway. "Ma, when we got here before, do you remember?"

"Of course I do," she answers. "I'm not senile."

"I know that, Ma." I sigh. "Look, I'm just trying to remember myself, okay? We showed up in the Matrix room, just like this time. I showed you down the hall and into the living room here. Then those things attacked us. Was there anything else that happened?"

She looks around. "Let me see." Here's the thing—Ma's got a memory like a steel trap. She has to, to have kept track of all of us and our activities and proclivities and alibis over the years. "We were in that football field of a room. I asked you why you needed such a big room, then what that thing was in the middle of it, then why it kept winking at me." Yes, the Matrix gets a little overly friendly sometimes. That's what happens when you're stuck walking in circles and talking to yourself all day. Trust me, I know.

"You told me that was the Matrix," she continues, "and then offered to show me the rest of the house. I noticed the couch and asked you about that, you told me it's where you sit and hang out to keep it company sometimes. Which is very sweet of you, but you've always been the sensitive type." Read here, "you're one of my only children who would have qualms about running someone over in the street—or at least, someone you weren't related to." That's right, I'm the *nice* one. Scary thought, isn't it?

"You led me down the hall, and I asked why it was so dark, were you trying to hide carpet stains or something? You fumbled at the light switch but it didn't seem to do anything, so you hit it again, then said, 'Damn, must be fried. I thought these bulbs were supposed to last until Hell froze over.' Then we—" She trails off when she realizes I'm staring at her, my bill wide open—which can be dangerous, at least for me, because I could get a whole zeppelin stuck in my craw if one flew low enough!

"That's it!" I grab her in a hug. "That had to be it. Fried and frozen— just like them." I point at the Blurry Binaries. Then I lead Ma back down the hall to about where we were before. Sure enough, there's a panel on the wall—and it isn't for the lights. That one's a few feet farther along, and a little bit lower, too. This is one I've never really noticed before; it kinda blends into the wall a bit, like it's recessed a little and has smooth edges and even a bit of glitter to it. Looks like it's pretty old.

And obviously it triggers something a whole lot different from the overhead fluorescents.

"Okay, so it's some kinda security system, maybe," I mutter, scratching at my bill. "Doesn't mind us walking around or talking but doesn't like electronics? Maybe it considers them a threat?"

Ma smirks at me. "Not a threat, Robert," she corrects smugly—yes, this is where I get it from. "A distraction. Like in school. Remember?"

Lord, how could I forget? Cell phones had already been around for a few years when I was in school, long enough that at least some of the kids had them. Which drove the teachers nuts, since all it took was one kid with a flip phone and Candy Crush and suddenly you're talking to the back of a whole room full of heads. So the school banned them. Completely. They saw you with a phone, they took it away, no exception. To make matters worse, you couldn't just reclaim it afterward. Oh no—you had to get your parent to come in and retrieve it for you.

After the second time doing that, Ma laid down the law. "They take your phone," she warned us, "they can keep it, 'cause I'm not going to bust my ass to get down there and get it back for you just so you can do it all over again." Not that she objected to our having the phones, of course— she's the one who got them for us, mainly so we could call and let her know if we were going to be at a friend's for dinner. No, she just wanted us to make sure that, if we did have them out during school, we didn't get caught.

Typical for our family, really.

She's probably right, though. Although maybe it's less about distraction—after all, why would they care if we were distracted?—than potential interference. After all, the Matrix has only been wireless for a year or two, long after the last time the Polar Opposites would've been activated. They're probably programmed to think about it in older terms and older tech. And a competing signal could interfere with the Matrix's functions. So they'd want to keep that from happening.

Problem is, even knowing that, how do I convince them otherwise?

I look at the panel again, but there isn't a big red "OFF" switch. I really wish more things had that. Then again, I know a lot of people who wish *I* had one of those. Might be nice, actually, for those nights when I can't sleep—no more lying awake or staring at the TV till all hours or teaching myself Fandalusian aerobic waffle-making just because I'm bored, just hit the button and turn off instead.

So I can't shut them down. What next?

I tell Ma this and she shrugs. "You just need them to know you don't have anything that interferes, right?" she asks.

"Pretty much, yeah."

"Got it." She stomps over to the nearer of the two—Blue Man Group—and taps it on the chest. "You got a scanner in there?" she demands. It cocks its head slightly, studying her. "A scanner," she repeats. "Scan for radio interference or whatever. You're not flying blind here, are you? You've got some way to tell if something's gonna cause a problem?"

It doesn't reply, nor does it produce a security wand or that doohickey from *Ghostbusters* or one of those big metal detectors you see on the beach all the time.

"Oy," she mutters, hands going to her hips. "Are you seriously telling me you don't even have a way to tell if something could be a problem?" She glares at it and at its partner, Mr. Red Hot. "How do you know *you* two aren't a problem, then?"

It looks at her a second more, then its head swivels around—a lot like Linda Blair if she were a store mannequin coated in graphite—to lock gazes with its counterpart.

"Ma," I warn, but she's already stepping back.

Good thing, too, since both Blurry Buddies' arms come up, their lights ramping up to blinding levels—and they open fire (and ice).

On each other.

Ice coats the one, causing the whole thing to crystallize and crack and crumble. Fire melts the other to slag. In a matter of seconds, there's nothing left but a small mound of dust and a strangely glossy puddle.

This is the power of my mother's disapproval. Now you see why I used to pay Terrence McAllister to swap report cards with me.

"Nice work, Ma!" I shout, giving her a hug. "That showed 'em!"

"Thank you, Robert." She hugs me back, briefly. "Now, where's your mop and broom? If you leave those there too long, they'll damage the floor."

I grab the implements in question and return, but pause before handing them over. "Why do you still call me that?" I ask instead. "It's DuckBob now."

"That's not the name I gave you," she answers.

"No, but it's the one I chose. Only you never use it."

She sniffs, sighs, takes the broom, starts to sweep, then stops. "I don't like to see you give in to them," she says finally. "I didn't raise you to let other people decide who you were."

I take hold of the broom, not hard but enough that she's gotta look up and meet my eyes. "Ma, I didn't change it to give in," I tell her. "I did it to take control. Get out ahead of it." I gesture at my bill, and the rest of me. "But this really is who I am now. And you know what? I like it. I'm pretty happy this way." Which I didn't even know for certain until recently when it looked like I might stop being this way, might go back to my old, normal, boring self. And I realized how much I didn't want that to happen.

She studies me close, the way only a mother can. "Are you sure?" she asks. "This is what you want?"

"It really is." And it's true. My bill and feathers, the Matrix, all of it—I love it all. "I wouldn't change it for the world," I tell her.

Ma considers that a second. Then she reclaims control of the broom and starts sweeping again. "Fine," she says softly. "But don't expect me to call you that when I'm annoyed. 'DuckBob Fitzpatrick Spinowitz' doesn't exactly roll off the tongue."

"Fair enough," I tell her, and hug her again. She lets me for a full three seconds before pushing me away with a little cluck of her tongue, but I can see she's pleased.

Which is why I don't even mind when she tells me to grab a dustpan and scoop up the dust, and then a bucket to help with the mop, and then a towel to dry the floor, and then some wax to bring back the shine.

That's how I know she loves me. Either that or she's training me to take over a cleaning business—or to cover up evidence of a crime, which is something else she drilled into us at an early age. But that's my mom, always looking out for us. Even when it violates federal statutes.

ON MOONLIT WINGS

MARY FAN

GEORGIA, 1910

CLUTCHING THE ROPE, ANNA SWUNG her legs over her hands until she hung upside down. The yellowing canvas of the big top glowed from the early morning sun beating down outside, and the scents of animal and human bodies thickened the air. She hooked her knee onto the rope, released one hand, and reached down—

"Point your toes!" Marcelle's sharp voice, which carried a light French accent, called up to her.

Anna tried to remember her feet as she grabbed the bottom part of the rope and wrapped it around her free leg and her waist. But, weary after two hours of practicing, her body dropped abruptly, and she barely managed to keep her grip.

"That's enough for today."

Disappointed, Anna climbed down and landed roughly in front of Marcelle, billed as "The Empress of the Skies."

"I'll get it next time," Anna said.

Marcelle nodded, her thick black curls, streaked intermittently with silver, bouncing by her thin, snowy white cheeks. "Your inverts are looking good. You only need a little more stamina."

Wiping sweat from her forehead, Anna smiled. Escaped tendrils from her gleaming black bun clung to her sticky neck.

Though the audience seats were empty, the ring was bustling with activity. Jugglers practicing their tricks. Clowns rehearsing their stunts. Trapeze artists warming up their swings. Instrumental voices swirled over the noises of people chattering and grunting.

Maja Lozanac, an acrobatic dancer billed as "Fortuna" for her abilities to dream of the future and see things others didn't, entered. Already dressed in her blue-and-yellow costume, she tied her signature blindfold over her eyes. "The ringmaster is on his way. You had better go put on your costume."

Anna started to leave, but agitation scratched at her heart. She hated that the last thing she would do on the rope that day was a failed wrap. She rushed back to the apparatus.

Marcelle pursed her lips, exaggerating the thin lines by her mouth. "I told you, you are finished for today."

"Let me do one last climb." Anna grabbed the rope.

Marcelle shook her head but didn't object.

Anna scissored her legs and scooped the rope over her hips. If this was to be her last climb of the day, she wasn't going to make it a boring one. After reaching above, she repeated the motion, then prepared to try turning upside-down again.

"Time to set up! Everybody out!" William Andley's voice boomed through the big top. Both co-owner and ringmaster of the Albers & Andley Traveling Circus, he commanded immediate attention.

Anna scrambled down the rope.

"You!" Mr. Andley, a blond man with a thick mustache dressed in a red waistcoat, glared at her. "What are you doing here? Go get dressed!"

"Yes, sir." But as Anna tried to rush past him, he grabbed her arm.

"I had better not catch you wasting time here again, understand? Stay with the ethnological exposition, where you belong."

Clenching her fists, Anna sped away without a word.

The moment she arrived at the costume tent, Kirsten Sigrist, an animal trainer, ran up to her with Rosie, Anna's two-year-old daughter, in her arms. Kirsten's blonde hair looked as if she'd tried to gather it in a bun but only managed half, and her green-grey eyes were frenzied. "Thank goodness you're back! Rosie's a delight as always, but I need to get my dogs ready for the show."

"Mama!" Rosie reached out with her tiny hands, which carried a cool brown tint that bore little resemblance to Anna's pale gold complexion.

Anna gathered the child in her arms with a smile. Though her muscles ached from practice, she never tired when holding her little girl. Yet looking into her daughter's soft brown eyes caused sorrow to drip into her heart. Every day, Rosie looked more like her father, and every day, Anna wished he could have met his daughter.

She made her way to the costume rack and grabbed her and Rosie's outfits for the ethnological exposition, more casually known as the human zoo. Though Anna had worn the same "Chinese Princess" costume for the past three years, she'd had to modify Rosie's every few weeks. The girl sat surprisingly still as Anna dressed her. Adorable as she looked in the pink-and-gold outfit with its flower-covered headdress, guilt stung Anna each time she dolled up her child for circus-goers to gawk at.

It wouldn't be long before Rosie was old enough to ask why she was made to spend all day in a fenced enclosure, forbidden to say a word of English, while onlookers stared and pointed.

Because some don't see us as people, Rosie. Anna dreaded the day she would have to explain that.

"What's troubling you?" Charles Sasaki, already dressed in his "Chinese Warrior" costume, approached her.

Anna whirled toward him. "How do you accept this? Your family came to America from Japan fifty years ago, yet you're made to masquerade as a Chinese man in his 'natural state.' I don't understand how you're never angry."

"This is the best-paying job I've ever had." Charles shrugged then smiled, his friendly black eyes crinkling. "Cheer up, Anna. You're royalty."

Anna made a face. "I'd rather be seen for what I can do than what people think I look like."

Tanya Mizrahi, a blue-eyed woman with short, shoulder-length hair, arched her brows at Anna. Though, like Anna, she was barely more than five feet tall, she seemed to take up more space with her strong presence. There was a reason why she was billed as "The Amazon Queen."

"If you want to defy their expectations, you have to be better than they imagine the best could be," Tanya said. "You must think about what you want to achieve more than what you want to escape. I did not become the only female lion tamer in the country by moping."

"Why are you not in your exhibits yet?" Mr. Andley stormed through the costume tent. He paused and stared at Rosie. "No. This is not working anymore." He snapped his fingers. "Sarah! Wrap this girl in one of your shawls. She's your daughter now."

"What?" Anna clutched Rosie to her chest as Sarah Barnes, a majestic woman with dark brown skin already dressed in her "African Priestess" costume, approached.

Mr. Andley huffed. "It was fine when the baby was swaddled and no one could see her face, but it's becoming too obvious now. I can't have customers asking why there's an African baby in the China exhibit."

"Because we're *American!*" Anna's voice rose. "She's *my* daughter! You can't—"

"Hand that girl over to Sarah, or I'll sack you right now." Mr. Andley glowered. "I can find another Chinese Princess in a heartbeat."

Sarah held out her bracelet-covered arms. "It's okay, Anna. I'll take good care of her."

Blinking back tears of fury, Anna complied. She wished she could storm out and never look back, but she barely had enough money to live off of as it was.

"Mama?" Rosie stared at Anna with round, confused eyes as Sarah took her.

"Hello, little one." Sarah's mouth curved. "Your Aunt Sarah has a new costume for you. Won't that be fun?"

Anna tried to give Rosie a reassuring smile as Sarah walked off. But she couldn't help feeling as if she was losing her daughter.

CALIFORNIA, 1907

The aerialist spiraled downward and stopped inches above the ground as her skillfully wrapped rope caught her. Anna gasped and clutched John's arm, both terrified and awed.

John flashed her one of his heart-melting grins. "She really is a sensation, isn't she?"

Anna nodded. "I wish I could do that."

"Well, why not? Let's run away with the circus!" His brown eyes danced, and the spring sunlight brightening the tent warmed his brown complexion. "You can dance in the chorus until you learn enough tricks to do an aerial act, and I can build sets or anything else they need."

As the aerialist climbed the rope for her next trick, Anna dared to imagine herself in the woman's place. She'd loved to dance as a child, but her father had ordered her to stop a few years ago, since he considered it inappropriate for a young woman of marriageable age. How wonderful it must be to dance in the air!

"You want to, don't you?" John's breath whispered across her face. "In all seriousness, what's keeping us here? I have no family, and yours will never see you for who you truly are."

Anna sighed. The future her father envisioned for her—full of domestic chores and obedience to a man just like him—felt like a nightmare. Now that she was almost twenty, she wouldn't be able to avoid it for much longer. Scarcely a day passed when he didn't bring up the topic of marriage. Yet if he knew about the man she wanted to spend the rest of her life with, he would kill them both.

She longed to agree to John's fantastical plan. But she shook her head. "Don't be foolish. We would run out of money and starve to death."

A heavy look descended on John's face. "Whatever happens, know that I love you."

The music swelled, but Anna didn't see what the aerialist did next, for her eyes closed and her lips found John's.

GEORGIA, 1910

Seated in a chair carved with dragons, Anna tried to focus on her calligraphy and ignore all the eyes staring at her. She hated that the skills her mother had so painstakingly taught her to honor their ancestral traditions were now being used to entertain the ignorant.

A few feet from her, Charles, her "husband," swung a prop sword in graceful arcs, punctuating each move with a fierce, "*Ha!*" No one would know that his movements were an art form he'd developed himself and not the "ancient Chinese sword-fighting techniques" advertised on the posters. At least he enjoyed performing.

And as much as Anna had grown to detest her ornately embroidered costume, at least she had chosen to wear it. She wasn't sure if the same could be said for the aboriginal Australians in the enclosure to the left.

Anna looked past the gawking crowd and glimpsed Rosie, now wrapped in a colorfully patterned shawl with her textured black hair teased out, playing with a cloth doll inside Sarah's enclosure. Several people leaned against the fence and pointed at the toddler. Through the mutterings of the crowd, Anna caught the word "savage." Her blood boiled.

I have to get us out of this "exposition." She gritted her teeth. *Tomorrow, I'll practice harder on the rope.*

CALIFORNIA, 1907

Silvery moonlight spilled through Anna's open window and traced the perfect contours of John's regal cheekbones. Lying in his arms and surrounded by a pool of her unbound hair, heart racing and skin tingling, she finally understood what true bliss felt like.

"Tell me one of your stories," she whispered.

"What kind?" Soft yet resonant, his voice felt like a gentle rain.

"Any kind."

In the blackness of midnight, she sensed rather than saw his smile. "Once upon a time, there lived a fairy princess with beautiful gossamer wings. She loved to fly across all the realms, including those of mankind. One day, she met a man who had no such powers, but whose voice soothed her soul. Though they fell deeply in love, it was forbidden for her kind to be with his, and the fairy king threatened to lock her in a tower if she ever saw her lover again. Desperate, the two sought the advice of a sorceress, who told them that the only way for them to be together was if the princess cut off her own wings."

Anna frowned. "Where did you hear this story?"

"I made it up. I call it 'On Moonlit Wings,' but I haven't written it down."

"Why not?"

"I can't decide how it ends. What do you think of it?"

"It's sad, but I like it. Maybe you could sell it to the papers—"

A scream exploded outside Anna's door. She bolted up, recognizing her mother's frantic voice. Heavy footsteps approached.

She scarcely had a chance to react before a booted foot kicked down the door. Her father stood beneath the frame, a gun in his hands. His long black queue swayed behind him like a snake.

"What they said was true," he growled, raising the weapon.

"*No!*" Anna rushed at her father.

Chunks exploded from the wooden wall as a bullet pierced it. Anna's mother grabbed her father's arm, pleading with him to stop. He shoved her off, sending her to the ground, and took aim again.

"John, run!" Anna tried to block her father, but he threw her aside. She fell in a heap on the floor.

As John scrambled out the window, Anna grabbed her father's ankle and pulled. He tripped but didn't fall. A bullet tore the window frame.

"He will not get far," her father said darkly. Five other men—her father's kin—appeared in the hallway outside. He turned to them. "Let us hunt down the beast that defiled my daughter."

"No, please!" Anna started to get up.

Her father seized her wrist with a cruel scowl. "You will return to China on the next ship and live with my brother's family until he can find a man willing to marry you. No one will ever speak of this shame again."

NEW YORK, 1910

The Albers & Andley Traveling Circus wouldn't open its doors to the public for another week, but already the big top was full. Hopeful performers waited in the audience seats for their turns to try out for the show. Anna waited among them, dressed in a glimmering leotard and tutu she'd borrowed from Marcelle, who sat beside her. Rosie was perched on Anna's knee, happily watching a young woman do somersaults on the back of a running horse.

Henry Albers, a portly man with a thick gray beard, strode across the ring, observing. William Andley walked alongside him with the air of a king observing his subjects.

The trick rider flipped off the back of the horse, landed before the two circus owners, and curtseyed, the colorful ribbons woven into her curls tumbling forward.

Mr. Albers nodded. "Well done, Miss…?"

"Nini Clementine."

"We'll take the act."

Nini clapped her hands with delight. "Thank you!"

"Next!"

Drawing a deep breath, Anna rose from her seat.

Marcelle marched ahead of her with a proudly lifted chin. "*Messieurs!* You know me as the Empress of the Skies. Now, allow me to introduce my protégé, the Princess of the Skies." She gestured at Anna, who scrambled to approach as Rosie fidgeted in her arms.

Mr. Andley snorted. "What is this?"

Anna handed Rosie to Marcelle and quickly patted her hair, some of which had come out of its updo after her daughter had tugged on her ribbons. "Sirs, I've been training with Marcelle for almost three years now. I—"

"You already have an act." Mr. Albers pointed one meaty finger at Anna.

"I won't be displayed like an animal anymore!" Anna inhaled deeply. "Sirs, imagine how much the crowds would love a double aerial act. Let me show you what I can do."

"You have some nerve," Mr. Andley growled. "I hired you for the ethnological exposition, and that's where you'll stay."

Marcelle ignored him and approached Mr. Albers with a smooth smile. "*Henri,* I was your most popular performer long before you brought *Guillaume* on board." She gestured at the other man. "In twenty years, I have never disappointed you, *oui?* I would not let *Anne* audition unless I thought she was ready. She could be great—someday, she could even be better than me. Give her a chance."

Anna's heart skittered. She was used to Marcelle lecturing her about crooked knees and clumsy inversions. This was the first time she'd heard such high praise.

Mr. Albers relaxed. "I suppose it can't hurt—"

"No!" Mr. Andley's brows gathered. "Henry, you came to me because your family's circus was about to go bankrupt, and you needed a fresh perspective. I brought this circus back from the brink. I know what it needs, and it's *not* the whims of an aging aerialist." He glared at Marcelle. "You were past your prime before I even joined. You're lucky that Henry is a sentimental man."

Anna scowled. "How dare you?"

Mr. Albers sighed. "I'm afraid William has a point. I'm sorry, Marcelle, but your talent is not what it once was, and, I fear, neither is your judgment."

Marcelle stared at him.

Mr. Andley took a threatening step toward Anna. "I told you to stop wasting time here. The next time there is an incident like this, I will sack you immediately."

Hot anger churned through Anna's gut. After years of hard training—and countless bruises, burns, sprains, and aches—to develop the strength and skills to appear weightless, she would not even have the chance to try performing.

She refused to go back to that garish enclosure, pretending not to understand the insulting comments directed at her. She could not watch people ogle her daughter and speak of Rosie as they would a captive cub.

"There will not be any more incidents because I'm leaving." Anna took her daughter from Marcelle. "Thank you for all you have taught me."

Marcelle narrowed her stern green eyes but didn't speak.

Cold pricks of fear pierced Anna's stomach as she wondered how she and Rosie would survive alone, but she did not regret her decision.

Mr. Andley laughed. "Where will you go?"

Marcelle gave him a withering look. "This is not the only circus in town." She turned to Mr. Albers. "And it is not the circus it once was. Good luck, *Henri*. When you see the papers lauding the phenomenal new aerial act that is the Princess of the Skies, remember this day and all you lost when you let this buffoon"—she glared at Mr. Andley—"start making the decisions. Come, *Anne*. Let us seek out a circus that still knows what talent looks like."

Anna blinked and followed as Marcelle strode out of the ring. "I... didn't expect you to leave too."

Marcelle arched her narrow black brows. "Did you think I would let you take everything I taught you to another circus and not come with you?"

"I…"

"Enough stammering, girl. Go pack your things and say your goodbyes. Let us not linger here a moment longer than we must."

"Yes, ma'am."

CALIFORNIA, 1907

So many tears had poured from Anna's eyes, she wondered how she hadn't drowned in them yet. An unrelenting pain crushed her heart. Though a week had passed since her father and the others had murdered John, it remained as acute as the moment she'd learned the news.

She wasn't sure how or why she was even still alive. Every day, she would cry until her body collapsed from exhaustion then wake only to cry even more. Unable to eat and barely able to drink, she felt as if she was fading to nothing.

She couldn't bear the thought of her John—her kind, beautiful, intelligent, imaginative John—lying dead at the bottom of the river, where her father had dumped his body. Locked in her room, whose window had been boarded up, she lay on her side with her knees curled in. If there were any mercy in the world, death would soon take her, too.

The door creaked open, but Anna kept her face buried in her hands. She recognized the sound of her mother padding softly across the floor, probably with another bowl of soup she hoped to entice Anna to eat.

But this time, a new sound accompanied the usual steps and sighing—that of metal jangling.

Tempted by curiosity, Anna peeked over her fingers.

Her mother rushed up to the bed, a large sack on one shoulder and a small bag in her hand. She shook Anna with an urgent look. "Get up! Hurry! We do not have much time before your father returns."

Anna blinked, puzzled.

Her mother shoved the two bags at her. "I packed some food and spare clothes for you, and I gathered as much money as I could. Go to the station. Take the first train out of the state, wherever it is going."

"What… What do you mean?"

"I will not watch my daughter waste away." She paused, hesitating. "I did not want to marry your father, but I had no choice. That will not be your fate. Run, *Xiao An*. Live."

Anna tentatively took the small bag of coins. "What about you?"

"I will be all right. I have often wanted to run as well, but I have your younger brothers and sisters to care for. Now, get out of here! You can cry more after you board the train."

Nodding, Anna stood. Terrified as she was of facing the unknown, at least the road ahead held possibilities. "Thank you."

"This country was built for opportunity. I agreed to accompany your father here because I wanted that opportunity for my children. You are American. Do not let anyone make you forget that."

ILLINOIS, 1910

As the hoop in her hands spun faster, Anna counted out four beats in her head and then hooked her knees onto it. Holding the other side of the apparatus, Marcelle did the same and released her hands, reaching for Anna, who took them.

Imagining the lilt of violins, Anna counted out another four beats, then, in sync with Marcelle, took one leg off the hoop and arched her back.

A child's babbling sounded below, and Anna tried not to think about what Rosie might be doing in the arms of the assistant who had agreed to watch her while the Empress and the Princess of the Skies auditioned for the Stein Family Circus.

As the piece progressed, Anna struggled to stay with Marcelle. A double act required precise timing to keep the hoop balanced. But she kept getting ahead, and she felt the apparatus wobbling.

By the time she and Marcelle finished, she was dizzier than she'd been in a long time, which seemed odd after all the hours she'd spent practicing to grow accustomed to the spinning. She nearly tumbled forward while giving her bow.

"Ah, Marcelle, you will always be a wonder." Eugene Stein approached with a wistful smile. "Ten years ago, I would have paid a pretty penny to steal you away from Henry Albers. But I'm afraid time withers even the brightest bloom, and while I was intrigued by your new 'Princess,' she is not as skillful as you were in your youth. I am sorry."

Disappointment dug its claws into Anna's chest. After eleven auditions in three towns, she should have been numb to hearing the same things each time.

Mr. Stein gave Anna an appraising look. "I am, however, putting together an 'Around the World' act and could use a representative of the Far East. Perhaps you could be my Chinese acrobat. And you, Marcelle, could represent France."

Anna's gut balked at the proposal, but she bit the inside of her cheek. After two months of searching for work, this was the closest she'd come to an offer that would allow her to perform. However, she hadn't left Albers & Andley to end up with yet another job that would treat her like an exotic animal. "No. I can't."

Marcelle scowled at Mr. Stein. "We are not museum pieces. We are artists. If you cannot appreciate that, then we will go someplace else."

Anna took Rosie from the assistant and rushed to catch up as Marcelle stormed away. *What happens now? Another city, another circus? What happens when we run out?*

The money she and Marcelle had spent on rooms and trains had been meant to sustain them through the winter hiatus, when circuses paused their traveling and performance jobs became scarce. Though Marcelle claimed she had substantial savings from a lifetime of fame, even that couldn't last forever.

If no one hired them soon, they wouldn't be able to feed themselves, let alone keep roaming.

TEXAS, 1907

In the days since she'd left her childhood home, Anna hadn't thought at all about where she was going. But now, she found herself in a state she'd never been to before, frightened and lost in a way she'd never imagined possible. What money she had left wouldn't be enough for a room that night.

Seeing a sign for the Albers & Andley Traveling Circus, she thought back to the joyful times when she and John would sneak away to explore menageries of amazing animals and watch acrobats perform incredible feats. She wandered toward the spot where workers were setting up tents, the sack of clothes and near-depleted food on her back. She could already imagine what the place would look like when it was completed—a portable town full of colors and delights. With the bright morning sun shining in her eyes, she could almost see John waving to her amid a sweaty crowd, greeting her with a breathtaking smile that left her helpless to his pull.

"What are you doing there, girl?" A blond man with a heavy mustache scowled at her from several feet away.

Startled out of her reverie, Anna quickly turned to leave.

"Wait!" The man strode to her, looking her up and down. "I'm in need of a Chinagirl. Last one quit without warning."

"What are you talking about?" Sweating from the heat, Anna suddenly felt sick.

"The ethnological exposition. It's a good job. You'll get a place to live, three meals a day, and decent pay, and I won't even ask what you're running from. What do you say?"

Whatever this job involved, at least she wouldn't have to sleep on the street. "Yes… Yes, sir."

"Excellent. I'm William Andley. What's your name, and how old are you?"

"My name is Anna Song. I'm nineteen—" Overwhelmed by a flood of nausea, she fell to her knees and vomited onto the dry grass.

"Whoa!" Mr. Andley jumped back. "Ah, so that's why you're running." He chuckled. "Not a problem. I'll have the seamstress make your costume extra-large and loose. A family exhibit would be nice, I think. Yes, this could work out well."

"What?"

He pointed at a large train car. "Go on, then. You have no time to waste if you're going to be ready for opening day. Tell them I sent you." With that, he walked off, leaving Anna kneeling in the grass.

She touched her belly, her eyes widening. She'd suspected but hadn't dared think about it. But now, she couldn't pretend any longer.

Trembling, she staggered to her feet and headed to the car.

ILLINOIS, 1910

Seated on one of the narrow beds in their rented room, Anna stroked Rosie's hair as the toddler played with her cloth doll. *Whatever becomes of me, you will grow up to be a capable and independent woman. I will make sure of that.*

Marcelle paced from the window to the door and back again. "Nobody values skill and experience anymore. All they want is spangles, spangles, spangles." She paused. "*Désolée, Anne.* I let you down today."

"What do you mean?"

"I could not keep up with you on the hoop, and that ruined our chances with *Eugène*. He was right about me. I am not the performer I once was."

"You are magnificent." Anna stood. "I'm lucky to perform with you."

Marcelle shook her head. "We must abandon the partner routines. You and I will each perform individually, side by side but on different apparatuses. I may not be able to invert as smoothly as I once could, but I still know what makes a good act."

"Marcelle…" Anna hesitated. The seed of idea had planted itself in her mind a few weeks back, but she hadn't spoken of it. Now, with their other options close to exhausted, she decided it could be worth the risk. "You have been performing longer than I have been alive, and you know more about creating a show than Stein or Albers or Andley put together. Perhaps, instead of seeking the approval of men who want spangles, it's time to start your own circus."

Marcelle paused, her brow furrowing. "I cannot deny that the thought has crossed my mind. I know enough performers who might be willing to take the risk. But even if I could corral them all, even if I could convince a bank to give me a loan, I could hardly build a menagerie, a museum, a sideshow. How could we convince the public to come to our tiny show when they're accustomed to so much more?"

"You could make it different from what they've seen before. Give them a story. Instead of only tricks performed by acts that have nothing to do with each other, make it like a play, or an opera, but with aerialists and acrobats instead of Shakespeare and Mozart."

"That would be interesting." Marcelle stroked her chin. "The public does love a good story. I have a pianist friend who has for years told me he wants to compose an opera. I could write to him."

Anna's pulse hummed with excitement. "It will not be easy, but if we succeed, we could give the world something truly beautiful."

She could practically hear the gears in Marcelle's mind clicking as the older woman began pacing again. "My name still means something to the world. It will be difficult to obtain a large enough loan or find investors, but perhaps I could convince the performers to accept an equal share of the profits in exchange for a lower payment. You and I are not the only ones who have grown tired of those smarmy bosses. Yes... this could work. Did you have a particular story in mind?"

Anna smiled. "Let me tell you a tale about a fairy princess who falls in love with an earthly man..."

KANSAS, 1907

"The Empress of the Skies" was a well-deserved name. Sitting in the empty audience stands, Anna watched Marcelle rehearse. The aerialist held the rope high above her with her hands wide and her legs free. She twisted her hips and bent her knees one at a time, as if walking on the air.

Thinking of the life growing inside her, Anna pressed her hand to her belly. A little piece of John, a little piece of herself, a little piece of the future. Though the thought of being a mother still frightened her, she already loved this child whose face she'd never seen. She couldn't wait to show the baby wonders like what she witnessed.

Marcelle twisted the rope around her waist, spread her arms and legs wide, and spun down toward the floor.

Anna couldn't help thinking of the last show she'd attended with John. Sadness blossomed in her heart. If only she hadn't so easily dismissed his idea of running away. She'd had to do so anyway—if she'd listened, he might have been there beside her, encouraging her to try learning to fly.

"You're the new girl." Marcelle lowered herself from the rope and waved. "You're always here when I'm rehearsing."

Anna stood with a self-conscious smile. "I love watching you perform, but, of course, I can't attend any of the shows. I hope I'm not intruding."

"Not at all. After a month of watching you watching me, I decided I should introduce myself properly." She held out a hand. "Marcelle Brodeur."

Anna took it. "Anna Song."

"You are part of the human zoo, *oui?*" Marcelle crinkled her thin nose. "Good luck with that."

Anna sighed. "I wish I could be a performer instead, but I don't have any skills."

"Why not learn, then?" Marcelle tilted her head. "I don't usually take on students, but you've watched me every day since you arrived here, and that shows you have dedication. I could teach you."

Anna brightened but then shook her head, placing her hand on her belly. "I can't. It's not safe."

Marcelle narrowed her eyes. "*I* will tell you what is safe. We'll begin with skills that can be done from the ground and start building up your muscles. After the baby is born, then I'll let you go up in the air."

Anna's lips split. "That would be wonderful."

OHIO, 1911

Anna wove through the bustling backstage area. With the show's opening night only a few days away, the atmosphere was growing more and more excited. She was supposed to play a background fairy in the next scene, spinning on a hoop behind Marcelle, who would be performing on the rope as the fairy princess.

After nearly a year of hard work—and Marcelle contacting every friend she'd ever had—*On Moonlit Wings* was about to become a reality. The rented theater had been transformed to accommodate aerial apparatuses and animal cages, and enough people were interested in the Empress of the Skies' new show that papers across America had written about it.

Standing by her lion cages, Tanya Mizrahi waved. "Have a good rehearsal, Anna!"

"Thank you!" Anna squeezed past Charles Sasaki, who would be playing the warrior who fell for the fairy princess, and Sarah Barnes, who would be playing the fairy queen.

They were hardly the only defectors from Albers & Andley. Kirsten

Sigrist had arrived with her ten dogs; they, along with Tanya's three lions and Nini Clementine's two horses, would separately perform animal acts to represent parts of the fairy kingdom. Numerous dancers and singers had also joined the show, as well as new acts eager for a chance to shine.

Maja Lozanac, who would, with her blindfolded acrobatic dances, play the role of the sorceress, stepped in front of Anna. "I had a dream about the show."

Intrigued, Anna asked, "What did you see?"

"If you are brave, you will carry us all."

Unsure what that meant, Anna continued on her way. When she arrived, Marcelle was already waiting on a catwalk above the stage. Her routine would begin with her climbing down, representing the fairy's descent to the earth.

"What took you so long?" Marcelle clapped. "Let us begin!"

Anna climbed a rope ladder to reach the hoop. She wished she could watch Marcelle bring her character to life with her famed strength and grace but had to focus on her own movements.

A thrill shot through her. She still couldn't quite believe that she and Marcelle had succeeded in putting this show together. Whether it was greeted with great fanfare or fizzled after a few performances, at least they'd created something that was their own.

A thudding noise and a cry interrupted her concentration. Startled, she looked down. Marcelle lay crumpled at the bottom of the rope.

Gasping, Anna rushed to climb down. "Marcelle!"

"I'm all right." Marcelle sat up, rubbing her ankle. "My grip isn't what it used to be. I may have been too ambitious with the choreography." She tried to stand but quickly plopped back down, cursing. "I won't be able to climb like this."

"What are we going to do?"

"You have to take the role. I should have given it to you in the first place. You are ready." She placed a hand on Anna's shoulder. "I said you could be great, and I meant it. This is your chance to prove me right, Princess of the Skies."

FLORIDA, 1908

Anna wasn't sure who was crying louder—her baby or her. Clutching the two-month-old to her chest, she tried desperately not to scream.

With the wet heat, she almost forgot it was still winter. Albers & Andley had called everyone back to prepare for the upcoming spring and summer tour. Anna had hoped that by now, she would have figured out how to be a mother. But with Rosie refusing to stop wailing, she wondered if she would ever learn.

"Shut that thing up!" Storming through the costume tent, Mr. Andley glowered at Anna. "Or I'll feed it to the lions!"

Tanya Mizrahi looked up from the costume she was mending and sniffed. "My lions do not eat infants. However, they do enjoy eating pigs." She gave Mr. Andley a pointed look.

"What's going on here?" Marcelle approached. "*Guillaume*, stop scaring the baby and let us do our jobs."

Mr. Andley's face purpled, and he walked off with a huff.

"Thank you," Anna said between sniffles. Having spent the winter moving between the homes of whoever had a bed to spare, Anna was beyond grateful for all the support she'd received from her fellow performers. She only wished she didn't have to be such a burden. "I-I'm sorry for all the trouble."

"Nonsense. Here, let me take her." Marcelle reached out for the baby. Rocking her gently, she sang a quiet French lullaby.

Anna wiped her eyes, watching in awe as Rosie quieted and eventually fell asleep. "How did you do that?"

"Experience. I may not have children, but I've looked after many over the years. We take care of each other here. Now that Rosie is asleep, I think it's time I teach you a drop. Tanya, would you mind looking after the baby?"

Tanya took the infant and cradled her. "What a sweet girl!"

Anna smiled. "Thank you… Thank you all so much."

"Someday, it will be your turn to take care of us," Marcelle said.

"Yes, of course. I won't let you down."

OHIO, 1911

Every seat of the theater was filled. The audience, promised an exciting new show from the great Empress of the Skies, watched breathlessly as Charles, playing the warrior, fought his way through various acts representing dangers in order to reach the enchanted fairy kingdom.

But they wouldn't get the Empress. Instead, they'd get the Princess—an announcement Marcelle, fearful of requests for refunds, had saved until after everyone was seated.

Waiting on the catwalk for her musical cue, Anna tried to still her quivering heart. Over the last several rehearsals, she had put her body through more than she had imagined it capable of. Her glimmering blue-and-white leotard, reminiscent of moonlight, and pale pink tights hid countless bruises and rope burns, and dull pain covered every muscle. If she wowed this audience, it would all be worthwhile. Everyone was counting on her to make their show a sensation, and she wouldn't let them down.

They all looked so amazing on stage.

Maja, with her blindfolded acrobatic dance. Dressed in a sleek black-and-silver leotard, she flawlessly transitioned from balletic spins to athletic tumbles as the narrator spoke of the power of fate and sorceress who knew its secrets.

Kirsten, with her ten playful dogs. Her long red skirt opened like a blooming rose as she whirled this way and that, directing the dogs to perform flips and jumps as the narrator described the delights of the fairy kingdom.

Tanya, with her three lions. Wearing her famed Amazonian armor, she commanded them to run over and under obstacles on cue as the narrator warned of the kingdom's dangers.

Upon hearing the opening melody of the song that would accompany her first performance, Anna gracefully climbed down and came into view of the audience from above. Still near the top, she swung her legs and lifted her hips to twist the rope around her waist. After wrapping it around her body a few more times, she let go, spinning downward at a dizzying speed. She stopped inches from the ground, caught by her precisely wrapped rope, and posed with an arched back as the audience screamed their approval.

It was the same drop she'd once gasped at while watching a show with

John. It felt like a lifetime ago, yet she still remembered his smile as if it were yesterday. *I did it, John. I wish you could see me now.*

Her wings may have been invisible, but the audience had seen them nonetheless. As she climbed back up, turning upside down, hooking her knee, and grabbing the rope above in a spider-like ascent, she wondered how he would feel if he knew she'd turned his story into a show.

She held the rope with arms wide, as Marcelle once had, and released her legs, pedaling them slowly. As the rope spun, she glimpsed the audience.

For years, people had stared at her, but never like this—never with awe and admiration. Though her hands were starting to burn, she felt she could stay in the air forever.

A face caught her eye—obscured by the shadows yet unmistakable. The gentle curve of his brow, the flawless contours of his cheeks... but it couldn't be John. It had to be her imagination putting his face onto someone who looked like him from a distance.

She wrapped her legs back around the rope, suddenly wanting to cry.

CALIFORNIA, 1906

Even inside the museum tent, Anna still looked around warily, fearful of spotting someone her father knew. He would never forgive her for wasting money on the circus. But having spent her entire life in his house, she'd yearned to glimpse the wonders of the world.

Behind a glass case sat an exquisitely decorated helmet—a relic of the ancient Greeks, according to the sign. It seemed impossibly old, and she marveled at its majesty.

A young man her age stared at it from across the case. Open-faced and handsome with the most beautiful brown eyes she'd ever seen... she blushed when he looked up and his gaze caught hers.

Flustered, she moved on to the next exhibit, an ancient sword. He wandered over to a nearby case containing a painted vase. As she wove through the exhibit, she kept glimpsing him and chastising herself for being so drawn to a good-looking stranger.

She was in the middle of observing a set of baubles that supposedly belonged to an ancient queen when he appeared beside her.

"That looks like something Helen of Troy would have worn." A soft voice, flowing like a clear creek, rippled past her ears.

She looked up with a start.

He smiled at her. "I apologize if I startled you."

"Not… not at all."

"My name is John Maxfield." He held out his hand.

"I'm Anna Song." Uncertainly, she reached toward him.

He took her hand and lifted it to his lips, sending delighted chills over her skin. "Pleased to meet you, Miss Song. Are you here with your family?"

She shook her head. "They think all this"—she gestured widely—"is frivolous, but I find it wonderful. It's all so amazing… so far from the ordinary life I'm expected to live."

"That's why I came, too. The world is so big, and our lives are so small. At least here, we get to experience a piece of all that's out there. And at least here, what's different can be celebrated. For someone like me, who doesn't belong anywhere, that feels special."

"I understand. I want more than I was born to have, and because of that, I'm considered strange. Here, everything is strange, and I'm no longer alone."

Their eyes met again, and for a long moment, they didn't speak.

Then, John jerked his head toward the tent's entrance. "Are you going to see the show in the big top?"

"Of course."

"Forgive me if this is too bold, but I would be honored if you would let me escort you." He held out his arm.

Blushing, she took it. "That… would be nice."

OHIO, 1911

Cheers and laughter swirled backstage. Glass bottles clinked as performers drank to their wild success. Anna squeezed past them, aiming for the dressing room so she could change out of her leotard.

"*Anne!*"

Hearing Marcelle's voice, Anna turned around.

Marcelle rushed up to her with a grin. "You were magnificent tonight.

You are no longer the Princess of the Skies—you may now claim the title of Empress. I relinquish it gladly."

Anna shook her head. "I can't. That's your stage name."

"You are a worthy successor. All the critics are saying so. I've spoken to a few investors, and they are very interested in our continued success. Soon, we will be able to tour the country."

"That would be wonderful."

"If you will excuse me, I must return to them. I just wanted to tell you before you left to go celebrate." Marcelle vanished into the crowd.

Anna's heart danced, but she wasn't in the mood to celebrate with the others. A heavy feeling still weighed on her as she thought about the one person she wished could have been there—and how impossible that wish was.

"Excuse me, I'm looking for Miss Anna Song. Have you seen her?"

Anna froze. That man's voice, watery yet firm, sounded just like John's.

"Yes, she went that way." It was Kirsten who replied. "You look familiar. Have we met?"

"I don't think so, ma'am. Thank you."

Anna almost didn't dare turn around. When she finally did, tears sprang to her eyes.

He was there—right there before her. Alive. Real.

His eyes widened at the sight of her. "It's—It's really you. I didn't dare hope…"

"John?"

He nodded.

The next thing she knew, they were in each other's arms. She held him close, scarcely able to believe what she was seeing and hearing and feeling. Questions tumbled through her head, but she couldn't stop sobbing long enough to ask any.

"If I'd known you were alive, I would never have stopped looking." His breath whispered across her hair.

"Wh-what?"

"While running from your father, I fell into the river and was swept downstream. By the time I made it back to town, word had spread that you'd killed yourself. Since then… no place felt like home. I wandered from town to town, picking up whatever work I could. Then I saw in the papers that the Empress of the Skies was putting on a show with the same name as the story I once told you... and that one of the performers had the same name as you... It seemed impossible, but I traveled two days to get here in case it was true, that you were still alive. And then I saw you dancing in the sky..."

"My father told me he killed you." Anna wiped her eyes. "I-I never stopped missing you. That's why I asked Marcelle to turn your story into our show."

He smiled. "I like the ending, how the fairy princess discovered the magic to give the man wings, how they flew off into the night. Did you come up with it?"

"Yes. It was my way of letting them run away together... like I should have with you."

"It's not too late, if you'll still have me."

Anna's heart leaped, but she stopped her tongue from answering too quickly. Rosie... he still didn't know about Rosie. Would he—

"There you are!" Maja rushed toward her, carrying a squirming Rosie. "I was asked to return her to you. I'm sorry, I would look after her, but she keeps trying to tear my costume."

"Thank you." Anna automatically took the child.

"Mama!" Rosie grabbed at Anna's face.

John stared with eyes rounder than Anna had ever seen them. Her heart clenched. What was she supposed to say?

He nodded at Rosie. "Is... Is that...?"

Anna lifted her chin and adjusted Rosie to face John. "John... this is Rosaline Maxfield Song. She's... she's yours."

A broad smile spread across his lips. "Well, isn't she a gift?" His expression sobered. "Please, Anna, wherever you go, let me come with you. Let me be there for you—and for our daughter."

Tears of joy streamed from her eyes. "Yes. Yes, stay with us."

He wrapped an arm around her waist and pulled her in close, kissing her deeply. Her heart hammered, and she thought she might dissolve in a swirl of light.

A sticky hand grabbed her bun, pulling her back to reality. Before her, John bent over sideways, Rosie's other hand tangled in his short black hair. The toddler giggled delightedly.

Anna and John both burst out laughing, their voices and Rosie's braiding together in a cord of happiness.

ABOUT THE AUTHORS

DANIELLE ACKLEY-McPHAIL
"Mama Bear"

Award-winning author and editor Danielle Ackley-McPhail has worked both sides of the publishing industry for longer than she cares to admit. In 2014, she joined forces with husband Mike McPhail and friend Greg Schauer to form her own publishing house, eSpec Books (www.especbooks. com).

Her published works include six novels, *Yesterday's Dreams*, *Tomorrow's Memories*, *Today's Promise*, *The Halfling's Court*, *The Redcaps' Queen*, and *Baba Ali and the Clockwork Djinn*, written with Day Al-Mohamed. She is also the author of the solo collections *Eternal Wanderings*, *A Legacy of Stars*, *Consigned to the Sea*, *Flash in the Can*, *Transcendence*, *Between Darkness and Light*, and the non-fiction writers' guides, *The Literary Handyman* and *LH: Build-A-Book Workshop*.

She is also the senior editor of the *Bad-Ass Faeries* anthology series, *Gaslight & Grimm*, *Side of Good/Side of Evil*, *After Punk*, and *Footprints in the Stars*. Her short stories are included in numerous other anthologies and collections.

In addition to her literary acclaim, she crafts and sells original costume horns under the moniker The Hornie Lady Custom Costume Horns, and homemade flavor-infused candied ginger under the brand of Ginger KICK! at literary conventions, on commission, and wholesale.

Danielle lives in New Jersey with husband and fellow writer, Mike McPhail and three extremely spoiled cats.

To learn more about her work, visit www.sidhenadaire.com or www. especbooks.

DEREK TYLER ATTICO
"What We Bring With Us"

Derek Tyler Attico is a two-time winner of the *Star Trek Strange New Worlds* anthology series, a screenwriter, and photographer.

Derek has a BFA in English and History from John Jay College of Criminal Justice, where he set aside his passion of contractual and entertainment law for his first love of writing.

His short work has appeared in various anthologies, and he has also contributed to projects for the Star Trek Adventures Role Playing Game by Modiphius Entertainment.

Derek currently lives in New York City, where he can be found striking up conversations with complete strangers. You can find him on Twitter @ DAttico, and his work can be found at www.DerekTylerAttico.com

TE BAKUTIS
"Pride Fight"

TE Bakutis is an award-winning author and game designer. His first fantasy trilogy, *Tales of the Five Provinces*, is complete, and *Analog Science Fiction and Fact* actually liked his grimsnark scifi thriller, *Supremacy's Shadow*, which he happily admits is filled with violently explosive nonsense. You can find excerpts from his work and his complete publication history at www.tebakutis.com, or read the start of his cyberpunk police procedural, *Loose Circuit*, for free at www.loosecircuit.com. When not writing, he is probably in Skyrim VR.

RUSS COLCHAMIRO
"The Hardwicke Files: The Case of the Full Moon"

Russ Colchamiro is the author of the rollicking space adventure, *Crossline*, the zany SF/F backpacking comedy series *Finders Keepers: The Definitive Edition*, *Genius de Milo*, and *Astropalooza*, editor of the sci-fi anthology *Love, Murder & Mayhem*, and co-author of the noir anthology collection *Murder in Montague Falls*, all with Crazy 8 Press.

Russ lives in New Jersey with his wife, two ninjas, and crazy dog, who may in fact be an alien himself. Russ has also contributed to several other anthologies, including *Tales of the Crimson Keep, Pangaea, Altered States of the Union, Camelot 13, TV Gods 2, They Keep Killing Glenn, Thrilling Adventure Yarns*, and *Brave New Girls*.

He is now completing the debut novel in a new sci-fi noir series featuring his hardboiled private eye, Angela Hardwicke, scheduled for publication September 2020.

Russ is repped by The Zack Company.

For more on and Russ's books, you can visit www.russcolchamiro.com, follow him on Twitter @AuthorDudeRuss, and 'like' his Facebook author page facebook.com/RussColchamiroAuthor.

PAIGE DANIELS
"Mr. EB's Organic Sideshow"

Paige Daniels is the pen name of Tina Closser. By day, she works as an Electrical Engineer and Mom mushing her kids from gymnastics and violin practice. After the kids go to bed, she rocks out with her headphones turned to eleven and cranks out books. She is an uber science geek. If she wasn't married to the most terrific guy in the world, she would be a groupie for Adam Baldwin.

Her books include the complete *Non-Compliance* cyberpunk trilogy, *In the Shadow of the Guild*, and *Project Eleutheria* (*The Singularity Wars, #1*). She is also the co-author of the *Brave New Girls* anthology series.

KATHLEEN O'SHEA DAVID
"She's a Real Cougar"

Kathleen O'Shea David started working with puppets when she was 2 and, over 50 years later, she is still "wiggling dolls" for fun and profit. Along the way, she picked up quite a few more skills and careers.

She has done just about everything from cancer research to rock and roll. Some of her favorite jobs have been in puppetry, theater, and publishing.

She is a published writer with a *Doctor Who* story in the Big Finish anthology *Short Trips: Qualities of Leadership*, among others. She worked on *Star Wars: The New Jedi Order* with Shelly Shapiro. She has had a number of short stories in published in various anthologies, and She created the series *Headcases* with her husband, Peter David.

Her costumes have won awards at a number science fiction conventions both for performance and workmanship. She has also created costumes for film and stage. She is a former employee of the Center for Puppetry Arts in Atlanta. Her puppets are in collections all over the world.

PETER DAVID
"Krysta, Warrior President"

Peter David is a prolific author whose career, and continued popularity, spans nearly three decades. He has worked in every conceivable media: television, film, books (fiction, non-fiction, and audio), short stories, and comic books, and acquired followings in all of them.

In the literary field, Peter has had over 100 novels published, including numerous appearances on the *New York Times* Bestsellers List. His novels include *Tigerheart, Darkness of the Light, Sir Apropos of Nothing* and the sequel *The Woad to Wuin, Knight Life, Howling Mad*, and the *Psi-Man* adventure series. He is the co-creator and author of the bestselling *Star Trek: New Frontier* series for Pocket Books, and has also written such *Trek* novels as *Q-Squared, The Siege, Q-in-Law, Vendetta, I, Q* (with John deLancie), *A Rock and a Hard Place*, and *Imzadi*. He produced the three *Babylon 5 Centauri Prime* novels, and has also had his short fiction published in such collections as *Shock Rock, Shock Rock II*, and *Otherwere*, as well as *Isaac Asimov's Science Fiction Magazine* and *The Magazine of Fantasy and Science Fiction*.

Peter's comic book resume includes an award-winning twelve-year run on *The Incredible Hulk*, and he has also worked on such varied and popular titles as *Supergirl, Young Justice, Soulsearchers and Company, Aquaman, Spider-Man, Spider-Man 2099, X-Factor, Star Trek, Wolverine, The Phantom, Sachs & Violens, The Dark Tower*, and many others. He has also written comic book-related novels, such as *The Incredible Hulk: What Savage Beast*, and co-edited *The Ultimate Hulk* short story collection. Furthermore, his opinion column, "But I Digress...," has been running in the industry trade newspaper *The Comic Buyers's Guide* for nearly a decade, and in that time has been the paper's consistently most popular feature and was also collected into a trade paperback edition.

Peter is also the writer for two popular video games: *Shadow Complex* and *Spider-Man: Edge of Time*.

Peter is the co-creator, with popular science fiction icon Bill Mumy (of *Lost in Space* and *Babylon 5* fame) of the Cable Ace Award-nominated science fiction series *Space Cases*, which ran for two seasons on Nickelodeon. He has written several scripts for the Hugo Award-winning TV series *Babylon 5*, and the sequel series, *Crusade*. He has also written several films for Full Moon Entertainment and co-produced two of them, including two installments in the popular *Trancers* series, as well as the science fiction western spoof *Oblivion*, which won the Gold Award at the 1994 Houston International Film Festival for best Theatrical Feature Film, Fantasy/Horror category.

Peter's awards and citations include: the Haxtur Award 1996 (Spain), Best Comic script; OZCon 1995 award (Australia), Favorite International Writer; Comic Buyers Guide 1995 Fan Awards, Favorite writer; Wizard Fan Award Winner 1993; Golden Duck Award for Young Adult Series (*Starfleet Academy*), 1994; UK Comic Art Award, 1993; Will Eisner Comic Industry Award, 1993. He lives in New York with his wife, Kathleen, and his four children, Shana, Gwen, Ariel, and Caroline.

For more on Peter and his fictional titles, visit his personal website, follow him on Twitter @PeterDavid_PAD, and like him on Facebook.

KEITH RA DeCANDIDO
"Materfamilias"

Keith RA DeCandido's "Materfamilias" takes place in the same world as his 2019 urban fantasy novel *A Furnace Sealed* and its forthcoming sequels. (Don't be surprised if the Rodriguez family shows up in one or more of those sequels, either). Keith has written in more than thirty different licensed universes from *Alien* to *Zorro*, as well as extensively in worlds of his own creation. Other recent and upcoming work includes *Phoenix Precinct*, latest in his fantasy police procedural series; *Alien: Isolation*, based on the movie series and hit videogame; the graphic novels *Icarus* and *Jellinek*; the collaborative novels *To Hell and Regroup* (with David Sherman) and *Animal* (with Munish K. Batra, M.D.); and short stories in the anthologies *Brave New Girls: Adventures of Gals & Gizmos, Thrilling Adventure Yarns, Pangaea III: Redemption, Across the Universe: Tales of Alternative Beatles,* and *Release the Virgins!* He has been writing about pop culture for the award-winning web site Tor.com since 2011. He's a third-degree black belt in karate, a percussionist for the parody band Boogie Knights, and probably some other stuff he can't recall due to the lack of sleep. Find out less at his woefully inadequate web site at DeCandido.net.

MARY FAN
"On Moonlit Wings"

Mary Fan is the editor of *Bad Ass Moms* and hails from Jersey City, NJ. She is the author of the *Jane Colt* sci-fi series, the *Starswept* YA sci-fi series, the *Flynn Nightsider* YA dark fantasy series, the *Fated Stars* YA high fantasy series, and *Stronger Than a Bronze Dragon*, a YA steampunk fantasy. In addition, Mary is the co-editor (along with Paige Daniels) of the *Brave New Girls* young adult sci-fi anthologies, which feature tales about girls in STEM. Revenues from sales are donated to the Society of Women Engineers scholarship fund. Her short works have been featured in numerous anthologies, including *Pangaea III: Redemption, Thrilling Adventure Yarns, Magic at Midnight, Tales of the Crimson Keep: Newly Renovated Edition,* and *Love, Murder & Mayhem.*

When she's not writing, she can usually be found singing alto at choir rehearsal, hitting bags at the kickboxing gym, swinging from a flying trapeze, or tangled up in aerial silks.

Find her online at MaryFan.com.

MICHAEL JAN FRIEDMAN
"Ruth"

Michael Jan Friedman is the author of nearly 70 books of fiction and non-fiction, about half of them set somewhere in the wilds of the *Star Trek* universe.

In 1992, Friedman wrote *Reunion*, the first *Star Trek: The Next Generation* hardcover, which introduced the crew of the *Stargazer*, Captain Jean-Luc Picard's first command. Over the years, the popularity of *Reunion* has spawned a number of *Stargazer* stories in both prose and comic book formats, including a six-novel original series.

Friedman has also written for the *Aliens, Predator, Wolf Man, Lois and Clark, DC Super Hero, Marvel Super Hero*, and *Wishbone* licensed book universes. Eleven of his book titles, including the autobiography *Hollywood Hulk Hogan* and *Ghost Hunting* (written with SciFi's *Ghost Hunters*), have appeared on the prestigious *New York Times* primary bestseller list, and his novel adaptation of the *Batman & Robin* movie was for a time the #1 bestselling book in Poland (really).

Friedman has worked at one time or another in network and cable television, radio, business magazines, and the comic book industry, in the process producing scripts for nearly 180 comic stories. Among his comic book credits is the *Darkstars* series from DC Comics, which he created with artist Larry Stroman, and the *Outlaws* limited series, which he created with artist Luke McDonnell. He also co-wrote the story for the acclaimed second-season *Star Trek: Voyager* episode "Resistance," which guest-starred Joel Grey.

Currently, Friedman is working on a variety of projects, including a contemporary fantasy novel featuring characters and themes from mythology tentatively called *Blood of the Gods*, a young adult fantasy novel set in Renaissance times, the true story of an extraordinary Little League team in 1955, and an epic-scale science fiction adventure.

As always, he advises readers that no matter how many Friedmans they know, he is probably not related to any of them.

For more on Michael Jan Friedman and his fiction, visit his personal website, follow him on Twitter @FriedmanMJ, and like him on Facebook.

ROBERT GREENBERGER
"Shoot Center"

Robert Greenberger is a writer and editor. A lifelong fan of comic books, comic strips, science fiction, and *Star Trek*, he drifted toward writing and editing, encouraged by his father and inspired by Superman's alter ego, Clark Kent.

While at SUNY-Binghamton, Greenberger wrote and edited for the college newspaper, *Pipe Dream*. Upon graduation, he worked for Starlog Press and while there, created *Comics Scene*, the first nationally distributed magazine to focus on comic books, comic strips, and animation.

In 1984, he joined DC Comics as an Assistant Editor, and went on to be an Editor before moving to Administration as Manager—Editorial Operations. He joined Gist Communications as a Producer before moving to Marvel Comics as its Director—Publishing Operations.

Greenberger rejoined DC in May 2002 as a Senior Editor—Collected Editions. He helped grow that department, introducing new formats and improving the editions' editorial content. In 2006, he joined *Weekly World News* as its Managing Editor until the paper's untimely demise. He then freelanced for an extensive client base including Platinum Studios, scifi. com, DC, and Marvel. He helped revitalize *Famous Monsters of Filmland* and served as News Editor at ComicMix.com.

He is a member of the Science Fiction Writers of America and the International Association of Media Tie-In Writers. His novelization of *Hellboy II: The Golden Army* won the IAMTW's Scribe Award in 2009.

In 2012, he received his Master of Science in Education from the University of Bridgeport and relocated to Maryland, where he has taught High School English in Baltimore County. He completed his Master of Arts degree in Creative Writing & Literature for Educators at Fairleigh Dickinson University in 2016.

With others, he co-founded Crazy 8 Press, a digital press hub where he continues to write. His dozens of books, short stories, and essays cover the gamut from young adult nonfiction to original fiction. He's also one of the dozen authors using the penname Rowan Casey to write the *Veil Knights* urban fantasy series. His most recent works include *100 Greatest Moments* series and editing *Thrilling Adventure Yarns*.

Bob teaches High School English at St. Vincent Pallotti High School in Laurel, MD. He and his wife Deborah reside in Howard County, Maryland. Find him at www.bobgreenberger.com or @bobgreenberger.

Glenn Hauman
"The Devil You Knew: A Scoubidou Mystery"

Before his relocation to the Fort Lee Home For The Tall, Threadbare, And Twitchy, Glenn Hauman was a pioneer of electronic publishing with the groundbreaking BiblioBytes. When the caretakers let him use writing implements, he also wrote numerous short stories; his *Star Trek* e-book, "Creative Couplings", got worldwide press coverage for its portrayal of the first Klingon-Jewish wedding. In addition to *Star Trek*, he's written other licensed tie-in works for *X-Men* and *Farscape*, and urban fantasy for Baen Books.

After they took the pencils and gave him crayons instead, he became the colorist for Mike Grell's *Jon Sable Freelance: Ashes of Eden* graphic novel and the award-nominated biography *The Original Johnson* by Trevor Von Eeden.

Now that electronic publishing is no longer considered crazy, he is slowly being integrated back into society and works at ComicMix, where they let him play with computers all day long.

For more on Glenn and his mental state, follow him on Twitter @ GlennHauman, read his personal website, and be sure to check out ComicMix.

Heather E Hutsell
"Shape Up, or Ship Out"

Heather E. Hutsell began writing stories at age eleven. Her first—a murder mystery—won her an award through the Young Authors program, as did two more detective mysteries in as many years. Already set on becoming an author, she published her first novella, *Awakening Alice*—a sequel to Lewis Carroll's *Alice in Wonderland*—in the collaborative work *Ghost on the Highway* in 2006. She went on to self-publish an illustrated version of *Awakening Alice* along with its sequel, *A Ticket for Patience*, in 2007. A willing prisoner to her many muses, Heather has since written and self-published eleven more novels, two novellas, and four short story collections, with her newest book being the second volume of humorous and macabre short stories involving dolls, marionettes, and automata. Her works include romantic horror, absurdist fiction, dystopian tales, fairytales gone awry, dark comedy, 1930's and 40's noir, and a steampunk mystery series, *The Case Files*. Heather has also written two historical documentary series, enjoys designing and constructing costumes, and just finished her Liberal Arts degree.

KRIS KATZEN
"Jupiter Justice"

Novelist and short story author Kris Katzen writes science fiction and fantasy, including "Kaboom, Ka-bye" for *Seattle 2072* in the *Shadowrun* universe and "Jupiter Jeopardy" for *Brave New Girls Adventures of Gals and Gizmos*. Fields of interest include theater, history, and all things feline. In Kris's latest novel, *Curai'Nal*, a newly-appointed starship captain must win the confidence of her new crew and solve an interstellar mystery before a ruthless, enigmatic enemy slaughters millions of colonists. Next up: the first novel in a new series *The Giant and the Gnat*. A ragtag assortment of renegades from various worlds run into each other—in some instances, literally—and wind up combining their diverse skills. All outcasts, the only thing more disparate than their abilities, is their respective sizes. It creates great opportunity, but also great difficulty, when the tiniest team member stands only two centimeters high, and the tallest measures over sixty meters. To see a complete bibliography and all the covers, as well as updates on upcoming works, please visit http://www.BluetrixBooks.com.

PAUL KUPPERBERG
"Come In, Sit Down, Have a Bite!"

Paul Kupperberg is the author of more than three dozen books of fiction and nonfiction for readers of all ages, including *The Same Old Story* (Crazy 8 Press), *Kevin* (Grosset & Dunlap), and *Jew-Jitsu: Hebrew Hands of Fury* (Citadel Books), as well as short stories and essays for anthologies published by Simon and Schuster, Ace, DAW, Titan Books, Sequential Arts, and others. Paul has also written over 1,400 comic book stories featuring characters ranging from Archie to Superman, including the 2012 Eisner Award and 2013 Harvey Award-nominated (and the 2014 GLAAD Media Award winner for "Outstanding Comic Book") *Life With Archie* series that culminated in the controversial "Death of Archie" storyline. He is the creator of the series *Arion, Lord of Atlantis, Checkmate,* and *Takion* for DC Comics, and numerous others for Charlton Neo Comics, publishers of *Paul Kupperberg's Illustrated Guide to Writing Comics.* You can follow him online at PaulKupperberg.com, on Facebook, and on Twitter @PaulKupperberg.

Karissa Laurel
"The Art of Crafting Resistance"

Karissa Laurel is a science fiction and fantasy author living in central North Carolina with her son, her husband, the occasional in-law, and a very hairy husky named Bonnie. Her favorite things are super heroes, *Star Wars,* Southern cuisine, and Hindi cinema. Karissa serves as an assistant editor at *Cast of Wonders,* a young adult speculative fiction podcast—part of the Escape Artists family. Most recently, she is the author of *Touch of Smoke,* a paranormal romance novel available from Red Adept Publishing. She's also the author of *The Norse Chronicles,* an urban fantasy series, and *The Stormbourne Chronicles,* a young adult, epic steampunkish fantasy series. Her short stories have appeared in various anthologies, including *Thrilling Adventure Yarns* (Crazy 8 Press, 2019), *Wicked South: Secrets and Lies* (Blue Crow Publishing, 2018), *Magic at Midnight* (Snowy Wings Publishing, 2018), *Love, Murder and Mayhem* (Crazy 8 Press, 2018), and *Brave New Girls: Stories of Girls Who Science and Scheme* (Brave New Girls, 2017). Her short fiction has also appeared at *Daily Science Fiction, Luna Station Quarterly,* and *Cast of Wonders.*

TJ Perkins
"Perfect Insanity"

TJ Perkins is a gifted and well-respected author in the mystery/suspense genre for YA and fantasy for teens. TJ has 8 YA mysteries under GumShoe Press, a 5-book fantasy series entitled *Shadow Legacy* with Silver Leaf

Books, and a Pagan picture book for ages 0-6, *Four Little Witches*, published by Schiffer Publishing 2015, which won the 2016 COVR Visionary Art Award. Her newest book is *The Healthy Witch*, New Age health/nutrition, Schiffer Publishing, Sept 2019.

TJ is always a strong presence at local author events, Fantasy Cons, and Fairy Festivals. Her short stories for young readers have appeared in the Ohio State 6th Grade Proficiency Test Preparation Book, Kid's Highway Magazine, and Webzine *New Works Review*, just to name a few. She's placed five times in the CNW/FFWA chapter book competition. Her short story of light horror for tweens, "The Midnight Watch," was published 2007 by Demon Minds Magazine. Adult short stories include: award-winning "Redemption," *The Reading Place*, 2014, "The Sapphire Circle," *Dark Luminous Wings*, 2017, "Thief in the Night," *FLASH*, 2017, "The Dark Defines Us," *Not Far From Roswell*, 2020, just to name a few.

AARON ROSENBERG
"Duckbob in: Running Hot and Cold"

Aaron Rosenberg is the author of the best-selling *DuckBob* SF comedy series, the *Relicant Chronicles* epic fantasy series, the *Dread Remora* space-opera series, and—with David Niall Wilson—the *O.C.L.T.* occult thriller series. Aaron's tie-in work contains novels for *Star Trek*, *Warhammer*, *World of WarCraft*, *Stargate: Atlantis*, *Shadowrun*, *Eureka*, *Mutants & Masterminds*, and more. He has written children's books (including the original series *STEM Squad* and *Pete and Penny's Pizza Puzzles*, the award-winning *Bandslam: The Junior Novel*, and the #1 best-selling *42: The Jackie Robinson Story*), educational books on a variety of topics, and over seventy roleplaying games (such as the original games *Asylum*, *Spookshow*, and *Chosen*, work for *White Wolf*, *Wizards of the Coast*, *Fantasy Flight*, *Pinnacle*, and many others, and both the Origins Award-winning *Gamemastering Secrets* and the Gold ENnie-winning *Lure of the Lich Lord*). He is the co-creator of the *ReDeus* series, and a founding member of Crazy 8 Press. Aaron lives in New York with his family. You can follow him online at gryphonrose.com, on Facebook at facebook.com/gryphonrose, and on Twitter @gryphonrose.

Jenifer Purcell Rosenberg
"Hellbeans"

Jenifer wrote her first story in the firm of a children's book for her 3rd grade G&T teacher. She's been hooked on writing ever since. She wrote and illustrated the book *Alligator's Friends*, which is about a socially awkward reptile trying to make new pals in the animal world. Her short story credits include "The Power of Five" from the 2018 *Brave New Girls* anthology *Tales of Heroines Who Hack*, "Waking Things" from the Crazy 8 Press anthology *They Keep Killing Glenn*, "Night Path" from *The Nature of Cities, Tales of Silver Green*, and "Evening Sonnet" in *Nisaba Journal 4*, and "Outsider" in *Thrilling Adventure Yarns*, among others. Jenifer has also written for online publications, and for the tabletop RPG industry.

When she isn't writing, Jenifer keeps busy with excessive volunteering, organizing charitable events, teaching paint classes, getting involved with Pride events, and learning new languages. Her garden is outfitted with a miniature fairy village that she has carefully cultivated. She also makes wine with her friends, loves to cook, and has been gaming since she was wee. Jenifer lives in the wonderful City of New York with her family. She is thrilled to be a part of this project and plans to write more paranormal fiction in the future.

Joanna Schnurman
"The Songbird and Her Cage"

Joanna Schnurman is an accomplished soprano and singing teacher with a deep and abiding love of all things literary. She has always been an avid reader and has enjoyed bringing many poems and literary characters to life on the stage. In the last few years and with the encouragement of dear friends, she began to explore another facet of her creativity through writing short stories and a novel-in-progress. Her work is primarily speculative fiction, although she relishes dabbling in many genres. Her short stories have appeared in *Brave New Girls: Tales of Heroines Who Hack*, *Brave New Girls: Adventures of Gals and Gizmos*, and *Brave New Girls: Tales of Girls Who Tech and Tinker*.

Hildy Silverman
"Raising the Dead"

Hildy Silverman was the Editor-in-Chief of *Space and Time Magazine* for 12 years. She is a short fiction author whose recent publications include, "My Dear Wa'ats" (2018, *Baker Street Irregulars II: The Game's Afoot*, Ventrella & Maberry, eds.), "The Lady of the Lakes" (2018, *Camelot 13*, French and Thomas, eds.), "Sidekicked" (2019, *Release the Virgins*, Ventrella, ed.), and "Divided We Fell" (2020, *The Divided States of America*, Bechtel, *ed.*). Her nonfiction articles have appeared in numerous legal and medical professional journals and blogs. In the mundane world, she is the Digital Marketing Manager for Oticon Medical US.

Denise Sutton
"Did THEY Do That?"

Denise Mizrahi Sutton lives in Brooklyn, New York with her husband, love of her life, Raphael, and their four sons. She graduated top ten of her class from Long Island University and has a doctorate in Pharmacy. She loves serving her community alongside her parents as a pharmacist at Supreme RX Pharmacy, but spends much of her time these days raising her 5-year-old twins, 2-year-old toddler, and new baby. Denise moonlights as a birthday party entertainer, possessing a natural-born talent for comedy and making children smile. She has always been artistic and imaginative, so Denise was encouraged by her husband Raphy to pursue writing. She is thrilled to have here her first-ever published story and hopes that this will be the beginning of a blossoming career as a writer. Denise just had her fourth child this April and couldn't imagine a better anthology to be a part of—one that gave her the freedom to portray all the joys and chaos of being a busy mom.

THANKS TO OUR PATRONS

We are deeply grateful to all those who made this project possible by contributing to and sharing our crowdfunding campaign. While we had 120 backers, we offered in-print acknowledgements to our Patrons, who are listed below. Thank you for your generous donations!

Alan J Brava

Anonymous Donor

Arthur Thomas

Brad Jurn

Chand Svare Ghei - Moonknight

David L. Webb

Edward Garou Linders

Eric Lentz

Jack Mizrahi

Jeremy Bottroff

Jill Peters

Kirsten Schwaller Sigrist

Lisa-Michelle McMullan

Lynda Foley

Raymond Mizrahi

Tina Good

Yonghua Wang

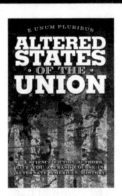